There is a way that seemeth right unto a man;
But the end thereof are the ways of death.

Proverbs 16:25
The Holy Bible

BOOK TWO **STORM CLOUDS**

Suicide Affair

A NOVEL BY
TONY STANFORD

outskirts
press

CONTENTS

1969

1. Friends, Flies, and Spirits............................3
2. BootShaker Quake 14
3. MedicineGirl 25
4. Uncommon Friends..................................34
5. In Time of Storm 51
6. Sunshine and Scarecrows........................72
7. Day Stalking..76
8. StormDancer and HoneySuckle 93
9. Dark Magic..115

1970

10. War-Pig Games.......................................151
11. Night Stalking...173
12. The Purple Heart Club............................198
13. Death Stalking..202
14. Dark Patriot..210
15. Once Upon a Foggy Night 227

16. Blood Test...258
17. Shades of Gray 277
18. Noblesse Oblige 301

1971
19. Paul and Julia 319
20. Wielding of the Wand 326
21. The Burning of a Scarecrow 332
22. Blossoming...342
23. That Girl Rita 368
24. Blakk Magick 391
25. Freedom...405
26. The Yorks..428
27. Till Death Do Us Part 435

1969

1

FRIENDS, FLIES, AND SPIRITS

A fly landed on the back of the seat in front of Rita Pierce. Pa hated flies. "The only good fly is a dead fly," he often told her. The more his mind eroded, the more obsessed he was with flies.

The fly crawled in a circle. Pa would scold her for not killing it. The thought of it riding the bus to her house, getting off with her, and following her into the house to torment her pa caused Rita to grin.

The school bus trip between school and home was long, but Rita enjoyed it. She lived outside the city in a small house surrounded by farmland and forest. Because of his hideous and scary looks, Pa didn't like being around people or going to town. They only went to town when it was absolutely necessary and stuck only to the business at hand. Most of NuSprings Rita still had not seen.

NuSprings began as an Indian settlement by a small band of Cherokee Indians who voluntarily left the Cherokee Nation before the Trail of Tears removal. To survive the 1800s and the Indian Wars, the Tribe of NuSprings closeted their Indian ways to adopt the white man's ways of life and society and built the town. A century and a half later, NuSprings, Missouri, has a population of 8,000 and growing. The mayor of the city is not only an Indian, but also the chief of the city's tribe.

On the bus, Rita got to spend time with friends. Growing up disliked, lonely, and friendless in Kansas for the first decade of her life, it felt strange surrounded by people who liked her. Sitting beside her was her best friend, Betty Brandt. Being in high school, they were the oldest on the bus.

"Wouldn't it be cool to go back in time?" Nancy Dayton asked Rita and Betty. Nancy, seated in the seat in front of them, was only nine. She was a little chatterbox sometimes. Rita liked her and she was a part of Rita's school bus "family."

Betty asked Nancy, "Where did that come from?"

Nancy answered, "Homework. We're supposed to write a paragraph about if we could go back in time and were able to change one thing in our lives, what would it be? And why."

Alex York, on the other side of the aisle and more toward the front, hearing the conversation, answered, "If I could go back in time and change one thing, I'd be born sooner."

"Why?" Nancy looked his way.

"So I could be older and in high school."

Rita saw Alex's stare go from Nancy to her. Making eye contact, a smile cracked his lips, but trying to hide it, he looked back to Nancy.

"Why?" Nancy asked again.

"Because. My brothers are in high school. I could be like them." Alex's eyes darted to Rita again and then away.

Rita had gotten to know Alex York and his older sister. Claire York was twelve and standoffish. She wasn't an unfriendly person by nature, but on the bus and especially toward Rita and the Brandts, she purposely kept her distance. There was animosity between the Yorks and Brandts. The Yorks thought themselves better than everyone, Betty had complained to Rita. Yorks weren't dirt poor like Brandts, Daytons, and Pierces.

Claire was staring forward and ignoring the conversation and everyone. She looked annoyed. Annoyed, because Alex was making conversation.

"What are you going to write about?" Betty asked Nancy.

"How she wishes she wasn't so ugly," Johnny Brandt said from the back seat. He and Nick Dayton laughed.

Nick was Nancy's older brother. Johnny was Betty's younger brother. Nick and Johnny were the same age. Rita considered Johnny a friend in spite of the pest he could be. He loved to aggravate people and often pressured Nick to take part in his ploys.

Rita saw the sunny disposition on Nancy's face fade, replaced by a hurtful concerned look.

"Shut up, Johnny!" Betty turned to scold her younger brother. Betty turned back to Nancy. "Ignore them. They're being stupid. As usual."

Nancy knew they were just being mean; nevertheless, it still hurt and made her self-conscious. Johnny and Nick were always saying hurtful things.

"Go on," Betty encouraged Nancy.

Inhaling a deep breath, Nancy said, "I wish my dad had never went to war."

Nancy's dad was in Vietnam and had come back with the "war sickness." Mr. Dayton lived in a state of depression and had nightmares. Sometimes, nightmares even in the daytime. He took pills for it. He drank all the time and had trouble keeping a job.

Rita understood all too well. Her pa lived in a state of depression and had nightmares. Pa drank all the time, was mean and abusive. Of late, he seemed to be losing his mind. Pa was never in a war. He had been in a fire that almost took his life. He was badly scarred and his face looked more monster than human.

Nancy was quiet a moment and then asked Betty, "What'd ya change?"

Betty shrugged. "M-maybe dat my d-dad didn't drink so much and wasn't so mean."

Just thinking about her dad and his drinking and the mean and violent temper he had caused Betty to become nervous. When nervous, Betty stuttered.

Nancy turned her gaze to Rita. "What'd ya change?"

Rita wanted to say, *My entire life!* or *That my pa was dead.* Shifting her gaze, Alex was looking and listening. Focusing back on Nancy, she answered, "That my mother wasn't dead."

Nancy looked down with a facade of sympathy. Looking up again, "How'd she die?"

"She was hit by a train."

"Oh."

The bus stopped in front of the York home. Alex and Claire stood up.

"Bye, guys," Rita said to be nice to Alex and to be annoying to Claire.

Claire ignored her, but Alex looked her way smiling. "Bye."

The York girls might be standoffish, but the York boys weren't. Rita, looking out the window, hoped to see Glenn or Denny. Sometimes they were home and out in the yard. Not today. Rita was disappointed. Denny, a senior in high school, was the first York to befriend her and her first ever "boyfriend." Other than Pa, he was the only other person she had been intimate with. Unlike Pa, she loved when Denny touched her.

Rita wanted to be a York. They were a perfect family. They had great lives.

Glenn was Denny's younger brother. Rita liked Glenn. Glenn liked her. They were more than friends. He was a "suitor." He and Paul both.

Paul Sumner and Glenn were best friends and also the same age. It was fun being Denny's secret girlfriend and pursued by two guys who were in a contest as to who would "get-the-girl." It was flattering watching them trying to outdo each other for her attention and time. They made her feel special, and feeling special was new to her. She had no plans of choosing either of them. She liked them both and was planning on keeping them both as lovers.

Rita lived down the road from the Yorks and would be the next stop. The bus, nearing her house, moved to the other side of the road to go around a car parked on the edge of the gravel road.

"Hey, what's with that blue car?" Johnny said as he moved toward a window.

"It's a Chevy Caprice," Nick noted.

Rita tried to see who was in the car as the bus went by, but couldn't get a clear look.

"Did you see who it was?" Rita asked Johnny.

"Some guy with a beard."

The bus stopped in front of Rita's house. Rita got off and the bus drove on. She went over to the mailbox, checking for mail, but mostly to watch the blue Chevy pass. Because of the beard and cap, she couldn't get a good look at the guy's face. He looked her way, but didn't act interested in her. Walking toward her house, Rita watched the car follow the bus.

Rita opened the front door of her house, and as she stepped across the threshold, the hand of monster-Pa grabbed her, jerking her inside and slamming the door closed.

Homer shouted, "Get in here, stupid. You're letting flies in!"

Rita's schoolbooks broke free of her hands and fell across the floor.

"We're under attack!" Pa shouted. "Flies everywhere." Pa rushed toward a wall and smacked a fly, leaving a gross bloody mark.

Cursing and swinging, he charged after one in flight. Rita ducked and moved to keep from being swatted herself. The fly got away, but Pa spotted one on the couch. Zipping over, kicking one of her schoolbooks across the floor, he annihilated it.

With an insane chuckle, Pa said, "Got the little black buzzy-buzzy! You see that?" He turned and looked at her.

"Yes, Pa." There was an excited, insane twinkle in his eyes.

Pa said, "The black buzzy was, but now he is not, buzzy wuzzy—get it?" He chuckled at his humor.

"What's happening?"

Pa, making sure no flies were sneaking up on him, jerked his head one way and the another. "We're at war, stupid! The flies are after us."

"Why?"

"Why? Girl, you're stupider than dirt. Stupid as a summer day is long. It's their spawning season. They want to lay eggs in our ears. So the maggots can feast on our brains. There's nothing maggots love more than to eat holes in one's brains. Where ya think the holes in Swiss cheese comes from? Do you want your brain to look like Swiss cheese?"

Pa pushed her aside, charging another. "Stay out of the way, Swiss Brains."

The room was a mess. Nothing in its proper place. Her schoolbooks lay scattered about on the floor as well as her cherished magazines and Pa's porn. There was fly carnage on the walls, the couch, Pa's chair, the floor, the window, curtains—everywhere. Obviously, Pa had been at this for hours.

Rita watched Pa annihilate another. Proud of the gory smear left on the couch, he reared back like some kind of animal and gave a beastly victory roar, then declared, "Harken, all ye black buzzy-buzzies, mess with me and you end up bloody wuzzies!" He laughed again.

Rita couldn't help but crack a smile. It was funny. Pa was in his "playful" mode. He had four basic frames of mind. When in the playful one, he was up and about and seemed to try to take some enjoyment to being alive. Another state was his "zombie" state. In his zombie state he was conscious, but not really aware of life around him. Or he didn't care. He was tuned out and turned off. He would stare, but seeing nothing. He was like he was lost somewhere in his mind. Another state was the "passed-out" state. Often following the zombie state and from too much whiskey, he would pass out. When passed out, he was usually dead to the world. It would be easy to kill him in that state, Rita often fantasized. His fourth state was the angry, crazy, violent state. In that state, he was delusional, suspicious, distrustful, and dangerous. His eyes were often dark and strange. Rita hated that state. She could expect a whipping or a smacking of some kind. Whatever state of mind Pa was in, he could be abusive and violent. Like obliterating flies.

Staying out of the way, Rita watched Pa search for another victim to slaughter. His flyswatter, she realized, was the metal cooking spatula bent out straight. The only spatula they had.

No surprise. The jerk.

Not seeing any flies and satisfied he had killed or chased them all off, Pa sighed, reaching into his pants pocket, pulling out a flask of whiskey. After taking a sizable sip, he looked at Rita. "Whew, what a day. I'm tired. I think I could use a bite to eat. Be a good girl, rustle up somethin'. You can clean this mess up afterwards." He stretched his arm toward her, handing her the spatula.

Rita took the offered weapon and utensil. It was gross.

He said, "You'll need to clean it up a bit."

You think?

Rita found the back door standing wide open. It was how the flies were getting in. It didn't surprise her. In Pa's way of thinking, a backdoor entry was an intrusion. He had the right to kill an intruder. Entrance through an open front door was an invitation and those who came in that way were guests. Killing guests wasn't proper.

Rita closed the back door. Opening the refrigerator, she grabbed a beer. She opened the bottle and took a drink. That first drink of the day was so pleasing. She loved the taste. There was nothing better than an after-school beer.

Food wasn't plentiful at the Pierce house. Pa didn't work, and the meager monthly disability check or whatever it was was never enough after bills to properly stock up on groceries. This evening, dinner would consist of warming up the pot of ham and beans left over from yesterday. Rita would fry some potatoes to go with it. After peeling and cutting up the potatoes, she decided not to clean the spatula and used it to fix her pa's potatoes. Looking around, she added dead flies and carnage to Pa's meal. She wished there were maggots to add. There weren't any, but she did find a dead roach and added it. After fixing Pa's food, she cleaned the spatula and fixed her food.

Feeling dirty and gross from cleaning, Rita took a bath while Pa napped. Clean and fresh again, she opened another beer and did some reading before going to bed. Beer and reading before bed helped her sleep better and not have nightmares. She had nightmares too. Nightmares in the sense of a foreboding lingering about on the outskirts of her dreamworld. A sinister presence she could never quite pinpoint. A shadow following her. Stalking her.

On occasion, during the reoccurring dream, she would be lying in a paralyzed state unable to move or scream. It was common for her to feel the presence of something next to her bed or standing in a corner.

Pa sleeping with her could sometimes be comforting.

Back in Kansas, the spooks living in the attic would come down at night. Rita couldn't see them, but they were real. Sometimes they would reach out and touch her. Their touch was cold and sent chills across her soul. When she would wake up in the night having to pee, and sensing the spooks in her room, she would pee on one side of the bed and sleep on the other.

Pa was the nightmare king. His nightmares were hellish. She understood why he often drank until passing out.

Finally, too sleepy to read more, Rita went to bed.

2

BOOTSHAKER QUAKE

IraQuake BootShaker, strolling the beach, saw his nineteen-year-old wife Tish upon the boulder, already partly surrounded by the rising tide. Her favorite place. Sitting cross-legged, she was reading the Bible.

Beyond Tish was the Pacific Ocean. The sky was purple, streaked with bright orange florescent clouds. On the horizon, the water mirrored the beauty above. The Heavenly Father was quite the artist. Ira lifted arms in celebration and praise. The purpose of all things created is to manifest the glory of God. Indeed, this ever-changing picture of beauty and wonder exhibited the glory of God. And this was just one small scene, in one small remote area of the world, lasting for a brief moment in time.

Tish, seeing him, closed her Bible and stuck it in her crocheted shoulder bag. She stood and leaped from rock onto the beach.

Meeting him with a kiss, she asked, "Out for a stroll?"

Ira nodded. "The sunset is beautiful."

"It is," she agreed.

With his arm around her and her arm around him, they ambled farther. Tish asked, "There's a look of burden in your eyes, what's wrong?"

"Nothing in the moment. Just the big picture of future things."

"What?"

"Times are changing. The world is changing. And not for the good. It burdens me. The fog of sin and evil is thickening. There's darkness on the horizon."

"Do you need to spend time with the Father?"

"I do."

They stopped walking. Tish gave him a hug. "I'll go and see how Mrs. Talbert is doing."

Ira kissed her forehead.

She pulled away.

Ira took a moment watching Tish walk back down the beach toward the house. For the most part, the life of IraQuake was much like the Pacific Ocean: peaceful, joyful, and abundant with life. By choice, he was a wanderer. He drifted where spiritual breezes took him. He lived to serve. It was his calling.

Looking toward the ocean, the sun, more red than orange now, touched the sea on the horizon. It created a trail of blood drifting back to the shore where he stood. A shiver ran down his back.

The wages of sin is death.

The shoreline was shrinking. Ira walked toward another large rock being surrounded by the ocean's tide. The rock, three to four feet in diameter, was like a stone platform. It was one of several large rocks scattered along the beach. Ira wondered about the rocks. There was probably a good Native American story offering an explanation, but he didn't know it. IraQuake BootShaker was a Cherokee from Missouri and didn't know the Native American folklore of northern California.

Ira took a seat upon the rock. Although jubilation eddied within, it was chased by burden. Crime was skyrocketing. Violence dominated the evening news. The country was ill with civil distress and upheaval. Across the nation, there were demonstrations and rioting over the Vietnam War. Rioting and demonstrations for and against the civil rights of blacks. Discord, rebellion, and violence was at an all-time high. Spirits of sex and licentiousness were running wild across the country.

A door had opened and evil was pouring in.

The youth seemed to hate their parents and parents disliked the youth. It seemed the more talk there was about love and peace, the more hate and violence reigned. Where would it all end? Was civil war on the horizon?

That was the frustration. It didn't have to be this way. The country was choosing to go down this dark senseless path.

Drug use was becoming epidemic. The youth, following the lead of rock-'n'-roll gurus, were turning on and tuning out.

Ira had attended "peace and love" festivals designed to bring awareness to the prospect of brotherly love and unity. The motto and sermon of these freedom thinkers was "Make love, not war."

The message of peace, love, and freedom greatly appealed to IraQuake. Not only the message, but the movement itself. The movement had a Native American mindset and spirit to it. Ira excitedly attended the festivals in hopes to be a part of a movement leading toward peace, love, and rightness. He hoped for a society of people open to and that would adopt the formula for a perfect society as laid out in the Bible. However, he found the movement disturbing and falling short of its meaningful intentions. The theme of peace, love, and unity was distorted in the stupor of free drugs, sex, and immorality.

The so-called "love" festivals were more of an ongoing party of rock-'n'-roll, drugs, and sex. Ira preached Jesus Christ and the "way" to anyone who would listen. Getting an audience wasn't hard. Jesus was popular amongst this movement, and many boasted it was a revisitation of the days when Jesus traveled about preaching the way of love, peace, and unity. However, as sincere as some of these people thought they were, they misunderstood who Christ was and had a false ideology of his ministry. Many taught Christ as a great teacher and philosopher, but not as God incarnate. People believed what they wanted to believe, distorted other things, and discarded what didn't appeal to them. Ira learned most people weren't really searching for truth and freedom, just a new religion to justify their "freethinking" and often immoral ideas.

No marvel. For Satan himself is transformed into an angel of light, calling that which is evil good and that which is good evil.

The one good thing that had come out of the experience was Tish. Tish, a convert to this new religion, was ordained as a "Commune Mother" at the age of seventeen. She was a naive girl with a big heart. Her duties as a "Commune Mother" were toward the caring and raising of the children. Children who were being born out of wedlock—the "love child" as they were celebrated.

Growing up with a big void in her life, Tish had forsaken home and family to go and "find" herself. To find purpose for her meaningless life. With rose-colored sunglasses, barefoot, beads, body paint, sundresses, and flowers in her hair, she was a poster child for the Flower Children.

However, the pills, marijuana, and LSD given to her to free her mind and enlighten her, brought even more uncertainty and confusion. Being a "mother" really meant her body was community property and her love should be freely given and shared by all. She had rarely slept alone and rarely with the same person. More often than not, the experience left her feeling dirty, used, and even emptier inside. Involvement in group orgies designed to celebrate the human body, to encourage unity and togetherness, brought with it a feeling of shame and disgrace. Tish felt that a group of naked acid-tripping people crawling around on one another on a sandy beach doing things that were unnatural seemed more about perversion than enlightenment.

After listening to a charismatic speaker on Hinduism and the possibility of a higher existence following this life, she consumed a lethal amount of drugs with the hope of elevating herself into the next life, where she was promised peace and fulfillment.

By a twist of fate, IraQuake happened upon Tish and rescued her from an overdose that would have taken her life. In her recovery, he stayed with her, looked after her, shared with her the Gospel. She answered the call of salvation, giving her heart and life to Christ.

In the weeks following, a romance between the two sprang up. After a brief courtship, they were married.

Ira leaped from the rock, now surrounded by water, back onto the beach. In the hours to come, the entire rock would be under water. He needed to get back and check on Mrs. Talbert. She was soon to depart from this world.

Along the way, a seashell lying in the sand caught his attention. He picked it up and raised it to his ears.

Standing on the beach, staring out across the ocean with the shell pressed against the side of his head, the sea looked like a lake of fire. The waves of the ocean inside the shell turned into screaming echoes of sorrow. Ira shuddered, casting the shell back into the sea. It disappeared from sight as an ocean wave rolled in to slap at his ankles. Like a chilling breeze, *the wages of sin is death* echoed in his mind.

Sin is a villainous lover with seducing looks and flattering lips, beguiling one into depths of darkness with traps and snares. Sin comes with a price tag. It carries properties of death, leading to the downgrading and destruction of one's life and happiness. The love of sin is a suicidal affair, yet people chase *Her Poisonous Majesty* with eagerness and desire.

People live to die.

At fifty-six years of age, Mrs. Talbert was dying. She had been an actress in her younger days. Never well-known or a star, she had a moderately successful career as a supporting actress and had landed many small and insignificant roles. She had been married three times, but never had had children due to her ambition and the grueling nature of the business. Her third husband divorced her over a decade ago for a younger woman. Mrs. Talbert had lived a wild, uninhibited, promiscuous life, and it was because of that lifestyle she was now without family, all alone and dying of cancer. Mrs. Talbert was reaping the rewards of the villainous lover.

Ira and Tish happened into Mrs. Talbert's life nearly a year ago and since then were caring for her. Getting back from his walk on the beach, Mrs. Talbert appeared asleep, but it was hard to tell sometimes. The expression on her face looked relaxed. At the moment, Mrs. Talbert wasn't in any great pain. Ira wouldn't disturb her. The food Tish had fixed for her earlier hadn't been touched. No surprise. She had hardly eaten a bite in days. Mrs. Talbert was withering away. The skin on her skeletal body was blotchy, wrinkled, and looked terrible. Such a shame. Throughout the house, pictures of her revealed she had been a beautiful woman. The nature of sin is to take beauty and turn it into ugly.

Ira found Tish in the kitchen.

"Would you like something to eat?" she asked.

"Not right now. I think I'll do some writing."

Ira went to the den where Mrs. Talbert had a typewriter. He took a seat at the desk and began tapping out the burden of thoughts torturing his mind:

The sky was purple
Streaked with bright orange florescent clouds
The sun was like blood
Bleeding across the sea

The wages of sin is death
And the sea grows deeper
And the tide keeps rising

Standing on the shore between life and death
A hell shell lay
I raised it to my ear
Echoes of sorrow, heard I
Souls tortured, but never dying

I cast the shell
Back into the lake of fire
Hell's waves of destruction
Rolling in, slapped at my ankles

Ira pulled the paper from the machine and read what was written. The message was dark, but he felt relief. Having it on paper, it no longer haunted his mind.

Ira abruptly awakened. He had fallen asleep on the sofa. It was the middle of the night. He rose and went to check on Mrs. Talbert. Tish in like manner was awakened, and she too was checking on Mrs. Talbert.

They entered Mrs. Talbert's bedroom and found her awake. She was staring across the darkness of the room. Ira went to turn on a light.

"No," she muttered in a raspy voice he barely heard.

He changed course and took a seat next to her bed. He leaned forward and took her hand. "Do you need anything?"

"Do you see them?"

Ira glanced in the direction she stared, but saw nothing. "What do you see?"

"They've come to take me home."

Ira saw nothing, but an air of peace as soft as a butterfly's wing was felt. He squeezed her hand.

"It's time for me to go," she muttered. "I didn't want to leave without thanking you for being with me in my darkest hours. You showed me the door of salvation and led me through it. Now I get to receive my reward."

They were her last words.

Ira leaned forward, resting his head against the side of her face as bittersweet tears leaked from his eyes. Tish joined him, sliding an arm around him. They had hardly known her, but felt a kinship with her. Ira would miss her.

His sorrow soon turned into a feeling of joy as he realized he would someday see her again. In heaven. And not the desperate lonely old woman dying in her pain, but a youthful woman of perfect health and glory.

IraQuake and Tish stood before the coffin of Mrs. Talbert paying last respects. There was no one else present. She had no family, and her friends and colleagues had long ago abandoned her.

As Ira and Tish were about to leave the funeral home, a man in a suit intercepted them.

"Are you Ira BootShaker?"

"I am."

"I am Daniel Gervais. I was or am Mrs. Talbert's lawyer. It was her last will and testament that you and your wife have what money is left after the sale of her estate and bills are paid. I estimate it to be around twenty thousand or so."

"I won't accept it," Ira replied.

"Mrs. Talbert figured you would feel that way. So she said for you to take the money and use it to help others in need. She said she lived a selfish life, but now wants you, in her behalf, to use the money to be a blessing to others." Mr. Gervais handed IraQuake the keys to Mrs. Talbert's Cadillac and a checkbook.

"But we don't want it."

"And yet you have it." Mr. Gervais smiled and said, "Spend it well and make her happy. Good day." Mr. Gervais turned and walked away, leaving Ira and Tish standing.

IraQuake BootShaker left the funeral home with a longing to see his own aging father. Ira, with his Californian hippy wife and with Mrs. Talbert's car, started toward home. Towards NuSprings, Missouri.

3

MEDICINEGIRL

Seated in a wooden swing built for two, Elizabeth Seeker's stare went up into the trees toward a fussing bird. She caught sight of it hopping from one limb to another. A blue jay. She wasn't welcome. She didn't care. Blue jays were rude and unsociable birds.

"Go away, stupid bird!"

This was her place. Her domain. No stupid bird was going to run her off. She wished she had something to throw at it. Squawking, the bird hopped to another limb and then took flight.

Elizabeth liked the morning birds. She liked their morning songs. Though a blue sky was visible beyond the web of limbs, a gray sky blanketed her soul.

Cushions made the wooden swing comfortable. It hung from a trellis-like structure in a far corner of the yard. It was a secluded and peaceful spot. Her quiet place. A place where she could think and meditate. She pushed the ground with her foot, causing the swing to swing.

She was depressed.

Confused.

Watching Tommy Morris die before her eyes affected her more than anyone had thought. She couldn't stop feeling responsible. His death was her fault. Jacky tried to get her to stay out of it. He tried to warn her Tommy was no good. That it was a bad idea to get into a car with him. But did she listen? No. She was stubborn. Thought she knew more than she did. Because of her high opinion of herself, someone died.

Someone died!

It went against everything she had ever believed about herself. Who she was. What she was. Wasn't she MedicineGirl? Wise beyond her age? A natural healer with the Seelot gift?

That's what they told her. That was what she believed. Lives would escape death's trap because she would be there.

Tommy Morris didn't escape death's trap. In fact, she led Tommy into the trap. His blood was on her hands!

The shocked look on his face in those last few moments of his life. His pleading eyes forever burnt into her memory. She was the last thing he saw. His last hope.

Tommy's death was her fault.

Everyone said it wasn't. But it was. The fight was over her. How was it not her fault?

Some healer she was. She couldn't even help the first person who truly needed her. Where was her gift? What good was all the knowledge she had acquired?

She was no doctor. She hadn't earned the right to bear the name MedicineGirl. She was just a stupid girl playing dress-up.

Tears slid down her cheeks.

Her tears were not only about Tommy, but about the loss of herself.

Who was she?

What was she?

She understood nothing. She no longer believed in herself.

Not only was Tommy dead because of her, but she almost caused her cousin to go to jail for murder. She almost destroyed his life. Luckily, that didn't happen. There were enough witnesses saying it was an accident.

The sudden appearance of RiverDawg startled her.

RiverDawg said, "It was said that in the beginning of the world Sky Woman was clothed in blue. That she had no sorrow. That she took great pride that her days were filled with sunshine and warmth. The lands beneath her were green and vibrant. A strong melody of life drifted on the currents of the wind like a song.

"But over time the rich greens of the land began to fade. Things became less green. Still later, that which was green turned yellow. And later still the land looked more brown than green and the song of life was but a hoarse whisper on the wind.

"Watching this change, Sky Woman became distraught. Witnessing the wonderful land beneath dying. No longer did the song of life fill her expanse with pride and zeal.

"Sadness seeped into Sky Woman's soul. Confusion covered her bluish charm with a blanket of gray depression. Worried and flustered, Sky Woman began to weep. As her sadness grew heavier, a flood of tears filling her expanse soaked the land beneath.

"Time passed. Rising from below, breaking through her soggy blanket of depression, a new and fresh song began to be heard on the currents of the wind. Its rich exuberant melody flowed with a joy of life that began to shatter Sky Woman's layers of doubt, confusion, and sadness.

"In time, Sky Woman's bluish charm came back. The land beneath had turned green again and a song of life filled her expanse with a renewed spirit of hope and wonder."

RiverDawg ended his talk.

"Your point being?" Beth wiped tears from her cheeks.

"A sunny world without rainy days eventually dries up and withers away. Spring follows winter."

"You bring me a message of hope?"

"I bring you a gift of truth."

"But why, RiverDawg? Why did someone have to die? Why did it have to be because of me? My depression is different from Sky Woman. She did nothing wrong."

"What is it you did wrong?"

"Ignored advice. Courted an insubordinate spirit. Rebelled against Jacky and Hedy because they made me do something I didn't want to do to start with. Being a spoiled brat.

"And it killed someone!"

"It was not your fault," RiverDawg comforted.

"Like everyone, you speak words, but not explanation."

"This tragedy was a long time coming. A storm that began years ago. Why did it come to a head at such a time you were present? I don't know. The spirits have their reasons."

"Perhaps the spirits were trying to tell me something. That I shouldn't be a doctor. That I'm no good. That there's evil in me." She looked away from RiverDawg, wiping her teary eyes again.

"No, child! Never think such thoughts! You are good! You are the MedicineGirl!"

"But—" She turned to look at RiverDawg. He was gone. Disappeared. "Seriously!" she called out to the wind. *Stupid witch doctor.* He had said what he had come to say. He had made his declaration and wasn't going to argue about it.

Ever since she could remember, RiverDawg would appear from out of nowhere to tell her a story or have a conversation and then be gone as suddenly as he'd appeared.

RiverDawg was a riddle no one understood. People feared RiverDawg. Hedy said he was more bad than good. Hedy said she should keep her distance.

But, RiverDawg was her father. She hadn't always known that.

Pushing at the ground to start the swing moving again, she couldn't remember how young she was—perhaps four—when she and her mom were at a tribal event. She was playing with kids. Some of the kids had daddies. She asked her mom if she had a daddy. Her mom replied, "No. Not all kids have daddies." Four-year-old Beth accepted the answer.

A couple of years later, when she was in school the subject came up again. Some of the kids in her class were talking about their moms and dads. She told them she had no dad.

Beth learned that day that everyone has a mom and a dad. The teacher unknowingly confirmed it.

That evening Beth told her mother that she had learned in school that everyone had a dad. She asked again, did she have a daddy?

Hedy told her, "It is true that it takes a mom and a dad to make a child, but you are a special child. RiverDawg did a secret magic spell on Mommy and you were created in Mommy's stomach."

Beth remembered her mommy getting serious and telling her it was a secret she was to keep and never talk about. At the time, proud to be special, proud to have been created by magic, she accepted the answer and kept the secret.

Growing older and learning biology, she began to doubt her conception was due to magic. She didn't believe it was possible.

She asked RiverDawg one day, "Are you my father?"

After a moment of thoughtful silence, RiverDawg answered, "That is a question for Hedy."

"I already asked her."

"What did she tell you?"

"That more or less you were," Beth twisting what her mother had actually said. "You and your magic."

"Not a lie."

"But, what is the truth?"

"What do you perceive the truth to be?"

"Hedy never uses the word *magic* concerning you. Her word for your 'magic' is always witchery. Through witchery, I was conceived. You and witchery computes. You, witchery, and Hedy doesn't compute. I believe that you, through tricks of witchery, took advantage of my mother. I believe I was conceived in the natural way as any other child is conceived. I believe," Beth stated with accusation, "Hedy would have never, *in her right mind*, slept with you."

Understanding the allegation, RiverDawg answered, "Hedy is not and never was a fan of mine. She disapproves of me. Of what I am. How I live. She always thought herself better than me.

"When she was younger, she was more arrogant than wise. There was this social event. It was a beautiful day and Hedy is a beautiful lady. I flirted with her as is my nature. She told me I was old enough to be her father. She told me I had no chance with her.

"I told her I did, if I truly wanted. She told me that her will was stronger than my witchery. I asked her if that was a challenge? She said, 'Sure, why not?' She told me, 'Give it your best shot.' So I did. I won the challenge. You were created. We both walked away winners."

The young twelve-year-old Beth, hearing the story, didn't know how to feel. How she was supposed to feel. She was confused. She didn't know if she was to be happy or angry? If she had been robbed and deceived? She had discovered she did have a dad and who he was. Although their relationship had always been a secret one, he had always been a part of her life. He was someone she could talk to. Shared her feelings and secrets. Someone who gave her advice.

After a couple of days of thinking about it, she finally decided she had been done wrong and allowed herself to become angry. She began lashing out at Hedy until Hedy finally asked her what her problem was. And Beth gladly, disrespectfully told her.

After a long and heated discussion, Hedy explained that, although she wasn't ashamed of Beth, she was ashamed of how she came to be. It was public knowledge Hedy didn't approve of RiverDawg.

She was outspoken about it. And then to have become with child by him, was more than her pride could handle. She didn't want anyone to know. Hedy told Beth that RiverDawg agreed to keep her secret out of respect because she was the tribe's new Beloved Woman.

Hedy explained, "I was a young woman who got pregnant out of wedlock from a one-night stand. No one knew RiverDawg was the culprit."

Hedy apologized. It was never her intention to hurt her, and she was as honest as she could be.

Hedy told Beth, "RiverDawg is not a person to take lightly. And as much as I detested it, RiverDawg taught me a lesson in humility I needed. A Beloved Woman should not be arrogant and I was. I hate to admit it, but RiverDawg made me a better person.

"Besides, I liked the idea of you being conceived by magic. You are beautiful, smart, and special. RiverDawg is right: although I lost the challenge, I came out the winner. I got you!"

The next day, after much thought, Beth told Hedy, "I don't like being angry and holding grudges. It's not who I am. I am better than that. I love life. I forgive you. And Dad too." As Beth and her mother embraced, Beth promised to keep the secret.

4

UNCOMMON FRIENDS

George Brandt, a self-employed carpenter, did good work but lacked ambition. Too often his workdays were short or he didn't make it to work at all. Such was the case today. Getting ready to leave for work, he spotted Homer Pierce crossing a field into the woods carrying a fishing pole. It was a perfect day for fishing.

Though neighbors, George had never met Homer. He hadn't cared to. He didn't see Homer as having anything to offer.

George had a roofing job to do. It was a nice day, sunny and not too hot. A good day for roofing. A good day for fishing too. Savoring a cigarette and the moment, George decided the roof could wait. The fish were calling. George flicked away what was left of his cigarette and got into his truck.

Stopping at a liquor store, George decided today would be a good day to get to know his weirdo neighbor. He had an idea where the freak was fishing.

By the time George found Homer, he was already annoyed. He had to walk through woods, weeds, and thickets. He found Homer in a ragged old adjustable lawn chair one could lie and nap in. George wasn't sure if Homer was asleep or not.

"Hey bud, how's the fishing?" George called as he approached.

Homer didn't respond. His pole and tackle box were lying beside the chair. The guy wasn't even fishing.

"Hey, I said, 'how's the fishing?'"

Homer's eyes opened. He must have been sleeping. George stopped in front of him and looked down. He'd never seen Homer up close before. The man was ugly. Severely scarred. A real freak in every sense of the word.

"Caught anything?" George asked.

Homer blinked as his eyes darted about. The freak didn't seem right. Was he drunk? Had the scarring affected his mind?

George dropped his gear. "Care if I join ya? I got beer!"

Homer didn't respond.

Growing more annoyed, George got a couple of beers, opened one, took a big gulp, and nudged Homer with the other. "Have a cold one."

Homer suddenly responded by jerking his head toward George, as if realizing for the first time he had company.

"So you are alive! Wanna beer?" George offered again.

Homer sprang up with eyes wide opened. He jerked his head around from side to side before settling his stare on him. Facial expressions usually gave George some idea as to what a person felt or thought. But this guy was different. He was scarred too badly. His face, what was left of it, didn't reveal information.

When it appeared Homer wasn't gonna take the offered beer, George pulled back his arm. "The name's George Brandt. Your neighbor down the road."

"Huh?"

"George. Your neighbor." George stuck out a hand, this time to shake hands.

Homer adjusted the chair back to an upright position. He looked at the stretched-out hand.

"Don't believe we've ever met," George said. "What do people usually call you?"

Homer reached out to shake George's hand. Making a face George didn't understand, he said, "Homer. Homer's my name. Homer Pierce."

"Well, Homer Pierce, it seems a fine day for fishing." George guzzled down more beer and then knelt to make ready his rod. "How's the fish biting? Care if I join ya?"

Homer mumbled something George didn't quite make out. He scooted out of his chair and stood up.

"Caught anything?" George asked.

Homer moved his head around in a way that appeared he was tracking a fly or something. *The man's crazy*, thought George, looking down at his tackle box trying to decide on a lure.

"Caught a fly!" Homer said with a slight shout.

"Really?" George said, almost startled.

Homer was holding his hand in a fist.

"He's a big one!" Homer's fist was slightly moving as if it was the fly moving it. "The black buzzy's gonna die too. Watch this." Moving lightning fast, Homer slapped his hands together.

Looking down at his hand, Homer gave a psychotic laugh and said, "Bloody little bugger. I bet it was my blood too. They wait 'til I fall asleep, then they attack me." Homer paused, then added, "Lots of blood. I killed him, though. I killed him dead!" The tone of his voice becoming vindictive. "I'll kill'em! I'll kill'em all! They think they own this place." Homer cursed, wiping his hand clean on his pants. "This is MY place! I'll kill'em all, I will."

George stood, wishing he had brought his pistol. Homer wasn't right in the head. Possibly dangerous. Sizing him up, George was bigger, and if he had to, he'd beat the freak-show to death with his bare fists!

Homer, staring at the stream, said, "Me and these fish, we got a deal. They let me catch'em and I don't kill'em. But if they resist me, by gawd, I'll kill'em! I'll kill'em all!"

"You sound like a dangerous man."

Homer snickered. A moment later he asked, "Wanna fish, do ya?"

"Only if you don't mind."

"I like ya, George, neighbor-down-the-road. Tell ya what, my bottle of whiskey against yer cans of beer there."

"A wager, Homer?"

"Ya a betting man, George?"

"Ya a sore loser, Homer?"

"I don't plan on losing."

"What's the game?"

"We venture upstream taking turns fishing. The man who catches the biggest fish wins."

"And what happens if I win?"

"You get my whiskey."

"No hard feelings?"

"It's just a game, George."

"Fair enough."

Homer started towards the creek. "Coming, George, neighbor-down-the-road?"

George, grabbing his fly rod and lucky lure, noticed Homer had left his rod on the ground next to his chair. "Hey Homer, you forgot your rod."

"Oh yeah. I do that sometimes when I fish."

Retarded Freak, thought George.

Serious fishermen went to Table Rock Lake, James River, and Bull Creek.

"The best way to fish a stream like this is to walk upstream." Homer stepped into the little meandering waterway wading ankle-deep water—deeper than his shoe tops.

George frowned. He wasn't wearing the right shoes either. The water was cold.

Coming upon a nice pool along one side of the stream created by a fallen tree, Homer stopped. When George got within range, Homer whispered, "There's a couple smallmouth. You wanna go first?"

"Be my guest."

Using a popping bug, Homer's first cast fell short and hit the pool like a rock. The bass scattered. Homer attempted to catch one anyway, but the fish weren't buying. He reeled his line in, stomped over to the pool, cursing, scolding, and threatening to kill them— kill them all! With a deep breath, Homer calmed down. "No point in trying this spot for a while."

"They're too scared to come out and play now." George stepped ahead of Homer in search of another fish hangout.

"They'd better be!" Homer snickered in a psychotic tone.

Fifty yards up, George signaled Homer to stop and be quiet. George eased forward, trying to see where the fish were without the fish seeing him. Bass weren't the smartest animals in the world, but they weren't the stupidest either. If sensing danger, they're less likely to go for bait. George hooked one, but before he could get it reeled in, it fought its way loose.

"Good try, George, neighbor-down-the-road."

Over the next hour, George caught three bass and two bluegills. Homer caught as many. Who had the biggest fish at this time was anyone's guess. They wouldn't know until they compared.

The two men reached what Homer referred to as Jonah's Bend because of a largemouth bass that lived there. George studied the area, stepped upon the bank, and went to the head of the bend above the fallen tree creating the hole. He cast upstream of the sunken log and weed bed and waited for his lucky crawdad to sink to the bottom. He began working it back toward him in short hops.

Without warning, the pole was almost pulled from George's hands. He stepped forward in reflex. A mistake! Already at the edge of the bank, he stepped into air, lost his balance, and went forward into the water.

Homer, hearing George hit the water, looked. George was splashing around trying to hang on to his pole and stand straight. Homer shouted, "Attaboy, George! Get down on their level! The fish love that sort of stuff! Don't let the fish reel you in, though: you'll be his catch and he'll get the beer!"

Managing to keep his head above water and one hand cemented to the pole, George got his footing and stood up. He was in waist-deep water. His line went tight as the end of the pole bent downward. "Fight if you will. I got you now!" George said to the whale on the end of his line with a few colorful words added.

George's reel went to screaming as the fish turned and swam a different direction. George reeled. The fish turned again. Back and forth in a tug of war.

George was making headway until the bass shot up out of the water in front of him. It was a beautiful sight, but the lure hanging on the corner of the bass's mouth was a little less than reassuring. The bass curled his body into a tight comma and shook its head back and forth with great vigor. The lure left the fish's mouth and went flying through the air back at George. George ducked. Having lost the fish, he threw his pole shouting obscenities!

Homer's big monster head bobbled back and forth as he stomped his feet in a river dance. He shouted, "You lost him, George! I'll catch 'em for ya!" Homer made a wild cast toward the bass. "Come and get it, Jonah, you big ugly lunker!"

No sooner had the lure hit the water, the big fish caught it and took off with it. Homer's line went to singing. "Whooppeee!" Homer yelled. "I got 'im, George! I got ole Jonah!"

"Reel him in!" George shouted back. *You ugly scarred-face turd.* He couldn't believe Homer's luck.

Pulling, tugging, and reeling at every possible moment, the bass splashed the surface of the water, darting this way and that way. Homer put more pressure on, hoping his line wouldn't break. Jonah turned again and headed straight toward him. Homer was reeling but the fish was faster. Jonah shot between Homer's legs. Homer's foot got caught in the line as Jonah swam a loop around him.

George Brandt's anger faded as the scene between Homer and Jonah became comical. The monster was hopping about while the fish swam circles around him.

"Careful, Homer, the fish is about to catch ya!" George hollered and hoped Homer would lose his balance and fall.

George got his wish. Homer fell backwards with a splash.

"I think Jonah's gotcha, Homer! Kick your feet and wiggle yer body, maybe you'll break free."

Having lost his pole, Homer crawled back to shallower water. To his surprise, the fishing line was wrapped around his foot and Jonah was still on its end. Homer grabbed the line and pulled. The bass fought, splashing water in every direction, but Homer was bigger and stronger.

Finally, Homer winning, he stood and held up the fish. Six, seven pounds, the fish still struggled. After showing off his catch, Homer carefully removed the hook and released the fish back into the stream.

Fishing trip over and walking back, George shook his head. "Never in a million years would I have believed such a tale. A fish taking down two grown men."

"That's Jonah for ya. He likes to come out and play now and again."

George almost forgot Homer was crazy until Homer said, "Old Jonah there, that lunker's my best friend. Sometimes I come down here drink whiskey and talk. He's a good listener, he is." Homer went silent a moment and then added, "Not a bad drinker either." Homer chuckled at the memories. "Someday, though, I'm gonna eat him. Fry him for supper. Nothing like the taste of a good friend."

Spoken like a true monster, George looked at Homer in wonder. Shaking his head, "Homer, you're a little scary, but alright."

"Well thank you, George, neighbor-down-the-road. You're not so bad yourself."

Back at "camp," Homer wasted no time in hitting the bottle. "Fishing makes a man thirsty."

George, tossing over to Homer what was left of his case of beer, said, "You won, Homer. There's your beer. Although I'm not so sure if you caught Jonah as much as it was Jonah catching you."

Homer looked down at the beer and frowned. "I guess I can give it to my wife."

"You married, Homer?"

"Not anymore. Had a wife once. She got hit by a train." Snickering, he added, "Like a bug on a windshield." *The man's a psycho!* "You said something about taking the beer home to your wife?"

"Huh?"

"You said you was gonna take the beer home to your wife."

"I did? Oh. I meant my daughter. She's the spitting image of her mother. I sometimes get'em confused."

Interesting.

Standing to leave, George said, "Homer, it's been fun, but it's time to party elsewhere."

Homer halfway waved his hand. "Good-bye, George, neighbor-down-the-road."

George took a few steps, stopped, and asked, "Wanna go for a ride, Homer?" He didn't expect him to want to.

"Okay," Homer surprised George.

Traveling gravel roads, taking turns sipping whiskey, George took Homer on a tour of the countryside. Homer hadn't seen much of the area. He preferred staying home or hanging out at one of his secret places like his fishing spot. He felt safe in the woods.

George pulled into the parking lot of a little tavern on the outskirts of town. "This is my oasis," George told Homer. "You wanna go in and meet some of the boys? We could tell'em our fish story."

"Rather not, George," Homer said uncompromisingly.

"I don't think the boys would be too hard on ya. Especially after they got to know ya some."

"Rather not, George."

George was quiet a moment. "Well if that's the way ya feel."

"It is, George."

"Hey, I understand." *If I was as ugly as you, I'd stay hid all the time too.*

George pulled back onto the gravel road.

"Up ahead," George sharing information, "lives a woman who attends the bar back there. Not a bad-looking gal. She's a cunt-friend," George bragged.

"She's married, but it means nothing. Her husband suffered a stroke a few years back, leaving him near close to a vegetable. Ninety percent paralyzed. He can't really talk, just utters noises and sounds. I call him Veg. He used to be a drinking buddy. We had some good times together. Now he just lies around in bed most of the time. And June, the poor woman, she tries getting him out into a wheelchair so he may sit some and stare out the window or whatever. When the weather's nice, she'll push him out onto the porch so he can get some fresh air. It's a struggle for June getting the lug out of bed and into a wheelchair. She ain't hardly strong enough.

"I check in on them regularly. Give June rides to work and places. She doesn't have a car and normally has to walk to work. I help her drag ole Veg out of bed and get him in his chair. I sit and visit with him some. Have a cup of coffee. A piece of June." George laughed. "No need in a good woman going to waste, right, Homer?" Chuckling more, George added, "Sometimes I do June right in front of Veg so he can watch. That turns June on like nothing else."

Homer took a drink of whiskey.

"That's terrible of us, ain't it," George stated. "That's where they live." George pointed as they drove toward the house. "Deep down I think she resents ole Veg for having a stroke. Having sex in front of him is her way of punishing him."

George pulled into the driveway. "Homer, I know you're not a people person or anything, but I feel I need to make a quick stop and see if June needs me to help her get ole Veg out of the bed." He turned the truck off. "You wanna come in and meet them? Ole Veg could use another friend. He's a lot like you. He doesn't say much." George opened his door. "Who knows, once June gets to know ya a little, she might spread her wings for you too. She's generous like that."

"I'd better stay here, George. It's better that way."

"Suit yourself. I'll not be too long."

George got out of the truck. Homer watched him go up to the house, knock on the door, open it, and say, "Anyone home? It's George!" George disappeared into the house.

Homer took another sip. George wasn't a bad guy, but what he was doing to his old friend wasn't right. But that's people for you. People are sinners. People love sin. Amen.

Recalling those first few months after being released from the hospital after the fire, Homer experienced just how cruel friends and lovers were. His mom and dad were dead and all he had were his friends. Friends who no longer had time for him. His best friend threw him a welcome-home party a few days after he had gotten out of the hospital. He was looking forward to the event until it was happening. Everyone was different. No one was friendly. Polite maybe, but not friendly. Homer realized he was a freak. A sideshow. He would catch people staring and whispering. When he would look their way, they'd turn their heads pretending to be socializing and discussing other topics. He knew better. He had been a socialite himself. He knew their shallowness. He knew their ways.

That was the last he'd seen of most of his so-called buddies. Two or three had come back around a few more times, but it wasn't long until even they quit stopping by. Day after day, in the big old house all alone. Day after day with nothing to do but drink whiskey, feel sorry for himself, and give in to the hate. Ugly scarred-face Homer, twenty-five years old, trapped in a prison of ugliness and disdain.

No one loved him.

No one cared.

Homer's attention was drawn to the house. George wheeled Veg out onto the porch. George getting the man in a comfortable position, a woman stepped out onto the porch. June, Homer supposed. She was nice to look at. George said something to her and she looked at the truck, smiled and waved. Homer ignored the gesture. George and June went back into the house.

Veg, slumped and leaning to one side, looked pitiful. Too bad for him. Homer had his own problems. His own demons to live with. Homer took a sip of whiskey.

Poor Veg. He didn't even have whiskey to keep him company. Homer and whiskey were best friends.

As long as Homer had his bottle, he didn't need anyone. Whiskey. Man's best friend!

The minutes passed. Homer wished George would hurry up. Veg had no friends either. George wasn't really his friend.

No friends. No whiskey. A whoring wife. Poor ole Veg. He couldn't even beat her. Homer used to beat his wife. He tried beating a soul into her. It was useless. She had no soul. Finally, he just killed her. Killing a whore was no sin. Stoning whores was in the Bible.

Poor ole Veg. God hated his soul too.

Homer got out of the truck and walked up to the house. He quietly stepped onto the porch. Veg's head moved a bit, but he was unable to turn it. Homer stepped in front of him and said in a quiet voice, "I'm Homer. George's friend. Sort of."

Veg didn't show much reaction to Homer's condition. Homer liked that. No shock. No shying away. He stepped over to the door. He could hear George and June getting it on. Veg could hear it too. Homer sat down in a porch chair and scooted Veg around so Veg could see him.

Homer said, "Women are whores." Homer took a sip of whiskey and looked at Veg. "Wanna drink?"

Veg uttered something. Homer had no idea what it was.

Homer stared at Veg. "A man should at least be able to have a drink. Without whiskey a man is nothing." Homer stood. "I'm gonna give you a drink." Homer put the open end of the bottle to the man's lips and raised the bottle up as he gently tilted his head backwards. Some of the whiskey was wasted as it failed to enter the guy's mouth, but Homer managed to get some down him anyway.

Veg coughed, gasped, and sounded a bit like he was strangling.

"It's got bite, don't it?" Homer said with glee. He wiped the spilt whiskey from Veg's chin. "Do you feel its fire inside ya? Is it warming your dead old bones?" The look in the man's eyes was different now. It wasn't the dead look of before. It was an awakened look. Like the man had felt something after being dead for so long. "Yeaah." Homer's lips formed a smile as he responded to the change in Veg's eyes. "You liked that, didn't you?" Homer took a quick sip. "Yep. This stuff is powerful medicine. What it don't cure, it makes you not care about. Here have another."

Homer helped Veg to another sip. Veg was good people. Homer liked him.

Homer wasn't hearing George and June anymore. George must have gotten his business done. He'd soon be back out. Homer leaned forward to speak quietly to Veg. "I like you, Veg. You're alright. I'll be leaving, but I'll be back. I'll be your friend. A real friend."

Veg made another utterance.

Homer had no idea what the utterance meant, but said, "I understand. Don't worry, friend, I'll bring the whiskey."

When George came out of the house, he was surprised to see Homer sitting on the porch with Veg. "Hey Homer, so I guess you met Veg?"

"Yeah George, we've been talking."

"You don't say." George looked back and forth at them.

June pushed open the door to step out onto the porch, but froze the moment she saw Homer. She wasn't prepared.

"June," George said, turning around and grabbing her hand, "step out here and meet my neighbor."

He pulled her out onto the porch. "Homer, this is June. June, Homer."

Homer looked at the woman. She reluctantly raised her hand for a handshake, trying with all her might not to look horrified. Homer gave her a half nod and shifted his eyes to George. "Time to go, George." Homer turned and walked toward the truck.

June dropped her arm.

George smiled. "He's a man of few words." He leaned closer. "I guess it's time to get the freak home. You gonna need help getting Veggy back to bed?"

"I'll manage," she answered, watching Homer crawl into the truck.

Stepping off the porch following Homer, George said to Veg, "Take it easy, friend. Don't overdo it."

George started the truck and waved to June as he backed out of the driveway. He'd had enough of freaks for one day. Going home to his own retarded family didn't seem so bad.

5

IN TIME OF STORM

The Cadillac was a fine ride and owning such a vehicle wasn't a sin, but IraQuake wasn't comfortable owning it. It seemed indulging. His flesh relished it too strongly. It made him feel exalted in a worldly way. One had to be on guard about the flesh becoming too brazen. The flesh, with its default Luciferian, self-god mindset, wars against the Spirit over control of a person's heart and mind.

The trip from California to Missouri would have taken only days, but Ira and Tish visited places of interest. Ira believed life was a gift and a person should take the time to enjoy it. He got that from his earthly father, who was a lover of life and enjoyed living. Ira was excited to see his dad and for him to meet Tish. Ira was sure his dad would be impressed.

In Kansas on a Sunday morning, Ira and Tish found a little country church to visit. Their presence wasn't welcome because of their hippy personas. Ira had long hair, a headband, tie-dyed shirt, and bell-bottom pants. Tish, also wearing a headband, wore a pair of rose-colored sunglasses atop her head. She had a small yellow daisy painted on her cheek. She was in a long dress, but wore no shoes. The good church people judged them anti-American and unworthy for the House of God. Ira and Tish humbly continued on their way.

Tish, offended and upset, asked, "What did we do that was so wrong?"

"We did nothing wrong."

"Why were we asked to leave?"

"They feared us."

"Feared us?"

"They feared we would corrupt their youth with our devilish charms."

"Devilish charms?"

"Things that go against set patterns of tradition are feared and even seen as being of the devil. Too many churches, too many Christians lack a true understanding of Christianity. And sadly too many lack enough divine wisdom to rightly discern good from evil. We should pray for them and not begrudge them."

With a deep sigh, Tish said, "I'll try."

Ira winked and smiled at her.

They hadn't gone far when they noticed an excessive amount of litter scattered along the sides of the highway. Ira believed it was a Christian's duty to be an example of social and moral excellence. Ira pulled over and as an act of worship to God, decided to clean up the litter.

Tish strode along with Ira in a joint effort to clean the roadside. She felt good about what she was doing. Ira never spoke ill toward those responsible nor complained about the deed they were doing. He told her those responsible had provided them with an opportunity to do good and honor God in environmental stewardship. Stewardship was one of man's divine purposes.

Tish was amazed how Ira was always thinking of ways to serve God and be a blessing to people. Serving God was not about being inside a church. The service was outside where the lost were. She paused in the good deed to give him a worshipful kiss.

"What was that for?" Ira asked.

"I love you is all." She pulled away and went back to work, aware of his stare and the temptation to take things further. Dropping another crushed beer can into her sack, moving toward the next piece of litter, her awareness of a vehicle slowing on the highway interrupted her thoughts of a playful seduction. The traffic on the highway wasn't heavy, but there was a constant zipping of vehicles. She turned her eyes to the passing vehicle: a pickup.

Someone shouted out the window, "Communists!"

The truck accelerated and drove on. Tish was offended. Why were they called communists? She looked toward Ira. He was ignoring it.

"What was that about?" she asked.

Ira shrugged. "Being Indian, I'm used to antagonistic remarks. It's usually best to ignore them."

"But that had nothing to do with you being Indian."

"They didn't see us as Indian. They saw us as being hippies."

Tish considered it. There was a definite association between the two. The hippy culture celebrated many civil-rights activists and lecturers who were friendly toward socialistic and Marxist ideology. Thinking about it now, she could see how the hippy counterculture was allied with Marxism and ignorantly adopted their socialistic views and ideas as a better way of life.

How blind she had been. How blind they all were. The flower children were about peace, love, goodwill, and freedom. In the flower children's pursuit of peace, love, and unity, social activists had engaged them in a civil revolution geared toward demonstrations, violence, and war. She felt disgusted and used.

The truck came back and pulled onto the shoulder of the road. Tish and Ira watched three guys get out and walk toward them. The guys looked to be in their early twenties.

"Hey, we don't tolerate commies in this part of the country!" one shouted.

Their country clothes, clean and pressed, revealed they were farm boys who had recently got out of church. Their flattop haircuts revealed them to be old-fashioned and patriotic. Their physiques suggested they were hard workers, strong, and were probably football players in high school.

Ira wasn't scrawny, but he didn't match the brawn of the three country boys. Not intimidated, Ira politely answered, "We're not communists."

"You're not American either!" The boys drew closer.

"They look commie to me," a second one said.

"We're not stupid. Hippies are of the devil."

No doubt, they were repeating a recent sermon. The boys stopped with only steps between them.

Ira put himself in front of Tish. "We are not communists! We believe in God. We believe in the Bible. We're Christians."

"How dare you call yourself a Christian! That's blasphemy!" one of the boys spoke.

"The Bible says, 'Whosoever shall call upon the name of the Lord shall be saved,'" Ira countered.

Flushed faces disclosed the anger building inside the boys. With clenched fists, the leader of the three threatened, "It's one thing to try to crash our church service with your stink, but it's another to twist and defile the Word of God!"

Another said, "It's that devil's charm trying to confuse us!"

"I think he needs a lesson in respect," the other boy suggested.

"The Bible says, 'The fear of the Lord is the beginning of wisdom' and hippies don't fear God." The first boy spoke directly to Ira.

Ira answered, "The Bible says to love thy neighbor and to be full of good works. Is this your idea of 'love thy neighbor'?"

The guy stepped forward, shoving Ira backwards a step. "Don't mock me, devil. I'm about to teach you some godly remorse for your wicked ways!"

Tish ran forward between Ira and the guy in a failed attempt to push the guy back. "Stop it! We've done nothing wrong and we've done nothing to you. We're just passing through."

The guy stood his ground and shoved Tish to the side. "Get this hippy whore out of the way!"

One of the guys grabbed her in a bear hug.

"Let me go!" she demanded, struggling to break free. Her cries went ignored and she wasn't strong enough to free herself.

"Let's teach this hippy commie some Christian respect."

Ira, in stance, took a step backwards, bracing himself for a fight he knew he couldn't avoid. They wanted to beat up a hippy and have another good-ole-boy story to brag about.

Ira let the guy throw the first punch. He dodged it. The second guy stepped forward also. Ira would have to defend himself against the two of them. Ira did his best to avoid fighting, but when not given a choice, you did what you had to do. He silently prayed that God would intervene or at least give guidance.

Ira dodged a punch from one and blocked the

punch from the other. He moved to create distance. He would not let them box him in.

"Looks like he's not gonna make it easy on you guys," the guy holding Tish called out.

"It would be a shame if he did."

IraQuake defended himself well against the two stout farm boys. His fight was one of defense, but he would land a good punch here and there to humble them and to teach respect. Finally, the guy holding Tish pushed her out of the way and went to help. Tish stood out of the way, astonished at Ira's ability to defend himself. He didn't need her. It was obvious Ira was a student of the martial arts. His moves were calculated and artful.

Eventually the good-ole boys overtook Ira, leaving him lying on the ground trying to catch the breath they kicked out of him. The leader of the group pointed a finger at Tish. "You best leave and never come back!"

Tish ran to Ira's side as the three went on their way.

"Are you hurt?" Tish knelt beside Ira, trying to help and check for wounds.

"I'll live," he answered with a smile.

With Tish's help, he got to his feet. "I don't think anything is broken." He took a step on his own. "I'll be alright. Sore. But alright. Grab those bags and let's go."

A sign declared a gas station and store ahead.

It was in the middle of the afternoon; Ira and Tish hadn't had anything to eat since early that morning. Ira was napping. The gas gauge declared the car was low on gas. Tish thought it wise to fill up while there was an opportunity.

Ira again surprised her. She had no idea of his fighting abilities. She'd feared he would suffer a beating. Instead, except at the last, he had hardly been touched. He told her he'd let them overcome him so they would feel they had won and move on. He didn't want to have to hurt them. Ira told Tish it was better to lose on his terms than to win on theirs. If he'd won and left the three on the ground, they would feel a need to avenge themselves. And that might lead them to attack someone else who might not have the ability to defend themselves as he could. By taking the fall, they got what they wanted, but because they had so misjudged his abilities, they would be less likely to do it again for a deep-seated fear of the unknown. Ira chuckled, saying that the lesson of respect had been on them and they didn't even know it.

She asked how he had come to study fighting in the first place, being it was not Christlike. "On the contrary," he told her, "being the best one can be is glorifying to God. Martial arts aren't about doing violence, but a defense against violence. It is also about discipline, health, and bringing body and mind into subjection. Which is very Christian. Martial arts, in a righteous mindset, is a very good Christian thing."

Tish pulled into the station and stopped at the self-serve pump.

Ira, waking up, looked around. "Where are we?"

"Still in Kansas, love. I thought we might fill the tank again and see what they have to eat. Hungry?"

"I am."

"I'll go in and shop around. Can you handle the gas? Are you too sore?"

"I'll manage."

Tish, barefooted as usual, headed into the store as Ira went to pump the gas. Filling the car, Ira watched an elderly couple pulling a plow over to their old but durable-looking pickup. At the back of the pickup, the guy Ira assessed to be in his sixties lowered the tailgate. The man and his wife attempted to lift the plow. They didn't succeed. It was bulky and too heavy for the lady. Before they made a second attempt, Ira called out for them to wait and he'd help. They did. Ira finished filling the car and then went over and the two men lifted the plow into the back of the truck. A task Ira discovered he was almost too sore to do.

Tish exited the store with a small sack of groceries and went to the car. Placing the sack in the car, she spotted Ira in conversation with an older couple. She went and joined him.

The couple, slightly taken aback by her hippy persona, quickly set judgments aside to be hospitable. Tish never realized how misunderstood hippies were until today, and the further east they went the more misunderstood she was. People treated her with suspicion and dislike. It was probably the media's negative presentation of them. Ira told her NuSprings wouldn't be so harsh. She hoped he was right. She liked her look.

After an introduction, Ira asked Tish, "Would you like a good home-cooked meal?"

"Sounds heavenly."

"I offered to help unload the plow."

The homestead of the Moores was modest, surrounded by farmland. Four trees provided ample shade and comfort from summer heat. A windmill, blades turning in the breeze, provided some of the electricity.

The house was built back when the couple was young and just starting out in life. Back then, they didn't have electricity or indoor plumbing.

Tish inhaled, filling her lungs with the clean and fresh air of Kansas. The air tasted almost sweet compared to the industrial smells of Los Angeles.

Behind the house, an abandoned outhouse stood within a short distance of a small barn housing an old tractor. At the side of the house was a storm cellar, and not far from it was a vegetable garden. The couple boasted that most of what they ate they grew.

Tish marveled at the life of the couple. They were simple folk, living simple lives, being mostly self-sufficient. They were "organic." They seemed happy, content, and had it together—much like how the commune was supposed to be. The back-to-nature life she'd left home to pursue.

Tish joined the commune in hopes to be a part of the new "enlightened" culture practicing brotherly love and living simple, self-sufficient, stress-free lives. A culture experimenting in organic farming and alternate fuel sources such as wind and solar energy. A culture getting back to nature and caring for the planet. A plan modeling a new and better society. So much dreaming and philosophizing went into the commune and its alternative lifestyle. It was to be a society of freedom and promise. A unified body of loving people, sharing all things, and helping one another.

The dream the commune offered greatly appealed to Tish. She grew up upper middle-class in a suburb of Los Angeles. Her childhood was stressful and fast-paced. Her mother and father, always bickering at each other, drank booze and took pills to cope with the demands of life. Materially, Tish had all she wanted. What she didn't have was a peaceful home or a happy life. She often felt depressed and angry for no apparent reason other than an oppressive atmosphere she didn't understand.

Standing in front of the Moores' home, she couldn't believe it. Here in Dorothy-and-Toto-land people were living the "new" and "alternative" life that the commune preached would be the future. In reality, there was nothing new about it. The Moores had been living like this their whole lives. It was simply life in Kansas.

A pleasant afternoon, followed by a wonderful dinner with homegrown dishes prepared in country fashion, was rich in aroma and flavor. Tish had never tasted such good food in all her life. It was hard not to gorge.

Mr. Moore invited them to stay the night. Ira and Tish felt the couple seldom had company and desired some. The Moores were church-going people. They enjoyed talking Bible and God's good blessings. Ira accepted the invitation. Besides, they promised a big home-cooked breakfast in the morning. Tish couldn't wait.

The bed in the guest bedroom came with a feather mattress Mrs. Moore stuffed herself. It was comfortable and it didn't take Ira and Tish long to fall asleep.

Ira and Tish were awakened by knocking on their bedroom door and Mr. Moore calling out to them from the opposite side. It was storming outside. Ira was surprised the thunder hadn't woke him. Ira pulled open the door.

"The storm has gotten bad, we feel it best to head to the cellar," Mr. Moore demanded.

A strong gust of wind against the house rattling the windows was convincing. Throwing on clothes, grabbing a blanket, Ira and Tish followed the couple outside into the violent storm. Thunder was loud and the lightning constant. The wind was fierce and challenging. In the flashes of lightning, they could see objects blowing across the ground and through the air.

Battling the wind, Mr. Moore struggled to open the cellar door as Tish and Mrs. Moore held on to each other for fear of being blown away. As Mr. Moore pried open the door, Ira took charge holding it open. The women entered first and Mr. Moore followed.

The storm was roaring. Ira didn't have time to focus on the oddity of it as it was taking every bit of his strength to hold open the door for himself. As he was about to step down into the cellar, Ira felt himself lifted into the air. The wind jerked the door from his grip. He reached to grab the handle, but it was out of reach. Everything was out of reach!

Like a merry-go-round zooming out of control, round and round he went.

Partnered with a storm in a dance of life and death, time and reality are different. Inside the vortex of a mighty swirling wind, in the blackness of darkness, the mind doesn't stop working, but the experience is so alien, the mind doesn't know how to process it. It's disorienting. You are suspended in time, but moving at a speed you don't understand. The noise is so loud it is almost silent. Everything is dark and black and the flashes of lightning are blinding. You don't just hear thunder, you feel it. You're a part of it. You are helpless and all seems hopeless.

No amount of self-will or wisdom does you any good. You are at the mercy of the beast! You know at any moment the beast may grow tired of you and hurl you through the air and to your death.

IraQuake BootShaker cried out to the Lord!

When the door slammed shut and Tish realized Ira hadn't followed them in, she shouted for him and raced back up the steps. The roaring storm outside was deafening. She wasn't strong enough to push the door open and cried for help. Together, she and Mr. Moore pushed open the door. The wind grabbed it, ripped it from its hinges. The door disappeared into the night. Fighting not to be sucked out, Mr. Moore, holding on to the handrail, pulled Tish back down into safety and against her will.

The violence lasted only minutes. To Tish it was hours. She did the only thing she knew to do: she cried in desperation unto the Lord. They all did.

The roaring moved on and atmospheric pressure normalized. Mr. Moore ventured up the steps to peer out. It was dark. Nothing to see but a wall of pouring rain. Tish, pushing him aside, ventured into unwelcoming elements shouting "Ira."

Her search was futile. Howling wind drowned out her yells. She couldn't see to get around. In the flashes of lightning, she saw glimpses of the tornado's destruction. The rain descended without mercy. It was cold. She was soaked.

Ira was nowhere to be found.

Mr. Moore begged her to return to the shelter. She refused, fought free of his grip, and continued without a plan. Without direction. What other choice did she have?

To her side, seemingly only yards away, a thick bolt of lightning struck the ground. Its charge held for an incredible second. The brilliant flash lit the entire area, burning the scene into Tish's brain like a photograph. The tremendous power and energy of it paralyzed her. She froze in fear, having never experienced such a thing before. It was so close. Too close! An instant later it was gone, leaving her engulfed in total darkness and perhaps blind. The *Ka-boom* of thunder nearly knocked her off her feet. Never had she suffered a noise so loud. The earth beneath her shook. Instinct—or something—took over. She, no thought of her own, raced over to the barn that hadn't completely fallen. She couldn't see it, but from the mental photograph taken with the strike of lightning, she knew it was there. Reaching it, she stumbled about, feeling for a place to huddle down. She found a corner that was dry and out of the elements. With her back to the corner, she slid down into a sitting position. She felt loose straw on the dirt floor around her and pulled it in for warmth. She wanted to pray, but couldn't remember how. She stared into the dark, cruel, angry night hoping for a glimpse of Ira in the flashes of lightning.

Where was God?

The light of dawn brought a complete picture of the storm damage. Debris and limbs were everywhere. The house still stood, but not without damage. The windmill wasn't so lucky. It was lying on the ground and parts of it were missing. The barn was severely damaged, but still stood. The old outhouse was gone. Everything that wasn't nailed down was either gone or lying elsewhere. Mr. Moore marveled at his truck. It wasn't sitting where he had parked it. Except for a little hail damage and a dent on the hood where a large limb had fallen on it, it appeared fine. Even more astonishing was the Cadillac. It looked as if it hadn't been touched. Not one dent. With the dust washed off it, it looked better than before. Overall, he considered himself and his wife blessed. They still had a home and each other. With time things would be put back to normal.

They found Tish. She seemed detached from reality. Her flimsy nightclothes were wet and she was shivering. The storm had brought with it cooler air. They got her inside and Mrs. Moore got her into dry clothes.

What power the house had was what was stored in the generator. Electricity use would be on rations until the power line leading up to the homestead was restored, or until the windmill was repaired. Mr. Moore shut off the natural-gas supply until lines could be checked for damage and leaks.

There was no stopping her: wrapped in a blanket, Tish wandered about in the fields surrounding the house looking for Ira. One moment she was numb, detached, and seemingly in shock, and the next she was sobbing. Mrs. Moore felt her sorrow and did her best to console her, but the losing of one's spouse at such a young age is a terrible thing. The heart and spirit is so torn and damaged.

Mr. Moore pulled away the limb lying on the truck. He told his wife and Tish they needed to check on neighbors. Tish was reluctant to go, but changed her mind when they added they would also be searching for Ira as well.

Following the storm's path, the first of their neighbors had fared well, having suffered only minor damage. They had no information concerning Ira, but would search their fields.

Mr. Moore drove on. The next home belonged to the Youngs, a couple who had just had their first baby. They saw the damage before reaching it. The homestead was hit hard and looked as if it had been put through a shredder. Nothing was left standing.

Tish, focusing on the open land and fields searching for Ira, pointed out a man and woman in the field. The woman acted frantic. Tish understood how she felt. She was barely holding on herself. Mr. Moore turned off the road and drove across the field toward them.

The couple was searching for their infant child. The mother claimed the child was pulled from her arms before she was hit by flying debris. Dried blood and an unattended gash on the side of her head gave credence to her story. The house collapsed on her husband before he got out. Joe had been trapped for a time, but eventually worked himself free, only suffering minor injuries. He found his wife unconscious and bleeding. The baby, however, was gone.

Fearing the worst, Tish and the Moores joined in the search. The mother was losing her mind and the father was panic-stricken. The baby could be anywhere in any direction. Perhaps miles away.

It was a dreadful and despairing situation. Tish wondered at the cruelty of God. She felt betrayed. Her own cloak of pain and despair hung heavily on her soul. Instead of seeking God for help and comfort, she joined the mother in a festival of tears, sorrow, and anger.

Her search gave sight of a man crossing the field toward them. Was it Ira? From a distance, it was a possibility. Tish directed the others to look. As he drew closer, Tish, deciding it was Ira, took off in a run toward him. The others followed walking.

With renewed hope and delight, Tish flung her arms around Ira in celebration of affection. Protecting his stomach, he stood letting her have her way.

Tish paused in her merriment as the sound of a crying infant penetrated her awareness. She pulled away from Ira, focusing her attention to his stomach where the cries came from inside his shirt.

"I found a baby."

Tish pulled the baby from his shirt and turned toward those coming. She held it up and shouted, "He found her! He found her!"

The mother and father, like Tish moments before, leapt into a run. Tish handed the crying infant to its mother. Tears of joy poured from the mother's eyes as she danced and celebrated. After Joe assured himself that the baby was all right, he grabbed Ira with a hug and wept in a tearful jubilation of gratitude.

After the moment of initial relief and joy subsided, everyone looked to Ira with questioning eyes looking for answers. Tish, clinging to his arm, asked, "I thought you were dead."

When Ira opened his mouth to answer, an anointing of the Holy Spirit bubbled up. He prophesied, "God is your refuge and hope in time of storm! Trust God."

It wasn't what Ira was going to say. The world seemed to have gone silent.

Joe fell to his knees. "It's my fault! I've been disobedient." Tears rolling down his cheeks, he continued, "God called me to be a missionary and I ran from the call. I was weak in faith and lacked trust in God's protection over my family and me.

"God is my hope. He is my refuge in time of storm." Joe looked at his wife. "This was God proving himself to me! Showing me just how much I lacked control in my life. How unable I am in protecting my family and myself. I couldn't even protect us in a storm. Yet God protected my baby inside a tornado."

Ira prophesied, "She was born for a time such as this."

Joe, who had grown pale, said, "I was reading in the book of Esther when the storm came." Bowing his head, "Oh God, forgive me! How arrogant I've been."

Joe continued on the ground in godly sorrow and repentance as he made his heart right. Ira knelt beside him, joining him in prayer. Tish, feeling the shame of her own lack of trust in God, followed Joe's example.

After a time, Joe stood and stared at the chaotic mess that was yesterday his home and refuge. "Well, one thing is for sure, God doesn't intend for us to spend another day here."

Mr. Moore offered, "Let's all return to my house. The three of you can stay with the missus and me."

The Youngs' infant had not yet been named. The parents couldn't agree. They told Ira, Tish, and the Moores how they were trying different names, but none seemed right. In light of what had happened, the Youngs named their baby Esther Tori Young. Esther, because it was the book Joe was reading when the storm came and Ira prophesied that the baby was born for a time such as this. Tori referenced the tornado she survived.

One week later, Joe, his wife, and Esther Tori Young left Kansas to pursue his divine calling as a missionary to the South Pacific islands. Ira and Tish gave Joe and his wife the Cadillac as a gift. Ira told him that when it came time to leave the States, he could sell the car to help with finances.

Although it could not be known at this time, Esther Tori Young would grow up full of the Holy Spirit and power. She would continue her father's missionary work in the South Pacific and would befriend a young island girl in captivity named Belle. Belle would one day find herself traveling across Missouri in the cab of a semi whose driver would be Nick Dayton.

After a month of helping the Moores with repairs and cleanup, Ira and Tish set out once again for NuSprings, Missouri. Mr. Moore took them to a nearby town to a train depot and bought them a ticket.

6

SUNSHINE AND SCARECROWS

The school day was over; Julia Brooks, sitting with her best friend, Cheryl, waited for Valerie and Dave to pick her up.

"How did you get Dave to start picking you up after school?" Cheryl asked.

Julia shrugged. "Flirting with him. He likes me flirting with him."

"What about Val?"

"I am discreet about it."

"Does she know?"

"She doesn't know how far I sometimes push it."

Dave Sumner's car came into view. Julia rose from the bench. "Boy toy is here. Play time," winked Julia.

Julia got into the backseat behind Valerie.

"Hey, Julia," Dave greeted, looking at her in the rear-view mirror.

Julia puckered her lips and gave him an air kiss.

Dave took the girls to the Wigwam for an afternoon snack of a malt and fries. Greeting Dave and Valerie, Denny York joined them. Taking a seat, he looked at Julia. "Lit'le Darling."

Denny always called her *Lit'le Darling*. It was a generic flirt. He was like that. Always hitting on girls. It was who he was. Most of the time, it meant nothing. Just fishing for bites. Julia's intuition told her that in the right place at the right time, he would make out with her just for kicks. Denny was a nice-enough-looking guy. Under the right circumstances, she would make out with him. Just for kicks.

Passing by, Quillpen greeted, "What's up." Pulling a chair from a nearby table, he joined them. Looking at Julia, he greeted her with, "Sunshine."

Julia didn't know why the high school guys always singled her out. Was it because she was younger? A tagalong? And not really member of the gang? Or was it her looks? Her looks often got her special attention.

"Hi," she greeted Quillpen. Tribe members now addressed her as Sunshine. Quillpen said she had Seelot blood in her. Seelot blood was special. And because so, she was considered tribal family. RiverDawg had given her the name Sunshine because of her blond hair and sunny disposition.

Quillpen's bright dark eyes, dark complexion, and long hair gave him a savage warrior look. His lips were full. Julia wondered what his lips felt like. If his kiss would be savage and aggressive.

Denny's lips weren't full like Quillpen's, but they didn't lack. Denny was a good kisser—the rumor was. Well-practiced. She would have to someday find out. Have a standard to judge by.

Dave's lips were well defined and masculine. But his eyes were his best feature. His eyes were blue and warm. They were heart-touching and made you feel safe and protected. A girl needed to feel safe and protected.

Julia, left out of the conversation, saw Denny's sister Jenny and a friend approaching. Jenny smiled to the group. "Have you heard about the scarecrow thing? They were talking about it on the radio."

"About scarecrows disappearing from gardens and stuff? Yeah, we heard," Denny answered.

"Weird, huh? The radio said if anyone has any information, let the police know. It's becoming a big deal."

"Like everyone these days, they're probably pro-testing," Denny offered.

"Yeah man, like they're tired of birdwatching and hanging about," Dave joked.

"Scarecrows have rights too, you know. Hanging on a cross isn't as fun as it might sound," Quillpen stated matter-of-factly.

"It killed Jesus," Dave added.

"And he was the Son of God!" Denny expressed.

Annoyed by their lack of seriousness, Jenny said, "We'll be outside. Don't forget and leave without us. Like you did the other day."

"Yeah, yeah." Denny waved her away with a hand gesture.

As the girls went on their way, Dave said, "Jenny's cool, why you always mean to her?"

Denny shrugged. "I don't know. She's alright. A bit churchy sometimes. Tries to keep me on the straight and narrow. Preaches at me too much. It's annoying."

"You got something against Jesus?" Quillpen asked.

"Not at all. Hey, I go to church."

"Your mom and dad make you go," Dave charged.

Denny defended, "Jesus is cool. He's the Way, the Truth, the Life. He like, walked on water and turned it into wine. Known to kick demon butt now and then. I dig Him. He died on a cross on my behalf to save me from my multitude of sins." Denny glanced at Julia with a wink. "Gotta love that."

Valerie addressing Dave, "Whacha think is going on?"

"Denny's young. Hasn't got his wild oats sown yet."

"I mean about the scarecrows!"

"Oh." Dave winked at Julia. "Probably some punks being mischievous."

"We used to do stupid stuff," Denny said.

"Used to?" Quillpen teased.

7

DAY STALKING

Homer Pierce's easy chair leaned to one side. Sitting, Homer did too. Anger stirred inside him. He wasn't sure why the angry feeling. It just was! Anger and rage was a part of his nature. It lived inside him. There was always something nipping at him. Even when there wasn't anything, there was something. He was tired of feeling angry all the time. Tired of frustration. Tired of hating. Tired of being alive.

Just so tired.

That pissed him off too!

He shifted his gaze to Rita lounging on the sofa reading a magazine. She was soft and warm. She didn't have the stormy spirit in her. She didn't know what it was like to be a slave of torment and anger. He wished he could be like her. He was once. A long time ago. A long, long time ago. Before he was turned into a monster. Before a spirit of hate and anger took residence inside him.

Even now, the thought of beating her seemed like the thing he needed to do. He didn't know why. But, why not? Life was mean, cruel, and unfair. She needed to know that. Resisting the urge to give Rita the whipping she somehow deserved, he swallowed the last few drops of whiskey from the bottle he was nursing.

Great!

Now he would have to get another one.

Inconvenience.

Everything about his life was an inconvenience. Everything constantly pissing him off.

He looked down at the bottle and label. Stupid bottle. Stupid, stupid bottle. He hated the bottle. He tightened his hand on it and squeezed. He wanted to crush it with his bare hands.

The hand of death!

He squeezed harder. And harder still. With all his might. He could feel the strain on the muscles in his hand. He could feel the muscles in his forearm and triceps. Even muscles in his shoulder were taut and straining.

He squeezed.

The muscles in his hand now aching. The strain caused his hand to shake. His arm grew tired.

He couldn't do it.

He relaxed his hand and arm. His arm ached with exhaustion. His hand felt like it wanted to cramp up. His other hand took the bottle, letting his exhausted arm go limp and rest.

Automatically—an instinctive move—he raised the bottle to his lips for another sip before realizing it was empty. He lowered it again.

Stupid bottle.

He only wanted another sip.

Just a taste.

He didn't know why suddenly another sip seemed so important. Why was his craving suddenly so great? But it was!

It was probably because the bottle was empty. It was the way life picked at him. Tormented him. He wanted something, but he couldn't have it. Oh, no! Wouldn't want Homer to have a second of happiness or peace, now would we?

His stormy spirit grew darker.

Hate thundered inside.

He just wanted another sip.

Whiskey was his friend. It medicated his anger. Helped him to tolerate living. Numbed his pain and frustration.

The bottle was empty.

His anger increased.

He glanced at Rita. He could have her go and get him another bottle. But that wasn't the point. The point was that the bottle ran out just when he didn't want it to. It was about the inconvenience of wanting something and not having it. Craving something and being denied.

Stupid bottle.

Stupid whiskey company for not putting another

sip or two in it. Like it would be such a major expense. Stupid company owners. Stupid rich company owners.

Homer hated them.

He stared at the label. It represented the company. Well the company had pissed ole Homer off! Homer grabbed the bottle with his throwing arm and hurled it across the room, smacking it against the wall. The bottle bounced off the wall and landed on the floor, happily spinning about.

It didn't even break.

Rage erupted!

Homer jumped up. Curse words flying. The bottle was mocking him. Laughing at him. Did the bottle think it was better than him? Stronger than him? Did the company think it couldn't be broken? He glanced around the room for something he could smash the bottle with. Rita was staring, wide-eyed and frightened. Stupid girl. He wasn't mad at her. Stupid dumb girl. He ought to smack her for her lack of sense.

His eyes roamed the room. There was nothing! He wondered if he were to grab the bottle and smack it against the dumb girl's head if that would break the bottle. More likely it would just break the dumb girl's head. He wasn't mad at the girl. He liked the girl. She was soft, pretty, and warm. She had a way of calming his dark stormy soul. She was the best possession he owned.

There was nothing in the godforsaken room he

could use to smash the bottle. Even the house was against him. He hated the house.

Anger exploding in his soul, he grabbed the bottle off the floor and swung it into the front door facing. The bottle shattered. Glass flew. The door facing was cracked and busted. He looked over at the girl. She had her book held up to protect her pretty face from flying glass.

Homer looked down at his hand at what was left of the bottle. A sharp jagged piece of glass that fit comfortably in his hand. A deadly weapon. The damage it could inflict on someone. Homer held it like a knife. He liked the way it felt in his death hand. He looked over at the girl. She was staring. She feared him. He liked that. It kept her obedient. He turned toward her and gave her a look like he was going to use it on her. He could cut up her face. Make her into a monster like him.

As if she could read his thoughts, she grew fearfully tense.

It was Homer humor. In his mind he saw himself smile. He wouldn't do that to her. Not as long as she was a good little pet.

The thought of cutting up her face appeased him a bit. He didn't feel as angry now. But he wanted another drink. Still staring at the girl, the dark voice inside said to her, "What're you looking at? Make yourself useful and fetch me another bottle!"

The girl couldn't move fast enough. She was well trained. In fact, she was convenient. He liked that about her. Pretty, soft, warm, and convenient.

She quickly returned, hesitantly handing him the bottle, glancing down at the weapon he had forgotten was in his hand. He slipped it into his pocket and snatched the bottle from her hand. She flinched. He said, "Clean this place up before someone gets hurt."

"Yes, Pa."

He patted her on the head. "I think I'll go for a walk. See what's abuzz in the neighborhood."

He stepped outside and stood on the front porch. He opened the bottle and took a swallow. Sunshine to the soul. He stepped off the porch and headed toward the back of the house.

Rita, picking up pieces of glass, watched her pa head around the house talking to himself. She went to the bathroom to look out the window. Pa crossed the small field and disappeared into the woods. What he did or where he went, Rita had no idea. Nor did she really care. She was glad he was gone. His walks and fishing trips usually lasted a while, sometimes hours. That was what she cared about.

She hurried cleaning up the broken glass. She swept the fragments. Scanning the room, everything looked in order. The *True Story* magazine she had been reading was still lying on the sofa. She loved magazines. Especially ones like *True* Story that taught her about life, men, love, and sex. Before Pa's outburst, she had been reading an article about the power of feminine charm and how to use it to secretly control the men in your life. She had read the article more than once. It was intriguing and she wanted to absorb the information.

Now wasn't the time for reading. Pa was gone. Now was her free time to live her life. Free time to take a walk of her own. She went to the bathroom and quickly brushed through her hair. After applying lipstick and a touch of perfume, she changed into a dress.

Leaving the house, her stroll took her toward the Yorks'. She hoped to see Denny. Hoping for some private time with him. She searched the field. No Denny.

She continued. Still no Denny. No Glenn either.

She would have settled for Glenn. He was different from Denny. She liked him too. He was good to practice her charms on. Even Alex would be fun to play with and tease a bit.

Reaching the York house, scanning the fields, hoping for the best, there was no Denny. No Glenn. No one. Disappointed, she started back home.

Back home again, she looked down the road at the Brandts'. She could pay Betty a visit. But, it wasn't a good idea. She looked at her own house and sighed. Maybe she would have herself a beer. Beer always made her feel better.

Stepping onto the porch to go inside, she heard a loud growl, and out of the corner of her eye something jumped onto the porch attacking. She screamed!

Johnny Brandt burst into laughter.

Going from fear to anger, she cussed at him and gave him a hard shove. "You stupid jerk, you scared me!"

Nearly tripping from the shove, he said, "That was the point, stupid!"

Johnny wasn't alone. Nick Dayton was with him. Laughing too.

Making a mocking face at her and sticking out his tongue, Johnny added, "Scaredy-cat dummy girl." He smiled and then spat on her.

Fury ignited. Rita charged with fists doubled and nasty words flying!

Giggling, Johnny jumped off the porch running. He yelled to Nick, "Spit on her!"

Rita stopped pursuit and turned to Nick. "You do, I'll pound your face bloody."

Nick backed away.

Rita chased Johnny around the yard, cussing and calling him names. Johnny ran onto the porch and into the house. Rita followed. Grabbing ahold of him with one hand, she began hitting him with the other. Falling on the sofa, he broke free of her grip, but she was on top of him cussing and punching.

For Rita, it felt good to punch someone. To release pinned-up anger, fear, and frustration. Hitting Johnny was just plain good therapy.

And fun too.

Blocking, punching back, and kicking, Johnny eventually gained the upper hand and made his way atop her. Johnny held her down as long as he could before she bucked him off.

She got back on her feet and stood. Johnny stood too. Staring at each other, they were both sweating and breathing hard. Nick was nearby and watching.

Johnny said, "You're bleeding," pointing at her arm.Rita looked. On the side of her upper arm was blood. She had probably cut herself on a shard of glass that escaped her cleaning.

Johnny stepped over to examine it. "It's just a small cut." Taking hold of her arm and leaning forward for a better look, he licked the wound. Looking up at Rita, smacking his lips, "I want to drink your blood," he said in his best, but bad, Count Dracula voice.

Rita shook her head. "You're a weird lit'le freak."

Johnny grinned, and when she didn't pull her arm away or resist, he leaned forward and covered the wound with his mouth. Rita could feel him licking and sucking and tasting the fresh blood forming at the small cut.

Johnny looked at Nick. "Hey Nick, come over here and be a vampire and suck her blood."

Nick was the same size as Johnny, but Nick was timid. Johnny was good at bullying him into things he wouldn't normally do.

Johnny leaned forward with another lick. He looked up at Rita and grinned.

Rita said, "You little pervert freak."

"Nick. Get over here and lick her blood or I'm going to punch you in the gut for being a sissy!"

Nick reluctantly stepped forward looking at Rita, fearing a threat. Rita made no threat. Her smirk challenged him to do it. He leaned forward, stuck out his tongue, and licked the cut that had almost stopped bleeding.

Johnny said, "We should start a secret club. We could be called, 'The Vampires'!"

Boys craved adventure. They loved being a part of something secret.

Reading was Rita's main pastime activity. Besides the radio, there wasn't much else to do. Pa had magazines that came monthly in the mail. Rita had magazines she bought when she went to the store. Pa usually allowed her one. She bought magazines about being a woman and issues women faced.

Rita also loved reading Pa's magazines. Pa's magazines taught Rita the nature and thoughts of men. One of Pa's magazines Rita liked reading was *The Gentlemen's Club.* Decorated from cover to cover with beautiful women skimpily dressed or naked, the magazine was about style, high-performance cars, beer, whiskey, cigars, guns, and hunting. There was always a manly cuisine featured revolving around some exotic meat cooked rare and often dripping with blood.

Men were meat lovers. Meat barely cooked and bloody.

Men had a thing for blood, and for Johnny and Nick to want to taste her blood was natural.

From Pa's magazines, Rita learned that men

were obsessed with the female body. From her magazines, Rita learned that women love to attract men and be pursued. It was fascinating to Rita learning about men and women. It was no longer a mystery to her why women, in the summertime, lay outside in bikinis for all the world to see. It was to attract the attention of men. And for men, a naked, dark-tanned, sunbaked girl was a fantasy cuisine.

Johnny, sucking on her arm, tasting her blood, was a natural thing deep within his male psyche. To want to start a secret club, to be a part of some secret organization, was natural too.

Homer liked Missouri better than Kansas. Homer liked trees. He liked the Ozarks. He felt at home in the forest. Traveling unseen behind a veil of trees suited him. Trees allowed him to watch people. Study people. Stalk people.

Hiding behind trees, he could watch people in their yards. Watch kids at play. Watch women hang clothes out to dry or work in gardens. Watch young women sunbathing in skimpy bathing suits.

Sometimes he could get close enough to hear talk. Hear conversations. Hear people's little secrets.

The first house on Homer's stalk was a newly constructed home sitting in the woods surrounded by forest. More and more houses were being built in the forest. People were moving to the woods. Homer both liked it and disliked it. He liked it because it made it easy and convenient to spy on and stalk people. He could sneak into people's yards and up to their houses without being easily noticed.

He disliked people moving into the forest because the forest belonged to him. His place in the world where he wasn't a freak. Where he could move about freely and not be stared at. The forest was his home. His playground.

Standing behind a tree, looking at the back of the house before him, all seemed quiet. Staying in the woods, he circled around to the front. There were no cars in the driveway. The garage door was open. Slipping from tree to tree, he made his way to the side of the garage. He peeped around the corner. No sign of people. He entered the garage and made an inventory of items. He would keep the items in mind in case he ever needed something.

He went to a door that opened into the house. He listened. Nothing. He slowly turned the knob. It was unlocked. Quietly and slowly he opened the door, listening for anything indicating someone was home. He heard nothing. He stepped into the house. He felt the rush of adrenalin. A few steps later, he stood in the kitchen. It had an electric stove. This is what new and modern kitchens looked like these days.

Homer went from room to room seeing the rest of the house. He envied the owners, feeling the pain of his sorry life and existence. When he was a boy, he had lived well. He had lived in a nice home with nice things. But that was a long time ago.

In the master bedroom, Homer found a watch he decided to keep. He couldn't remember the last time he'd had a watch. He didn't have a big need to know what time it was. He didn't even know if the watch had the correct time. It didn't matter. Morning, evening, or night was all he needed to know. The sun told him that.

He went through a woman's jewelry box and found a necklace for Rita. A pretty toy for a pretty girl, Homer mused to himself. Going through the house was like going to a store. There were many things he would like to have taken, but he wasn't a thief. An opportunist maybe. He mostly took things out of need, not out of greed.

On an end table was a magazine. It looked like a woman's magazine of some kind. He grabbed it for Rita. The girl loved to read. Exiting the house, he disappeared back into the woods again.

Homer soon stood at the edge of a neighborhood that only three years ago didn't exist. The new development carved out of the forest already had a dozen houses. Another one was being built and more were likely to come. It was midafternoon and Homer didn't want to risk being seen, so he kept his distance. He would come back at night. At night he could wander into the yards and get close to the houses. At night he could peep into the windows and the people in their cages. The human zoo, Homer joked with himself.

Staying in the safe cover of the woods, he moved

around seeing what was going on. At a couple of the houses, people were doing yard work. Looking from house to house, Homer saw six kids. At one house, a couple of preteen boys were playing basketball. They were loud and obnoxious. Homer especially hated those types of humans.

In another yard, a boy was digging in a pile of sand with a stick. The sand was construction sand left over from the building of the house. The boy's lips were moving. Talking to himself, Homer assumed. That was Homer's childhood. Alone. Playing by himself. Entertaining himself with a stick. Homer's childhood was spent in Kansas on a large farm. There was no neighborhood. No neighbors. Just boring old farmland. It was just him and his invisible pals. Boy with a stick was a good human. Homer would have to come back at night and hide a surprise in the sand for the boy to find.

A few houses down, a mother, sitting on steps leading to the front door, watched and played with her toddler that had recently learned to walk. Homer could hear the woman's laughter even where he stood. He could also hear the loudmouth basketball players down the street. Homer glanced back down the street at the boys. Stupid loudmouth punks. Why, he ought to cut out their tongues. That would make the world a better place, by gawd.

At another house, a young boy and girl were playing on a swing set with a slide and glider. Spoiled brats. They were laughing and having fun.

Happy was the neighborhood.

Happy were the kids.

Unhappy was Homer 'cause Homer hated happy kids.

He should trap one. A young tender one. Gut it. Fillet it. Taking the fresh meat home for Rita to cook. Homer's lips smiled at the fantasy. He amused himself with it. It was more Homer humor. He could just see Rita preparing a nice tasty roast of child, having no idea what she was cooking. He would comment on how good it tasted and brag on her cooking. She would be proud of herself. Happy and pleased with his positive comments. She would savor the meal with delight, wondering where he had gotten such a delicious sweet-tasting roast.

Happy was the neighborhood.

Happy were the kids.

Unhappy was Homer 'cause Homer hated happy kids, but the thought of a roast of kid brought respite.

Homer faded back into the forest as his interest in the neighborhood waned. There was one more person on today's stalk he wanted to check on before going back home. He traveled through the woods until he reached another little isolated house on the edge of the forest. Keeping to the trees, he searched for the old woman living there. She wasn't too old, but she was retired and lived alone. What Homer liked about her was that she was nearly deaf. She didn't hear well at all.

Seeing her nowhere outside, Homer stealthily made his way to the side of the house. He could hear the TV. The old lady kept her TV volume way up. Homer snuck over to a window and peeked in. There she was. Watching television. Homer went around to the back of the house. He didn't have to worry about being too quiet. The back door was open and covered by a screen door. Homer eased open the screen door. It squeaked, but the woman would never hear it. Homer stood in the kitchen and listened for any movement by the old woman. All he could hear was the TV blaring.

He looked around. Sometimes there was something good to eat on the counter. No luck today. He went to the refrigerator and opened the door. There was fried chicken. He grabbed a leg, took a nibble, and then stuffed it into his pants pocket. There was a pitcher of tea. The woman made good tea. Homer raised the pitcher and took a drink. He put it back. Taking another small piece of chicken, he closed the refrigerator and went over to the kitchen's entrance and listened. Besides the television, he heard a cough. The woman was still in her place.

Homer tiptoed from the kitchen into a dining room, crossing over to the entry into the front room where a large heavy curtain hanging was used to block drafts and "seal" off the other part of the house. Homer hid behind the curtain peeking around it. He could feel his heart hammering. His blood pumping. As long as the woman didn't turn her head, she wouldn't see him. Homer could almost reach and touch her. He stepped closer into the curtain, moving toward her. He stretched his arm out toward the back of her head. He could touch her if he wanted. He moved his hand to lightly touch her hair. She moved her arm and swatted at what she thought was probably a fly. Homer was amused. She was a fun old gal. Ugly as a wart. But fun. Homer decided not to press his luck and snuck back to the kitchen and left as he came. He would go home now. Have a snack of chicken on the way.

8

STORMDANCER AND HONEYSUCKLE

Waking up to the morning, RiverDawg blinked his eyes open. He didn't want to. Land-of-Dreams was a pleasant place to be. He closed his eyes to will himself back to the place he had just been. Where was that? What was he doing? How could he not remember? He was just there. He thought harder. Was he sharing a meal with someone? Yes. With who? It was with a woman. A special woman. He couldn't remember who she was or what she looked like. Was her name HoneySuckle? Perhaps. It smelt right.

It had been a pleasant dream. The more he tried to go back, the less he could. His eyes were open again. RiverDawg grumbled, *"An old man should be allowed to wander Land-of-Dreams as long as he wishes."* He shut his eyes in aggravation. To dream of feasting with friends, especially with a lady, was a sign of love and appreciation. Commodities of wealth.

In Land-of-Dreams, he was younger, stronger, and irresistible. In Land-of-Dreams, it was better times, a better world. The air was fresher. The water sweeter. The ladies were pretty and flirty.

With eyes shut, Land-of-Dreams had fled far away. Instead of dreaming, RiverDawg was thinking about the new day. The things he might or might not do. Outside, the birds were up and busy with chatter and song.

RiverDawg watched a bug busy in journeying across the ceiling to wherever bugs journey. Bugs have their own lives. Their own world of survival and struggles.

It was morning.

Time to get up.

It was a struggle going from lying down to standing, but RiverDawg did it easy enough. At his age he could take pride in his agility. Many people his age were dead. He slipped a robe over his naked body and grabbed a towel. He would go down to the river, greet Mother Dawn and Brother New Day, and cleanse his body and soul from yesterday's sins to make room for today's new ones.

Opening the door to the new day, RiverDawg stepped out onto the porch gazing about. Mother Dawn was looking lovely today. He took in a breath of her fresh, clean morning air. Air was cleaner and sweeter in the morning.

Inhaling, he detected something. Not really from the smell of Mother Dawn, but in an intuitive way. Brother New Day was up to something. Scanning the forest about him, he saw nothing out of the ordinary, but in spirit, something was out of the ordinary. No bother, he would know soon enough. He stepped off the rustic rickety porch heading toward the river only a rock-throw away.

RiverDawg walked past him without seeing him, but suddenly stopped. Intuition. He turned, his eyes dropped to the ground. IraQuake BootShaker was sitting on the ground leaning back against a tree. A woman seated between Ira's legs leaned back against him. At first RiverDawg was startled, but quickly got over it to pretend he wasn't. RiverDawg wasn't afraid of much, but his son sometimes scared the devil out of him!

"Morning, Father," Ira greeted.

"Back again?" RiverDawg said without fanfare. He started toward the river again. "Join me in my morning homage?"

"We've already greeted the Creator with praise and prayer."

Ira watched the old man stop at the river's edge. RiverDawg shed the robe he was wearing. Ira looked at Tish to see her expression. Her eyes widened with surprise. Once nude, the old man stepped into the cold river, wading out until the water was up to his waist. Tish turned to Ira with a surprised and slightly embarrassed expression.

Ira said, "Yeah, he's not bashful."

Tish didn't comment and turned her attention back to her father-in-law.

In the tradition of the "old" religion, RiverDawg did as his grandfather had done and as all the grandfathers before him. In Cherokee, he spoke a greeting followed by a prayer with hand gestures, turning his body towards the four directions.

After a short river bath, RiverDawg emerged from the water, stepping back onto the bank where he began drying off. Tish was staring. Not because the sight of the naked and wrinkly old man was appealing, but because it was educational. A glimpse of the past still alive in a modern world. There was no condemning spirit with RiverDawg or Ira she was doing wrong by staring. She had been to nudist camps and seen nudity of all ages. She had listened to speeches about the beauty of the naked body and how it ought to be celebrated and flaunted instead of covered. Watching RiverDawg didn't seem indecent as much as it did natural and real.

RiverDawg, pulling the robe together in front, walked toward them. Tish, looking at his face as he approached, suddenly, without a conscious action, dropped her stare to his midsection to an opening where the robe wasn't closed as it should have been. Curiosity caused her to linger longer than she should.

"Like what you see?" RiverDawg's face was humorously lit.

Tish felt the heat of flush. "Oh my God! I'm sorry. I didn't mean to look." Now she felt a spirit of condemnation.

RiverDawg chuckled. "No need to apologize." His

words were spoken softly and soothingly. "You honor an old man. Any time my manly parts can attract the attention of a young lady, it's great flattery."

Tish turned to Ira. "I'm so sorry! I didn't ..."

"It's alright. It's of no consequence," Ira waved it off. "You were probably a victim of a charm anyway." Ira looked up at his father. "Maybe an old man should be more modest around a young lady."

"Life's too short for boring." Closing his robe properly, he offered Tish a hand. "Shall we break fast?"

Tish looked to Ira for instruction.

Ira nodded. "Meet your father-in-law."

Tish took his hand and rose to her feet in uncertainty.

Holding her hand, looking at the freshly made headband of braided honeysuckle crowning her long straight light-brown hair, RiverDawg said, "You smell tasty." His eyes dropped to the daisy painted on her cheek before stopping at her eyes. "Eyes of green. Child of nature. They speak of a free spirit." His stare dropped to her mod-color psychedelic tunic dominated by green, purple, and yellow that could double as a short dress. Underneath the tunic, she wore denim jeans that ended in bells with embroidered butterflies going up one leg. Sandals admitted view of her rainbow-colored toenails.

"You're one of those hippie-chicks, ain't cha? One of Mother Nature's daughters." RiverDawg's smile hinted approval.

Ira stood. "Pure California-bred flower child."

"I like her. I met her in a dream." RiverDawg lifted her hand, leaning forward with a kiss. "Welcome, my dear. I shall call you HoneySuckle. I take it that you have married the pup?"

Tish glanced at Ira. Her eyes humorously expressing hesitation. Looking back at RiverDawg, she nodded.

RiverDawg's gaze went to Ira in scrutiny. "Turning hippy too?"

"It's the look these days."

"Umph." RiverDawg began leading Tish arm-in-arm toward the shack. "I half feared the pup was never going to become a man and know the comforts of a woman."

The shack was only one room with minimal furnishings. The back wall featured an oversized fireplace that served as a cook fire. There was no stove. No refrigerator. No electricity. A large makeshift cupboard dominating one wall housed most of RiverDawg's possessions. In one corner of the room was a pallet for sleeping. The pallet appeared to be an old mattress covered with quilts. The furniture was rustic, homemade, and low to the floor. For sitting, there were chairs in the shape of *X*'s made from using two planks of wood, one passing through the middle of the other. Other "X" chairs were stacked over against a wall next to the shack's only window. The walls were decorated with items of necessity like fishing poles, pans, traps, a bow with a quiver of arrows, and so forth. Tish took a moment to take it all in.

RiverDawg said to her, "Someday, my dear, all this will be yours and the pup's."

IraQuake put his arm around her. "Makes your heart swell with pride, don't it?"

Her expression betrayed her lack of enthusiasm over the idea.

"Here. Have a seat." RiverDawg offered her an "X" chair.

Tish reluctantly ventured over and eased down onto it. It was surprisingly sturdy and balanced. What really amazed her was how comfortable it was. She had figured, it being wood, that it wouldn't be comfortable. She was wrong. The angle reclined you and supported the back. She exhaled, giving in to the comfort of it.

"Nice, ain't it?" Ira grabbed one off the top of the stack. "These were the chairs of the frontiersmen. They come apart for easy carry. They're very durable and surprisingly comfortable."

"I would not have imagined." Tish relaxed.

His face expressing pleasure and approval, RiverDawg said, "Relax. Make yourself at home. I'll go and see what's for breakfast." RiverDawg exited the house.

"Where's he going?" Tish asked.

"To check traps for meat and gather whatever else is available. He lives off the land."

It took a bit of time to prepare and Tish was

ready to fill her griping stomach. Her father-in-law and husband made various trips out into the woods gathering this and that for one dish or another. The meal before her in her opinion was questionable at best. The meat, roasted on a split, did smell appetizing. "Bird provided by Mother Earth" was all she was told. Also with the bird was a roasted fish. The bird, not knowing what kind, she questioned. The fish seemed safe enough. She was hesitant about the salad. "Wild edible greens," she was told. Weeds in her opinion. It did have sliced radishes, carrot, and apple in it.

RiverDawg's special *Gumbo Surprise* worried her. The ingredients and preparation had been done in secret. It was suspicious looking and not at all appetizing. She feared it to be an insect dish. Her inquiries were answered with smiles and, "Trust us."

RiverDawg conceded to Ira the offering of thanks for the meal. Tish was the last to begin to eat. She started with the fish. It was good, as she'd expected. She sampled the bird and found it acceptable. The salad wasn't great, but better than she had figured. Apart from what she recognized, she was told it contained cattail parts, lamb's quarters, wild rose, clover, and wild lettuce. She figured the honey/vinegar dressing poured on top of it made it tastier than what it would have been otherwise.

RiverDawg's red clover tea was drinkable. A touch of honey made it better. She would have preferred Lipton.

"Are you gonna try the gumbo?" Ira asked her.

"I don't know." Her answer suggested, probably not.

RiverDawg chuckled.

"It's Dad's specialty. He's known for this dish."

"What is it?"

"*Tsgoya* soup." RiverDawg spoke in Cherokee.

"See, that's what scares me. You know that if I knew what it was, I wouldn't dare."

"It's healthy stuff. It's good for you," Ira said.

"It doesn't look good."

"Looks can be deceiving."

"What's in it?"

"*V-le dosvda li*." Again, RiverDawg spoke in Cherokee.

"What's that mean in English?" Tish demanded.

"Trust me and take a bite," Ira encouraged.

"I'd rather not."

"Tish!" Ira's tone was stern. "I thought I married an open-minded woman big on nature and being organic. This is one of the most natural, healthy, and organic dishes one can possibly have."

"But ..."

"If you don't try it, you will disappoint me, being one who preaches getting back to nature."

Tish's deep breath spoke of her displeasure at being cajoled into something she didn't want to do. With her fork, she picked at it looking for a bite that didn't look so disgusting. Finally, with as minimal an amount as possible, she raised a bite to her frowning mouth and willed it open. She touched it to her tongue first, before actually committing herself to eat it. Deciding it wasn't too repulsive, she went and took the bite and quickly swallowed. She considered the taste a moment.

"Well?" Ira asked.

"I don't know."

"Admit, it wasn't that bad."

Tish glanced at RiverDawg. He was enjoying the show.

"Take a real bite," Ira ordered.

She wasn't used to Ira being demanding and didn't know if she liked it. He sounded like her father, instead of her partner. Hoping her expression revealed her displeasure in his attitude, she picked at the dish again, raising another small bite to her lips. She met the bite first with her tongue. She didn't swallow it as quickly as the first bite, but didn't take time to savor it either. There was nothing in the bite she hated. Nothing that seemed to make her sick. Although somewhat different, it was familiar. "What is it?"

"Do you like it?" Ira asked.

"It didn't make me throw up."

"Try some more and tell me what you taste."

With another breath of protest, "I'm only doing this because I love you and trust you with my life." She picked another bite. A bigger one. This time, she was even slower in swallowing it. "There's sort of a shrimp taste to it with a hint of something like pineapple. Lemon, maybe? Is it some kind of river shrimp?" she asked RiverDawg.

"*Tsgoya*." RiverDawg's grin was not comforting.

"It's a secret recipe." Ira took a bite of his *Tsgoya* dish. "Eat some more. It's good. Show Dad you're a true daughter of Earth Mother."

Although Tish ate a few more bites of the dish to be a good sport, she didn't finish all of it. It wasn't that she hated it, she didn't like eating something in which the ingredients were secret.

Breakfast was followed by a time of lounging outside in the "X" chairs. Mild breezes kept the warm day comfortable. The sound of the wind moving through the trees and other forest sounds was peaceful and soothing. Beyond the canopy of limbs, the sky was blue with puffs of white clouds.

This was happiness.

Ira looked more contented than normal. Did he grow up in the woods in a shack eating whatever? Was that why he had no problems sleeping under the stars, nor worried where his next meal might come? He seemed too educated, too refined, to have grown up this way.

Ira seemed too young to be RiverDawg's son. Grandson maybe. A look of pleasure showed on his face. Tish figured he was happy seeing his son again.

Time passed. Tish didn't actually fall asleep, but her meditation was like a form of sleep. True rest. A spiritual rest rejuvenating one's vitality.

The soothing song of nature was interrupted with

movement from RiverDawg. Tish turned her attention his way. He held a pouch and an old Indian-style pipe—something he would have. He filled the bowl from the pouch, saying, "The only thing that would make this moment better, is a good smoke." He lit the bowl, sucking in the smoke, holding it briefly and then exhaling. He stretched out his arm, handing it to Ira.

"Dad, you know I don't smoke."

"Bah. Hippies are smokers."

"Not this one."

"Why not?"

"Smoking is bad for you."

"I'm a hundred and ten years old! Smoking hasn't hurt me none."

"You're not that old."

"How would you know?" RiverDawg countered. "Was you there when I was pulled from my ma's belly?"

"I know you're not a hundred and ten."

"You know nothing." RiverDawg raised the pipe to his lips again. "You should honor the requests of an old man at death's door. You should honor your father. Is that not the Jesus way?"

"You're not dying."

"Only because the angel of death can't catch me. He chases me, though."

Ira sniffed. "No. It can't be. You're smoking pot?"

"It's the thing these days." RiverDawg grinned, raising the pipe to his lips. "I like to refer to it as spirit weed." RiverDawg offered Ira the pipe again.

"I don't smoke."

"Not even the peace pipe? You make for a lousy Indian as well as a hippie!" RiverDawg grumbled, looking past Ira to Tish. "Dear, would you honor your father-in-law and share an important moment with him?"

"Sorry," Tish apologized with facial expressions.

"Bah! You both disappoint me." RiverDawg grudgingly put out the pipe. "What's the harm in a little spirit weed?"

RiverDawg was silent for a time. Finally, he asked Ira, "Tell me, boy, what is your name?"

"StormDancer!"

Tish raised an eyebrow. Ira was full of surprises.

"StormDancer?" RiverDawg questioned.

"One night in Kansas while we were asleep, Storm Man came in the darkness of night with warriors of fury. As we were fighting our way to safety, Wind Man grabbed me, pulling me up into the clouds with him in a dance of life and death. Around and around we danced. Wind Man hurled objects big and small, familiar and foreign at me. Never once hitting me. When Wind Man learned of Who I am, Wind Man, shaking in his boots, gave me a gift and put me gently down and returned to the clouds."

"Umph" was RiverDawg's comment.

RiverDawg's reaction surprised Tish. Did he not believe Ira? Ira glowed. Proud with himself. Was there some sort of rivalry between the two? Did

Ira have something to prove to his father? Ira didn't even mention Esther Tori Young.

After a time of silence, RiverDawg spoke: "You should talk with your sister. A dark wind of confusion swirls about in her mind."

The *Dragon Slayer* had a distinct low rumbling sound akin to thunder. Elizabeth Seeker first heard the car before seeing it. Glancing over her shoulder, it was a block away, but coming. Jacky would certainly pester her. She continued walking.

Pulling toward the curb next to her, Jacky called out, "Hey Beth, wanna ride?"

"No," she answered, keeping her pace.

Quillpen idled along. "Where ya going?"

"Walking."

"Hop in. Let's do some cruising."

Beth sighed. Why not? She didn't have anything else better to do. Besides, she was determined to be less stubborn about things. What did she know anyway?

She got into the car. Jacky pulled away from the curb. "Besides walking, whatcha doing?"

"Nothing."

"You gotta be doin' something?"

"Hedy ran me out of the house. Told me to take a walk. Told me I needed some fresh air and sunshine."

"Mother knows best."

"Mother knows nothing."

"Whatcha been doing lately?"

"Not much. Watching TV. Keeping up with current events mostly. What's up with the scarecrow thing?"

"Scarecrows disappearing from people's gardens?"

"Yes. That. I heard Hedy talking about it."

"Who knows? Probably someone having fun."

"Weird."

"You ain't been studying?"

"I read *Time* magazine. *National Geographic*. I've always been so wrapped up in my own world, that I didn't know much about the real world. Man has finally walked on the moon! Until recently, I never thought how incredible that is. There are other things like Woodstock and the hippie movement. I mean, the world is in a major state of change. A new age is dawning. There's a new awareness. The nation is on the brink of civil war! What about the gruesome murder of Sharon Tate and her friends? She had her baby cut out of her stomach! Who would do such evil? How could people be such monsters?"

"What about biology? Medicine? You ain't been studying that stuff?"

"Not much."

"Why not? I've never known you not to be studying or researching something related to medicine."

"Time to grow up."

"What's that supposed to mean?"

"Just what I said."

"Yeah, but you're MedicineGirl!"

"Was."

"What'd ya mean by that?"

"Can we change the subject? Gawd! Either everyone's on my case for studying too much or they're on my case for not."

"I was just making conversation."

"You can tell Queen Hedy I'm fine."

"Are you?"

"Where's all this fun you talk about all the time?"

"Whatcha mean?"

"For years you told me to live a little bit. Get out of the house and have some fun. Enjoy some life."

"I can do fun."

"Well let's do some. Show me a good time."

RiverDawg was dressed in a thin red suit vest over a long-sleeve white cotton shirt with dangling beaded cuff links. The vest might have at one time been a part of a stylish three-piece suit. If it weren't for it being such a warm day, he would have worn his old dark-gray frock coat. The faded black top hat on top of his head gave him the look of a nineteenth-century politician. The band going around the hat was a bright mod-color rope belt he'd borrowed from Tish. The belt's tails hung down his back with his long hair he had taken the time to comb. In place of his normal Indian necklace, a large gold-metal "peace" symbol decorated his chest. His trousers were a charcoal gray, and although old, weren't as worn as most of his clothes. Sandals protected his feet.

Ira's denim jeans, flared at the bottom, covered sandals. His shirt was a blue tie-dyed. His long hair was held off his face by an Indian-style headband. A leather thong necklace with a wooden cross hung on his chest. Wire-rimmed circular grandpa sunglasses made him look more hippy than Indian.

Tish was wearing a psychedelic tunic with a crocheted rope belt, bell-bottom denim jeans, and sandals. Her honeysuckle headband had been replaced by an Indian-style headband with a wild daisy stuck in it. Her sunglasses were like Ira's, but rose-colored.

They stood on the street corner of a busy intersection. RiverDawg saluted people with the "peace sign." To most people, RiverDawg was the crazy Indian witch doctor that lived in the woods. RiverDawg told Tish he was life's spice. People expected him to add a bit of flavor to their lives. They'd be disappointed if he didn't.

When Homer Pierce passed through the intersection taking Rita into town to take care of business, RiverDawg saluted him with the peace sign. Homer began a dialogue of curse words preaching a philosophy of prejudice and hate against hippies.

Rita stared at the three Indian hippies. The hippy look was cool. Hippies were about freedom. It was their religion. Rita would like to be a hippy and taste the cake of freedom.

"Freaks, sinners, and dopers they all are!" Homer proclaimed a block and a half later. "The country would be better off if they were all gathered up, lined up, and gunned down. I'd bite into that one, I would. I'd buy me the biggest, baddest gun they make and explode their heads like melons! The freaks! The L.S.D.-taking commie weirdoes. It's all a communist plot to destroy this country. Instead of sending people to the moon for cheese, the government ought to be making bombs to blow up communists." Homer went silent for a moment. Then he suddenly reached over with a hard slap to Rita's head. "If you ever turn commie, I'll slice your throat, fillet the meat off your bones, and barbeque you for supper!"

"No, Pa! I hate commies and hippies. I wish they were all dead!"

Homer grunted an approval. He then popped the back of her head again. "That's so you don't forget."

I wish you were dead! Rita thought. *Dead and burning in hell like my momma!*

Coming up to the intersection, Beth saw RiverDawg, BootShaker, and a girl she didn't know. Her dad was not only giving people the peace sign, but to some, he gave wild daisies. When they stopped at the stoplight, RiverDawg stepped over to the car. He smiled at Beth and handed her a flower. In her head, she heard him say "Wigwam."

RiverDawg said, "Make love, not war. That's my motto."

"I hear ya, man," Jacky answered. The light

turned green. Glancing up at the rear-view mirror, "Man. I can't believe it. RiverDawg and BootShaker gone hippie."

"Let's go to the Wigwam."

"The Wigwam?"

"I could use a malt. Perhaps some fries. You're buying, right?"

"I guess so."

When Beth and Jacky entered the Wigwam, Beth should have been surprised to see RiverDawg, BootShaker, and the woman already there. She wasn't. They were seated in a "horseshoe" booth that could comfortably seat five adults. RiverDawg waved them over. He occupied the center seat. The woman was seated at his left and BootShaker left of her. Beth entered the booth on the right, scooting toward RiverDawg. Jacky slid in behind her, greeting BootShaker with a nod.

BootShaker, returning the nod, said to Tish, "This is Quillpen Jack and his cousin Elizabeth Seeker. She is MedicineGirl. Last time I saw them, they were kids."

"We've grown some," Quillpen said.

"This is my wife, Tish, known as HoneySuckle. We met in California."

"Nice to meet you," Beth said.

"Likewise." Tish smiled.

Beth assessed her new sister-in-law was some-one she might like. Beth thought perhaps she should turn hippie. Why watch change? Be a part of it. Give Hedy something new to nag about.

"Married! How long?" Quillpen asked.

"Almost a year."

The last time Beth saw BootShaker, she didn't know they were brother and sister. Did he know she was his sister? He was older and different. How hippie was he? Was he still into Jesus? Did he do drugs?

Sedges appeared. "Well, look who's back! If this isn't a Kodak moment, I don't know what is."

A smile curved RiverDawg's lips. "Would you by any chance have a camera? I'd like to order a picture."

"Sorry. Fresh out."

RiverDawg snorted a sarcastic, "Umph. You never have what I want."

Sedges asked RiverDawg, "You turning hippie?"

"I like the motto. Besides, Indians are natural hippies anyway."

Sedges looked at BootShaker. "Tokin' the Bible or tokin' other things?"

"The Bible of course."

Good, Beth thought. He was still into Jesus. It was what set him apart.

Sedges' eyes drifted to Tish.

Ira said, "My wife, HoneySuckle." To Tish, Ira said, "Meet Sedges."

"Nice to meet you," HoneySuckle greeted.

"Likewise." Sedges looked back at BootShaker.

"I thought you went on a name quest, not a wife quest."

BootShaker shrugged. "I found both."

"So what are we to call you now?"

"StormDancer."

"StormDancer?" Quillpen's boyish enthusiasm breaking through his normal shell of cool and mature. "What's the story?"

"Wait. I wanna hear. But first, I need to take orders and give the cook sump'in to do." Sedges made a quick scan of faces. "What can I get you all?"

"I would like a *tsgoya* burger," RiverDawg answered.

"Sir, we don't offer anything *tsgoya.* Or opossum, or coon, or rabbit, bird, frog, deer, bear, nor wolf."

"Bah. This place ain't Indian. It's Hollywood. The Big Chief Burger should be a feast of meats!" RiverDawg pounded the table for emphasis.

"Oh, hush. You're being difficult." Sedges was not intimidated. "I can serve you a flaming buffalo burger if you'd like."

"Was the buffalo wild?"

"As wild as a southwestern Missouri buffalo gets."

"Excuse me," Tish interrupted addressing Sedges, "could you tell me what *tusguyia* is?"

Sedges smiled at her attempt to pronounce the word correctly. "Have you tried old grumpy's Gumbo Surprise?" Before Tish could answer, the smirky expressions on RiverDawg and BootShaker's faces told her she had. "Of course you have." Sedges' face melted into a warm smile. "You're definitely one of us, now."

Sedges, never giving answer to Tish's question, took orders, and before long everyone was enjoying their burgers and fries. Conversation revolved around BootShaker's travels and adventures. BootShaker sought updates. When he went to explain the name StormDancer, RiverDawg stopped him.

"I have a better idea."

Everyone's eyes turned to RiverDawg. He said, "Celebration at my place. T'night. A homecoming for the pup. I'll fry up some *Tsgoya* cakes and serve a real Indian burger!" A challenging stare was thrown Sedges' way before he turned to BootShaker. "You can tell your story then."

BootShaker consented with a nod.

Shortly afterwards, Beth found herself agreeing to go shopping with Sedges and HoneySuckle. Springfield had a new plaza. *Far Out* was a new store offering mod and psychedelic clothing and accessories. Sedges wanted to check it out. Possibly go a little hippie herself. Perhaps Beth would too. Maybe it was time for a change. A name quest of her own might be in order. After all, she was no longer MedicineGirl.

9

DARK MAGIC

Darkness swiftly came as the sun dropped below the hills. The rhythmic night song of the *tsgoya* had begun. Over the next couple of hours their forest melody would grow fuller and louder.

Tish had been gone for hours. Ira missed her. When they were apart, he didn't feel complete. He was sitting in an "X" chair beside RiverDawg on the shack's porch. Ira was surprised at the number of people trickling in. Most of the people Ira didn't know. It was a crowd of younger people. A mix of Indians and whites, male and female. RiverDawg was popular these days.

Ira and his dad spent the afternoon preparing for the celebration. Mostly preparing *tsgoya* corn patties. The patties were small by common burger standards, but enough for what they were. RiverDawg was known for his *tsgoya* dishes. Stacks of patties wrapped in foil stayed warm by an outside campfire a few feet from the front porch. Someone Ira didn't know was playing maître d'.

Ira wondered why such an old man was so popular with the youth. RiverDawg was color-ful. Entertaining. Mysterious. Mischievous. Taking a studious look, this was a party crowd. The wild bunch. The long hairs. Those with side burns, tie-dyed tees, bell-bottom jeans, and dingo boots. These were Ozark hippies. RiverDawg was no doubt their "Indian" guru, filling their minds with Native-American wisdom and philosophies disguised as wise, pure, and enlightening, but dark and deceiving nevertheless.

RiverDawg's silence and solemn look told Ira he was in meditation and up to something. Ira suspect-ed a mental connection to the spirit world. Ira said, "This is my night. So you say. Keep your dark magic out of it."

RiverDawg turned his head toward him. "You have your spirits."

"I have the Spirit."

"Spirits are spirits."

"No. There is the Spirit of God and then there are spirits of darkness. Spirits you play with. 'Friendly' spirits up to no good."

"Bah. You and your beliefs. What do you know?"

"Your magic is dangerous."

"Always with the Jesus talk. Always trying to spoil an old man's harmless fun. You make an old man's head ache. People come to experience a witch doctor's party." RiverDawg rose to his feet. "Shall I not give them what they want? Now I remember why I sent you away to start with." RiverDawg stepped off the porch and disappeared into the woods, into a wall of darkness.

It seemed as soon as they started down the trail to RiverDawg's, day switched to night as if by a switch. It was eerie. Discomforting. Beth was feeling a range of emotions. Excitement was one, although she would never admit it. Mostly, she was nervous and self-conscious. What started out as three ladies shopping, ended up with Sedges and her new sister-in-law giving her a makeover. It began with the older ladies discussing her natural good looks. How she was a diamond in the rough and with a bit of polishing and glamorizing, she would sparkle with heartbreaking beauty. Sedges and HoneySuckle were determined to flaunt the treasure hidden under Beth's modesty.

Ignoring Beth's argument of wanting to be who she was and not wanting to be made up and superficial, Sedges told her, "Feminine beauty is a woman's power. And you're full of it! It's time you learn to exploit it!"

Except for a little lipstick now and then, Beth never wore makeup. She wasn't one for trying to be pretty. She didn't care about boys or having a boyfriend.

Beth gave the ladies a minuscule fight, allowing them to do what they wanted. Secretly, she too was curious as to how she would look glamorized and sparkly.

Beth's young face, naturally smooth and blemish free, needed no foundation. Eye makeup made her brown eyes bigger and brighter. Lipstick and liner gave her lips definition and voluptuousness. Instead of the common yellow hippie-daisy on the cheek, a small white Indian symbol resembling a flower was painted on by Sedges.

The miniskirt was provocative. Beth had never worn such a short dress before. It was designed to accent the figure and stir the imagination. The idea of it was risqué. Sedges and HoneySuckle bought it for her and insisted she wear it. The dress, white and sleeveless, was a great contrast to Beth's dark Native-American skin. The V-neck was revealing and Beth was glad that her young breasts weren't larger than they were, but yet wished they were.

The dress, a part of the '69 Mod Pop-Culture Collection, had nothing to do with an Indian or the hippie look by itself. But accessories transformed it. A thin sterling silver chain serving as a headband gave sparkle to Beth's forehead. It was so light Beth could hardly feel it atop her head. Dainty feather earrings dangled from her ears. A white bead choker with a hanging sterling silver dream catcher decorated her neck. White suede-leather wristbands with twelve-inch fringe made her outfit even more exotic.

Beth had never been to her dad's place before. The deeper they traveled into the woods, the spookier it seemed. The darker it became. Walking was difficult. She was glad for the flashlight Sedges was carrying. Hiking through the woods in the dark and not tripping was hard enough, and Beth was in new platform sandals with white suede-leather spaghetti straps twisting their way up and around the ankle and calf to mimic boots. The footwear wasn't Indian, but because of the straps and her overall look, it looked Indian.

Knowing she would soon be among people and on display, Beth was feeling anxious. Her sexuality had never been so exposed before. Was this the new Beth she wanted to be? "I don't know about this," Beth reconsidered.

"You look great," Sedges encouraged her.

"Drop-dead gorgeous!" HoneySuckle agreed.

"You'll rule the night," Sedges told her.

"You're like an Indian princess from the future," HoneySuckle declared.

Beth trusted Sedges and her new sister-in-law, but they weren't dressed flauntingly. Sedges' new outfit, a long skirt, blouse, and shawl, was gypsy-like. Tish's new outfit was hippie, but subtle. The earth-tone crocheted skirt touched her knees. Her blouse was a sleeveless pullover with a laced-up V-neck. Over the blouse, a light and airy crocheted cardigan with bell sleeves matched her skirt. A turquoise belt with matching necklace, earrings, and bracelets dressed up the outfit while sandals kept it casual.

Arriving at their destination, it seemed the dead of night, although it wasn't late. RiverDawg's shack was small and rustic, but Beth expected that. A campfire and numerous lanterns lit up the area around the shack and down to the river. At least a couple dozen people were mingling about. Almost immediately they were noticed and the staring began. Beth felt the touch of a hundred eyes. Tish spotted BootShaker and the three ladies headed his way.

"You like the new outfit?" Tish greeted Ira with a smile and twirl.

Ira looked her over. "It's down to earth. Fashionable. Kind of elegant. It becomes you." He gave her a good-to-have-you-back kiss.

Tish pulling away, "What do you think about Beth? Is she not beautiful?"

Ira's eyes traveled from Beth's face to her feet and back up again. "Too much so."

Beth's smile came with a blush.

Ira said, "For a young woman to be so beautiful and so alluring is dangerous. To stir the savage desires of men is unsafe."

"Oh, leave her alone," Sedges told Ira. "The girl needs to know she's beautiful. And feel beautiful. To have a few guys drooling over her tonight will do her some good."

Paul Sumner, Glenn York, and Wally D. pulled the jon boat upon the bank. Turning, they looked toward the lighted area of RiverDawg's home. The boys didn't know the witch doctor personally and had never been to his home. They had heard the wild tales. Anything could happen. Anything was possible.

BootShaker was the son of RiverDawg and supposedly a real-to-life prophet of God. Father and son: one of darkness, one of light. Both said to have supernatural abilities. The evening promised to be eventful.

Hiding apprehensions of the unknown and the dark and spooky surroundings, they put on a brave if not haughty front and started toward the lighted area.

"So we're just gonna march up and eat a bug burger?" Wally asked.

"Dave says they ain't bad," Paul answered.

Glenn added, "Denny says it's kind of an initiation thing to become welcome at RiverDawg's."

"I wonder what kind of bugs they are?"

"Crunchy ones," Paul imagined.

Drawing closer, the boys caught sight of Beth. They paused, stepping off the path into the shadows for a secret session of gawk and lust.

"Wow! Is that Beth Seeker?" Paul asked.

"It looks like her," Glenn agreed.

"She's hot!" drooled Wally.

"I've never seen her attempt to be sexy before," Glenn remarked.

"Neither have I," Paul thinking back. "I'm gonna hafta get a closer look."

"I wonder if she's open for business?" Wally hopefully aspired.

"She's open for something." Glenn relishing the idea.

"I get first crack at her," Paul declared.

"Forget that," Wally contested.

"Every man for himself!" Glenn ruled.

Hearing a rush of commotion coming from the woods, the boys turned their attention that way. A towering group with tattered straw hats and plaid shirts took hold of the boys before they had time to react. The "scarecrows" wrestled the boys to the ground while they fought and struggled to break free. Making quick work of binding and gagging the boys, the scarecrows carried them off into darkness.

Quillpen Jack, Dave Sumner, and Denny York arrived via the trail and were immediately summoned by a group gathered in a gray area between light and darkness. Manning a cooler filled with ice and Coca-Cola, the group was passing out drinks. Quillpen, Dave, and Denny each took an offered bottle.

Quillpen and company stopped at the campfire. "Chef, dude, what's on the menu tonight?" Quillpen asked.

"Burgers for the general public." The guy, stepping a little closer and in a quieter voice, "But for a select group, there's the Magic Shroom Burger. Interested?"

"Whatcha think, boys?" Quillpen asked Dave and Denny.

"Groovy." Denny speaking for the three of them.

"You know my motto," Chef said. "Life's a song, but with shrooms, it's a symphony."

Paul, Glenn, and Wally, bound and gagged, were shoved back and forth between the scarecrows. The sounds coming from the creatures were weird and nonhuman. A couple of the straw men with long pipes blew smoke in their faces. Between the shoving and coughing, Paul could hear the beating of a drum and chanting in the background.

After hearing how IraQuake BootShaker's dance with the tornado earned him the name StormDancer, Denny asked Quillpen, "Do you think the story is true, man?"

"For someone of StormDancer's status, to tell such a lie would be shameful. A disgrace. He wouldn't do it. That in itself would earn him another name. A name of shame and dishonor."

"So IraQuake is BootShaker's real name?" Dave asked Quillpen.

"RiverDawg used to barter with the Quakers," Quillpen began. "During visits, a young woman provoked his desire. Over time he beguiled her and she ended up pregnant. It caused a terrible scandal since these were very religious and devout people. Shame caused her to leave the village and live with

RiverDawg. For the sake of religion and reputation they were married. RiverDawg said it was a charity marriage, but nevertheless he was fond of the girl."

"I didn't know RiverDawg had a wife," Dave stated.

"He doesn't now. She died when Ira was young."

"What did she die of?"

"All I know is that she became ill and eventually the illness killed her. The Quakers blamed it on her sin.

"When the baby was born, she named him Ira. On the day he was born there was an earthquake on the east side of the state. So RiverDawg thought it was only right to add 'quake' to the name. The name Quake worked well because of Ira's grandfather. His grandfather was known as Quaker James, a member of the Society of Friends.

"As far as the tribe was concerned, IraQuake was the boy's official name. Ira wasn't born in a hospital or anything, so there was never a birth certificate on him.

"For the next few years and until her death, Ira's mother lived back and forth between RiverDawg and the Quakers. It was her desire Ira be educated and taught the Bible. Though she had shamed herself and family, she, as a form of repentance and reconciliation to her faith and God, gave Ira to God. It was her hope God would take what was a weakness of flesh and turn it into something for His glory. Ira probably bears an official last name in the Quakers' record of baptisms, but I don't know what it is.

"Growing up, Ira spent most of the year living

among the Quakers. At other times, and mostly during summer months, he and his mother lived with RiverDawg.

"The first few years of Ira's life, RiverDawg referred to Ira as the 'pup.' So Ira was known as RiverPup.

"Then, when Ira was around six or seven, he began doing this routine where he would put on a pair of RiverDawg's boots—boots way too big for him, but that was a part of the comedy—and perform this amusing little dance in which he would bob his head around and hop about. Periodically lifting a leg and shaking his foot. The boot would twist about on his foot, making his foot look like it was turning in circles. People say it was hilarious and that's when people started calling him BootShaker.

"However, at the conclusion of the dance, he would sometimes stop and look at someone with a soul-piercing stare and call out their sin. It was prophetic and quite disturbing to people. When asked why he did it, Ira said he didn't mean to, it would just happen."

"So his 'prophetic' statements caused people to shake in *their* boots?" Dave understanding.

"Exactly. It got to the point that when he would start his dance, people would discreetly slip away for fear of being exposed for things they were guilty of.

"There was this one time, at a Quaker meeting that BootShaker began doing his dance. Of course in the middle of the dance he stopped. His eyes focused on this woman. He just stared at her. Just long enough for everyone to notice who he was looking at. He then turned his stare onto one of the prominent members of the Society of Friends, pointed a finger at him, and said, 'Thou shalt not judge, unless thou be judged. Thou shalt not covet thy neighbor's wife!'"

"Wow!" Dave exclaimed.

"Yeah," Quillpen agreeing. "It caused quite a scandal. The woman was pregnant. It eventually came out that the man and the woman were having an affair. After that, BootShaker was brought to RiverDawg and told that a boy should be raised by his father."

"Sounds like they wanted to get rid of him," Denny suggested.

"Yeah. The Quaker village was never the same after that. Rumor has it that RiverDawg did some dark magic that invoked the affair between the Elder and the woman. RiverDawg can be quite the matchmaker when he wants to be. He did it to get back at the Elder and the Society of Friends for the shame and guilt they placed on BootShaker's mother and then claiming her death was the result of her sin."

Paul, lying on his back on the ground, tried to pull free his wrists and ankles that were tied to stakes driven into the earth. Unable to break free, he raised his head and neck straining to see. Holding torches, the scarecrows stood in a group a few yards away. They were whispering and moving about, but staying in the same spot.

"Hey, Paul," Glenn asked. He and Wally were also staked down. The gags around their mouths had been removed.

Paul answered, "What?"

"Can you see what's going on?"

"They're just standing in a group watching and whispering."

"What are they gonna do with us?" Concern in Wally's voice was evident.

Paul raised his head and neck again, looking toward the scarecrows. He called out, "Hey, man, what's up? What's going on?"

The scarecrows didn't answer. Their tattered clothes rippling with the breeze.

"The shrooms have kicked in. Am I hallucinating?" Denny pointed out Beth.

"Wow!" Dave stared.

"That is Beth Seeker, isn't it? In a hot little mini?"

"Well, if you're hallucinating, I must be too."

"I think I'm in love," Beth heard a voice whisper in her ear.

She turned. It was Denny York.

"Really? And who's the unlucky girl?" The sarcasm plainly understood.

"That's not nice."

Beth shrugged.

"You're beautiful!"

"Me? Then perhaps you mistake love for lust."

"Perhaps I've never seen such beauty before?"

"You're the type of guy mothers warn their daughters about. Not necessarily mine, but most would."

"C'mon, Beth. Elizabeth. Give me a chance. I adore you. Compared to all the women here tonight—all the women I know—you are a goddess!"

"Well then, why would I want to waste divinity on such a shallow project as you?"

"MedicineGirl's tongue is like a scalpel wielding cutting words slicing my poor bleeding heart."

"Impressive! How long have you been waiting to say that? MedicineGirl shall save your heart by walking away. Don't follow and you'll suffer no more cuts to your poor bleeding heart."

Beth walked away.

Denny stared after her.

"Give it up, man," Dave advised Denny walking up. "Besides, I doubt you could handle the girl."

"I could handle the parts that interest me."

"Now that's why she's beyond your reach."

"Beautiful and smart!"

Beth turned. A guy known as the *Inada* was leaning against a tree, hiding in its shadow.

"If you're not a goddess, you should be," the *Inada* softly and soothingly declared, obviously having overheard the conversation with Denny.

The *Inada* was taller. Older. Beth's stare was drawn to dark eyes that sparkled though there was no light. They were piercing and hypnotizing. Sinfully beautiful. She could think of no response as her resolve melted.

Drowning in the abyss of his consuming stare, a silent communication of attraction reared itself. The drumming of Beth's heart began a new beat.

"Walk with me?" The *Inada* reached down, taking her hand into his, and gently pulled her in a direction opposite the crowd and into the darkness.

Beth followed.

"Who is that and where is she going?" StormDancer spoke with protective alarm.

Sedges looked. "Hmmp! What do you know? She's charmed the Lucy!"

"The Lucy?"

"That's what some of the girls call him. He's mostly known as the *Inada*." Sedges looked at HoneySuckle. "It means snake. The Lucy is the town's star D.J. He's got a soothing, tranquil, romantic voice that can melt a girl's heart."

"Why Lucy?" HoneySuckle asked.

"Short for Lucifer."

"Lucifer!" StormDancer was outraged.

"Calm down. Gee, you act like you're her father or something," Sedges mocked. "He's not called the Lucy because he's evil. He's called the Lucy because of his male perfection. He's gorgeous! Has eyes to die for."

"How old is he?" StormDancer demanded.

"Seventeen."

"He looks older."

"He does," Sedges agreed.

"I don't like Beth being where I can't see her. Especially with a guy known as Lucifer." StormDancer began walking toward the darkness where Beth had disappeared.

"She'll be fine," Sedges assured HoneySuckle, amused with StormDancer's protective stance.

"How do you know?"

"As gorgeous as the Lucy is, he's a gentleman. He's a lot like Beth actually. He doesn't date and keeps distance between himself and the ladies." Sedges stared blankly toward the edge of darkness. "Sad, really."

"Why?"

"Half the girls in town are in love with him. Even I would jump at the opportunity to go out with him."

HoneySuckle saw the fondness in Sedges' expression.

"When he was like thirteen, fourteen, a group of high school girls took notice of him. Noticing how fine and mature-looking he was. His pretty face, dark complexion, and soul-stealing eyes. His hard and chiseled warrior's bone structure. Deciding that such a fine-looking boy should be a warrior of love, they began to teach and trained him in the art of wooing and romancing a woman. To make a long story short, over a time of private 'lessons,' they taught him how to talk, kiss, hold, and conduct him-self around women. In short, they taught him how to steal a woman's soul.

"The sad thing is, after he was trained to be what every girl wants, he didn't seem interested in dat-ing. In trying to create a 'Lucifer-of-love,' they some-how damaged him. Perhaps he was too young when the lessons began. Not emotionally mature enough to handle such an adult teaching and relationship. Whatever it was, he made himself unattainable. And that has made him that much more desirable. He has broken many a girl's heart simply by being unattainable."

So far all that Beth and the Lucy were doing was talking. Other than her hand, he hadn't touched her. RiverDawg didn't hear StormDancer as much as he felt his presence.

StormDancer asked, "Spying on your daughter?"

"Spying on your sister?"

"What do you know of him?"

"Local celebrity of sorts. Talks on the radio. He's mostly known as the *Inada*. Whites call him Viper. Some call him the Lucy. Some say his eyes are en-trancing like the Cobra's. Some say his kiss is just as poisonous. Some say he has the power to steal a woman's soul."

"Sounds dangerous. What do you see?"

"A dark cloud. Snakes are not evil, but they should be respected. And sometimes snakes are deadly. Isaac Connesawga is as such. He is not evil, but I fear he could be dangerous."

"That doesn't help."

"You are BootShaker. The StormDancer. A prophet of God—what does your spirit tell you?"

"The Spirit. That I should pray more. God is in control. Through prayer, God acts. Through prayer, faith grows. In God, peace is found."

"Bah. You know nothing."

"Why do they call you the *Inada*?" Beth asked.

"Do you know what Genesis 3:1 says?"

"Not right offhand."

"Read it and beware."

"Beware?"

The *Inada* smiled. His stare dropped from her eyes to the dream catcher on her chest. He reached out to handle it, touching naked skin at the valley of cleavage. His touch stirred Beth. He said, "You and I have things in common."

"Yeah? What?" Was he looking at the dream catcher or her breasts? Was he purposely making contact with the exposed skin between her breasts?

"We have dreams. We protect our dreams from bad ones." "What are your dreams?" Beth found his touch pleasurable.

"Law." The *Inada* let go of the dream catcher. His eyes met hers with a probing stare.

"Law?" She wanted to run a finger along his cheekbone.

"I wish to study law. Become a lawyer. It is said I have the eyes for it." With a smile, his eyes shimmered naughtiness and arrogance. "It is said that I can charm, hypnotize, and manipulate by my stare alone."

Beth perceived a challenge. However, the cleverness of it intrigued her more than offended. She countered, "Such a commendable ambition for such a superficial reason."

His visage changed into one of honesty. "I have a fascination with the world of law and politics. It's where the power is. Where a real difference can be made.

"This will be my last semester in high school. I will graduate in December and come January, I will start my first semester at Yale University. After college I hope to return and practice law where I may serve our people and tribe."

"What else do we have in common?"

"Well"—the *Inada* paused—"we both have a no-date rule. We purposely keep ourselves off limits because we have purpose. We both dislike superficial, shallow people having no purpose or direction. Living for the day without regard for the morrow."

"Interesting predicament you boys are in." StormDancer looked down at the three boys staked to the ground.

Paul, having heard no one walk up, looked in the

direction of the voice. Someone Paul didn't know towered above him.

"Who are you?"

"Some call me BootShaker. Some call me StormDancer."

"What are you going to do to us, man?" Glenn asked.

"Nothing."

Paul raised his head and looked toward the group of scarecrows. They were still there. Quiet, still, and watching.

"Why then are we staked to the ground?" Wally asked.

"Couldn't tell you. How did you come to be in this pickle?"

"Those dudes over there did it." Paul pointed with his stare.

StormDancer looked. He saw a collection of scarecrows. Regular ones. Old clothes sewn together with a cloth head and button eyes stuffed with straw and leaves mounted on wooden crosses driven into the ground. StormDancer looked down at the boys. "Did you boys do some L.S.D. tonight?"

"What?"

"Are you boys on drugs?"

"No, man! We don't do drugs," Paul stated sharply.

"Interesting." StormDancer pondered, looking toward the stuffed people. What were scarecrows doing here in the woods anyway? So this was the old man's harmless fun. He looked down at the boys. "Enjoy yourselves." StormDancer began walking away.

"Wait!" Paul called out. "Aren't you gonna free us?"

"And spoil your fun?"

StormDancer disappeared among the trees. Paul looked toward the scarecrows. Had some left? The group seemed smaller.

The *Inada*'s stare was consuming. He said, "Against my better judgment, I have a great desire to kiss you. Against your better judgment, you desire to be kissed."

He stepped toward Beth, leaving only inches between them. She could smell his pleasing masculine blend of forest, campfire smoke, and a hint of cologne. She could almost feel his breath. She wanted to step closer and inhale. She stepped backwards. "Did you think it would be that easy?"

"I would have been disappointed if it were. Easy girls are fun. Loveable. Popular. Guys love easy girls. However, guys fall in love with hard-to-get girls. Especially those worth the wait. You, I suspect, are worth the wait." He lifted her hand to his lips with a light kiss.

"However, another thing we have in common: you don't want to fall in love and neither do I. You and I, we are professionals. Career motivated. We have callings and don't want distractions. You want to be a doctor. I intend on becoming a lawyer. Both demanding. Therefore, I don't need a girlfriend. I don't need to fall in love. I don't need that kind of distraction in my life just yet. For you and I romance is forbidden fruit."

The *Inada* paused, his eyes hypnotizing. "But there's something about you. Something begging me to touch and kiss you. The desire is overpowering. So"—he stepped in close again—"just for tonight, this one time, in the cover of darkness, for the common good of our future and careers, could you not play so hard to get? Will you be just a little bit easy? I don't want to have to wait to kiss you. I don't want the risk of falling in love. I only want a kiss. Maybe try to bring some kind of relief to the craving of wanting to taste you. Of all the girls I've known, you're the first to tempt me in such a way."

This was Beth's moment to say, *Sorry. This dish is not for sampling*, and step back again. Walk away. But she didn't. She couldn't. His voice was persuasive. His smell alluring. She didn't move and knew her silence and lack of action was an invitation.

He leaned in, allowing his nose to gently caress the side of hers. "I should be the one wearing the dream catcher, protecting me from the dream of you." He slipped arms around her, and though she wasn't pressed against him, there was no space between them. He pressed his lips against hers.

The first kiss was short, gentlemanly, and promising. Just pleasurable enough to spark desire and want. Promising enough to invoke temptation. Innocent enough to eclipse doubt and reservation.

This was Beth's first kiss. She liked it. She wanted another. She initiated the second kiss.

The second kiss lasted longer and was indulging.

When they broke the kiss off, they stayed in each other's arms. They didn't speak, but stared into one another's eyes. They met each other halfway for the third kiss.

Beth's heart and mind whirled within. How could a kiss flood one's soul with delightful sensations? Was it chemistry? Chemistry on a metaphysical level, causing a spiritual reaction with the connecting of two souls? These thoughts and feelings were new to Beth. She was beginning to understand the appeal of dating. How it might be consuming and addictive. How it could be delightful and destructive at the same time.

The third kiss lasted longer than the second. When it ended, they remained embraced. There was no need for words. The oneness of their souls said all that needed to be said. What they were doing was blissful. Refreshing. Welcoming.

A mistake! A major distraction factor that could short-circuit their purpose and goals. But, the fruit had been tasted. Instead of doing what they both knew was right, they gave in to the forbidden fruit of desire and indulgence and took another bite. As they kissed, their spirits danced.

Paul raised his head to look at the scarecrows again. Where were they? He strained to look in all directions. Were they gone?

The *Inada* had to leave to go to work. Beth stayed. She needed to think. Leaning against a tree in the shadows outside the campfire's light, she stared toward the fire and mingling people. Her heart and mind reeling. One moment she was feeling bliss and joy, the next confusion and uncertainty. She seemed unable to focus. She had always been able to focus. She had always been levelheaded, insightful, and centered. What happened tonight?

Who was she?

MedicineGirl would have never been tramping about in the forest at night. Nor at a party! MedicineGirl would have never worn such an outfit. Wouldn't be displaying herself in such a provocative way. MedicineGirl would have never kissed a guy, nor experienced the wondrous pleasure of making out. And it was pleasurable! And fun.

The thought of the *Inada*'s lips pressing on hers caused her heart to leap with excitement. The *Inada* had made her feel sexy. She relished in his approval of her. But it was MedicineGirl the *Inada* liked and approved of, not the flaunting floozy she was being tonight. It was the dedicated and studious nature of MedicineGirl the *Inada* liked.

Suddenly, Beth wanted to be MedicineGirl again. She had liked who MedicineGirl was. She liked that the *Inada* liked who MedicineGirl was. She smiled. The *Inada* had such wonderful eyes. Such an intimate stare. When he stared into her eyes, he saw into her soul. He made her feel exposed, but in an honest way that allowed her to be who she was without feeling she had to justify herself.

Another thought invaded Beth's thinking. The *Inada* didn't want a girlfriend. He didn't want to be in a relationship. The power of her physical appearance provoked a savage beast of lust within him that overcame his better judgment and resolve. And though he liked MedicineGirl, it wasn't MedicineGirl he was quenching his fiery desires with. It was the new Beth. The floozy shallow Beth willing to give herself to the lustful desires of a man she hardly knew.

MedicineGirl would have never done that. MedicineGirl would have never been easy. MedicineGirl would have played hard-to-get. MedicineGirl would have made the *Inada* wait. She would have made him fall in love with her.

What had she done? She had given into lust and had fallen for someone who point-blankly told her that all he wanted from her was a "one-night stand" per se.

Stupid! Of all the times, of all the people, she chooses to want a relationship with someone who didn't want one back. Anxiety, fear, and confusion swirled within. Tears were sliding down her face.

"Is everything alright?"

Beth jumped. Startled by the sudden presence of someone. She turned: StormDancer stood before her.

Beth wasn't sure how to answer. She tried to formulate a proper and honest response. She wanted to be honest. Honesty was a part of who she was. However, she feared being vulnerable. She sifted through her range of emotions for the dominant one. She wanted to answer she was fine. That everything was great. And it sort of was. But it mostly wasn't. She wanted to cry. She wanted to see the *Inada* again. She wanted him to kiss her again. She stared at StormDancer. She wanted to be witty and sarcastic. But silence prevailed.

"I perceive turmoil. I am the StormDancer. Let me help."

StormDancer was her brother. Since he had been back, they hadn't been able to talk about it. He stepped closer and pulled her into a cautious embrace. A boyfriend, brother, a sister-in-law—it was too much. Beth began to sob. She wasn't able to stop them. StormDancer remained silent and held her, allowing her to cry.

Soon, Beth, feeling foolish, took control of her emotions and forced her tears to stop. With a quivered voice, "They say God speaks with you—explain to me why Tommy Morris died?"

StormDancer had already heard the story, but wanted to hear Beth's point of view. "Tell me what happened."

Paul, hearing movement, raised his head. Dave, Denny, and Quillpen came into view. "Dave! Over here. Help us."

"What's up?" Quillpen asked, seemingly amused.

"Free us, man!"

"Who did this to you?" Dave asked.

"Those scare ..." Paul looked in the direction where the scarecrows had been standing. They were no longer there. "Let me up, man!" he demanded.

Quillpen reached down with a knife and cut the cords binding him. Paul jumped to his feet. Standing, he turned in all directions searching for the scarecrows.

"They were here, man!"

"Who?" Dave asked, looking about.

Glenn jumped up. "The scarecrows, man!"

"Scarecrows?" Denny questioned.

"For real, man. A group of scarecrows ambushed us as we were walking up the path to RiverDawg's. They carried us out here and staked us down."

"He's telling the truth!" Paul demanded.

Wally stood up and nodded in agreement.

"They ate the wrong burgers, man," Denny said to Dave.

"Did this happen before or after a magic burger?" Quillpen suggested.

"Huh?"

"Whatcha mean? Scarecrows?" Dave asked.

"Scarecrows, man. Straw men. The kind that people put in their gardens to scare away crows." Paul looking about hoping to see one.

"Like the ones that have been disappearing from people's gardens," Glenn explained.

Glenn, Dave, and Quillpen glanced back and forth between each other. Their expressions spoke doubt.

"You guys didn't take anything, did ya?"

"No!" Paul starting to get irritated. "We are not high—on dope or anything!"

"For real, man," Glenn backing Paul up. "We're straight."

"We're telling the truth, man!" Wally declared.

"Yeah, man. That dude BootShaker saw them," Paul remembered.

"Really?" Quillpen said.

"Yeah, man. He was here," Glenn added.

Quillpen, Dave, and Denny looked at each other.

"Let's go ask him," Quillpen suggested.

After reliving the memory, Beth explained how her presence not only led to the cause of Tommy's death, but with all her knowledge and "special" abilities, she could not save him and he died. And it was her fault.

After a moment of mental deliberation, StormDancer said, "You weren't the cause of Tommy's death. You were the source of his hope. God knew Tommy was going to be stabbed. The fight between Tommy and Quillpen was a long time coming. You didn't cause it. It was bound to happen sooner or later. God led you there that night because of all the people that could be present, you were the one that could have saved Tommy's life. You knew and understood the type of wound Tommy had. You knew the knife needed to be left inside him. When he went to pull it out, you *DID* do something—you yelled to him not to. You told him what he needed to do to live. The problem wasn't you. You were his hope! The problem was that in his own wisdom, he thought he should pull it out. The basic instinct in human nature is to remove such a thing as quickly as possible. In most cases it is the best thing to do. However, in this case, it was the wrong thing to do. A deadly thing to do. And if Tommy would not have pulled it out, someone else might have, trying to help. But you were there with the proper advice telling him or whoever not to pull it out.

"The problem wasn't you. It was him. He didn't listen. He ignored your knowledge, understanding, your gift and reputation. He did as he willed. It was his will, his wisdom that killed him."

StormDancer paused to let the message sink in. With an embrace and speaking softly, "You and I are both in the business of saving lives. Your calling is toward physical salvation. Mine is toward the spiritual salvation. We can't make people do what is right, we can only advise, inform, and encourage. Ultimately, the decision is up to the individual as to what direction they will travel. Most people travel toward death and misery. Death is the way of fallen man.

"Someday you will be telling people they need

to quit smoking or they'll end up with lung cancer or emphysema. Or they'll need to stop drinking because the alcohol is slowly killing them. Or that they need to completely change their diet if they want to avoid heart disease or diabetes or whatever. And though you see the things that are destroying their lives, and you'll know how to help them live longer, better, and healthier, you'll not be able to make them do what is right. They will either listen or they won't. If they don't listen, it's not your fault. People do what they want to do.

"You were not the cause of Tommy's death. God placed you there to be his second chance. However, he trusted in his own wisdom and it killed him. You did what God led you to do.

"As a doctor you're gonna see death happen. Too often it will be needless. Too often out of your control. It's the dark side of your calling that you'll have to deal with. You and I must not let the dark side stop us from saving the many lives that will listen—that you and I are called to save."

It was what Beth needed to hear. What she wanted to hear. She had been unable to see the big picture. Liberation rose inside her soul. She was there because God was using her? It was an awesome concept! However, who was she that God would use her? As much as she wanted to believe it, she wasn't sure. She asked, "Could it not have been a coincidence?"

"The first law of science is *Cause and Effect*.

Everything that happens happens because of a cause. To say something is random or coincidental is not scientifically or divinely correct. And therefore not true."

Beth was skeptical. "Do you really believe God gets involved in people's lives? I believe in God, but I'm not like a religious person."

"God wants to be involved in your life. The problem is that most people don't want Him involved. Most people want to live their lives according to their own wisdom and ambitions. God reaches out. People pull away.

"People see an ugly world resulting from the consequences of man's decisions and wonder where God is. A man looks at his miserable life that is the product of all his bad decisions made according to his wisdom and then wants to blame God for it."

StormDancer hugged Beth. "Elizabeth, you are a beautiful person. Yield yourself to the person God knows you can be and hopes you'll become. In Him you will find joy and happiness."

Beth hugged StormDancer back. It all sounded so simple and beautiful. She pulled away and wiped her eyes. "Thank you." She looked up at him. From deep inside she felt a freedom she hadn't felt in a long time. She giggled. "I feel much better."

She looked up at StormDancer. "You are my brother."

"And you are my sister."

After a tight hug, StormDancer said, "And, you

are the MedicineGirl. Someday, you will be a great doctor."

After telling what had happened to them, people, making fun of Paul, Glenn, and Wally, were accusing them of drugs and asking them if they had any left that they might share.

StormDancer and Beth appeared from the woods smiling and looking happy. "Hey, StormDancer," Quillpen called. "We've been looking for you."

StormDancer and Beth walked toward the group. "What can I do for you?"

"My friends here claimed they were attacked by a group of scarecrows that staked them to the ground. They say you saw the scarecrows. Is that true, man?"

RiverDawg, seated on the porch, was listening. The witch doctor's smirk was suspect. StormDancer answered, "Well, I don't know what they claim, but I did see some scarecrows tonight."

"Were they alive?" Dave asked.

"They were real. They weren't alive."

"See! We were telling the truth," Paul declared.

After a talk of how for weeks scarecrows had been coming up missing around the town, Quillpen, Dave, Denny, Paul, Glenn, Wally, and others went on a scarecrow hunt searching the woods.

They found nothing.

Beth, dressed for bed, lay atop her bed listening

to the radio. Listening to the *Inada*'s intimate and romantic voice. It had been an extraordinary day. A wonderful night. She felt excited. For the first time in months she felt whole again. Once again she knew who she was and what she wanted to be.

She wanted to be a doctor.

She had been home and listening to the radio for an hour now. She glanced at the clock. Midnight was minutes away. Isaac told her to be listening at midnight and he'd play her a song. So far, since she'd been listening, he hadn't said anything about her or the night. She was feeling apprehensive and hoping he hadn't been leading her on. She was hoping the song he played would give her some kind of indication of his feelings toward her. She was hoping good news and not bad.

Finally, the *Inada* said, "The midnight hour is upon us. That wraps up another day for the history books as we step through the door of tomorrow. What will tomorrow bring? Who knows? I trust you'll face it with anticipation.

"I'd like to end this day with a smoke signal. I have delivered many smoke signals over the last couple of years, but never have I personally sent one myself. But that changes tonight.

"In a few weeks, your favorite group and mine, the Beatles, will be releasing a new album, *Abbey Road*. I have in my possession the first single off the album. The song is titled *Something*. My smoke signal to a special one. You know who you are."

1970

10

WAR-PIG GAMES

At night, in the jungles of Vietnam under a moonless sky, darkness penetrates everything. It is as if all things dissipate into nothingness.

Your ears become your eyes.

Garth Rygersmith entertained himself by silently holding his hand inches before his face. It wasn't there. He brought it closer. Nothing. Finally he touched his hand to his nose for a weird comfort he still had it.

After enlisting, Garth did basic at Fort Benning, Georgia. From there he went to Fort McClellan for military occupation specialty training. And then Vietnam.

He arrived in Saigon with a different mindset than most. He had joined the army and was there by choice; most had been drafted and just wanted to go home. Garth was now a hunter with a license to hunt human, and Vietnam was the hunting ground. The North Vietnamese Army and Viet Cong guerrillas, known as the VC or Charlie, were the prey and Garth was ready to go in, get his limit, and make his country proud.

The first thing Garth learned during his first days in Vietnam was that he was going to die. It was the repeated message the combat survivors who had done their time in the jungle told the new arrivals. When and how was the question. After hearing the same pessimistic message over and again, Garth, with his white skin, fresh uniform, shiny black boots, retaliated by explaining his philosophy of war and hunting to a group of homebound soldiers. The veterans found his dialog amusing. One of the guys said, "Check it out, Uncle Sam recruited Elmer Fudd." The guy slapped Garth on the back. "You're alright, Fudd. Naïve. Perhaps even stupid, but crazy enough to survive."

Another guy told him, "But you got it backwards, man. In the jungle, you're the prey. Charlie's the hunter!"

A third guy said, "And smart as ole Bugsy himself!"

From Saigon, Garth was transported to Dau Tieng. Here he got to see the effects of war on a city. The city had seen combat off and on for twenty years. Garth's stay at Dau Tieng was for one night.

The next day, Garth along with about thirty others were put aboard helicopters to be taken into the combat zone as reinforcements for a base that had suffered heavy losses.

The choppers flew low to the ground, dodging and jumping over the tallest of trees. The pilots were daredevils. Had to be. A chopper flying too high or too slow was an easy target. Garth's legs dangled from open doors. His fatigues rippling from the wind. He held on for dear life, fearing that one of the quick sudden jerks from the daredevil pilots would cause him to slide and be tossed out. It wasn't so uncommon.

Colored smoke indicated the landing zone was hot. The choppers flew in low and fast, hovering over the ground low enough and just long enough for Garth to barely have time to jump out. Though Garth understood they were being fired upon, with the noise from the choppers and his focus to run for safety, he never heard nor saw where the attack was coming from.

Reaching cover, Garth turned his attention back to the landing zone, searching for the enemy. The helicopters were already up and leaving. As they disappeared, their noise fading with them, everything grew eerily silent except for a piercing, anguish-filled voice, crying and begging for life. The wounded soldier was sometimes crying out to God, sometimes to his mother. He didn't want to die. He wanted to go home. Garth watched as a couple of guys raced back out into the open area of five-foot elephant grass to grab hold and pulled not one, but two guys, to cover. One was dead.

No more shots were fired. Charlie, the hunter, went undetected.

Welcome to Vietnam!

Jagged Hills Base was a series of bunkers dug into the ground fortified with sand bags and connected by trenches deep enough to move from one area to another without being a target. The area around the base was flat and cleared. The only structure was a tower standing in the center of the base. Beyond was the jungle—Charlie Land.

The new guys, known as NGs, were separated out and placed with the more experienced soldiers for real-life on-the-job combat training.

Another big attack was coming. The North Vietnamese Army (NVA) failed in their first attempt to take the base, but the word was, they would try again. It wasn't so much that the base was strategically important as it was about principle. The generals of the NVA were determined to take the base, and the generals of the U.S. Army were determined not to let them. It was a war-pig game. A pissing contest.

Garth didn't get any sleep his first night. The periodic incoming mortar and rocket attacks on the base kept him stressed and paranoid. The night was Charlie's playtime. Every night, throughout the night, random mortars, rockets, and sniper fire. It was Charlie's nighttime harassment directed to keeping the soldiers unnerved and unable to get proper sleep. Sleep deprivation was one of Charlie's war strategies.

Garth was told, "Here you don't sleep. You nap a little, but mostly learn to function without sleep."

The next day Garth headed out with his squad for the daily sweep and search for Charlie's hiding places and munitions caches. During sweeps there was always the danger of being ambushed, but the greater danger was the booby traps Charlie might have set during the night. Charlie was big on booby traps. Another big threat was the occasional sniper that for target practice would take someone out. Garth was told to keep alert with one eye up in the trees, one eye on the ground, and one eye on the squad leader for signal and communication. When you weren't looking, was when Charlie would strike.

At the end of Garth's second day on the battle-front, he was exhausted. He hadn't had sleep for more than forty hours. He was told that after mess and before the beast of night swallowed the land was the best time for sleeping. Garth followed the lead of those he was bunked with and tried to sleep. It seemed no sooner had his eyes shut than he was knocked from his bunk from an explosion nearby that rocked his bunker. Within seconds he was armed and running with his squad to their battle station. To Garth's surprise it was night. He had actually gotten some sleep, but it had gone by so quickly he hadn't felt like he had and his brain was hurting because of it. He watched another rocket sail into camp and explode with the earthshaking thunder of the previous one. Then all became silent and calm again. After a while he followed the rest of his group back to the bunk. The big attack wasn't tonight.

Garth crawled back into his bed.

"Don't get too comfortable, Fudd," Benideer said. Benideer was the squad leader.

"Yeah, man," agreed Piper. "You need to keep an open ear for sounds of digging." Piper's real name was Jimmy Otto. He was a colorful guy and liked to talk philosophy. He was called Piper because he smoked marijuana from a fancy-looking Asian pipe he'd purchased in Saigon. Piper was second in seniority. Garth would soon learn that Piper didn't trust the government nor high-ranking officers. He regularly referred to generals and senators as *War Pigs.* Piper liked hard rock music and his new favorite album was by a group called Black Sabbath. He had obtained a recording of Black Sabbath's album *Paranoid* and played it daily. Religiously. He seemed to be able to connect much of the lyrics and music to the Vietnam experience. Every day Garth heard at least one song off the album. The music, dark and devilish, seemed to define the Vietnam experience.

Garth didn't like his brothers in combat. But he didn't like most people anyway.

"Tell him, Worby."

Garth turned his stare toward Worby. Worby Jones rose in his bunk. He was a black guy, a combat veteran of six months. Here in Vietnam seniority determined social class. And Garth was the squad's NG.

"Last month, right 'afore one of da nearby bases got attacked, a group a' guys tryin' ta get some sleep got woke up by some commotion inside da bunker. They woke up ta find Charlie done tunneled underneath da base and was comin' up into they bunker! Two guys got kilt before Charlie disappeared underground."

Piper added, "Rumor was that Charlie was making a secret tunnel into the base, but misjudged their location and ended up in the bunker."

"Charlie's like a mole," Worby said. "He gat tunnels runnin' everywhere. All over dis land."

"They're vermin. Rats," Piper said.

"Or for you, Fudd, he's like Bugs Bunny, you never know when or where he's gonna pop up and say, 'What's up, doc?'" Benideer smirked.

"The guy who writes the Bugs Bunny and Elmer Fudd cartoons must be a Vietnam vet," Piper rationalized.

"All we're saying, man, is when you sleep, stay awake."

"Charlie never sleeps." Worby lay back down.

Benideer reached over and turned off the lantern. "Lights out."

Being called Fudd and compared to a cartoon

was a putdown. Once again Garth was being made fun of. Made to feel bad for who he was.

Garth fell into a restless sleep, dreaming of fighting and killing VC who were tunneling up into his bunk. Again, he was jolted awake from a round of mortar fire. Within seconds he was back at his battle station. This time the guys in the mortar pit answered back with a couple of mortar rounds themselves.

"If we're lucky, Fudd, we may get to watch a mortar's game of volleyball," Piper said.

"The team with da mos' casualties loses," Worby chuckled.

Piper pulled out his pipe and loaded it. He lit it, took a strong drag, and handed it to Benideer. Benideer took a toke and passed it to Worby. Worby followed suit and handed it to Garth. Garth took his turn and handed it back to Piper.

For the rest of the night, Garth watched a sporadic volleying of mortars. Charlie would send one over. The mortar pit would answer back. Every twenty to thirty minutes, just when you thought the game had ended, another would sail in. And so it went. For Garth, it was mostly another long, sleepless night followed by another hot tiring day of tromping around in the jungle. The mortar game apparently ended in a draw.

By Garth's third week in the jungle, things had become routine. At the end of another miserable day of search and seek and placing mines, Garth was hot, tired, and hungry. At night the enemy was Charlie and Charlie didn't like you sleeping. During the day, the enemy was the jungle and the jungle wasn't friendly at all. Early in the day the temperature would reach the hundred-degree mark. After that, it just got hotter. The heat index was usually about a thousand degrees. When Garth tried to combat the heat by going shirtless or wearing only a T-shirt, bloodthirsty mosquitoes and jungle flies were there to feast and add another form of torture. Each day that passed, Garth felt less human. Vietnam was turning him into something he wasn't familiar with. He hating that his bunker was beginning to feel like home and his squad like family. A family he had assigned each with a bullet bearing their name.

Day Twenty-eight:

After a miserable, hot, hard day of stomping around in the jungle searching for caches of rotting rice and rusty rounds Charlie no longer cared about, Garth and his squad returned to the base to enjoy another meal of C-rations. Benideer was called to the command bunker. Garth quickly ate his food and smoked some pot with his "brothers," hoping to get in an extra few minutes of sleep before the night games.

Pot took the edge off and helped a person relax a bit, to feel human again, and see the beauty of the land around them. It gave a person a false sense of well-being, helped one to fall asleep faster, and sometimes allowed a person to have dreams rather than nightmares.

During these times when the pipe was being passed around, Piper would have some kind of philosophical dialogue to offer. This evening's discussion was on the real world. Piper's fantasy about life back home after the war. He was engaged. He showed a couple pictures of his fiancée. A pretty girl with long blond hair. In one of the pictures she was wearing a cute smile, bell-bottom jeans, a short airy blouse revealing her belly button, and a floppy wide-brim hippy hat. In the other picture she was posed in a bikini showing off her body. She was built nicely. Garth gave rise to the fantasy of boning her. Piper said, "She sent me this one so that I'd have something to dream about." Tonight she gave everyone something to dream about.

Garth fell upon his bunk, relishing the mild euphoric feeling of the marijuana high. Piper's transistor radio blared out the song "American Woman / No Sugar Tonight" by the Guess Who. A sweet taste of home. With a slight smile on his face and thoughts of Piper's fiancée and cute American girls in general, it was perhaps Garth's best moment thus far in Vietnam.

Garth drifted off to sleep thinking of Lois Hoffman. She had been a pretty girl too. Thoughts of her stirred him. He had really enjoyed her company.

He wished he had her company now, molding his hard tired body into her soft comfortable one.

Garth hadn't been asleep long before being awakened. Benideer had returned from his briefing. "Wake up, Fudd," Benideer commanded. "Get suited up."

Pulling his mind back into reality was painful, but Vietnam was a painful place. Garth rose, swinging around, planting his feet into his waiting boots.

Benideer said, "There're reports of heavy movement in the jungle coming our way. The CO thinks the NVA has gotten a regiment of reinforcements and is coming to pay another visit. Two, maybe three thousand strong. Maybe more. Tonight's the night."

A short time later, Garth was settled in at his battle station armed and ready and staring toward the jungle. Staring at the darkness. Seeing nothing. It was a moonless night. Charlie used moonless nights to their advantage.

Garth stared forward, envisioning thousands of short Vietnamese soldiers slipping through the trees and crawling through the grass toward their camp of less than a hundred men. Nearly half of which were NGs. Garth felt fearful and tried to fight off the sense of terror trying to take over his will.

"It's kill or be killed!" Piper told him as if Garth needed any encouragement to kill.

Garth would have to kill between twenty to thirty men. That was tonight's odds. For every American there were twenty to thirty enemy soldiers. That was the way the war pigs liked it, according to Piper. Piper said, "If we survive and hold the fort, we're heroes because we were outnumbered thirty to one. If we all die and lose the fort, we die heroes because it's the Alamo all over again. Win or lose, live or die, either way we're heroes and the war pigs come out smelling like a rose having a good ole story to talk about. And that's the bottom line, man. Good ole American politics and good ole dinner conversation for the generals and politicians." Piper's cynicism plainly evident.

Piper hated the war. Hated Vietnam. Hated the government for making him do something he didn't believe in. Hated the fact that he was most likely going to die when he wanted to live. When all he wanted to do was marry his girlfriend and give her children. In a few weeks he was supposed to meet with her in Hawaii for some R&R.

Radios crackled as reports came in from the tiny squads of listening posts that were outside the camp watching and reporting on the advancement of enemy troops. According to the reports, the enemy was everywhere. Approaching in droves.

Soon the radios went silent as the listening posts were ordered back to the base before becoming trapped.

The night became completely silent with anticipation for the battle to begin. Everyone waited, staring with their ears. Garth stared down the barrel of his gun at the night. At the beast of darkness with its poisonous bite of death. His finger positioned on the trigger, ready to start squeezing away. How could the advancement of thousands of men be done so silently?

Garth felt a nudge on the shoulder and turned. Benideer offered him a tiny glass vial. "Drink this. It could be the difference between living and dying."

"What is it?"

"Doesn't matter."

"War-pig juice, man," Piper said. "Special weapon. A CIA secret recipe designed to make one into a fighting machine."

Garth took the offered vial. Benideer said, "This doesn't exist. You've never heard of it. You've never seen it. And you definitely never took any of it. Got it?"

The look in Benideer's eyes was more convincing than his words. Garth drank the concoction.

Garth positioned himself again, putting his finger on the trigger of his M-16 and staring forward at the darkness.

Death was out there. And coming. It was perhaps only yards away and crawling closer. When Garth joined the war, he never imagined he'd be fighting an invisible enemy.

It seemed to Garth the enemy was more phantom than real. So far to Garth the enemy seemed like an apparition of sorts. Never really seen, but always present. Always watching. Haunting you.

Toying with your mind with the anticipation of a sudden appearance followed by death. The enemy was death stalking, and it wanted to be the last thing you saw while dying.

Garth felt fear. His stomach was churning. He had always expected to feel braver on the battle-front. Once in Vietnam, he realized he wasn't as brave and tough as he always thought. But he didn't feel like he was fighting something human either. It was more like he was going up against something supernatural. Something living in the darkness that wasn't tangible. Wasn't visible. The type of stuff horror movies were made of. Garth was at war in a nightmare. Terribly outnumbered. The battlefield was darkness. The enemy was invisible and deadly and floated silently through the dark. Neither Hollywood nor basic ever told him combat would be this way.

Garth now realized what the soldiers meant the day he arrived in Vietnam and was told he would die. The odds of surviving a year in Charlie's world were small. This wasn't America. This wasn't Hollywood's portrayal of the American way of war and life. This wasn't a war against Germany. This wasn't the South Pacific. Nor Korea. Garth wasn't in Kansas anymore.

The silence was unnatural. Like a suspension of time in which everything had stopped. Frozen in time, Garth stared at the dark void in front of him; his heart was racing inside. Sweat was running down his face. He just wanted the fighting to begin so it could end. So he could either live or die. At this point it didn't matter which.

It was odd—the only person Garth thought about while waiting for death to appear and claim his soul was Lois Hoffman. Of all the people he could spend his final thoughts on, it was Lois. Like she was the love of his life. The one person he would miss. Or perhaps be missed by. He began to feel regret for killing her, before realizing it was coming from a fantasy. Lois didn't love him. Lois hated him. Garth quickly squelched the pain of reality with a deep-seated rage. He killed her and she deserved to die!

Suddenly, over loudspeakers penetrating the silence, kickstarting time again, *"I AM IRON MAN!"* Giant spotlights came on to blind the enemy as dozens of flares were launched, igniting the sky above the enemy's head.

The music of "Iron Man" began blaring through the darkness like a secret weapon wielding occult power, able to slice and dice the invisible apparitions floating into camp.

Rock-'n'-Roll, man.

It was America.

It was the Calvary!

Inside, adrenalin erupted like a spell of magic. A rush of power flooded Garth's mind and thoughts. A joyous feeling of rage and invincibility. A feeling of victory! The song brought a reveille of spirit and supremacy. Garth was now ready to fight. Ready to kill. He could hardly wait to sing along with his gun.

As the spotlight and flares made visible the invisible, Garth now saw the enemy. Scores of nonhuman dark shadows swarming forward, many already at the barricade of wire that protected the perimeter of the base. Garth's finger began squeezing the trigger of his machine gun before he consciously thought to do it.

The enemy immediately launched their own assault. Thousands of bullets, hundreds of mortars, rockets, and rocket-propelled grenades poured into the base.

Garth instinctively dropped, taking cover. There were explosions everywhere. Some were thunderous. The earth shook. Fire, smoke, dirt, bullets, and shrapnel filled the air. It felt and sounded like the end of the world!

When the barrage lifted, the music was still blaring, but sounded weak and distant in Garth's ears. Garth heard his sergeant barking out orders to begin fighting again. Garth took position. The spotlights were gone. The flares too. If that weren't bad enough, the air was filled with dust and smoke. The enemy had become invisible again. Garth began spraying the darkness with bullets, having only the picture of the enemy and battlefield his mind took moments before. With that mental picture to go by and "Iron Man" playing in his mind, driving his zeal, Garth, although being on the defense, took an offensive attitude. Even the enemy bullets that were screaming overhead and the green tracers slashing across the sky didn't deter Garth's determination to kill and slaughter the tide of enemy forces.

The fighting was intense. Kill or be killed! Garth often grabbed images of the enemy from the continuous explosions from the onset of mortars, rockets, and bombs offered by both sides. Like flashes of lightning, the explosions offered pictures of the battlefield and the enemy's progress. In different places, the enemy had penetrated the perimeter barrier and wire and was flowing in like water from a cracked dam. At one such opening, Garth concentrated his efforts in hopes to stop the inflow.

Reality didn't seem like reality. Although Garth was in one of the most dangerous environments one could be in, it didn't seem that dangerous. He knew better. But what he knew and what he was feeling were two different things. He felt like leaving the protection of his bunker, running over to where the enemy was pouring in, and giving him an up-close and personal greeting with an M-16. He wanted to soak his uniform with the blood of the enemy. He wanted to taste their blood. He wanted to feel their death.

The enemy was nonhuman black shadows and silhouettes. Creatures of darkness and death having no souls or value and needing to be exterminated. And Garth was an exterminator. An iron man. His mind was rushing with clarity of determination while his heart pounded in his chest, pumping adrenaline like crazy. He felt powerful. Unconquerable. If the

Black Sabbath music was still being broadcasted, Garth couldn't hear it, but nevertheless, the song "Iron Man" continued to play over and over in his mind, giving him rhythm and attitude.

The experience was like nothing Garth had ever had before. He was having the best time of his life. This was what war was all about. Killing and slaughtering. He could only hope they would keep coming so he could keep gunning them down.

Worby's gun jammed. In frustration, he threw it down. With the same sense of invincibility Garth was feeling, he climbed out of the bunker. Garth yelled up to him, "Go get'em, you big black beautiful warrior!"

Benideer paused from his concentrated efforts and ordered Worby back down. Worby, standing in the open, smiled and took a hand grenade. He pulled the pin, an enemy bullet took half his head off, and Worby fell dead back into the bunker. The grenade exploded!

Garth came to dazed and confused. He was bleeding. He rose to his feet. The noise of *boom, boom, boom* was deafening. The ringing in his ears was nearly as bad. He remembered he was in combat and wasn't actually dreaming. He looked down at the blood covering his uniform, but could not find a serious wound. His eyes traveled around the bunker. Worby was in pieces. Piper, on his back crying, was both cursing and praying to God to live. He was bloody all over. Garth realized he was missing a leg. Garth looked to where Benideer was. Benideer lay slumped over his gun. Garth stepped over Piper and went to Benideer. He was dead. A bullet to the head.

Garth turned to look at Piper again. Something hit Garth in the head with the force of a baseball bat. Garth fell to the earth again.

A Vietnamese soldier jumped down into the bunker. With his bayonet he finished off Piper and began running down the trench line toward the next bunker of machine gunners.

When Garth came to again, it took a few moments to regain his faculties. It took longer to stand up, but eventually he remembered how to do it.

Was he dead?

Was he in hell?

Fire was everywhere. Not just regular fire, but intensely hot burning fire. He could still feel the effects of the War-Pig juice in his system. It was what was perhaps keeping him going.

Garth realized the fire was napalm. Yeah, he was in hell, but he wasn't dead. Yet.

Garth found his helmet. The large dent in the side showed where a bullet had ricocheted off. Garth put it back on. The helmet was never comfortable, but now it didn't fit right and the dent was irritating and painful against the major bruise and cut at the side of his head. Garth had a head wound and was bleeding from it. He left the helmet on anyway. He found his M-16 and began walking down the trench. Every bunker he came to, everyone was either dead or dying. He still heard fighting going on and wondered who was left.

Garth came upon a wounded enemy soldier. The soldier tried to raise his gun to point it at Garth. Without a second thought, Garth shredded the man with bullets. Garth moved on.

Suddenly, enormous explosions erupted everywhere. An airstrike, Garth realized. Didn't the friendly pilots realize they were dropping the bombs right on top of the base? It wasn't so much a conscious thought as it was an involuntary act of training; Garth fell to the ground, hunkering against the trench wall.

Hunkered down, Garth's last thoughts before his mind shut down were that his own government was trying to kill him.

When his mind began to work again, Garth wasn't sure if he was alive or dead. It was all mixed up. It all seemed the same. He was bloody all over, but not in any real pain. He felt like a zombie. As far as he knew, he was dead and his spirit wandering. Maybe he was in hell after all. Maybe this was his eternity. A lonely soldier trapped in darkness in an eternal battle against demons that didn't die.

Garth didn't know how long he sat there. Minutes? Hours? Years? Time was irrelevant. It seemed like it had been an eternity. It seemed like it had only been minutes ago the battle had begun. Garth simply just didn't know.

Reasoning and rationalizing didn't seem to be a part of who he was anymore. Something inside had shut down. He felt primitive. Acting out of instinct. Nothing was real. Nothing mattered. There was no tomorrow. There was no past. Just now. Just darkness, death, fire, and thunder.

When dawn became apparent, Garth realized the bombing, explosions, and fighting had stopped. How long ago it had stopped he didn't know. It was like he was waking from a dream, but still disconnected from reality. He repositioned his gun and rose to his feet. In a combat stance, he began moving again down the trench. Moments later, he realized he hadn't stood yet. He had only been moving in spirit, but in reality, he was still sitting, hunkered against the trench wall.

Garth and only a handful of others survived. They had won the battle. Won the pissing contest. The NVA failed in yet another attempt to conquer the American base. The American army's firepower was superior to the NVA's massive ground troops.

Garth stared about. Ash, debris, and mangled burnt bodies from both sides covered not only the base, but the area beyond. He had seen scenes like this in the movies, but in reality it was truly disturbing. A thought, rising from the ashes of Garth's distant past, surfaced: Garth wondered if this would be what Armageddon would look like? Armageddon would be God's judgment on the war pigs.

Detached, hardened, and zombielike, his head bandaged, Garth was barely aware of being loaded aboard a chopper and taken away. He wasn't aware he had taken Piper's pipe, pictures of his fiancée, and recent perfumed letters she had written him.

11

NIGHT STALKING

Loaded down with camping provisions, two eleven-year-olds made ready for a promising night of fun and adventure. It was the boys' first campout. They spent the day making plans and preparing. Saying good-bye to their mothers, they headed out the back door and traveled across the backyard into the woods. They took a path they had worn down, and a few yards later, they were at the campsite. With the tent already up, they rolled out their sleeping bags. Next thing to do was to make a fire.

Rita Pierce, lounging on the couch, listened to the radio while flipping through a magazine she had read before. Pa looked asleep in his chair. She wasn't for sure. Sometimes he pretended sleep. A game he played to spy on her. A game she used to her advantage, playing the part of a loving and obedient daughter he could trust whether he was asleep or gone. Pa was mean and dangerous, but she had learned how to survive him.

Rita loved magazines and bought one every opportunity she got. She kept them and read them repeatedly. They taught her about life and relationships. They taught her how to be a woman, how to dress, how to have sex appeal, how to use her womanly charms to her greatest advantage. She liked the stories too: *I was Sixteen He was Twenty-eight*, *Midnight Lover*, *Torn Between Husband and Boss*, *Single and Free*, and so on.

She wished she were "single" and "free." She considered life without Pa. How different her world would be. Freedom. It rolled off her tongue tasting like honey.

Pa moved. She looked his way out of the corner of her eye. He yawned, stretched, and rose from his chair. He took a swallow of whiskey and then stuck the bottle in his hip pocket. He walked to the door and went outside.

Listening, Rita followed his footsteps. She went to the bathroom to peer out the window. Her pa was heading toward the woods. It was getting dark. He would be gone for hours. Where he went and what he did, she didn't know. She didn't care.

She washed her face, brushed her teeth, and combed her hair. She put on lipstick and gave herself a squirt of perfume Pa had brought home one day. As mean and hateful as he was, he was good about bringing her little gifts, things he "found." He occasionally surprised her with makeup, perfume, jewelry, and even dresses a couple of times. Those little gifts made it hard to hate him completely, but she managed well enough.

Outside, Rita looked toward the woods making sure Pa was gone. She couldn't see much. It was more night than day. After satisfying herself, she went to the front of her house and stood at the road and began walking toward the Yorks'.

She wanted to spend time with Denny. Or Glenn. She liked them both. Denny was her boyfriend. He liked having sex with her. Glenn liked her too, but unlike his older brother, Glenn was careful not to touch her in certain places.

When she got closer to the York house, Rusty ran out to greet her. Rusty was the Yorks' dog. A playful Lab acquainted with her. She took a moment to greet him with a pat and a hug, and for the moment pretended like Rusty was her dog.

Leaving the road, she cut across the yard to the side of the house. Peeping through windows, she looked to see where people were. No Denny or Glenn. Their rooms were upstairs. She wished they had bedrooms on the ground level. She stepped quietly down the side of the house toward the front. As she got to the front corner, she heard talking. She paused and listened. Someone was on the front porch. Peeking around the corner, Denny and some girl were sitting on the porch swing.

Rita stood quietly and listened.

"Stop it," the girl demanded.

"I'm not doing anything," Denny replied.

"I told you, I'm not that kind of girl."

"But, I can't help myself. Your beauty causes me to touch you."

Rita felt jealousy. Denny was with another girl.

"Oh, please. Do I look stupid? You say that to all the girls."

"What girls? There are no other girls, but you."

He told me that too, Rita thought. She accepted it because she wanted to believe him.

"Oh come on. You're Denny York. You have a reputation."

"Reputation?"

"Stop it, I said!" Rita heard some commotion and then a slap. "Everyone knows you don't really care about a girl's feelings. We're just toys to you. You tell us lies to make us feel special. And then, after you've had your fun, you toss us aside like trash."

"Well, if you know me so well, then why are you here?"

"Rumor is you're a good kisser. I like kissing."

"Well then, my toy, what are we doing here?" Rita heard Denny stand up. He said, "Let's go someplace where we can do some real kissing. I can work wonders with lips and hands."

The tear forming in Rita's eye surprised her. Sexual freedom and indulgences were shown to be healthy according to some of the world's leading and progressive psychologists and marriage counselors.

Rita spied Denny leading the girl to his car. They got in and left. Rita started back home. Wiping her eyes, she was disappointed. She wanted to be with Denny tonight. Someday, they would get married.

The brave young boys roasted their "wild animal" Oscar Meyer hotdog meat held over the campfire by sharpened sticks. It was truly dark now. The forest sounded and looked different at night. It wasn't friendly anymore. Bloodthirsty creatures of the night were up and on the prowl.

Homer Pierce was a creature of the night. A creature of the forest. Darkness was his cloak. He needed no light as he made his way through the woods to his favorite neighborhood.

Homer stepped out of the woods and onto a freshly mowed lawn. The commercially sown lawn was lush and cushiony underfoot. *Fancy lawns for fancy people*, thought Homer. The place belonged to an older couple that rarely did anything entertaining. He stopped and examined their small vegetable garden. Homer knew gardening. The garden wasn't much, but he looked forward to when he could come by and grab a tomato or two, pick a few radishes, a cucumber, some peppers, and whatever else they were growing. Why hadn't he and Joanna planted a garden this year? He just simply didn't think about it. With a chuckle about his absentmindedness, maybe next year, he thought.

Homer regarded the scarecrow guarding the garden. It wasn't doing its job. Homer wasn't the least bit scared. It was store bought. The classic straw man in "old" patched clothes crucified on a cross with "loose" straw hanging out in the traditional places. It had a simple professional drawn-on face with button eyes. Its expression wasn't too intimidating, but not friendly either. Nor was it as large as homemade ones like Mr. Scarecrow he and Joanna had back in Kansas. Mr. Scarecrow truly had scary eyes. Homer stared at the toy hanging on the cross. *Fancy people and their fancy things.* Suddenly, he lunged at it and said, "Boo!" To scare a scarecrow. The idea amused Homer.

At the second house, Homer ventured stealthily up onto a wooden deck and peered into the house through the French doors. The kitchen area was dark. He could barely see into the family room where he suspected the family was. The family consisted of a man, woman, and little girl Homer figured was around five.

The family had gotten new deck furniture. He took a seat in one of the cushiony chairs and nodded in approval at its comfort. The chairs in his own house weren't as comfortable. *Fancy people and fancy things.* This was the good life. He wished he had a cigar. He pulled out the whiskey and kissed the bottle with satisfaction. "Aah," he cooed. He was once a fancy person with fancy things. He once had money.

Homer stood. He had places to go and people to see. Standing out in the yard he looked back and thought, *I ought to burn this place down. Burn this fancy house with the fancy people in it.*

It would be a neighborhood bonfire. However, little girls should never be burned. They were assets. Pets for training. He could raise himself another wife.

Be like the Mormons.

Yes.

That would be nice. Mormon Homer.

Mormons had the right idea. In Mormonhood, women were raised to honor and serve men. Women who didn't respect the man were beaten for their sins. It was their religion.

The collecting and trading of young girls like baseball cards was an intriguing idea. He'd enjoy a collection of young women serving and worshipping him. Trading the ones he grew tired of for new ones. New ones, fresh and full of lust and sin.

By gawd, he liked the idea of being Mormon. Mormon it is! He would let Rita know. They were Mormons.

Peeping through a window of another house, a woman crossed the room and disappeared into a hall. He didn't see anyone else. He went around the house peeping in all the windows. It seemed the woman was alone. Where were the kids? Homer knew she had a boy nearing adolescence and a teenage daughter. A girl full of lust and sin for sure. Girls were sinners from birth.

The woman had a mate, but Homer had rarely seen the man. Homer made a complete circle around the house. When he found the woman again, she was in the kitchen getting something to eat. She was dressed in a baggy lounging suit that hid her figure and showed no skin. Boring.

Lacking for entertainment, Homer left the neighborhood. He had a friend to visit. Walking back into the woods, he heard laughter. He paused and listened. There was talking.

Homer squatted behind a tree. Two brave boys were spending the night away from Mommy out in the big bad woods. He felt around on the ground until he found a good throwing rock. He tossed it over their heads into the woods on the other side.

The boys jerked their attention toward the sound.

"What's that?" one said to the other in a slightly alarmed voice.

"I don't know."

They stood and gawked at the darkness beyond the fire's light. They stood quietly without moving or making a sound. Homer found their intensity amusing. The brave little boys weren't feeling so brave now.

After a few moments of silence and not hearing anything else, one of the boys said, "It was probably nothing."

"Probably."

They sat back down, but remained silent for a moment longer.

As apprehension melted away, one of the boys stated as if he'd never felt any concern at all, "It was nothing. A coon probably."

Homer could see the tension leaving their faces.

"Maybe it was a scarecrow!" the other said in a voice intended to disquiet his friend.

"Yeah, right."

"I'm serious, man."

"No you're not."

"It could be."

"I doubt it."

"Scarecrows have been disappearing from people's gardens for months."

"My parents said it's probably teenagers up to no good."

"Yeah, but what if it ain't? What about that story of the three high school guys at the witch doctor's party? A group of scarecrows carried them out into the woods and staked them to the ground? My cousin was there. He said they said the scarecrows told'em they were gonna skin 'em alive and eat'em."

"That didn't really happen."

"Yeah, it did! That Injun-preacher dude, BootShaker StormDancer, confirmed it. He saw the scarecrows. He don't lie!"

"My dad don't believe in that Injun preacher. He has long hair. My dad says that long hair on a man is a sign of sin and rebellion. If he was truly a man of God, he wouldn't have long hair."

"All I'm saying is, what if there really are

scarecrows out here?" The boy gazed into the blackness of the forest. "Other people have seen them. A friend at school said he saw one in his backyard."

"What happened?"

"The scarecrow took off running." The boy looking around asked, "What if they attack us tonight?"

The other boy looked down at the fire. "We'll fight 'em off with fire!" He reached down and carefully picked up a branch burning on one end.

Homer remembered Rita telling him about scarecrows and some boys who were kidnapped by them. He hadn't really paid her any attention when she was telling him. She was stupid and gullible. It was sinful to be stupid and gullible the way she was. He had tried slapping some of that stupidity out of her, but it was useless.

Homer slipped away.

The house was dark. Homer, looking into the window, couldn't see much. He went to another window, having the same results. June would be working. He went to the window where Veggie stayed. It looked like he was in bed.

The back door was locked. Homer rammed his shoulder into it, knocking it open. He first checked June's bedroom to be sure she wasn't home. She wasn't.

Veggie's room stank of urine. He was in bed. His eyes shut. Homer stepped over, reached down, and gave him a shake. Veggie's eyes opened. "It's me.

Homer." Veggie grunted something Homer didn't understand. "Can you use a drink?"

Rita sat on the edge of her porch drinking a beer. Why couldn't she have been a normal girl with normal parents? Why couldn't she have lived in a decent house and had friends? She took a drink to take the edge off her depression.

There was yelling from the Brandt house. She stood and looked. Betty's pa was in one of his rages. Someone was in trouble. Probably Johnny. Johnny was always in trouble over one thing or another. Rita watched as Betty's pa, holding Johnny's wrist with one hand, was smacking him with the other. They were too far away for her to hear what was being yelled, but Johnny's pa was giving it to him good. They went around in a circle as Johnny tried pulling away. Johnny's pa let him go with one final slap, sending Johnny to the ground. His pa, continuing to shout, stormed back into the house.

Rita felt sorry for Johnny. He got far more beatings than he should have. Johnny lay on the ground not moving. Was he all right?

She began to walk in that direction, but hadn't gotten far when Johnny got up. She stopped. Johnny stomped around for a minute in his own rage. He reached down and picked something up. A baseball bat? He went over to his pa's truck and began smacking the tailgate. She could hear the banging easy enough so he had to be hitting it hard. *Johnny, ya dumb little fool! What are ya doin'?*

As Rita feared, Johnny's pa stormed out of the house again in a cussing rage. Johnny dropped the bat and ran to a safe distance. Johnny's pa picked up the bat and headed toward Johnny. Johnny ran from the yard into the field. Johnny's pa threw the bat at him and went back to his truck. Mr. Brandt pulled out a rifle. Johnny raced further out in the field. Johnny's mother, standing at the door, was yelling. Johnny's pa shouted back at her and pointed the gun at her. She retreated into the house. Johnny's pa went to the edge of their yard. Johnny was out in the field dancing. Mocking? *Johnny, ya stupid fool! Whacha doin'?* Johnny's pa aimed the gun and fired it. Johnny went down.

Rita ran back to her house fearing being next. Entering the house, slamming the door shut, she squatted down against it. After a few minutes, she cracked open the door and spied out. Johnny's pa was seated on the tailgate of his truck. She couldn't see Johnny anywhere. Was he dead?

Veggie didn't weigh much, but over the long distance, he got heavy. Homer needed a break. Veggie was secured to Homer's back, and Homer went down on his knees and gently released Veggie. Veggie slid off and fell over onto the ground. Homer pulled him back up, positioning him against a tree for support.

Homer wiped his face of sweat. "Whew! We

need to put you on a diet, buddy." Homer stood and stretched his back, twisting around until it popped. "That's better."

Homer sat down and pulled out the whiskey. He took a sip and then helped Veggie to a sip.

"It's a good night to be alive," Homer said. "Don't you think? Yeah, I agree. Who would have thought? A couple of freaks like us out and enjoying the night life." Homer chuckled. He liked the company of Veggie. Veggie didn't say much. The only opinion Veggie had was the opinion Homer gave him. Homer liked that about Veggie. Some of the ideas Homer had, he gave credit to Veggie. He enjoyed thinking for Veggie. Veggie was the kind of friend Homer could respect. They were going to have some fun times together.

Rita's house was dark except for a candle burning in the front room. Peeping through the window, Johnny saw Rita was up. He didn't see her old man anywhere. He snuck in through the back door and found Rita peering out the front door. "Got a beer?"

Rita jumped and jerked around. She stood dumbfounded a moment, before asking, "Are you okay? I thought you were dead!"

"I ain't dead, stupid. Where's ya old man?"

"Out."

"Out where?"

"I don't know. Snipe huntin'."

"Snipe huntin'?"

"Snipes only come out at night."

"What's a snipe?"

"Some kind of bird, I think. Pa says they're good eatin'. Taste like chicken."

"When's he comin' back?"

It was just past midnight. Rita shrugged. "Couple hours, maybe."

"I need a beer?"

Johnny was only thirteen, but Rita shared beer with him. He didn't like the taste, but like smoking, it made him feel manly.

Rita stepped past him to the refrigerator. "What happened? What'd ya do?"

"It wasn't me." He went to the door, cracked it open, and looked toward his house. He couldn't see his old man. Hopefully he was probably passed out. Lying on the ground or in the back of the truck.

"What happened?" Rita repeated, handing him an opened beer. He had cuts and bruises on his face. She reached out, but he knocked her hand back.

Johnny took a drink and made a face. Although they stood in semidarkness, he could see well enough to see Rita grinning. "Stop laughing at me or I'll knock your teeth out!"

"But, it's funny."

"Yeah? Is this funny?" He punched one of her breasts. "Stupid girl!"

"That hurt!" She glared, taking a step backwards and bringing up a hand to rub it.

"I meant fer it to! I'm in no mood to be messed

with!" He swelled up, pushing out his chest in a cock stance.

Normally Rita would have laughed, but refrained this time. She didn't want to be hit again. Johnny was in a violent, thunderous mood, full of turmoil and frustration. He would take some of that rage out on her if she gave him an excuse. It was how men were. Violence was a man's answer for having a lack of control. It was why Johnny was there. To blow off steam. To find some control. To regain self-respect and importance.

Magazines taught Rita that men needed to feel in control. It was their ego. It was a woman's job to boost a man's ego. To make him feel masculine, smart, and in control. "Sorry," she apologized, not so much because she was, but Johnny's need to feel manly and in control.

Johnny took another drink. Although he tried hard not to, he still made a face.

Rita pretended he didn't. "What happened?"

"The tyrant's drunk on whiskey." Johnny sat down on the couch and sipped the beer again.

Rita joined him.

"When he drinks whiskey, he gets mean. Meaner than normal." He raised the bottle to his mouth again. He still made a face. "He wanted Betty to read some joke he'd tore out of a magazine or something. As Betty tried reading it, she went to stuttering. Betty's stuttering made him mad 'cause it was ruining the joke. He cussed at her and made her try to read it right, but she still stuttered. The madder he got, the more she stuttered and cried."

Johnny tilted the bottle and took a big gulp. Rita ignored the bitter face. "The creep told her she was going to learn not to stutter or he was going to beat her to death! He kept making her read and slapped her when she stuttered. Mom tried to reason with him, but he finally knocked her flat on the floor. He made Betty read again. She was no better, probably worse. He grabbed her and started whacking her in the head.

"Mom tried to stop him, but he punched her in the stomach and then pushed her headfirst into the wall. He made Betty try again. She was crying so bad she couldn't even get the first word out. He started slapping her head again. He was hitting her hard too. I got scared. Betty being a girl and retarded."

"Betty's not retarded."

Johnny took another drink. "The old man says she's weak minded. Mentally lazy. That she don't apply herself."

"Stuttering comes from being nervous."

"How would you know? You a scientist? You're a stupid dumb girl yourself."

"I read magazines. You can learn about lots of stuff from magazines."

Johnny turned his stare from her to her pa's collection of porn magazines. Johnny liked looking through those magazines. Rita and he sometimes looked through them together. She found it fun to poke and tease him through his trousers when they did. It was another reason he liked coming to her house. He saw the stack in the normal place, next to the chair her pa always sat in. "Yeah? Have you learned a lot from those magazines?"

He had no idea. "So, then what happened?"

"Betty didn't have a chance. I felt sorry for her and was afraid the old man was gonna hurt her real bad. Maybe even kill her. I knew it was up to me to protect her. I ran over and shoved him as hard as I could. He stumbled and fell. He got up madder than a hornet. He came for me telling me he was gonna give me the best beatin' of my life!

"I knew I had a better chance outside, so I went runnin' fer the door. He caught me at the door, but I managed to get outside and into the yard while he was clobbering me. He kept hitting me in the head with his fist."

Johnny turned his face toward the light for show-and-tell. Rita reached out with a tender touch. Johnny pulled back and took another drink. "When he let go of me, I fell to the ground, dizzy. I couldn't think straight. I soon realized he was back inside cussing and beating on Betty again. She was crying and trying to beg him to stop, but was stuttering so bad, she couldn't get it out. The tyrant wouldn't let up. I was so mad. I went over and started hitting the truck with the bat, yelling and calling him names. I was trying to make him madder at me than at Betty. It worked and he came for me. That's when I headed out in the field. I wanted him to chase me. I knew I could outrun him. Instead, though, he got the gun. When he shot, I hit the ground and went crawling."

Johnny took another gulp. Lowering the bottle, he looked at Rita. "I hate him! I hate him to death! Someday I'm gonna kill him."

Rita felt his pain and understood his frustration. She scooted against him, putting an arm around him. "I hate my pa to death too." She kissed the side of his head. When Johnny didn't pull away, she kissed one of the small cuts on the side of his head and licked the cut with her tongue. He seemed to like being licked. She licked another cut.

After chatting with Veggie, telling him about coming across a couple of boys camping in the woods, Homer was struck with an idea. The more he thought and talked about the idea with Veggie, the more he liked it. Being the good guy he was, Homer told Veggie, "That's a great idea, Veg." He slapped Veggie on the back for praise. Veggie grunted, falling over face-first to the ground. Homer pulled him back up right. Dirt around Veggie's mouth caused Homer to laugh. "Hungry?"

The campsite was dark and quiet except for an occasional pop from the smoldering campfire, where scores of tiny red lights lit up when touched by a breeze. The two eleven-year-old boys were asleep in their tent. Hearing something, one of the boys raised his head looking toward the door and beyond. He saw nothing out of the ordinary. He listened. He heard movement. He reached over and shook the other boy. "Hey," he whispered.

Groggy, the other boy answered, "Huh?"

"Did you hear that?"

"What?"

"Listen. I heard something."

The other boy drifted back to sleep again.

Rodney strained his hearing. There was a quiet shuffling of leaves. Something was prowling about the camp. In his imagination, he saw a wolf. Perhaps a bear. He calmed himself down. It was probably a coon.

He slid out of his sleeping bag and crawled to the tent entrance. Face pressed against the screen door, he looked about. It was too dark to see much. He turned his stare toward sounds of movement. He was hearing something, but could not see anything. With more demanding effort than before, he shook his sleeping friend.

The sleeping boy responded with a grumble.

"Zack. Wake up! There's something outside."

"Huh?"

He shook him again. "Wake up!"

"Why?"

"Something's outside."

"What?"

"I don't know. An animal or something."

"So." Zack willed himself awake. Sleepily, he joined his friend at the door. "I don't hear anything."

"Listen."

Seconds passed. "There's nothing out there. You're just hearing things."

"I'm serious, man. Something's out there!"

The sleepy boy grabbed his flashlight and shined it around. He saw nothing. He unzipped the door.

"Whatcha doing?"

"Gotta take a leak."

Rodney, realizing the need also, grabbed his flashlight and followed Zack out. The boys stood in front of the tent, their small beams of light scanning the area. Nothing seemed amiss.

"See. There's nothing out here. You were dreaming."

"There was something out here."

"Well it's gone now." Zack moved forward to a place to do his business.

The other lingered, continuing to search. Hearing the snap of a twig off to his side, he shined the light in that direction. He saw something lying on the ground. "Hey, Zack."

"What?"

"I see something."

"What?"

"I don't know."

Zack, finishing his business, zipped up his pants. He turned around to his friend. "Where?"

"Over there." He pointed with his light.

Zack went to investigate. To his surprise, there was something lying on the ground.

"What is it?"

"I don't know." Zack proceeded slowly and saw what appeared to be a body. He cautiously took another step forward. Then another. Shining his light, he saw straw sticking out at places. The thought occurred to him that his friend was playing a joke on him, trying to scare him with a scarecrow.

Zack stepped closer and said, "It looks like a body."

"A body?"

"Yeah." Zack stepped closer. "There's straw sticking out of its shirt."

"What?"

"I think it's a scarecrow."

"What?"

Zack bent down and picked up a stick. "If it is, I'm gonna burn him." He would show his friend he was too cool to be fooled.

"I think we should get out of here!"

"What? Are you kiddin'? I ain't scared of no dumb scarecrow." Zack stood next to the scarecrow shining his light down on it. It was lying on its stomach. Zack poked it with his stick. He was surprised how solid it felt. "It's a scarecrow alright." Zack glanced back at his friend. "A dead one," he stated for drama.

"Let's get outta here, Zack!"

"Scared?" Zack mocked.

"Yeah."

"Well, I ain't." Zack reached down to the scarecrow's shoulder area to turn it over. He was surprised by the weight of it and how real it felt. Having second thoughts, but too cool to stop, he rolled the scarecrow over. Staring down at its face, Zack saw a face staring back at him. Its mouth opened and it grunted. Zack froze in fear. Then fainted.

Fear gripped Rodney's soul as he watched Zack suddenly go limp and fall to the ground. Then from the darkness beyond where Zack was standing, another scarecrow, yelling something demonic, came rushing forward floating through the air.

Rodney, peeing himself, went fleeing for his life!

Homer was beside himself with laughter. He had never seen anything funnier. He picked Veggie off the ground, and holding on to the store-bought scarecrow he'd stolen from the old folks' garden, he raced away.

Rita woke up and cursed herself for falling asleep. It scared her to have done such a dangerous thing. She was lucky this time: it was past three o'clock and her pa hadn't come home. Johnny was asleep, lying on the couch with his head in her lap. He had drifted off to sleep while she tenderly caressed and ran fingers through his hair. She had meant to stay awake so she could hear her pa coming and get Johnny out of the house.

Running fingers through his hair, she had calmed

his stormy spirit. Subdued the angry animal. She felt proud of her accomplishment. More and more she was learning how easy it was to manipulate men. From magazines, she'd learned men had simple drives: food, control, and sex. These basic drives made them predictable. Women were different. Women were unpredictable, driven by a variety of complex emotions.

She and Johnny had much in common and understood one another. With Johnny, she didn't feel shame. She didn't worry about being stupid or embarrassing herself. Johnny knew she was stupid, poor, and of low class. He didn't care. He liked her for who she was.

Rita caught herself nodding off again. She woke herself up and heard talking. Pa was back!

She shook Johnny. "Code red! Wake up. Code red!"

Johnny, coming to life, was out the front door almost instantly. Rita marveled at his quick response. She shut the door and ran to bed.

Hearing Pa coming in through the back door, she closed her eyes and pretended to be asleep.

Johnny, keeping to the shadows, made his way back home. He found his dad passed out in the back of the pickup. The rifle at his side.

Johnny wanted to kill him. The Dark Knight would. Johnny quickly ran a gambit of ideas through his mind on how he could do it and not go to jail. He went over to a small pile of concrete blocks left as extras from one of his dad's jobs. With a flashlight and a pair of his dad's work gloves, he quietly moved the blocks around searching for what he knew was there. When he found it, he carefully reached out and grabbed it and held it in his gloved hand. He went back to the tyrant and stuck the black-widow spider under the tyrant's shirt.

Hours later, a very sick George Brandt was taken to a Springfield hospital for a spider bite.

Betty was left in charge.

Knowing their old man was in the hospital from a black-widow spider bite and with the hope he would die, there was an air of freedom in the Brandt house. In spite of the bruises and cuts on his head and face, Johnny felt happy as he went about doing chores and helping Betty with the running of the house.

Even Betty, who looked like she needed to be in a hospital with her face bruised and swollen as it was, was in good spirits and joked around. She seldom made jokes. Johnny noted in all her talking and bossing, she never once stuttered. He felt bad for the way she looked and how she was limping from a hurt leg suffered from the abuse of their old man.

When some guy stopped by to talk to their dad about some work he had for him, Johnny dealt with the man so that Betty could hide. They had strict orders not to let anyone see how she looked.

To Johnny, Betty, and little Jimmy's disappointment, their old man only spent a couple of days in the hospital before being released. Hearing the truck, Betty looked out the window. Johnny saw the life leave her eyes. "M-m-mom and D-d-dad b-back h-home."

Johnny stood with clenched fists as his parents entered the house. The Dark Knight had failed to assassinate the tyrant. Underneath his cloud of depression swirled a wind of suppressed rage. Someday the Dark Knight would kill the tyrant.

12

THE PURPLE HEART CLUB

P ushed by a nurse, Garth Rygersmith was returned to his room via a wheelchair after
another session of psychotherapy. For the
reason of the therapy, he wasn't sure. It didn't make
sense. But, this was the army: nothing ever made
sense. He could have walked back to his room, but
the hospital staff wouldn't hear of it.

Taken from the "Jagged Hills" battle, Garth was
brought to the hospital for medical treatment and
observation. He'd suffered numerous wounds from
the battle; most were minor. The worst was the head
wound where an enemy's bullet ricocheted off his
helmet, knocking him out cold and severely bruising
his head and perhaps his brain as well. The hospital
was keeping his head bandaged and him under close
observation.

The semi-attractive nurse insisted on helping him
into bed. Garth didn't understand the fuss. He didn't

feel he was hurt and yet they were treating him as if he were. The pampering was totally unnecessary.

Back in bed, all tucked in, he was left to rest, heal, and think. He reached for his cigarettes.

Garth didn't mind being in the hospital. It was a nice vacation from the hells of the jungle. Here he had nurses to wait upon him and take care of him. Nurses to lust after and make suggestive remarks to.

But still, he had witnessed men with more serious injuries come in, receive treatment, and be shipped out again.

Why was he still here?

And what was up with all the psychoanalyzing?

A man, first pausing at the door, glancing in, and then appearing to recheck the room number, entered Garth's room. He was civilian. A checkered sports jacket and tie. He looked to be in his thirties. A little on the plump side. Wearing a camera like a necklace, he smiled and said, "Good day, sir. Garth Rygersmith?"

"In the flesh."

"Great. Glad to meet you." The guy stepped over to the bed and stuck out a hand. "Ben Arnold—freelance journalist."

Garth stared at his hand a moment before deciding to shake it.

Ben Arnold continued, "I'm part of a team working on this year's annual Veteran's Day magazine, *American Soldier.* The theme this year is *The Purple Heart Club.* We're honoring those who have received purple hearts. I'm told you've recently received a Purple Heart. A survivor of the Jagged Hill Offense. The Vietnam's Alamo of sorts. Took a bullet to the head?"

"Could've been serious, but I'm a bit hardheaded, ya see."

Ben Arnold let out a small chuckle. "Good one. If you don't mind, I'd like to hear your story of the battle. Ya know, your side of it. What you saw and experienced. And I'd like to take a few pictures."

"He won't mind at all!"

Standing in the doorway, in military stance, was a captain.

Before Garth had a chance to move, salute, or anything, "As you were, Soldier," the captain told him.

The captain's stare went to the journalist. "The good people back home need to hear from their boys. Their heroes. The soldier will be happy to fully cooperate." The captain's gaze shifted back to Garth. "Right, Soldier?"

"Yes, sir."

"Good deal," the journalist said.

Garth told his story. Ben Arnold recorded it and in certain places, embellished it. Photos were taken. The pictures were staged showing Garth lying down instead of sitting up. Showed Garth to be seriously injured. The captain had red dye smeared onto the bandage to give the appearance of a wound still bleeding.

Garth understood Arnold wanting to hype the story up, but was surprised when the captain began speaking of his post-traumatic stress problems from the battle. Garth was a bit confused, since he didn't have any. Nevertheless, he knew better than to refute the captain on the matter.

The captain told Arnold that Garth was soon to be transferred to a special hospital in Europe for study and treatment of his PTSD. His release and transfer papers were in the works even as they were speaking.

13

DEATH STALKING

Seated at the kitchen table, savoring a cup of coffee, watching a fly, Homer Pierce's mind was in the past, but his coffee sipping was in the present.

He was waiting for Joanna and for breakfast.

Anger was building inside. He didn't know why. He just felt the need to be mad. Perhaps it was because it was a new day. Another day of misery in his miserable life.

Maybe, it was because he didn't have time for waiting. Waiting got on his nerves.

Joanna, in the bathroom, was getting ready for the day. She wasn't much of a wife. She wasn't much of anything.

Homer took a sip of coffee. The fly zipped by his head. He hated flies. Flies were pests. Tormenters. Following it with his eyes, he stalked it. The little bloodsucking buzzy-buzzy didn't know its life was about to end. Homer was going to kill him. Kill him good!

Death is stalking you, said Homer to the fly in his mind.

The fly landed on the refrigerator. It sat there a moment, cleaning its little fly hands. Then it crawled around in a circle before taking to the air again.

Joanna's perfume interrupted Homer's death stalk as she entered the room. The look on her face was pleasant.What was she happy about?

Opening the refrigerator, she got out the eggs and milk, placing them on the counter next to the stove. Her back was to him. Her pretty blond hair, brushed, hung down the back of the flannel shirt she wore as a robe.

In lustful stare, Homer raised the cup of coffee to his lips. His eyes falling to her legs below the shirttail. She had nice legs.

She turned his way, bringing the coffeepot to warm his cup. She looked as young and pretty as when he first took her as his wife. She was sixteen then and still she didn't look any older.

Her beauty was a torment.

She returned to the stove.

Why was she dolled up? Was she going somewhere? Was she going to go whoring today while he labored in the fields trying to make her a living? Was that why she was in a pleasant mood?

The whore.

The voice within told him he should beat her.

The fly landing on top of her head interrupted the fantasy of how to hurt her. Or was it a different fly? He wasn't sure. They all looked alike.

Wait a second. Had the fly crawled out of her ear? It wouldn't be surprising. Crawling atop her head, she raised an arm and shooed it away. The rising of the shirt's tail at her upward movement exposed the upper back side of her legs.

Homer took a sip of his coffee.

He caught another whiff of Joanna's perfume.

Her womanliness was powerful.

Seducing.

He stalked her every move, watching to see if flies were coming out of her ears. She stepped over to a nearby cabinet on the wall to get something out. The shirt went up. Her panties were beige.

The effect was torturing.

She was torturing him on purpose.

She didn't love him. She hated him. She flinched at his looks. Held her breath when he touched her. Nearly gagged when he kissed her.

He hated her!

You should beat her, the voice in his head spoke again.

She wouldn't look so pretty then. She wouldn't feel like going out and whoring then. She would stay home like a wife was supposed to.

Beating her was his right.

He should beat her and rape her.

Raping her was his right. What she wouldn't freely give, he would take! She was his wife. He owned her. She was given to him fair and square.

His eye was drawn to the buzzy-buzzy landing on the table in front of him. It walked about in front of him. Teasing him. Provoking him.

Soon the buzzy-buzzy would be dead.

That's right, buzzy-buzzy. Death is coming. It's just around the corner.

Joanna's sexy thighs grabbed his attention again. She pranced about in front of him.

Looking so young. So sexy.

Teasing him.

Provoking him.

Torturing him.

The fly crawled closer.

Homer watched it. He would wait for the right moment.

Now!

At the move of his hand, the fly flew—zipping right in front of his face. So close Homer could hear it laughing.

Homer's anger increased.

He inhaled a deep breath and sipped his coffee. He was trying not to lose his cool while tracking the fly as it flew about.

The fly would soon be dead.

Homer's stare was drawn to Joanna again. Her pretty legs flirted with him. Stirring him. She wanted him to want her. She loved knowing her looks and body tormented him. She loved rejecting him. Loved causing him pain.

Evil she is, said the voice in his head. *You should kill her.*

That would teach her.

Looking up at the back side of her head, he saw the fly. Or had another crawled out of her head? He cussed himself for not having been watching. It was Joanna's fault he had not been watching. She had caused him to be staring down at her legs.

He was angry before. He was pissed off now.

Homer hated flies!

Homer hated his wife!

Homer hated everyone!

Hate flowed through his soul like blood through veins. He quietly rose from his chair. Moving stealth-ily toward his wife, lifting an arm, his slap came down hard upon her head the fly was sitting on.

Joanna, knocked forward into the hot stove, pushed the skillet off the burner. Hot grease and fire threatening to burn her. She instinctively pushed herself back and fell to the floor.

Towering over her, she looked stunned. He couldn't tell if he had killed the fly or not. Flies were tricky little creatures. He stood with clenched fists debating his next move.

Beat her! Beat her good! Throw the hot grease on her face, the voice in his head demanded. It made sense. Joanna moved into a defensive position, raising an arm to shield her from whatever was coming next.

Stupid woman, Homer thought.

Grab her arm and snap it in two! commanded the voice in his head.

It sounded like a good plan and instead of grabbing the skillet, he reached down and grabbed her by the arm.

With desperate eyes, she shouted, "What did I do, Pa? Please don't hurt me! I'm sorry! I won't do it again! I'm really sorry!"

Pa?

Joanna had disappeared. It was Rita staring up with fearful pleading eyes.

Rita?

Homer continued to looked down. It wasn't Joanna! It was Rita. Easing his iron grip, he pulled her to her feet, and said, "There was a fly on top of your head. I wanted to kill it. You know how I hate flies."

Letting go of her, he went back to the table to sit down. He felt a moment of confusion. It wasn't really him that had done it.

Rita was confused too. And crying. On shaky legs, she raised a trembling arm to examine it. She had been burned.

Not bad.

Bad enough.

No burn was fun. Homer knew burns. Burns turned pretty people into monsters.

He rose from his chair, went to the refrigerator, and got an ice cube. He gently took the frightened girl's arm and pressed the ice to the burn. No one should ever be burned.

Rita was a good girl. She wasn't a whore. He kissed the top of her head. "I'm sorry for hitting you. I didn't mean to hit you so hard. It was the fly's fault."

After eating his breakfast, Homer went to the front room and sat down. Rita, making herself ready for school, came out of the bedroom to wait for the school bus.

She acted leery of him.

She was in a dress.

Her pretty legs started flirting with him again.

He took a drink of whiskey.

When had Rita become such a woman?

When had she become her mother?

Homer sipped his whiskey in lust.

Outside, the school bus honked and came to a stop. Rita, grabbing her purse and books, hurried out the door letting a fly in.

She was getting too old for school.

Boys would be buzzing around her.

Buzzing already, most likely.

Boys were bloodsucking flies.

Rita was stupid. She had a head full of maggots. She would be easy prey.

Homer sipped his whiskey, giving it some thought.Boys would stalk her. Buzz about her. Get into her head.

The fly caught Homer's eyes. Homer hated flies. He hated flies to death! He followed the fly with his death stare. Soon the maggot-maker would be dead! The buzzy-buzzy would become the buzzy-wuzzy.

14

DARK PATRIOT

Garth was pushed out on a gurney and loaded in a medical van for transfer to an airport to be taken to Europe to a special hospital for PTSD treatment. He could have walked out, but the medical personnel insisted he stay on a gurney. Garth felt it was all a charade—for what reason, he had no idea. He complied.

The driver and one other person, both in medical garb, sat up front, leaving Garth in the back on the gurney. Surrounded by medical equipment, Garth assumed the van was an ambulance of sorts. There were no windows to look out of so Garth didn't see the need to sit up.

En route, a short time later, Garth felt the van come to a stop. He heard the doors open and his escorts get out. Garth sat up, looking toward the front and out the windshield in hopes to see what was going on.

The back doors opened. One of the medical guys leaned in. "The Captain wants a word."

Garth looked past the guy, seeing the captain. It was the same man who had been present during his interview with the journalist from *American Soldier.*

"Out here, Soldier," ordered the captain.

Garth got out of the van, took a step toward the officer, and went into a salute. The captain, ignoring protocol, said, "Follow me."

Garth followed. He didn't know where he was. It was an isolated place. Jungle all around.

Stepping from the road, the officer led Garth down a jungle trail ending on a beach. Garth followed the captain along the beach to a bench. The captain sat down, offering Garth a cigarette and seat beside him. Garth took the cigarette and sat down.

"It's a beautiful day," the captain said.

It was midmorning and before them was a blue sky and a sparkling ocean. "Yes, sir," Garth agreed, lighting the cigarette and exhaling smoke.

"A fine day indeed," the captain half whispered, staring out across the ocean.

Garth, relishing the moment as both men sat silently staring at the sea, caught sight of a couple of birds circling above the water some distance away. Hunting, he reckoned.

Disrupting the tranquil vibe, the captain said, "It is of my opinion, Soldier, you have talents. Talents I wish to capitalize on. I'm here to give you options. You can volunteer to join my special team, leave this godforsaken land to serve your country in an elite way. Or, you can tell me to go screw myself, rejoin your company, and go back to stomping around in the jungle until your tour is up or they haul you out of here in a body bag."

Suspiciously, Garth looked at the captain.

"The choice is yours, of course," the captain assured. "But, to help you to make a thoughtful choice, let me give you a debriefing of the situation. Are you the type that likes history, Soldier?"

"History, sir?"

"Most people don't. Most people are stupid. History is important. Knowing history can be very advantageous."

Garth didn't respond.

The captain said, "You need to understand the big picture. This war here, here in Vietnam, isn't the war. What you see here is a battle. This is the Vietnam battle in the real war. The war between the United States and the Soviet Union. The war between West and the East. Between freedom and slavery. Between capitalism and Marxism. Between liberty and suppression.

"The United States and the Soviet Union are global superpowers. And for the first time in history there truly is a global war. A war being waged on every continent, in most every country, and on all levels of life and society. It's a war like no other war. A war being waged on multiple fronts: social, intellectual, political, economic, and military.

"This great world war was birthed in 1917 with the violent seizure of the Russian government by the Bolshevik party led by Vladimir Lenin. The triumph of Marxist socialism in Russia electrified sympathizers, supporters, and radicals around the world. The Marxist/Soviet ambition is global control. Soviet leadership then and now has no concept of 'peace' as the West understands it. Soviets have no plan for coexistence. They want to destroy the American way of life, dominate the world, and enslave the masses and control their every thought and deed.

"Back home, socialism is being preached. How our country is in need of more social reform and programs. 'Power to the people,' the left-arm preaches. But socialism has nothing to do with social balance, equality, and justice as their speeches allude. It is not about empowering the people. But just the opposite. It is about dominating the people. Controlling all aspects of their lives."

The captain's words held truth. When Garth was attending college, he heard the doctrine of Socialism preached everywhere. There was a definite movement to create sympathizers and supporters. It was the true agenda behind all the "peace" rallies.

"Soviet mentality is that of bullies," the captain went on. "They have seized Eastern Europe. They have generated revolutions in Latin America, Asia, and Africa. They aid aggression as they did with North Korea and now with North Vietnam. They train and subsidize guerrillas, disrupt elections, shoot down unarmed planes, sponsor coups, shoot refugees, and imprison dissidents. They threaten, connive, conspire, subvert, bribe, intimidate, terrorize, lie, cheat, steal, torture, spy, blackmail, and murder."

The captain wasn't saying anything Garth didn't already know. His mind wandered from the captain's words as he strained his eyes. Across the ocean, on the horizon, a vessel came into view. A war boat? A fishing boat, perhaps? Garth couldn't tell. He couldn't imagine trying to maintain a life and raise a family in a war zone. The stress, fear, and hardship would be too much. Yet, for the Vietnamese people, it was their way of life. Their world. What choice did they have? They were born in the wrong place at the wrong time. It wasn't fair. But life wasn't fair. Garth understood the unfairness of life all too well.

"Focus, Soldier!" the captain commanded. "This stuff is important. Knowledge is power."

Garth turned his attention back to the captain. "Yes, sir."

"The Soviet machine has no true master plan, no timetable for world conquest, but rather a constant pushing and shoving and strengthening of military forces and a consistent exploitation of every opportunity to expand their own power and weaken the Western Alliance and its power.

"The United States of America is its chief rival. We stand in their way of world domination. For that reason Soviet intentions are to destroy America. Our values. Our freedoms. Our way of life. The American dream. The Soviet machine is vicious, but patient. The Socialists are driven and calculating. They understand a victory, no matter how small, is still a victory. They understand that multiple small victories create a platform for large victories."

Small victories create a platform for large victories—that was something to write down and remember. *Patience is what wins in the end*, Garth remembered reading somewhere.

"The Soviet Socialist takeover in America began in 1919. The Socialists preach social justice. What the Socialists preach and what they do are two complete opposite things. To gain acceptance they tell the people what they want to hear. They rally their hearts with false promises. And then when they get the upper hand, they turn monster. Vietnam is full of stories where the Communists have gone into a village, took prisoner the chief and his family. And then starting with the youngest, even the babies, slowly peeled the skin off their bodies in front of the chief and his family and all the villagers. A slow agonizing torturous death. Doing this one by one, from the youngest and ending with the chief. Doing this to create fear for anyone who would stand up against them. Doing this to create control. Doing this in the name of social justice."

Social justice. A concept Garth had always wanted to believe in. All he had ever wanted was a chance to make his mark. To achieve a dream. But life's not fair.

Life is like a villain and can be cruel. Throughout his life, Garth had to deal with social injustice. He was dealt a bad hand at birth. He was judged trash and looked down upon not because of who he was or the possibility of what he could achieve, but because of his family and the environment he was unluckily born into.

Social injustice was the handicap Garth had to live with and endure. The disability he had to overcome. Social injustice was why the pretty, perky Lois Hoffman deemed him unworthy of her time.

Social justice didn't exist. It was a noble idea, but not a true concept of evolution. Survival of the fittest. Kill or be killed. That was truth. That was life. That was evolution.

"Back in the 1920s"—Garth focused on the captain's speech again—"abrasive tactics of terrorism backfired and the U.S. government retaliated, arresting and deporting hundreds of Communists for advocating anarchy and violent revolution. For survival, the American Communist parties went underground and out of sight."

Underground. Out of sight. Invisible. A rallying of inspiration started taking place in his thoughts.

"They later joined forces and resurfaced as the *Communist Party of the United States of America*—CPUSA. Realizing the integrity of the American people and that a direct and hostile takeover would not be possible, they had to develop a new strategy."

Garth's mind was at work. The captain's dialogue was important. The captain's intention was that of a history lesson. A debriefing as he put it. Somewhere in this history lesson, there would be a point that the captain was working toward. However, in Garth's mind, dots were being connected. A vision was being created.

The captain looked at Garth. "Do you know what a 'water' strategy is, Soldier?"

"No, sir." But, he was interested.

"Water can take a strong, structurally sound building and if there is a weak spot, a spot where the water can infiltrate and create a leak—that leak and seepage over time can compromise the integrity of the structure and eventually bring it to collapse.

"Soviet methodology against the strong, against our great country, is like that of water. Presenting itself as harmless. Even something good and noble, like peace, love, and equality."

The captain paused for a moment to let it sink in. "That's the Soviet plan for America. By the 1930s, seeking weak spots and leaks, the Communists had gained control over many labor unions. Presenting themselves as nonthreatening, telling the people what they want to hear, presenting themselves as champions of social justice. The Communists infiltrated dozens of organizations, dealing with every aspect of American life. Just small harmless drops of water seeping in. Even the American Youth Congress, a federation of the largest youth groups in the United States, was led by a Communist advocate preaching social reform.

"Although most Americans remained suspicious of Communists, some were becoming open-minded to the sugar-coated ideas. Many movie stars and celebrities were closet Communists. CPUSA was secretly working at putting people into government offices. A takeover from within. And then the CPUSA's support of Roosevelt's *New Deal* and his new social policies, bought them friendship with certain left-wing liberals in Congress. The CPUSA, discovering a door cracked open, stepped forward to ally itself with these congressional liberals in forming a new coalition. For the first time, the CPUSA, although small, became a true political force. Every small victory is still a victory nonetheless. They were gaining ground.

"By the mid-forties, the CPUSA had a hundred thousand American members, making it big enough and influential enough to merge itself with the Democratic Party. In certain key states the CPUSA was in control of the American Labor Party, the Farmer-Labor Party. They were also in control of the Washington Commonwealth Federation. The Soviet-Socialist strategy was paying off."

And there it was! Dots connecting. The mindset between industry emperors and homicidal killers was frighteningly similar, and now, along with business and homicide is the art of war. Garth realized the building of an empire, whether business or political, creates war. An advanced business strategy is a war strategy.

The captain said, "Today's average young American is a spoiled, clueless, naive, television zombie and music airhead, buying into anti-intellectual idealisms sponsored by Soviet-Socialist advocates who have seized control of television and music entertainment, creating a mighty propaganda weapon devoted to brainwashing and indoctrinating the upcoming generation. Soviet-Socialist advocates have infiltrated and seized control of many of the college campuses and classrooms, preaching a religion of "pseudo-social equality, pseudo-justice, and pseudo-liberation" which is aimed at dividing the country into fractions and undermining the government's power and ability to wage a proper fight against Soviet advancement of global conquest.

"The strategy is to seize control of our country 'peacefully' and from within. Using our Constitution and political system against us.

"The truth, Soldier, is that we're only one, maybe two, generations from becoming a socialist nation! While the United States Armed Forces are over here fighting for the freedom of Vietnam, the Soviets, our enemies, invisible to the common person's eyes, are fighting a better fight back home in our towns and cities. They are creating divisions. They have instigated a social war between whites and blacks. Between men and women. They are creating fractions and divisions in all walks of life. Ten years ago, there was no such thing as a generation gap. Now parents and children no longer respect nor trust each other. The Soviets know all too well—even better than the American people themselves—that united we stand, and divided we fall.

"The Communists are aiding and promoting violent protests and demonstrations against this war. Soldiers who do their tour, served their country heroically, are returning home to find that they are despised. They are called names and spit upon. They have been made into the enemy. And from the socialist mindset, they are the enemy.

"Those who understand the big picture, those who understand the 'real' war, understand that the United States of America is falling into jeopardy. We have become a divided nation. For the first time in our history, there is a real danger that the Soviets could actually, eventually, seize control of our great nation without military force."

The captain paused again, making eye contact. "How do you fight an invisible enemy?"

Garth's mind rushed back to the night of that horrific battle he barely survived. He remembered thinking that the enemy was both silent and invisible. More phantom than real. An apparition of sorts. Never really seen, but always present. Always watching. Haunting you. Toying with your mind with the anticipation of a sudden appearance followed by death.

The captain's next statement was firmly spoken to wrap up the history lesson: "Soviet 'water' is pouring in and the American way of life is being compromised and growing weak at an alarming rate.

"And this is where you come in!" The captain's stare intensified. "I want to take you out of this hellhole of a battle, and put you on the real front line. I'm asking you to volunteer for a special team that is so covert it doesn't exist.

"It's not because you're some great soldier that survived the 'Alamo.' It's not that I think you're some great patriot. I doubt you're much of a patriot at all.

"But it's like I said a while ago, I feel you have talents. The right kind of talents to get a special job done.

"What you are, which may be more important than being a patriot, is a capitalist. An ambitious freethinker who believes in free enterprise. A creative thinker who wants to create wealth and not share it with freeloaders and those who lack ambition enough to earn it themselves. You want your piece of the pie and to have it with cake and ice cream. And that, my friend, makes you an enemy to socialism.

"You are a man who understands poverty, but is driven and determined to rise out of it. And again, that puts you at odds with socialism.

"You're a man of conviction. A man willing to live or die for what he believes in. And that's the makings of a true patriot. Because you dream and believe in the American dream, you are a danger to the Soviet agenda.

"You're independent. Not dependent. Socialism creates dependency and poverty. That's how they maintain control. A hungry person is a submissive person. People on food stamps will eventually do as they are told whether they like it or not.

"You are a man who works better alone. You see others as getting in the way, rather than helping.

"You generally don't like people. Don't care whether they live or die. You're cynical. Suspicious. That keeps you watchful and alert. It causes you to be calculating, giving you a dangerous edge.

"You're a Darwinist. With you, killing a person is no different than killing an animal. You don't believe in an afterlife. You don't believe people have souls. No God that will someday judge you. You have no moral foundation to get in the way of a necessary dark deed. You have no moral hesitation or dilemma within yourself over it. You believe in survival of the fittest. Again, more of capitalism ideology than the socialist idea that everyone should be in the same boat with the same economic status.

"You have survivor instincts. You don't lose your head when all hell breaks loose. You've been through one of the most hellish and horrific battles a person can experience and you survived with little physical injury and no real detectable PTSD. That's amazing and says a lot. That tells me you have the mentality for the job that America needs you to do."

A spirit of patriotism was rising in Garth, not so much because he was, but because the captain's speech was inspiring, passionate, and dark. Garth asked, "And Sir, what's the job?"

"Protecting America's back door. While the U.S. Army is stationed out front of democracy warring off Soviet military aggression, the enemy, once only slipping in through open cracks, is now pouring in through the back door. The back-door aggression needs to be confronted and if possible—stopped! We need sentries to stand guard. Snipers to take out the aggressors. I'm asking you to volunteer to become an invisible dark patriot. To defend democracy's back door."

"Sounds dangerous. Sounds illegal."

"We are talking about war. Real war. Freedom at all cost. There are no rules on this level. And it's not as dangerous as the battle you were just in. Not any more dangerous than marching around in the jungle waiting to be ambushed or taken out by sniper fire from an enemy you don't see.

"You know what a 'hit' man in a war is called?" The captain didn't wait for an answer. "A sniper.

"The real war, Soldier, is the 'cold' war between the USSR and the USA. The 'cold' war is another word for covert war. The fighting that goes on behind the scenes. A war waged through espionage and covert operations. An invisible war being fought and in many cases right in front of everyone.

"I'm going to be point-blank honest with you right now. The job I'm asking you to volunteer for is that of a homeland hitman. A cold-war sniper. I want you to go back home and defend the great house of America."

The captain asked again, "How do you fight an invisible enemy? By being invisible too. You will work alone. A phantom soldier within a phantom team. A specialist by rights. There will only be me and one other person knowing who you are and what your job is. The other person will be your contact. Giving you names and information on Soviet covert soldiers to be taken out. You will be aided by the team, but you'll never know them. You will only know your contact. At times there will be an orchestration of groundwork put into place for you to be at the right place at the right time to execute a perfect extraction."

The captain looked down at Garth's forearm. On the underneath side there was a tattoo of a group of stars. "What is that tattoo?" he asked.

"It is the constellation Drago, the great celestial dragon of the sky and night."

"You'll be known as Drago. You'll serve your country covertly. You'll defend democracy as a warrior phantom. You'll never be acknowledged. You'll never earn a medal. No one will ever know of your heroism. Or the difference you made. If you are caught, you will be on your own. There will be no Calvary. This team does not exist. I don't exist. I may or may not even be a captain. I could be a colonel. I may be CIA. I might just be a figment of your imagination. You may be right now sleeping on a gurney on your way to an airport to a special place to help you with your head injury and illusions.

"If you are ever caught, arrested, the response of the government will be that you are delusional. A hero gone rogue. A man suffering from severe post-traumatic stress disorder encountered from your time in the war. Your PTSD and treatment have been well documented. Soon, the whole country is going to be reading about you in the *American Soldier* and the battle that caused your PTSD. They're going to be reading how you were in one of the most horrific battles ever, shot in the head, and the complications of such an injury.

"My advice to you, Soldier, is not to get caught. But, if you do, and you do go to prison or an asylum or whatever, you probably deserve it. Before picking you, I did my homework. I find it interesting you were in college, majoring in business. And suddenly, out of the blue, you join the army. And on the day you joined the army, a fire caused the death of two prominent people who had rejected your application into their elite fraternity. And not only rejected you, but brought great humiliation upon you, ruining your reputation.

"But, hey, that's just me thinking. Creating scenarios.

"But, if it is true, and you did kill two people, and you did join the army to get away with it, it proves to me you are the right man for the job. A man who is willing to do what it takes to get a job done.

"However, with all this having been said, let's get down to business. You are a capitalist. You were in college majoring in business. The question running circles in your head right now is, what's in it for me? What shall it profit me?

"I operate from a budget. Covert operations have expenses. You'll be one of the expenses. You will be generously paid for your 'acts of patriotism.'

"I'm going to give you a few minutes to decide. Before we leave this beach you will decide whether to join the 'team' or go back to being an ordinary soldier and complete your tour. If you decide to join the 'team,' you will be taken to a secret place in Europe for specialized training. As far as the army is concerned, you will be in a hospital for PTSD and treatment. After your training is completed, because of your injury and PTSD, you will be discharged from the 'regular' army and sent home where you will pick your civilian life back up as any normal ex-soldier would and wait until contacted."

The captain stood. "I think I'll take a stroll along the beach. It's a fine morning. It'll give you some time to think."

Garth watched the captain walk away. He really didn't have to think about it. It was a dream job. But, drag-gon it, it was more than that! It was the missing link to his ultimate business plan.

15

ONCE UPON A FOGGY NIGHT

It was scarcely four o'clock and the predicted fog was settling over the land and getting thicker by the minute. Night would come early. Homer was excited. He turned from the window, anticipating the good night ahead. His gaze unintentionally fell upon Rita.

Or did it?

He wondered.

She had a way of attracting a man's attention. She was witchy like that. On the sofa, reading a magazine, she leaned against the arm rest in a lounging position. One leg was stretched out across the rest of the seating area, the other was drawn back with the knee raised in the air and her foot flat on the sofa, exposing her entire thigh. As late as it was in the day, she hadn't bothered about dressing. She was wearing an old large flannel shirt as a house coat. Homer liked the look. With the position she was in and the place Homer was standing, he could not only see her exposed upper thigh, but even panty.

It aroused him.

She was causing him to have dirty, sinful thoughts. That was the nature of women. They beguiled men into sin while the whole time playing innocent. Homer stared, fighting temptation. In rare clarity of thought, she was his daughter. She was forbidden fruit.

But they were sinners.

Sinning was what sinners do, the voice in his head gave counsel.

Sinners were damned to hell anyway.

All Rita ever did was read magazines. She never read the Bible. She never prayed. She was a sinner through and through. He turned his lusting eyes away, but they found their way back to her again. It was her fault he was having lustful thoughts and had reached into his pants.

She was provoking him.

The beguiler.

The witch.

Well, he would fight against her witchy powers. He pulled his hand out of his pants. Getting the old family Bible that had belonged to his mom, he wiped the dust off it with his forearm. It was time for Bible teaching.

He took a seat in his chair and opened the book up to the second chapter of Genesis. He looked Rita's way with a feasting eye. "Put the magazine down, I'm gonna read some Bible to ya."

"Why?" She lowered the book, annoyed by the idea.

"Why?" he growled back. "Because we're not heathens! That's why. Decent families read the Bible. Decent parents teach their kids the laws of God!"

"I thought you didn't like God. You said God was mean and vengeful-like."

"Are you being sassy with me?"

"No, Pa."

"You have an option. You can sit there and listen as I read the Good Book to ya, or you can take a beating for your sinful ways."

"What sinful ways, Pa?"

Always playing innocent. Ignoring her question and not being in the mood to beat her, Homer began to read the verses he had underlined in the past: "And the Lord God took the man, and put him into the Garden of Eden to dress it and to keep it. And the Lord God commanded the man saying, Of every tree of the garden thou mayest freely eat: But of the tree of the knowledge of good and evil, thou shalt not eat of it: For in the day that thou eatest thereof thou shalt surely die.

"And the serpent said unto the woman, Ye shall not surely die. For God doth know that in the day ye eat thereof, then your eyes shall be opened, and ye shall be as gods, knowing good and evil.

"And when the woman saw that the tree was good for food, and that it was pleasant to the eyes, and a tree to be desired to make one wise, she took of the fruit thereof, and did eat, and gave also unto her husband with her: and he did eat."

Homer closed the book. "You see that?" He pointed a preacher's finger at her. "Woman is the original sinner. Eve was friendly with the devil. Man talks to God, but woman talks to the devil. Not only talks to the devil, but listens to him. Eve disobeyed the law of God and became a sinner. And then she beguiled Adam with her witchy charms into sin also."

Leaning forward, his stare traveled from her thigh to her panties. His lust was her fault. She was causing him to sin. "Man was the innocent victim." He stood up. "You hear what I'm telling you!"

"Yes, Pa."

"Good."

He marched over and put the Bible back in its spot. The shelf it was kept on was dusty. The shelves above and below it were clean of dust. Rita never dusted the Bible or the shelf it sat on. It was deliberate disrespect. More evidence she had witch's blood in her. More evidence she was hell-bound. He glanced her way. She was staring at him. Still in a lounging position, she was still invoking desire and challenging him to sin with her. "I'm afraid, girl, you're destined for hell. There's no hope for you." He turned back to the shelf and blew in hopes of blowing some of the dust off.

He looked her way again. She was still staring. Still inviting him to sin. *Witches are supposed to be burned*, the voice within encouraged. A smile crossed his lips at the humor of burning her alive. She answered with a smirk.

As eager as Pa was about going out for the night, Rita was more eager. She couldn't wait. She acted as if she had nothing better to do than to read magazines. However, she had plans of her own. Glenn and Paul were camping tonight. She had seen the signal. Since they couldn't come to her house to see or talk to her, they had devised a system to communicate with her. There was a certain fence post in the Yorks' field she could see from her house. Different-colored ribbons tied to the post meant different things. She checked the post for messages daily. A pink one meant Glenn was thinking of her. She liked Glenn. Although Glenn tried not to show it, she knew he was jealous of her and Paul's relationship. She often saw the jealousy in his eyes.

Rita liked Paul too. Paul was daring. A sinner. He seemed to enjoy her sinfulness as well. Rita reckoned she and Paul would make for good sinners together.

Glenn didn't have the sinful nature Paul did. He went to church and was proper and more apt to do the right thing rather than the sinful thing. Rita had fun pushing Glenn to do sinful things.

Earlier, before the fog moved in, she noticed a yellow ribbon dancing in the wind. A yellow ribbon meant campout. She answered by sticking a shovel in the ground at a particular place in her yard, which meant she got the message and would come if she could.

Another torturous hour passed before Pa headed out the back door. *Finally!* Rita, tossing the magazine aside, went and peeked out the back-door window. The fog was thick. Visibility was short: Pa quickly faded in the watery mist. She looked in all directions, seeing only the gray blanket of cloud. Tonight's fog would hide the sins of a sinner.

She would be a sinner tonight.

Pa had inspired her with his Bible lesson. She went to Pa's pile of porn magazines, looking for the one featuring a layout entitled "Adam and Eve." If there was no hope for her, if she was destined for hell, she wasn't going to go to hell alone. She would have her lovers with her. Tonight, she would step up the game with Glenn and Paul. Like Eve, she would beguile her lovers. Cast upon them a spell of lust and sin. Tonight, she would offer them the apple.

If someone were standing in the road looking toward the house, all they would see was the faint glow of the porch light. They would have to venture closer before the scarecrow and Veggie would materialize. Homer, sitting in the porch rocker, was wearing a homemade scarecrow costume made from the old scarecrow that once stood guard over their garden back in Kansas. Rita insisted on bringing Mr. Scarecrow to Missouri. Mr. Scarecrow was her friend, she argued, and they would need him to protect the new garden. They never got around to doing a garden, and Mr. Scarecrow had spent its time in

Missouri in the outhouse shed. But, Mr. Scarecrow wasn't in the shed no more. Homer had freed him. Homer had become him. Or had Mr. Scarecrow become Homer? Homer didn't really know, but they were blended.

Homer sighed. "Ain't it a wonderful night, Veg? Just about right." Homer sipped the whiskey, gazing at the damp swirling cloud engulfing them.

There was a grunt from Veggie, who was slumped toward one side in his wheelchair.

"I agree. I too love the fog. You know, I think it might just be my favorite weather." Homer stared forward in contemplation. He broke the silence a moment later, adding, "I bet we could get away with walking the streets of town tonight."

Homer turned his scarred scarecrow head toward Veggie. "Whatcha think?"

There was twitching with some of the muscles on Veggie's face.

"Sounds exciting, don't it?" Homer chuckled, staring into Veggie's zombie eyes. He added, "Imagine us proudly walking down a foggy street and someone from the opposite direction passes us. Why, I bet they'd piss their pants at the sight of us!" Homer chuckled again. "Might even faint!" Homer scooted to the edge of his chair. "I'm telling ya, buddy, it's hilarious to see a face freeze in terror, eyes about to pop out of their face and all. And then *BAM!* They just drop to the ground as if they were dead!

"You've heard of people being frightened to death, ain'tcha?" Homer laughed. "If looks could kill," Homer said as an afterthought, staring forward into the cloud. "Why, I betcha they could." Mr. Scarecrow Homer turned his gaze to Veggie. Homer's old, half-rotten straw hat had straw poking out from underneath it. There was straw poking out of its top and other holes as well. On the scarred side of his face, he had drawn what was to look like stitches or where sewing had taken place.

"Here. Have another good swallow." Homer stood and tilted Veggie's head back. Homer was wearing an old, raggedy plaid shirt with straw poking out at the wrists and other places. He poured whiskey into Veggie's mouth. As usual, there was a bit of coughing and choking that took place, especially with such a large amount, but Homer had learned how to pour whiskey down his friend's throat without wasting much.

Hearing it before seeing it, a vehicle was approaching. "Hear that, buddy? Someone's coming down the road." Homer listened. The vehicle drew closer.

The glow of headlights materialized in the fog. Homer stepped off the porch into the yard. The vehicle drove forward and pulled into the driveway. Homer stepped deeper into the fog.

Homer couldn't really see what was going on. The vehicle sounded like a truck. The engine was turned off and two doors opened. By the giggling, laughter, and comments of making it home safely, it was the voices of a woman and man. Homer discerned they were a bit drunk. The woman was Veggie's wife.

Hiding in the fog, Homer listened as June stepped up on the front porch and stopped. "Why? How'd you get out here?" she spoke to her husband.

"What did you do, June? Push him out here before you left today and forgot about him?"

"Of course not."

"Really?"

"I wouldn't have done such a thing. Here, help me get him back inside. He'll catch his death out here."

"Probably already has. If you're lucky."

"You shouldn't say such a thing."

"We both know it's true."

Homer listened as they wheeled his friend back into the house. Homer walked away disappointed and angry. *There is no sin in killing a sinner*, Mr. Scarecrow said to Homer.

The campfire crackled and popped, flickered and danced, in combat against the watery vapor trying to smother it. Seated on a couple of bales of hay pushed together, Paul and Glenn poked and played in the fire, relishing their accomplishment of getting the fire going.

The air was wet and chilly. The fog engulfing them was getting thicker all the time. Visibility was low. The smell of damp earth was strong.

"Man, can you believe this fog?" Paul looked about to see what was no longer visible. "If it gets any foggier, we won't even be able to see the tent."

"I bet visibility is less than twenty or thirty feet," Glenn reckoned.

"You don't think Rita could get lost, do you?" The thought occurring to Paul.

"From her house to here? Hardly."

"The fog's thick, man. And it's dark on top of that. No landmarks for guidance."

"There's the glow of the fire," Glenn argued.

"Maybe. Maybe not."

Off in the distance, Glenn could hear the Brandts' dog whining. "If she called out, we'd hear her. The fog doesn't stop sound."

"I suppose," Paul agreed. He looked in the direction of her house. Not being able to see it meant not knowing what was going on. He didn't know if she was on her way or still at home. He didn't know if she was still even coming. Unknowns were a nagging pest.

Rita had changed the game. She had become the party. Before Rita, Paul and Glenn could have a campout and have the time of their lives. Just the two of them. Now it was different. Now all they were doing was sitting and trying patiently to wait for Rita to show up so the fun could begin.

Rita was a contradiction. She was clueless about so many things. Sometimes totally lost. Other times, she was smart and wise beyond her age. She presented herself as both a girl and a woman. She was shy, backwards, and lacked self-confidence, while at the same time she could be flaunting, aggressive, and intimidating. She could be controlled and controlling at the same time. With Rita, it was sometimes hard to know who was actually in charge. You always seemed to do what she wanted, but it was always your idea. Paul was baffled by her. And obsessed. She was a riddle he couldn't figure out. When she was around, good common sense was lost in a fog of siren spell.

"Do you think she's still coming?" Paul voiced concern.

"I hope so. It'd be a drag if she didn't."

"I hear that."

The boys, given to lustful thoughts, poked at the fire in silence. Breaking the silence, Paul asked, "You gonna try making out with her tonight?"

"Are you?"

Paul shrugged as if it was no big deal. The truth was, it was all he could think about. Rita knew about making out. She was the queen. Advanced in the subject. She had taught them things. She had let them see and touch things. "What ya think she'll be wearing?"

"Something short, sexy, and see-through, I hope," Glenn answered.

"If I could choose, it'd be nothing."

"With Rita, it's possible."

The more Homer thought about it, the more he relished the idea of walking the streets of NuSprings. Materializing in front of someone. Watching them freeze in bug-eyed horror and dropping to the ground as if dead. It would almost make his damaged, monster-scarred scarecrow face worth it. At last it would be useful for something.

Homer found himself heading through the woods in the direction of town. It would be a long walk. Too long really, but Mr. Scarecrow had committed Homer. He had already covered too much distance to go back and use the pickup.

Dave Sumner was driving while Valerie Brooks, seated next to him, had her left arm entangled around his right. The car's bench seat allowed for her to be scooted against his as was the custom for young lovers on a date.

The fog made driving adventurous. There was splendor and mystery in the swirling fog spotlighted by the car's headlights. The fog isolated structures like a gallery, creating a sequence of individual sights and scenes to be viewed one by one without the distraction of nearby places and upcoming sights.

Dave found the Wigwam and pulled into the parking lot. Inside, Quillpen Jack and his girlfriend Tianna RedBird were sitting in a booth. An order of fries, fish nuggets, two warm delicious-smelling apple turnovers, and two drinks sat on the table in front of them. Dave guided Valerie to their table. "Hey, what's up?" Dave greeted.

"You know, filling the basic needs of a man. Food for the belly. Woman for the heart," Quillpen answered.

Dave motioned Valerie to sit and scooted in after her.

"Please, join us," Quillpen offered after the fact.

"You're so kind," Dave countered, reaching out and helping himself to one of the apple-pie turnovers, popping it into his mouth.

"Help yourself to some pie," Quillpen offered—again, after the fact.

"Most generous of you."

"So what are you two up to?" Tianna addressed Valerie with an inviting smile.

"Enjoying the weather. I guess." Valerie's eyes and expression spoke of uncertainty.

"I know, crazy, right?"

Valerie agreed. "I can't remember the last time the fog was this thick. If ever."

"Spooookyyy," Dave dramatized.

"The fog scares ya, does it?" Quillpen jested.

"Hey, all I'm saying is, it's an Alfred Hitchcock kind of night."

Quillpen was leaning back in a relaxed position with one arm around Tianna. "I was thinking more like *The Twilight Zone*." He began to vocalize *The Twilight Zone*'s theme song. He sat up straight and leaned forward. "Here we are: two couples in a diner. Isolated amidst a thick cloud of fog." His stare traveled from eye to eye. "Look out the windows. Do you see any other places? Are you even sure they still exist? We've just entered the Twilight Zone!

"Our known reality of our town outside has disappeared. Go ahead. Walk out that door. See if you can find another building. It won't be there. Your search will take you further away from the only place you know exists. Deeper into thicker fog you'll go. You'll find yourself roaming. Soon you'll discover yourself lost. You'll turn back for the diner and friends you recently left. But you can't find it. You see only fog. You wander in a state of confusion. You become anxious.

"You hear something.

"Something animal.

"Something"—Quillpen pauses, his gaze jumps from eye to eye—"something monster.

"It knows you exist. You become aware that it's hunting you. You're frightened. Your heart pounds in your chest.

"You run.

"It chases!

"You trip and fall and break a bone. You cry from the pain. You hear the monster closing in. You get back on your feet, dragging your wounded leg, trying to ignore the pain.

"You hurry along. There's no place to hide. Only obstacles to crash into. Obstacles to trip over. It goes on and on. Bruise after bruise. Cut after cut. Broken bone after broken bone. It never ends. You need rest. But, you can never rest. Rest brings the monster closer.

"You're out of breath. But you have to keep going. "You're plagued with intense fear. You're in great pain. Bleeding in numerous places. It's your worst nightmare. You're forever alone. Forever isolated. Forever lost. Forever hunted. Forever tired. It becomes your eternal hell. There's no rescue. There's no repentance. There's no time. And why?"

Quillpen turned his gaze to Dave. "Why you? Perhaps, it was the sweet slice of apple pie you just had to have. Forbidden fruit that wasn't yours, but you just had to taste. That superb, delicious-looking, wonderful-smelling, appetizing, satisfaction-guaranteed piece of apple pie."

Quillpen ended his dialogue with a moment of silence. Dave responded, "I was just thinking it might be a scarecrow kind of night. A night in which scarecrows would be on the prowl. Wow." Dave looked at the girls. "Guess I shouldn't have ate the apple."

"Sin, brother, it always costs you in the long run," Quillpen chided.

Valerie added, "My grandfather says, 'Sin, in the end will do you in.'"

Hearing before seeing her, Rita materialized out of the fog carrying a sack in her arms. "I made it," her voice rang with a sigh of relief.

Paul and Glenn stared. Rita was more naked

than not. Her costume was like a bathing suit. From a bedsheet with a broad-leaf tropical plant print, she had cut out the leaves and fastened them together with safety pins. One set of leaves wrapped around her waist. The other set was pulled snug around her chest to cover her breasts. Having become damp from the fog, the leaves were clinging to her breasts.

Rita stopped between them and the fire. Spellbound by the provocative and scandalous outfit, Paul and Glenn were focused on the woman more than the person. The light of the fire behind her made her costume even more scandalous.

"It is okay for me to be here, isn't it?" Rita asked, suddenly paranoid from the staring and the lack of a greeting. Perhaps she wasn't welcome. Perhaps she should have dressed differently.

"Certainly!" Glenn forcing eye contact. "We've been waiting on you."

"Wow! Love the outfit," Paul complimented.

Paul's exuberance chased away Rita's paranoia. She said, "Thanks. Sinful, isn't it?"

"Delightfully."

Rita smiled. She could count on Paul to love her sinful ways. "I was hoping you'd like it. It was a last-minute creation. I thought it'd be fun. I want to be your Eve tonight." Although she was standing close to the fire for warmth, she shivered. "It's much colder than I thought. It didn't seem this chilly when I first stepped out of the house."

"It's the fog. It cools a person off," Glenn informed.

"Yeah, the water in the air pulls the heat from your body."

"Oh. I didn't know that." Rita's face spoke of her ignorance of such matters.

"No fear, our lovely Eve, your Adams are here to keep ya warm and cozy," Adam Paul offered.

"Yeah. Our pleasure," Adam Glenn agreed. "Come. Have a seat. Squeeze yourself between us. Let our bodies warm you."

Eve obeyed. Stepping forward, handing her sack of goodies to Glenn, she seated herself between the two boys as they scooted themselves against her.

"What do we have here?" Glenn peeked into the bag.

"My contribution. Beer and a magazine." Rita leaned toward Glenn with a kiss on the cheek. "Thanks for inviting me." She did the same to Paul.

"The pleasure is ours, I assure you," Glenn answered, pulling a beer out of the bag.

Scarecrow talk brought Dave, Quillpen, Valerie, and Tianna to talk about the two young boys camping out in the woods behind their house. The boys reported scarecrows floating through the air to attack them. The story made the news and called for a more serious investigation. The traumatized boys were now in therapy.

Whether true or false, rumors of sightings and

encounters with scarecrows were being reported. Scarecrow hunting was now a thing with the city's young adults. Taking the Dragon Slayer, the two couples decided to scarecrow hunt. Quillpen gave Dave the keys. Dave drove along city blocks lit by streetlights, parking-lot lights, and the accent lighting of businesses and homes. They saw no scarecrows.

Dave turned onto the heavy forested route with hills and curves, taking them along the back side of the city's lake and park. In such foggy conditions, the route would spark an adrenaline rush and a heightened sense of adventure and awareness.

Rita, tightly sandwiched between her Adams, held the porn magazine for the boys to look at, leaving their hands free for drinking and touching. Rita, turning the pages, controlled the conversation. She commented on the images displayed, the bodies of the nude women and their sexual positions. She asked her Adams questions about their likes and dislikes. She was amused by their bashful and often hesitant answers. They sipped beer in reaction to their nervousness and their revealed lack of knowledge and understanding. She comforted them with her charm. She made them feel manly in spite of their timid boyish ways. She challenged their imaginations. Guided their thoughts. She tutored them. Stealing their innocence was fun and intoxicating.

Dave, barely able to see the road well enough to stay on it, drove slowly. Dipping down into a valley, the density of the fog brought visibility to nearly zero. There were no streetlights, only the headlights of the car which didn't help much. The thick fog was more challenging than Dave had imagined. It was dangerous. He fought to keep his cool and maintained a confident front.

Mr. Scarecrow Homer, making his way through a part of the forest he had never been, drew closer to town. The fog was thick and moving in the right direction was difficult. He stopped and looked about. He was surrounded by trunks of the trees. He could just be going in circles and not know it. He didn't think so. He had an instinct about these things. He continued.

Making his way up a hill, he topped it and found asphalt. It had to be Highway 5. The city lake and park wouldn't be far.

The route along the south side of the city and lake normally didn't take long. Tonight, driving between ten and twenty miles an hour, it seemed to be taking forever.

Driving, Dave caught a glimpse of a person appearing suddenly out of the fog on their right. He lifted his foot off the accelerator.

Valerie yelled, "Scarecrow!"

Dave hit the brakes. The abrupt stop threw its

passengers forward. On recovery, everyone swung their heads. The scarecrow was still there.

"Back up," Quillpen said.

Dave eased backwards until the Dragon Slayer was beside the figure with a potato sack head, button eyes, and a painted-on mouth. The scarecrow, mounted on a cross, had on a brightly colored plaid shirt and pants stuffed with hay.

Quillpen, opening his door, said to Dave, "Let's check it out."

The guys got out and cautiously approached the scarecrow. It appeared to be your normal inanimate homemade garden-variety type. Quillpen reached out and touched it. There was no reaction from the scarecrow.

"Really?" Dave questioned.

Quillpen shrugged. "Never know."

Realizing how silly they were being, how much they had gotten caught up in the urban legend of monster scarecrows, Dave and Quillpen looked at each other.

"What are we doing?" Dave laughed.

"Like you said, it's scarecrow kind of night." Quillpen laughed with him.

"We done a good job of scaring ourselves, I'd say."

"We have to take it. After all, we are hunting scarecrows, are we not?" Quillpen suggested.

Dave and Quillpen stuffed the scarecrow into the trunk of the car.

"Adam and Eve" was the featured layout of the issue. It was where Rita wanted to go. Where she wanted to camp out. Where she got even more personal and provocative, somehow managing to invoke the idea that the Eve featured in the pictures was her. Although Paul and Glenn clearly understood the model in the magazine was not Rita, somehow she charmed them with the idea, making it easy to imagine, especially in their inebriated state. When they looked at the Eve in the pictures, they were seeing Rita. "Could you see me in that position?" asked Eve Rita, directing her question to Adam Glenn, making eye contact. "What would you do to me if I were?"

That called for Glenn to take another sip of beer.

Turning her gaze to Adam Paul, "Tell me," she softly and sweetly spoke, "would it excite you?" Paul answered with a sip.

Dave, Valerie, Quillpen, and Tianna finally reached the back entrance to the city's park. Quillpen announced, for pretense, "I think a time of parking is in order. It is customary for warriors, after a hunt, to be rewarded with the love of a woman."

"Customs are customs." Dave turned into the park and slowly made his way to his favorite make-out spot.

Once parked, Dave suggested, "Hey, we should get the scarecrow out and have him stand guard."

"Good idea," Quillpen agreed.

The girls watched as Dave and Quillpen got the

scarecrow out of the trunk and erected it at the back of the car to stand guard.

Getting back into the car, Dave moving toward Valerie, "Now that we're safe and secure, how about a kiss for your brave warrior?"

"Warrior's don't ask, they take," Quillpen declared, taking hold of his date.

Closing the magazine, Rita let it drop to the ground. With exciting, challenging eyes, she looked at Glenn. "Now, my Adams, which of you"—her head and gaze turned from Glenn to Paul—"is gonna be the first to bite the apple?"

Paul's eyes declared his uncertainty of her meaning. "What apple?"

Rita pushed up her leaf top to expose a breast. She had drawn an apple around her nipple. "This apple." She stared into his eyes. "One for you"—she turned to Glenn and exposing the other breast—"and one for you."

Glenn stared in disbelief, raising the empty bottle to his lips. The drink didn't hide the look of uncertainty crossing his face as his stare went from her apple drawing to her eyes. "Well?" she asked, her gaze leaving Glenn's and swinging back to Paul.

Paul, staring at her breast, looked interested but insecure. He needed coaching. "You, then." Rising to her feet. Taking hold of his hand, "Come, my Adam. I've got something to show you." She pulled Paul to his feet. "Something for you to taste."

Rita pulled Paul to the tent. She crawled inside first and flopped down on her back as Paul crawled in behind her. Pulling him down on top of her, she said, "Come, my love, taste the apple. Sin with me."

Mr. Scarecrow Homer finally made it to the south side of the park.

Soft romantic music filled the car. The music was low enough to encourage intimacy, but up enough to drown out whispers and other private sounds. From the Jackson 5 to Sugarloaf, the radio played a series of love songs. "Love Grows (Where My Rosemary Goes)" had just finished and now "Close to You" by the Carpenters was playing.

Tianna RedBird, on her back in the back seat, had her eyes closed, relishing the music and the intimacy and feelings stirred by wandering hands and having her neck kissed and sucked on. Quillpen would leave his mark on her neck as a testament of their time together. It was customary. The proof of conquest. A form of boasting. After he was finished with his mark, she would make hers on his neck.

Dave and Valerie were doing the same in the front seat.

Tianna heard the whispering voice of Quillpen in her ear. Engrossed in music and imagination, she didn't hear what he said. Opening her eyes, there was movement beyond Quillpen's head. Focusing her eyes on the movement beyond the window outside of the car, she saw a hideous monster face staring down into the car. The monster opened his mouth and growled.

Tianna let out a bloodcurdling scream!

Suddenly there was pounding on the car's roof, followed by violent shaking of the car. Pandemonium filled the car as Tianna and Valerie went to screaming. Quillpen and Dave, trying to understand what was taking place, scrambled to sit up and look out the windows.

As quickly as it began, it was over. Staring out the windows, Dave and Quillpen saw nothing.

Locking the doors, the girls, still in a panic, were calmed down by the guys, who tried to comfort them and figure out what was happening. Getting Valerie and Tianna calmed down, Quillpen looking at Tianna, who was still crying but trying to be quiet, "What happened? What did you see?"

Sobbing, she answered, "I saw a monster looking in the car watching us."

"Whatcha mean, 'monster'?" Quillpen asked. Outside the car was silence and fog.

"A scarecrow monster!"

Quillpen's eyes looked to where they had erected the scarecrow to stand guard. "It's gone!"

"What's gone?" Dave turning his gaze in the direction of Quillpen's stare.

"The scarecrow."

They all looked out the back window. The scarecrow wasn't there.

They searched the fog and listened.

They heard nothing. Saw nothing.

"I want to get out of here!" Tianna tearfully begged, on the verge of a panic attack.

Valerie, with her own fear expressed in her eyes and tears still sliding down her face, held Tianna's hand while searching for movement in the fog.

"See, I told you! Please, Dave, let's get out of here!" begged Tianna.

After staring about and searching, "C'mon," Quillpen suggested to Dave, unlocking his car door and opening it.

"No!" protested Tianna, pulling back on Quillpen's shirt.

"We got to," he justified.

"Please," Tianna sobbed.

"Let's just go," Valerie told Dave.

"It's okay. Whatever it was is gone now," Dave said.

Valerie, still in the front seat, held Tianna in the back seat in a hug. The girls watched the guys slowly and reluctantly get out of the car. At first they only stood beside the car with open doors for a quick retreat.

They searched the thick fog. There was nothing outside the ordinary. Cautiously, they went to the back of the car, expecting the scarecrow to be lying on the ground. The scarecrow was gone.

Talking, Tianna suggested to Valerie the scarecrow had come to life and attacked them. It seemed the likely explanation. She began to sell the idea to Valerie.

"Let's go!" Tianna called out to the guys.

"We're trying to figure out what's going on," Quillpen answered back.

"I know what happened," Tianna said.

"What?"

"The scarecrow came alive and attacked us." The possibility of it suddenly appearing out of the fog with another attack was frightening. "Please, Quillpen, let's get out of here before it attacks again."

"Dave," Valerie called out. "She's right. Let's just go."

The girls, becoming more convinced, became panicky. To appease the girls, Dave and Quillpen got back into the car. Dave said, starting the car, "Let's get the girls home and come back with a search party."

"Sounds like a plan," Quillpen agreed.

Homer, carrying the scarecrow in his arms, reveled in delight as he scurried from the park, dodging trees.

Once he decided he was safe, he paused to catch his breath. He leaned the scarecrow up against a tree and bent forward to breathe better, taking in deep breaths. He played back in his mind the terrified look in the girl's eyes as she looked up at him. He snickered and wondered if she'd pissed herself. If he had scared the piss out of her. Out of them all.

He hoped he did.

He looked around. He wasn't sure where he was. In the excitement he had lost his bearings. The fog was thick. He was still in woods. He had to be on an east or southeast travel which was going away from the park and town.

He looked at the scarecrow leaning against the tree. "Ain't we got fun." He snickered.

After a rest, Homer tossed the scarecrow upon his shoulder and began walking, hoping for another opportunity to frighten the piss out of someone.

Paul Sumner returned to consciousness after momentarily passing out from the euphoric explosion of release. He lay atop Rita, who was still working her hips in response to her own building climax.

He imagined sex to be great, but never imagined it to be so intensely joyous. Truly there was no greater single act of pleasure than this. This was the stuff of addiction.

Rita, moaning in climax, drew his attention to the blissful expression on her face. Pleasuring her brought him a deep sense of fulfillment and accomplishment. Still joined together, he relished the experience. With closed eyes, Rita pulsated in her own current of bliss. She was exquisite. Women were exquisite.

Mr. Scarecrow Homer wandered upon a house. Nothing new. Nothing fancy. Still carrying the scarecrow on his shoulder, he walked around the house. The house and yard were manicured and kept up. There was a car in the carport.

Homer did his best to peek in the windows, but could see nothing. All was dark and quiet. Whoever lived there was in bed and asleep.

At the back of the house, he discovered a patio with furniture. He decided to rest his weary old bones. He stood his scarecrow friend up against a pole at the edge of the patio facing the sliding glass patio doors. Homer then took a seat in a patio chair next to a patio table. Homer was disappointed not having come across another situation to scare the piss out of someone. "You just can't count on people for nothing," Homer complained.

In a one-way conversation, Homer said to the scarecrow, "All in all, you're not much different than ole Veggy. You're a lot easier to carry around. Veggy's dead weight." Homer stared at the scarecrow and added, "I think I'll call you, 'Mr. Straw Head.'"

Suddenly a patio light came on. Caught off guard, Homer jerked his head around toward the door. A woman's scream filled the air from behind the glass door. Homer, jumping to his feet, saw the curtain falling back into place as the screaming woman ran from it.

Homer grabbed Mr. Straw Head and disappeared into the fog and woods.

Homer wasn't sure how long he had been running, but tired and out of breath, he stopped. His heart, beating hard, was pumping adrenaline. He felt alive. And beastly! He looked toward the sky and roared from the excitement. Breathing heavily and trying to catch his breath, he looked about. Fog and trees. He had no idea where he was.

He guzzled some whiskey. He looked at Mr. Straw Head leaning against a tree. Homer laughed and said, "That woman nearly scared the piss out of me!"

He chuckled from the humor of it. "I hope she pissed herself in return."

Rita woke up after temporarily dozing off. She was lying between her Adams. Their breathing and mild snoring were evidence of deep satisfactory sleep. Her work here was done. Her Adams were true sinners now. They partook of the fruit. They had sinned with her. They would be in hell with her.

She rose to a sitting position. With a flashlight, she checked Glenn's wrist for the time. It was after two. She needed to get home before her pa came dragging in from his night out.

With the flashlight, she found her costume. It would have to be fixed again before she could wear it. She cussed. She didn't have the time and was tired. She threw her Eve costume to the side, deciding to return home naked.

Looking out the tent door, the dense fog still blanketed the land. Rusty was sitting nearby. He hadn't been around earlier. Rusty got up as she crawled out of the tent. She patted Rusty on the head as he greeted her with sniffs and licks. Slipping on her shoes, she headed home with Rusty following.

Making it home, Rita went around to the back. Treading quietly, she stepped onto the porch and put an ear against the door. Hearing nothing, she quietly opened the door and cautiously entered the house. Her heart pounded with the fear of her pa being home. The deadly beating she would surely receive. There would be no way of explaining being out so late. No way of explaining being naked.

Hardly making a sound, she tiptoed through the house. Pa hadn't made it home yet. She relaxed with a great sigh of relief.

After a quick bath, she took her tired soul to bed. Waiting for sleep, she thought about her Adams. Paul would make a good husband. Glenn would make a good father. Her daughter would need a good father and that was the most important thing. But she wanted a good husband. A man who would sin with her.

Considering the dilemma, wasn't she a Mormon? Her pa had said so. She didn't know much about being a Mormon, but in the Mormon society, a man could have multiple wives. So why couldn't a woman have multiple husbands? It was only fair.

Days later, during a gathering at the Wigwam, RiverDawg listened to stories of the scarecrow invasion of NuSprings. Old stories were retold and embellished. There had been numerous sightings. He listened to Tianna RedBird tell her story of the foggy night. She told of the scarecrow they had found and how it had come alive and attacked them. She spoke of its hideous face. The beating and shaking of the car while trying to get at them. She spoke of having nightmares and asked RiverDawg if he could stop the nightmares.

He felt certain he could. He had charms for such things.

RiverDawg listened to the story of that same night of a woman awakened from sleep by talking. Investigating, she discovered scarecrows on her back patio. She called the police, but the police found nothing. The encounter made the local news.

Tianna agreed that the scarecrow monsters were able to float through the air.

RiverDawg contemplated all that was being told. It was both amusing and disturbing. He had started it. But somehow, it had taken on a life of its own and was getting out of hand. He needed to put a stop to it.

But how?

How does one stop a conjurer gone rogue?

16

BLOOD TEST

Passing the Pierce house, the school bus stopped in front of the Brandt house. Stepping off the bus behind his sister, Johnny, instead of following his sister, stood at the edge of the road as the bus moved on. Staring toward Rita's house, he wondered why she hadn't gone to school. It wasn't like her to miss. It called for an investigation.

He raced through his chores so he could make a quick trip to Rita's house before his dad came home. Staying out of sight, he made his way to the edge of Rita's yard. He focused his hearing, listening hard for anything coming from the house. He heard nothing and couldn't detect whether Rita's monster-pa was home or not. Studying the house and surroundings, he decided to take the risk and darted across the yard to the side of the house.

Standing next to the house, listening hard, Johnny still didn't hear anything. He moved down to the only window on that side. Listening, he heard nothing. Slowly and cautiously, he peeked through the window into the bedroom. His face pushing against the screen, he searched the room. Things weren't clear because of the screen and the darkness of the room. Someone was in bed. It was Rita. She wasn't covered. She looked naked. With greater focus, stretching his vision if that were possible, trying to will sight beyond its ability, he studied the situation. She looked tied down with each wrist and ankle pulled and tied to the nearest corresponding bedpost. Satisfied the monster wasn't there, Johnny lightly tapped on the windowpane with a finger.

Rita turned her head. She stared a moment and then shook her head to say no. Johnny understood. The monster was somewhere around. He nodded in understanding.

He needed to find the monster. He went down the side of the house to the front. Peeking around the corner, he saw no one.

The only window in front of the house was on the opposite end from where he was. Feeling it was too risky to cross in front of the house, he decided to go back around the entire house to get to the other side.

The only window on the back side of the house was the bathroom window. In passing, he heard talking. He dropped and sat frozen. Ready to flee if need be.

Hearing nothing indicating he had been seen, he

slowly stood. From the other side came mumblings and sounds of someone taking a bath. The monster was taking a bath and talking to himself.

Knowing the monster was awake and alert, it was too risky to try anything. He would return home and come back later.

When bedtime came, Johnny willingly went to bed. The house was a two-bedroom house. Johnny and his two siblings shared a room with two beds. Betty and Jimmy slept in the twin bed and he slept in the single.

Pretending sleep, waiting for his sister and brother to fall into a sound sleep, he ran schemes and scenarios through his mind. Once everyone was asleep, he would sneak out in hopes to help Rita.

Waking up from having fallen asleep, Johnny sat up. He wasn't sure of the time. There was no clock in the room. He looked toward the other bed. The deep breathing of his sister and brother told him it was safe to get up. He quietly slipped out of bed and peeked out the door. The TV was on but down low, which meant his mom was probably napping in her chair. She often took a nap before going to bed. Such a weird thing, Johnny always thought. It also meant his dad was still gone. His dad had left after supper to drink beer and play cards.

Johnny picked his pants and shirt up off the floor, leaving the bedroom quietly. Cautiously, he tiptoed to the back door, making sure he didn't step on weak spots in the floor. Years of sneaking about had revealed the soft spots in the floor that would alert his parents.

The night was chilly, clear, and full of stars. Johnny slipped into his pants and threw on his shirt. He had forgotten his shoes. It didn't matter—his feet were tough and he could move about quieter barefooted.

He traveled the road for only a short distance before entering into the field adjacent to Rita's house. The field offered covering.

The monster was unpredictable. Although there were patterns to his behavior, there was no true rhyme or reason of daily activities. There was no schedule he followed. He didn't do certain things on certain days at certain times.

According to Rita, her pa acted on random thoughts given to the voice in his head. His pattern of behavior was drinking, meditating, and philosophizing. Some days he went fishing. Some nights he went hunting. The specific hour and time of a day was irrelevant to him. It was either day or night.

Hiding at the edge of Rita's yard, Johnny searched for the monster. Monsters were trickier at night than in the day. They could hide in the shadows. Squinting his eyes, straining to see, he attempted to conjure super night vision like a superhero in a comic book.

Not seeing anything, he sprinted across Rita's yard to the side of the house like he had done earlier. He listened, but only heard a symphony of night bugs and tree frogs. He snuck down to the window of Rita's bedroom. Peeking in, the room was dark. Maybe Rita was in bed, maybe not.

With his back against the west side of the house, he looked back toward his own house. Off in the distance he heard the hooting of an owl.

Johnny stopped at the bathroom window. All was dark and quiet. On the east side, the kitchen window was too high for Johnny to look into, but there was no light on. No sounds either. He continued.

Peeking around the corner at the front porch, Johnny saw the monster. He jerked back. Hearing only snoring, he carefully looked around the corner. The monster was seated in an old chair, and by the rhythm of his breathing and snoring, the monster seemed sound asleep. Johnny picked a pebble off the ground and tossed it upon the porch. There was no reaction from the monster. Johnny found a larger one and tossed it upon the porch. The monster didn't respond. Feeling confident, Johnny ran back around to the back door and entered the house.

Leaving the door open for a quick getaway, he tiptoed to the bedroom. The room was dark and he couldn't tell if Rita was in bed or not. Stepping closer to the bed, his heart pounding, he pulled a lighter out of his pocket and flicked it on.

Rita was in bed and tied down. She had no cover and was wearing only panties. Johnny's eyes feasted upon her. He wanted to touch her breasts, but this wasn't the time. He feared the monster.

There was something on her shoulder near her neck. He moved closer with the lighter. A big black slimy leech came into view. He shuddered. It was freaky.

Rita's eyes popped open with a jerk and a gasp escaping her mouth. She instinctively tried raising her arms, but they were tied down.

"Shhhh," Johnny whispered, "it's me, Johnny."

A confused Rita took a moment to figure out what was going on.

"What's going on? Are you alright?" Johnny asked her.

Rita tried looking about. "Where's Pa?"

"Asleep on the front porch."

"Asleep or passed out?"

"Don't know. Rita, you got a big leech on your neck!"

"Get it off!" Rita commanded in a loud frantic whisper.

Johnny took ahold of the nasty thing. It was well attached to Rita's neck and took a bit of effort to pull it free. Blood trickled down her neck. Looking around for a place to put it, he dropped it into a cheap metal ashtray on the nightstand.

Rita cried, "Get the others off!"

"Others?"

"There's two others!"

Johnny began searching. "Where?"

"I feel one on my left thigh."

Johnny moved the light to her thighs. On the

inside of her thigh near her panties was another one. Johnny worked it free and dropped it in the ashtray.

"Where's the other one?" Johnny whispered, moving the light back and forth lighting different areas of her body.

"Not sure. Can't feel it. But, my pa dropped three on me!"

"Why?"

"'Cause he's crazy!"

Moving the flame around, searching, "I'm not seeing it." Looking up around her head and face, he noticed tears in her eyes.

"Untie me! I'm 'bout to pee myself."

Johnny set the lighter on the nightstand and started untying her wrist.

"Hurry!"

"I'm trying."

Loosening one, he went around the bed to the other one. When he freed that one, Rita rose up and stretched forward to untie an ankle as Johnny worked on the other. When she was finally free, she quietly and hurriedly got out of bed and went to the bathroom.

Johnny, looking toward the ashtray of leeches, went and picked it up. Staring down at them, he hated them. He stuck the flame of the lighter under the metal ashtray. The leeches began to squirm and move. "Die, hideous creatures," whispered Johnny in a killer's voice.

When the ashtray got too hot to hold, Johnny

set it down. Closing the lid on the lighter, he tiptoed to the front room of the house and looked out the window. The monster was still there and still asleep.

Rita came out of the bathroom and hurried back into the bedroom. Johnny followed her in.

She asked, "Where'd ya go?"

"Checking on your dad."

"Where is he?"

"Still asleep on the front porch."

"Where's your lighter?" Rita turned. "The thing is on my hip!" She tried pointing behind her back at her hip.

With the lighter, Johnny discovered the third leech. It was small, but no less gross. It was on her right hip just above her panties. Johnny removed it with less effort than the others. Holding it above the flame, allowing the flame to lick its head, he dropped it in the ashtray.

Turning toward Rita, his eyes fell upon her breasts. Breasts were lovely. She said nothing, but with a quivering hand, pulled the sheet from the bed. Closing the sheet around herself, she quietly said, "I'm freezing. Thanks for getting those things off me!"

She looked pale. Her eyes swollen from crying. "What's going on, Rita?"

"Pa's insane is what's going on." Shivering, she sat down on the edge of the bed.

Johnny, closing the lid of the lighter, sat down beside her and put an arm around her. She pressed herself against him for warmth and kissed the side of his head. She said, "The other night Pa saw a black cat run across the yard and under the house. The next morning, he discovers the cat had given birth to a litter of kittens under the house. All black. Later that day, after getting rid of the cat and kittens, he sees a black snake slithering by the house and it ended up going under the house. After meditating on it, he decides it's because I'm a witch."

"Witch?"

"Pa says I was conceived in lust and sin-born."

"What's that mean?"

"Don't know. He says I cause men to have dirty and sinful thoughts and that's a sign of witchery."

Johnny understood. She was always causing him to have dirty thoughts.

Rita went on, "So he's thinking on all this and the voice in his head tells him to tie me down and put leeches on my body. If the leeches die sucking my blood, it's proof I have witch's blood."

"Your dad is psycho!"

"You want to know why he's on the front porch? He's out there watching for bats. He wants to see if bats fly about the house at night. Bats are a witch's bird, he says."

"What are you gonna do?"

"I don't know. What can I do?"

Johnny tightened his arm around her, wanting to help her.

"I wish he were dead," she whispered.

Her despairing whisper wrapped itself around Johnny's heart. She was right. The monster needed to die. And he wanted to be her hero.

Searching through thoughts for a plan and solution on how he could kill the monster, he heard the sound of a vehicle. As it drew closer, Johnny recognized it was his dad.

The vehicle slowed to a stop in front of the house. Johnny's heart began to race again. His dad would wake the monster up. Then came a blast of the horn. Two times.

Rita cussed and jumped up. "Hurry, you got to tie me back up!" She pulled Johnny off the bed and lay back down in her earlier position, stretching out her arms and legs toward the bedposts, revealing her body as the sheet unfolded from her.

Johnny stared.

"Johnny! Tie me back up before he comes checking on me," commanded Rita.

Hearing the monster coming to life on the front porch, Johnny began tying Rita back down. It didn't seem like the right thing to do, but he didn't know what to do.

He rushed from ankle to ankle, wrist to wrist. It was a sloppy job.

Outside, Johnny's dad had turned off the truck for conversation.

"Put the leeches back on me!"

"What?"

"Johnny, you have to put the leeches back on me or my pa will know someone was here!"

Johnny's heart was racing. Too much was happening too fast. He wasn't given time to think. Johnny looked over at the ashtray of leeches.

"Just do it, Johnny! And hurry!"

Johnny took the ashtray, picked up a leech, and dropped it on her hip. He placed another on her thigh where it had been sucking. It fell off her thigh to lie between her legs. He set the final one on the side of her neck. It slid off onto the bed beside her neck.

"Get outta here before ya get caught!" Rita ordered.

Outside, the monster and his dad were still talking. Johnny didn't want to leave. He wanted to help Rita, but had no idea how.

Cussing him, Rita demanded, "Get outta here while you have the chance."

He wanted to take care of her. Protect her. But, she was right. Before exiting, he pulled the sheet over her body for warmth and because he didn't want her dad or anyone seeing her breasts.

Outside, darting from shadow to shadow, Johnny made his way home. Back in his own yard again, he stared back down the road toward Rita's house. His dad was still parked out front.

Rita tried listening to what was being said between her pa and Johnny's dad, but it was too muffled. After a bit, the truck started up and drove on. The front door opened and her pa entered the house. She heard his footsteps coming. Entering the bedroom, he flipped on the light.

He stared at her. Finally, he said, "How did you get covered up? You weren't covered before?"

"I thought you came and covered me up when I was sleeping. Since it's so chilly tonight."

She saw a confused expression in his eyes. He stared, contemplating her answer. After a moment, he spoke: "I don't remember such a thing."

"All I know, is when I woke up a while ago, the cover was on me."

His eyes spoke of disbelief, but he had no explanation. Stepping over to the bed, he pulled the sheet from her body.

"Please, Pa," Rita whined. "It's cold. I'm cold."

"I gotta check the witch worms."

Rita, knowing the leeches were no longer attached, feared her Pa's reaction. How he might perceive such a thing. He wasn't logical in his thinking. She stared into his eyes while he did his examination, trying to read his thoughts.

Reaching down beside her neck, he picked up the leech lying on the bed there. He held it up before his eyes, examining it. "It looks dead."

He dropped it into the jar on the nightstand he had used to carry the leeches in with. Reaching between her legs where he knew one had been sucking, he found the second one.

He looked it over. "This one's dead too!" Making eye contact, "You know what this is proving."

The blackness in his eyes told her she wasn't talking to her pa. "No, Pa."

"I'll whip you for playing dumb, girl!"

After dropping it into the jar, he found the third. It was dead. He dropped it into the jar. With an accusing stare and devious smile formed on the good side of his face, he gave a slight nod. "Just as I suspected." Placing hands on the bed and leaning forward, staring in her eyes, he said in a quiet and calm voice, "You's a witch girl! Proof positive. Witch's blood and all. Those worms died sucking your blood!"

A crazed look of satisfaction sparkled in her pa's black eyes. He straightened up and stood tall again. "What to do with you now?"

Lustful eyes roamed her body. He said, "The Christian thing to do would be to burn ya."

Fear swept Rita's heart. He was serious and likely capable of such a thing. With a sob, she begged, "No, Pa! Please! I am a good girl. I want to please you! Give you satisfaction."

"You're a witch girl! Hell spawn."

"No, Pa! Please! I'm a good girl." She cried, "If I'm a witch, I'm a good witch."

Staring down, eyes roaming, he said, "Quit bawling. I said the Christian thing to do would be to burn ya. But, we're not Christians. You and I are sinners. Sin-loving, God-hating sinners. You'll burn soon enough fer your sins. For being born a witch. You'll burn alright. Forever and ever. Amen!"

He picked up the jar of witch worms and started for the door.

"Pa, please, I'm a good girl. Aren't you going to untie me? Aren't you hungry? Would you like me to fix you some supper?"

Pausing and looking back at her, "Use your witch's power to untie yourself like how you did when you covered yourself up. It'll be another test." Flipping off the light switch, he walked away.

"Please, Pa. Let me up. I'm cold!" she begged.

Homer ignored her.

Anger flooded Rita's soul. In rage, she cussed, kicked, and jerked her legs and arms. Johnny's poor tying job didn't hold up. She was grateful.

Getting out of bed, simmering with anger, she went to the wardrobe for warm clothes. Her pa was mean. Making her lie there uncovered was torturous. She started to put on a certain outfit, but stopped. If her pa wanted her to be a witch, then fine, she would be a witch!

She pulled on a pair of black pantyhose. In the corner beside the wardrobe was a stack of boxes with outdated clothes that belonged to her mother. One of the boxes had a black blouse with batwing sleeves. Finding it, she put it on. It was also thin and not warm at all. But her anger inside was warming.

In boxes under the bed was her mother's collection of dress shoes with heels. Rita had worn them in play growing up. Pulling out a box containing a pair of black pointed-toe dress boots with a heel, she slipped a foot into one. It was snug. She forced her foot in anyway. She put on the other. They were nice boots.

Examining herself in the mirror, it wasn't the witch's look she'd hoped for. The batwing blouse stretching across her breasts was revealing. It ended with an elastic band around her waist just above the hips, left an inch of exposed flesh above the panty hose. The see-through panty hose gave little to the imagination. The boots added height and gave her legs a sexy shape. She stretched out her arms to the side. It was more of a naughty sexy bat look than a witch's look. However, the spirit was there. She needed a witch's hat to help transform it. But, she didn't have one. She did have an old cartwheel hat that was of fashion in the fifties. It had a bowl-type crown and a very wide brim. She put it on. The hat gave the look a witch's flavor. It was the best she could do.

Turning from the mirror, it was time to find Pa.

She had heard him go out the back door after leaving the bedroom. Walking through the kitchen, she grabbed the broom in hopes to enhance the image. Quietly opening the back door and stepping out onto the little porch, her eyes searched the darkness. Pa was digging a hole. Quietly stepping off the porch, she walked softly toward him. She wanted to surprise him. Create the idea she had just suddenly appeared.

Approaching his back side, she heard him in conversation with himself. Stopping within a few feet of him, she stood in silence. Her heart pounded.

He stopped digging and stared into the hole. Sticking the shovel in the ground, he reached into a pocket and pulled out a bottle and took a gulp. Putting it away and stooping over, he picked up the jar of dead leeches. He held the jar up and chuckled.

Rita spoke as calmly as she possibly could: "Whatcha doin', Pa?"

Pa jerked around. His eyes showed shock. He acted like a little boy caught with his hand in the cookie jar.

It was empowering. "Whatcha gonna do with them witch worms?"

He seemed lost for words. His bugged-out eyes darted about. He was trying to sort things out in his mind.

His eyes, traveling up and down her body, finally settled on her breasts. He lifted his stare to her eyes. "Where'd you come from?"

Fighting to stay calm, "Whatcha mean, Pa?"

"How'd you get untied?"

"You were right, Pa! I am a witch. Leaving me lying there tied up and cold, I started shivering. I got mad. Real mad! I concentrated with all my mind on the ropes, and when I jerked my arms, they came untied and fell off. I passed the test, Pa! Pa, how come you're so smart?"

Pa looked confused. A struggle between truth

and delusion warring in his mind. He was trying not to believe her, but seeing is believing.

"What's the hole for, Pa? You going to bury them witch worms?"

He didn't answer. He was trying to process things. Trying to make sense of it all.

"I want to bury'em, Pa. Can I?" Letting go of the broom, allowing it to fall to the ground, she fought the fear trying to overpower her as she stepped toward him. Trying to keep her hand from shaking, she reached and took hold of the jar. "Can I, Pa?" She pulled on the jar. Pa released it.

"Thanks, Pa." She surprised herself when she hugged him. It was a short and quick hug. Pulling away, his eyes were a dark void of confusion.

Pa was unpredictable. That was his superpower. At any moment, he could go off. Attack her. Beat her for being a sinful witch.

She had to stay cool. Keep in control. She took a deep breath and smiled. It took everything she had to turn her eyes from his. She opened the jar, held it up to the stars, and began to speak—not from anything she had planned, but from inspiration that wasn't her. "Witch worms, witch worms, suckers of blood. Witch worms, witch worms, you found death in my blood. Witch worms, witch worms, my blood offering to the lord of hell. May he have mercy on my soul." She lowered the jar from the stars. Turning it upside down, dumping the leeches into the hole, she added (it was her voice, but not her words),

"Witch worms, witch worms, in the ground you go. Witch worms, witch worms, may your souls burn in hell instead of me." Producing a wad of spit, she spat into the hole. She dropped the jar, took the shovel, and covered the jar with dirt.

Sticking the shovel into the ground with a push of her boot, she turned and looked at her pa. The dark cloud of confusion still swirled. A rush of power and excitement coursed through her. Maybe she truly was a witch. The words she had spoken were not her words. They had just flowed out of her lips naturally.

Maybe she was a daughter of the devil.

As quickly as the power and excitement came and coursed through her, it left. All of a sudden, she began to feel vulnerable. It all seemed too real. As a fog of confusion began forming over her own mind, Rita said, "I'm cold. And tired. I need to go to bed. I have school in the morning."

Picking the broom off the ground, she walked away. Stepping upon the porch, she looked back at her pa. He was standing there watching her. She opened the back door and entered the house. She leaned the broom against the wall and took a deep breath of relief. Her whole body shivered. Her hands were trembling. She needed to lie down.

She undressed, crawled into bed, and covered up with a blanket. She felt exhausted, but her mind wouldn't stop. Something had changed tonight. Was she a witch for real? Was she hell-spawned?

Conceived in lust and born in sin? A trueborn child of the devil? Was it a good thing? Was it a bad thing? What were the possibilities?

Before falling completely asleep, Pa entered the room. Getting into bed, he crawled on top of her, establishing dominance. Looking into black eyes, she submitted. The normalcy of it somehow felt comforting.

17

SHADES OF GRAY

I t was closing time. Looking around, the Wigwam was clean and ready for tomorrow. It had been a slow night and Sedges Vannhorn was looking forward to getting home early. Normally, by the time the last patron left and cleanup was done, it would be eleven thirty or twelve before she would get to leave.

Her plan was to go straight home, have a quick shower, get into comfortable night clothes, eat a bowl of ice cream, do some reading, and go to bed.

Sedges stepped into the back to check on Otis's progress. Otis, the cook in charge of cleaning up the back and mopping, was getting rid of the mop water and rinsing out the bucket. "Done?" asked Sedges, stating the obvious.

"I will be in a few seconds," Otis answered.

Sedges looked around making sure nothing was overlooked. The door-tone sounded, alerting them of someone entering the restaurant. Otis looked up with disappointed and pleading eyes. Feeling a spirit of aggravation, Sedges reassured him, "We're closed!"

Wishing she had locked the door already, she went back out to the front to confront the customer. Standing in the middle of the room was Jared Seelot. Her spirit of aggravation heightened. Jared would not simply turn and go away. He would have to debate the issue. Insist he got there before closing time and had the right to be served.

Trying to be professional, trying to hide her aggravation, she announced, "Sorry, we're closed for the night. I was just fixing to lock the door."

"I was afraid of that."

Jared's acceptance and the humbled tone in his voice took Sedges by surprise. It wasn't like him.

"By chance, do you have anything left over, something I could take with me? I just got in town. I'm hungry, haven't eaten all day."

Sedges looked into his eyes. He didn't look right. She felt her defenses go down. "I don't think so, let me check with Otis, maybe there's something."

"I'd be obliged."

Sedges turned and stepped into the back. Otis was standing by waiting for the verdict. She said to him, "It's Jared Seelot. He's hungry. By chance do you have anything left he might take with him?"

"Sorry. It was slow tonight."

The door-tone sounded again. Sedges and Otis

looked at each other. "I can't believe this," Sedges complained. She checked the time: it was eleven o'clock. She looked at Otis. "Clock out and get out of here. We are closed!"

"You're the boss."

With Otis making his escape while the getting was good, Sedges went back out to the front to witness Jared telling two guys the Wigwam was closed for the night. He practically escorted them out.

As the guys left out the door, Jared turned back around. Seeing her, he said, "You need to lock the door."

"Thank you." Grabbing her keys, she went to the door. "Sorry, there wasn't anything left over. It was a slow night." With the door locked, she turned. There was only a foot or so between them.

Disappointed, he said, "It's cool. It's not been a good day. Thanks anyway. I'm sure you're ready to get home. I won't keep you. If you'd like, I'll follow you out—not saying you need me to, but it might make me feel better doing something honorable." He added, "Wouldn't want you attacked by a scarecrow or whatever."

"Sure. I guess." Perplexed, Sedges moved past Jared gathering her things. He wasn't acting right. He was being genuinely nice. That wasn't like Jared. Something was wrong with him.

Crossing the parking lot, subconsciously scanning the area for scarecrows, she asked, "So you had a bad day?"

"More or less."

"What's wrong?" Normally she would have taken pleasure over Jared "Thunder" Seelot having a bad day—karma and all—but, her spirit told her that something important was going on.

"Nothing."

"I know better than that."

"Whatcha mean?"

Sedges paused at her car. "You're not yourself."

"In your illusion of me, how would that self be?"

"I don't understand."

Jared shrugged. "It doesn't matter. Take care. Have a safe trip home. I'm going to go and find something to eat. Or maybe something to drink."

Take care? Have a safe trip home? When had Jared ever talked to her in a good civil manner? In good conscience, she couldn't just let him go his own way without knowing what was wrong. She was cursed that way. She truly enjoyed helping people.

As Jared walked away, the words sprang from her mouth: "Would you like to follow me home? I could fix you a roast-beef sandwich and some chips?"

Jared paused, turning around. "I don't want to put you out and impose upon your family. It's late."

"It's no imposition. Mom and Dad are on the road. Don't expect them back for another week or so. I was going to have a bite to eat anyway, so you wouldn't be putting-me-out." With a bit of humor to lighten the moment, "Just as long as you don't expect me to 'put-out.'"

A smile crossed his lips. "Wouldn't consider it."

"It's settled then." Opening her car door, "See you in a few."

Driving home, Sedges considered Jared's words: *Wouldn't consider it.* The words bothered her. Almost hurtful. Why wouldn't he consider it? Was she that unappealing to him? It wasn't like he was choosy. He wasn't pure. He had a reputation. Why was he so against her? It was true they were lifetime rivals, but she had thought it a contest of provocation. Weren't they really friends at heart?

Jared parked his car on the curb. The neighborhood, clean and decent, was adorned with early-century two-story traditional homes with manicured lawns. Some of the oldest in town. Sedges stood at the front door, waiting for him to join her.

Entering the house and turning on lights, Sedges said, "Make yourself at home. If you don't mind, I'm going to get out of these clothes. I feel all smelly and greasy."

"Sure. Take your time. There's no hurry."

Sedges disappeared.

The home expressed a warm and inviting ambiance. It was solid, well-kept and -maintained. The traditional old-style furniture looked heavy and sturdy. Thick rugs and draperies gave the room a rich and cozy feeling.

Jared walked about the room. A lot of fine and interesting things, some of which were probably antique. They told the story of who the Vannhorns were.

The Vannhorns were respectable people. Originally from the Oklahoma reservation, they migrated to NuSprings with hopes and dreams. They were never a "wealthy" family, but they were hardworking and money-wise. They never had a lot, but never did without. They were patient people who invested in themselves and in their lives.

Standing in the Vannhorn home, this was the America Jared knew. The America he understood. People who stood for something. People with morals, values, and convictions. Good hardworking honest people achieving their dreams. People who were the backbone of this country making this the greatest country on earth. People like the Vannhorns were why Jared went to law school. Why he was majoring in political science. He wanted to help, defend, and protect these people. These concepts. He wanted to defend and protect the American Way, the American Dream.

But what he found, what law school revealed, was that there was ugliness in this country. A growing ugliness like a disease attacking and threatening the moral fabric of the nation. A disease of the spirit that would cripple and eventually destroy the American Way, the American Dream.

Hearing Sedges entering the room, Jared said, "You have a nice home. Comfortable and reassuring." Her hair was wet.

"Yeah," she agreed, stepping closer. "I love this house. It's home." Directing Jared to a picture of her grandparents, "My grandfather, great-grandfather and a great-granduncle or two built this house back in the twenties. There're pictures of them working on it in one of the photo albums."

A clean, pleasant, powdery smell radiated from her.

"My dad grew up in this house." After a pause, she continued. "When my dad got married, he moved out and bought the house on Eagle Street. But after my grandfather passed away and my grandmother's health started declining, Dad sold our house and we moved in to help Grandmother and to keep the place up.

"With the passing of my grandmother, Dad inherited the house. After I graduated high school, Mother, wanting to see America, started going with Dad on the road. For the most part, this seems like my home. Follow me and I'll fix us a bite to eat." Sedges led the way to the kitchen.

An island in the middle of the kitchen had a bar on one side. Jared took a seat upon one of the barstools. Sedges busied herself with the task at hand, asking him questions as to what he liked and wanted with his sandwich.

Sedges' pajamas, although modest and not very revealing, fit her in a flattering way. She had a nice figure. Movement on the floor caught Jared's attention. He make eye contact with a mouse before it quickly scurried away.

"You have mice," Jared said.

"Not mice. A mouse. Was it white?" Sedges set a plate with the sandwich on the bar before him.

"I think so."

Getting her plate, she said, "It was a gift from RiverDawg. It used to be in a cage, but one day, I came home and it had escaped." She took a seat beside Jared. "I often see him. Especially late at night. He don't eat much. Keeps the floor clean of crumbs," she laughed. "I sometimes find comfort late at night in seeing him. I guess it keeps me from feeling like I'm all alone."

As they ate, Sedges did most of the talking. She sometimes could get the mouse to take food from her fingers. She shared stories about the home, her family, and experiences. Jared listened, commenting when it was proper.

Jared enjoyed the pleasant, peaceful, late-night atmosphere. Sedges was a proud woman and proud of her home and family. He needed this. He needed to be reminded of what he was. What his mission in life was. He needed the solidarity the Vannhorn home and family offered. He hadn't realized it until now, but he had sought out Sedges on purpose.

He needed honesty.

He needed to hear truth from someone honest and strong enough to give it to him.

Finishing his sandwich, Sedges offered, "Would you like another?"

"No, I'm good. Thanks. It was a great sandwich. I appreciate you doing this for me."

"You're welcome. No problem." Sedges got up and began clearing the bar, removing the dishes.

"It's getting late—what time is it?"

"A little past midnight. It's early still. I'm a bit of a night owl," Sedges said nonchalantly.

Setting the dishes in the sink, she turned and looked at him. Out of the blue, in a tender non-threatening way, she asked, "What's wrong?"

"Ummm, what do you mean?"

"You seem troubled. Burdened."

She was staring into his eyes. Jared shook his head. "Nothing. Just tired, I guess." He smiled.

"Follow me, I got something for you." Her cheeriness was refreshing.

Jared followed her back into the living room.

"Have a seat. Relax. I'll be right back."

Jared chose a dark-brown faux-leather recliner with a padded back and armrests. It was a man's chair and looked comfortable.

Sedges returned carrying a couple of glasses and two different bottles. She placed them on the sofa table. "You said something earlier about needing a drink. Are you man enough to try some moonshine?"

"Moonshine? What are you doing with moonshine?"

"Someone gave it to my dad. He's had it forever." She poured a swallow into a small round glass and stretched out her arm, handing it to him.

Jared reached out and took it. He held it before his eyes. It was not going to taste good. Not at all!

Sedges sat down on the sofa to watch. It was a challenge Jared understood. Was he going to be man enough? This was a moment when his past arrogance had come to haunt him.

"Have you ever tried it?" Jared stalled.

"Dad says it'll definitely put hair on your chest. I really don't want hair on my chest." She stared with delightful anticipation.

Dreading it, Jared smelt it in procrastination.

"Scared, aren't you?" she provoked.

Knowing she had him and he had no choice, he opened his mouth and sucked it down. There was no playing it cool. It was as he'd expected—the worst, most vile-tasting stuff ever. There was no fighting the horrible facial expressions he knew he was making as his face rebelled against the invasion. As bad as the taste was, the burning was equally as bad. It was like he was swallowing fire. He coughed, hacked, and broke out into a sweat. Through watery eyes, he saw Sedges smiling from ear to ear, truly enjoying the show.

After getting back his composure, but still in much discomfort, he said, "Not bad." He forced a smile. "Hit me again." He stretched out his arm toward her.

Her expression displayed surprise. He'd not only met her challenge, but was going to go beyond. He was not only man enough, he was man enough for a second round.

She poured him another. "Wish I had a camera."

"I wish you did too."

She had given him more this time. The second couldn't be as bad as the first. His taste buds were either numb or dead. He winked, raised the glass to his lips, and poured it in. If it wasn't as bad, he couldn't tell.

He broke out into a sweat again, his throat and stomach burned, his heart pounded, tears blurred his vision. There is a reason why this stuff was illegal. It wouldn't take much to kill a man.

Sedges dared, "Want another?"

"Only if you'll have one."

"No thank you. I prefer wine." She reached for the other bottle and filled her glass. The bottle was fancy and had no label. Jared asked, "What kind of wine is it?"

"Homemade berry."

"Homemade? You made it?"

"Mostly my grandmother did, but I helped. It was one of the last things we did together." Sedges raised her glass to her lips and took a sip. Jared could tell she liked the taste. She licked her lips.

"Explain something to me," she said. "Earlier, you said something about my 'illusion' of you. What did you mean?" She sipped her wine again.

Jared debated whether or not to go there, but decided to. "Your perception of me based on what you have observed and the bias programmed into you."

Sedges considered what he'd said. "Why 'illusion'?"

"Who you think I am and who I think I am are probably two different people."

Jared could see she was considering the validity of what he said. He proposed, "What is truth? What is reality? Am I the person you think I am or am I the person I think I am or am I the person others may think I am? Who am I? What am I?"

Jared looked into her eyes as she stared into his. He was challenging her. Challenging her on an intellectual level to play a philosophical game. The game of politics.

The ball was in her court. Jared waited for a response, still feeling a lingering burning inside from the moonshine that had awakened a warrior's spirit.

She repositioned herself on the sofa, leaning back and bringing a leg up to sit on it. She sipped her wine again.

Jared wanted to add more, but didn't. He was going to force her to respond. A lawyer had to learn patience and control. He lacked patience and control. They were virtues of Sedges.

Breaking the silence, she said, "Wow. Now I know."

It wasn't the response he'd anticipated. "Know what?"

"What's wrong with you."

"Whatcha mean?"

"You've not been yourself t'night. You have not fit into the frame of my 'illusion' of you."

"What is your illusion of me?"

"You are arrogant, demanding, haughty, and macho. At least that's the cloak you wear to create the 'illusion' you want everyone to perceive."

Jared smiled. "Well said." She was such a smart woman. Always a worthy opponent. Besting her was always a challenge.

"Now my turn," she declared. "What is truth, what is reality? What is the point of these questions which carry no great weight? To what end do they serve?"

So this was the game? Truth or dare. Fine. Why not? Jared leaned forward for the bottle of moonshine. He poured himself a swallow, leaned back, raised the glass in examination, and then swallowed half of it. It wasn't quite as bad this time, but not pleasant either. He felt manly doing it and hoped it would give his tongue freedom to speak what his heart was feeling. He needed to vent.

He set the glass down. "I've always believed overall, people were good. That the government, overall, was good and in the end did the right thing. Kept to an honorable path. That's how I was raised. My father, as you well know, is an honorable man and one of great integrity. He truly serves the people. I've often seen him put the needs of the tribe and city above his. That is the way of government. I was taught, *A government for the people, by the people.*

"My grandfather was a hero in the first World War and served in the House of Representatives. He too was a great man of honor and served not only our tribe, but the entire Native American culture, pushing for bills and laws that help our city and tribe to prosper.

"I've grown up understanding I will someday be chief of our tribe. I've been groomed for the position. I've hoped to be great and honorable as my fathers before me.

"But, the country is changing. There's a new mindset. An ugliness. There's a powerful movement rewriting—'updating,' they call it—the old law textbooks with the new, modern, and progressive way of thinking and doing law. The old law books spoke of law in terms of black and white. Things were either right or wrong. The old books promoted and encouraged a high standard of morality, teaching that law and politics had a moral obligation toward truth, honesty, and rightness. That man's law was to reflect Divine Law. That there was a Creator to answer to.

"The new textbooks, replacing the old, 'outdated' ones, are teaching a new philosophy. Many of the quotes and lessons of our forefathers are being rewritten, their messages diluted. Things regarding God, spiritual wisdom and concepts, and rightness are being removed and replaced with new and abstract ideas and concepts.

"The world of Law and Politics is no longer being taught as moral obligation, but instead, more of a game. And in this game there is no black or white.

There are only shades of gray. In this game, truth is irrelevant.

"What is truth?" Jared reached into his pocket and pulled out a quarter. "Catch." He tossed it over to Sedges. She attempted to catch it, but she didn't have enough time to prepare. The quarter landed on her chest. Jared said, "Hold the quarter up and look at it." Sedges obeyed. "Describe to me what you see."

"I see the head of a man. George, maybe. The word 'Liberty.' 'In God we trust.' Nineteen sixty-nine."

"Toss it back to me."

Sedges tossed it back. Jared caught it and held it up for examination. "You saw the head of a man. I see an eagle. A man and an eagle are two different things. Yet both descriptions are true.

"See, there are two sides to every coin. Two sides to every story. Which one is true? Or are both sides true? And if both sides are true, which side do you defend?

"Humans are biased creatures. As children growing up we are taught to think about certain things in certain ways. When we see a matter, our perception of it is in conjunction with the bias we've been taught. And that creates an illusion we see as truth, but in most cases is not exactly true, although based on facts.

"Historically, in most countries, including this one, laws are based on that country's religious beliefs. Laws are more about religious principles and ideology rather than human rights. Religion therefore dictates national and civil laws.

"So now the great debate is that of human rights versus religious law. Am I to be a champion of human rights or a champion of religious law?

"Nowadays, to earn a degree in law, one must have the required course of philosophy. The foundation of philosophy is to get you to think abstractly. To cause you to consider the possibility that there is no absolute right or wrong. That truth and wisdom are abstract ideas differing from person to person. From culture to culture. Truth, therefore, becomes a many-sided coin.

"The foundation of philosophy is to get you to think in abstract terms in which there is no absolute right or wrong. A foundation resting upon a footing of a greater debate—did God create man or did man create God?

"Lines of right and wrong become blurred. Things that were once black and white are now shades of gray."

Sedges spoke: "So, do you now doubt the existence of God?"

"I don't know. Our ancestors were polytheistic. They believed in multiple gods and spirits. Tribal laws and customs revolved around those spirits and gods and their attempts to honor them. Then the white man came, teaching us that it was not truth. Superstition. That there was only one God. Our children were made to go to school where the white man's idea of only one God was instilled in their way of thinking. And so generations later, our bias is toward the belief of only one God and the idea of many gods seems ignorant and foolish to us. But now, in the ranks of higher education, the idea of even one God is being taught as superstition. Will my great-grandchildren believe in God or will they see God and religion as superstition?

"My family was never what you would call churchgoers. To me the church religion is too restrictive. But I believed in God. I believed in Jesus. It's a good concept. Something to believe in. But is it the truth? I want the truth. I want to believe in the truth. I want to know if God created man or if man created God. If man created God, that changes everything!"

Sedges interrupted with an offended tone, "You're just trying to be intellectual, Jared Seelot. You know better. Us no longer believing the 'Old Religion' is not exactly true. The white man's teaching wasn't that there weren't different 'gods,' but that there was only one true God and Creator of all.

"RiverDawg still believes and practices the Old Religion. And no one, including you, doubts the realism of his 'superstitious' ways. RiverDawg has powers. His magic defies the natural. True?"

Jared nodded in agreement.

Her glass of wine was nearly empty.

She went on, "The truth is, because of the way we've been taught, most of us consider the Old Religion as a mixture of truth and superstition. It's not that we deny the truth of it, we see it as the dark side of the religion coin and that it is bad. But we still believe in spite of what we have been told. Real is real. As smart as some of these men may be, there are things they cannot explain."

Sedges raised the glass to her lips again and sipped to give him an opportunity to disagree. The visual was sexy. She was a sexy lady.

Jared found himself taking in her assets, her figure, lusting from her face down to her pretty painted pink toenails. Looking down at her foot, movement out of the corner of his eye caused him to shift his gaze. The mouse under the sofa was looking at him. When he looked directly at it, it moved out of sight.

"Your problem is that you're suffering from an identity crisis," Sedges stated sternly and point-blankly.

Jared looked up. She said, "You're allowing clever men, probably men who are champions of debate, to *bully* you into what they want you to believe!" She was offended by the idea of it.

It made sense. The skill of a lawyer is the ability to create doubt and confusion.

"You need to take your questions and confusions to StormDancer. Unlike your 'intellectual' teachers who only know about God, he knows God!"

She raised the glass to her lips again. Jared watched her finish the drink in her hand. He liked the protective hostility in her voice. It spoke of loyalty.

Loyalty, in higher education, was being taught as a commodity to be purchased.

Holding the empty glass, she was silent and staring, patiently waiting for him to speak. The ball was once again in his court.

"I don't know if I'm cut out to be a lawyer. Or a politician." He tossed the ball back to her.

"Why?"

"It's becoming too dirty of a game."

"How's that?"

"Truth is irrelevant. Unless it's to your favor. With nothing being black or white and everything shades of gray, it all comes down to the skill of illusion and the twisting of facts.

"If your job is to defend a bad guy, then you add enough white to his character to create the lightest shade of gray possible. Even bad guys have good sides. Or if your opponent is a good guy, you add black to his character to create the darkest shade of gray possible. Every good guy has a dark side that can be capitalized on.

"Would you like to know why I told you earlier that it's been a bad day?"

"I would."

Jared picked up the glass he had been drinking from. There was a swallow of moonshine still in it. He raised it to his mouth and emptied it. After a good hack and cough, he said, "I'm done with that stuff!"

Sedges was again grinning.

"You enjoy it, don't you?"

"It's funny," she agreed.

Jared rose forward, took hold of the wine bottle, stood and said, "Drink with me."

Sedges didn't protest as he filled her glass to only about a third of the way. He set the bottle back down and took his seat again.

"Okay, here it is. In one of my classes, as a class project for a large percentage of the semester grade, we were divided up into legal teams. The scenario was that our team, our firm, took on a new client. A political case in which our client was running for office, but the person holding the office was an honorable man and well liked. We were given a detailed folder of the man, his life and campaign. The whole scenario was based on real people and a real election. Our job was to make the incumbent look bad. Destroy his good character, giving our client a chance. We were to create the idea that the incumbent's good character was an illusion he created to hide his true self.

"So me and my 'colleagues' went to digging. We got creative. We discovered or perhaps uncovered things that could be twisted to look like something it was not. So we played the game. Created the illusion. We presented it before the judgment panel for a job well done and a grade.

"We got an 'A' and were praised for our work. At first we were all happy and celebrated. Then we heard that our presentation was adopted and used by a real law firm and against the real incumbent.

"What we did, what I was a part of, was used to take a good and honorable guy like my dad and your grandfather, and made him out to look fake with a dark side and dark intentions. With the help of the media, the whole thing has turned into a scandal. This good man's reputation and career that took a lifetime to build was destroyed in a matter of weeks. And not just him and his career, but his family and their good name are being destroyed. And I'm partly to blame."

Sedges offered, "Can you not speak up on this man's defense? Go public and explain it is not true?"

"I could. But there would be retaliation. In the end, my career as a lawyer and politician would more than likely be destroyed before it ever started. They would not only attack me, but my family. Our tribe and city would go under the microscope. Depending on how far they wanted to take things, it could destroy not only my family, but other people. It could seriously hurt our tribe and its control over our city.

"So what do I do? Heed the warning and turn a blind eye? Or do I try to fix something that is more than likely unfixable and in the process possibly destroy a precious way of life for our tribe and city that took more than a century to build?

"What is the right thing to do? And would the cost be worth it?

"Just this morning, my instructor told me, 'This is the world of law and politics. It's a hard and mean game. You have just learned more in the last few weeks than you can imagine. You have witnessed and experienced the real-life game of law and politics. Are you up to it? Are you in or out? And if you're out, you best walk away silently.'

"He told me, 'Consider the Kennedys. They were assassinated in broad daylight, in the public before thousands of witnesses, and no one even knows what really happened or who is really behind it all. That is the mastery of illusion.'

"He told me to go home and think about things. He hopes to see me back in a couple of weeks. He said I have promise."

Jared looked at Sedges. "So now you know." Jared looked down at his empty glass. He picked it up and reached for the bottle of moonshine.

Sedges asked, "You sure you want to do that?"

Jared poured another swallow into his glass.

Sedges said, "I just wanted you to loosen up and talk so I could figure out what was wrong with you."

"It worked." Jared sat back down. "You always were a smart girl." He raised the glass up to display it between them. "This drink is like law and politics. It's bitter, awful, hard to swallow, and very intoxicating. Cheers." He gulped down the swallow. He took it better this time with less of a show. Feeling the burn from throat to stomach, he said, "Woo, I think I just felt some hair pop out on my chest."

Sedges gave a small giggle.

"So smart girl, words of wisdom?"

She took a drink of wine. "I don't know."

"Nor I."

An awkward silence filled the room as they stared into each other's eyes.

Jared said, "You know what?"

"What?"

"It's late. I'm a bit drunk. And if I don't get up and leave, I'm going to make a serious effort to take advantage of you."

Sedges replied, "You know what?"

"What?"

"It's late. I'm tipsy. And if you stay and try to take advantage of me, I will let you." After a moment's pause she added, "It's about time, don't you think?"

The mouse hiding in the shadow underneath the furniture watched Jared leave his chair to join Sedges on the sofa. If a mouse could smile, it did.

RiverDawg broke his spirit-bound from the mouse. His eyes came to focus back on his tiny one-room shack. The night had been a success. His lust-casting had finally got those two together. Their combined genes would create the necessary leader for the storm darkening the horizon.

RiverDawg, moving from the position he was sitting, found his old body stiff and uncooperative. He was getting too old. He crawled to his pallet and lay down.

"It's too late for an old man to still be awake,"

he complained to himself, getting as comfortable as an old man his age could get. He soon fell asleep, dreaming again of a fox jumping from tree limb to tree limb.

18

NOBLESSE OBLIGE

A monument to a surviving culture and, in many aspects, a thriving culture, the concrete teepee was modern and futuristic. Tish BootShaker was proud to be part of this wonderful culture. Proud to be the wife of a Native American man. Proud to be known as Tish HoneySuckle BootShaker.

She followed Ira into the Wigwam. They were the only customers. They seated themselves in one of the booths. Tish said, "I love this place."

"You do?"

Looking at the Native American decor on the walls, she answered, "I guess I like the reality of how your people and culture are still alive in these modern times. It's the past mingled with the present."

"Our people," Ira corrected her. "And yes, we are a blessed tribe. The Seelots have been wise and visionary leaders."

"I would someday like to own this place."

"You want a restaurant?"

"Not so much the restaurant as much as the building and what it represents. It could make for a cool home."

"So you want a modern home that looks like a teepee?"

"Yes. It would be fun. Symbolic."

"What about my father's place? He has already said that when he dies, it will be ours?"

"Yeah, but it's lacking. It's not a teepee. And it's very small. There's no utilities, no bathroom. Running water and a bathroom is very important to me. Besides, I'm not so sure his little shack will outlast him."

"Well, you may have a point. So Ms. California, from a well-to-do family, would this teepee home come with an in-ground swimming pool?"

"And a fire pit. We definitely would have to have a fire pit."

"Hi, you-all," Sedges greeted. "Glad you could make it. Jared's on his way. How's things?"

"Good," Tish answered. "And you?"

"Never better."

"We were just talking about how this place could be a cool home," Tish said.

"Yeah?" Sedges glanced about. "I'm not seeing the vision so much."

"Oh, I do," Tish remarked.

"You have to imagine it with an in-ground pool and fire pit," Ira teased.

"In-ground pool and fire pit, hmmm."

Tish said, "Consider a Native American city, like this one, with modern homes fashioned with teepee concepts. A futuristic Indian encampment."

"Interesting idea." Sedges wasn't convinced.

"I see sparks of new life flickering in your eyes," Ira observed.

Sedges' grin spoke of a secret. She evaded with, "Can I get you anything?"

Jared, entering the Wigwam, made his way to Ira and Tish. Sedges, sitting on the edge of the seat opposite them with a serving tray in her arms, stood as he walked up. He made heartfelt eye contact with her. *"Osigwotsv?"* he spoke softly in Cherokee, asking how she was.

Humbly stepping aside, Sedges answered, *"Osd!"* It was Cherokee for "great."

Jared turned from Sedges to Ira. "StormDancer." It was a warrior's greeting.

"Thunder," StormDancer returned in like manner with a hand gesture of invitation.

Thunder, taking a seat, greeted Tish with, "HoneySuckle."

"Good afternoon." She smiled.

"Can I get you anything?" Sedges asked Thunder.

Noting StormDancer and HoneySuckle having water, he answered, "Water would be fine, thank you."

"So what's new in Thunderville?" StormDancer quested for personal information.

"Ahh, the roller-coaster of life. Sometimes I'm up, sometimes I'm down, sometimes going round and round. Some days it's fun, some days it's scary, but with every day, I get closer to the end."

"How's your love life?" StormDancer being more direct, discerning a new level of affection between him and Sedges.

"Who's got time for love?" Thunder denied.

"Warriors make time for love."

"If by love, you refer to physical needs, I do well."

If something was going on between him and Sedges, they obviously weren't ready to go public.

Sedges placed a glass of water on the table before Thunder and left.

"What can I do for you?" StormDancer asked.

"Answer me a question."

"Ask your question."

"How can you be so sure there is a God?"

"Because I know Him. Because I experience Him."

"That is an easy and convenient answer. But it proves nothing to me. It proves nothing to the world."

"The question, Thunder, is whether or not you want to know God."

"What do you mean?"

"Early in mankind's history, there was no question or debate on the issue. But man wanted to make his own rules. Do his own thing. And so man pushed God away."

"That proves nothing. That is your belief. It might be true to you, but it's not truth to me."

HoneySuckle said, "I think I'll go and keep Sedges company and let you guys talk."

StormDancer slid out of the booth, allowing Tish to exit. When he sat back down, he asked Thunder, "Do you seek truth or just justification for what you want to believe?"

"I want to know what the reality is."

"What would it change in your life?"

"How I live. How I do law."

"Why?"

"Because in the end, the account would have to be settled."

"So if there was no question, no doubt, you would serve and honor God with your life?"

"Yes."

"Why not live like that now?"

"Because, StormDancer, life is complicated. The lines of right and wrong have become blurred."

"Is that truth or your attempt to justify selfish motives?"

"What do you mean?"

"What is your true objective in life and becoming a lawyer? What do you want to get out of it? What do you want to accomplish? Do you want to honor God, serve your people, or do you want to have a comfortable living and make a name for yourself?"

After a moment of thought, "Both."

"The reality, Thunder, is that there is God. A

Creator of heaven and earth. And someday you will stand before him and be judged and your account will be settled."

"If there is a God as you speak of, as the Bible teaches, then why doesn't He just reveal Himself in a very real and physical way in which there would be no doubt? No confusion? No debate? Why play games? Why play the game of faith? It makes no sense."

"God is a God of love. A God of freedom and choice." Thunder disputed, "Your words do not answer the question. They do not settle the issue. You talk in circles, but still haven't proved anything."

"You've heard the old proverb, 'If you love something, let it go and if it comes back, then it is yours'?"

Thunder nodded.

"That's God's philosophy. If God were to 'put an end' to the debate as you say, then—as you attested a while ago—people would serve Him out of obligation and fear rather than love. The freedom of choice would be lacking.

"People would serve God out of intelligence, because it would be their wisest and best selfish thing to do in the long run.

"God wants to be chosen because of love. He wants you to choose Him because you desire a relationship with Him. He wants a relationship with you built upon love and desire. Not fear.

"However, God has, in fact, revealed Himself. He has in fact, made an appearance. God made an appearance upon Mount Sinai in a very vivid, super-natural, and dramatic way. The way of a 'god.' Upon Mount Sinai he appeared before millions of people.

"Then again through Jesus Christ. Performing great miracles to prove who he was.

"God has not only revealed Himself, Thunder, in a real and tangible manner that you desire, but there is a historical written record of it. It is man who chooses not to believe in God. People choose not to believe in the record or the evidence. But that is the way God desires it. God offers enough evidence for those who want to believe to be able to believe with-out doubt, but at the same time, withholds enough evidence that a man, in the council of his wisdom, cannot say for absolute fact that there is a God. God chooses faith rather than fact to create doubt. God uses doubt to expose the hidden truth and desire of the heart. As long as there seems reasonable doubt to His existence, it becomes easy to reject him and the idea of him. If that is what is in your heart.

"And that, my friend, creates the freedom of choice.

"Now it becomes a matter of choice. A matter of the heart. Do you want to believe in a God that created man or do you want to believe that man created God? If you want to believe that man cre-ated God, then man becomes god. Which do you truly want to believe? Which will you choose to be-lieve? God has given you the freedom of choice. You have the divine right to not believe in God. He has allowed an avenue of doubt to give you that choice. But that choice comes with consequences. God gave you the right to choose, but He also spelled out the consequences of your choice.

"Can I prove to you without a shadow of doubt that God exists? No. God has fixed it so that it cannot be done.

"You are given three choices: atheism, religion, or relationship.

"Relationship with God is the only one that matters. The only one that will save you. Only God can prove Himself to you. Those who seek Him will find Him."

"I don't know, StormDancer. Your words make sense. Maybe. But, it sounds too simple. It's hard to wrap my mind around it. Intellectually it doesn't really compute, being such an important eternal matter."

"And that's your problem, Thunder. God does not honor intellectualism. Man's desire of knowledge and independence is what led to the fall of man in the first place. What separated God and man to begin with. God does not have to prove himself to you. God does not have to prove that He is worthy of your love or loyalty. By faith, you please God. Without faith, it is impossible to please Him. By faith you choose God for the right reason. By faith you choose relationship with God. And because of your act of faith, and a desire to know him, He will reveal Himself to you.

"The question, my friend, is, do you want to know Him? I know God exists, because I experience Him. He has revealed himself to me."

The Wigwam's door-tone sounding gave alert to someone entering the building. StormDancer and Thunder turned their attention to the door. Chief KnifeWater Seelot entered, followed by Beloved Woman Hedy Seeker.

"So there you are!" Chief KnifeWater declared in a tone strongly accusing. Marching over to where the two warriors sat, the Chief, glaring at his son, demanded, "Where have you been?"

"Around," Thunder answered with a touch of defiance.

"I've been looking for you."

"So now you have found me. Why the buzz?"

"One of your professors from college called and wanted to speak with you. He said something about you were considering dropping out of law school. Is this true?"

"I don't know. It was a thought. I haven't decided anything."

"The man I talked to said you left school days ago. Where have you been?"

"I've been around. I felt the need for a sabbatical. I needed to think."

Tish and Sedges, standing in the distance watching the drama, were startled when RiverDawg appeared next to them, asking, "What's going on?"

"Where'd you come from?" the tone of Sedges' voice revealing an unnerving spirit.

"From the back."

RiverDawg was wearing his long-sleeve white cotton shirt, red vest, top hat, and good trousers. His "business" suit. Knowing RiverDawg as she did, something was up. Sedges asked him, "What are you doing here?"

"Looks like the place to be."

"What's going on?" Sedges sought for information.

"You tell me, I just got here."

Elizabeth Seeker, leaving school and crossing the parking lot toward Quillpen's car, noticed an unusual buzz of activity going on. There seemed a universal directive. People appeared focused, in a hurry, and on a mission.

A guy hurrying by her paused. "Hey, Medicine Girl, you heading to the Wigwam too?"

"Why? What's going on?"

"You haven't heard? Something big has happened or is going down! Chief KnifeWater, your mother, Thunder, BootShaker, and RiverDawg are all there! Everybody's heading there."

The guy hurried on.

Beth hurried to the *Dragon Slayer*. Quillpen had the Catalina painted a deep black-cherry. The chrome piece down the middle of the car running from headlight to taillight was removed, giving the car a more boss look. On the rear fenders of each side, near the taillights, *Dragon Slayer* was painted. Underneath the name *Dragon Slayer*, a dream catcher was painted. A couple of feathers tied to the antenna gave it Native American flare.

Beth walked upon a conversation between Quillpen, Dave Sumner, and Valerie Brooks.

Dave said, "We have to pick up Val's sister, but we'll be there."

"Cool." Quillpen turned to Beth. "Hope you got time for a visit to the Wigwam."

Beth shrugged her shoulders. "Sure."

Hedy, looking out the window to the gathering crowd, said, "Things are turning into a circus."

Chief KnifeWater ordered the doors locked. "We need to move this meeting."

Thunder said, "Really? We're not done? What more is there to say?"

"You don't seem to understand the magnitude of the matter, Son."

"I get it." Thunder looked at his dad. "I was born a Seelot. Tribal Law declares the firstborn of a Chief is to be groomed to be the next Chief. The yoke of chieftain is upon my shoulders. It's my destiny."

"You make it sound as if it is a curse." Chief KnifeWater's words had an edge of disappointment.

"It is an honor, Thunder," the Beloved Woman admonished.

"I didn't say it wasn't."

"You state law, Son, but do you understand the reason for the law?"

"Seelots carry the Seelot 'Gift,'" Thunder responded.

"Yes, but explain the significance."

Thunder sighed. "The 'Gift' is a weapon giving the chief an advantage in leadership."

"The 'Gift' is a supernatural benevolence aiding the Seelot Chief in the leading of the Tribe," the Beloved Woman corrected. "It creates an advantage. It is why our tribe has survived and flourished."

"But I don't possess the Gift," Thunder reminded.

"You have the calling," the Beloved Woman declared.

"The yoke, you mean." Thunder spoke with a bit of rebellion. He was growing weary of the whole conversation.

"You will not disrespect the Beloved Woman!" The Chief, showing a bit of temper, also growing weary.

Stepping forward from the sideline, RiverDawg addressing the Chief, "May I interject?"

"No," the Beloved Woman answered. "Why is this old fool here anyway? He's no part of the council. We have no time for magic tricks!"

Chief KnifeWater frowned at the Beloved Woman. "Say your peace, RiverDawg."

Giving the Chief a nod of respect and gratitude, RiverDawg stepped forward into the middle of the room. He turned to the young chief. "Thunder, my eyes have been upon you since you were a child. In a pack, you're the alpha male. You always take a leadership position. You're always the one out front, leading a charge. You do it naturally. By instinct. You do it because it is who you are. You are of strong opinion, born with the talents of leadership. People automatically follow you. Not because you are of royal blood, but because you stand tall, poised with arrogance and confidence. People follow you because they believe in you. That is why you have the *Calling.*"

Outside the Wigwam, the crowd parted as MedicineGirl and Quillpen made their way toward the doors. Reaching the door, she tried opening it, but found it locked. She pounded on it with her fist and yelled to StormDancer on the other side, "Can I come in?"

StormDancer turned to her and shook his head no. "Please. My mom is in there."

Having heard the pounding on the door and commotion, Chief KnifeWater asked StormDancer, "What's going on?"

"The Beloved Woman's daughter wants in."

"Tell her she has no business here. Tell her to go home. Tell'em all to go home," Hedy ordered.

"No," the Chief said. "This meeting is over. This is a place of business. Time is money. We will not cost the business any more time." The Chief looked at Thunder. "You will come home with me. We will discuss this further as father and son."

"Chief KnifeWater," RiverDawg called out, "may I say one more thing?"

"If you must."

"I must."

"Keep it short."

RiverDawg addressed Thunder. "My son, I know your concerns. Times are changing. Nothing ever remains the same. The spirits brought you forth for just this time. This tribe needs a strong leader who understands the modern game of law and politics. Finish school. The knowledge and understanding will become your weapons. With them you will defend our tribe, and the Tribe will survive another generation."

The Chief, the Beloved Woman, and Thunder exited the building. The crowd parted a path for them. The Chief, Hedy, and MedicineGirl went to the Chief's car. Quillpen Jack and others followed Thunder to his car.

"Hey Thunder, what'd ya do now?" someone called out to him.

"Yeah, Thunder, what's going on?"

Thunder pulled open his car door and turned to the crowd. "No biggy. Someone told the Chief I was dropping out of school. It stirred him up a bit. False information."

"Hey Thunder, speak some law to us, man!" TwoCents called out.

Thunder looked in TwoCents direction. "*Noblesse oblige.* The nobly born must nobly meet his fate."

"That sounded lawyery," Quillpen remarked.

"Greek philosophy, man. I'm not in college just for the party." Thunder got in his car and shut the door. Lowering his window, he said, "Gotta go, man. The Chief isn't done lecturing me. Listening to lectures is what college is all about." Thunder started his car, saluted Quillpen and the crowd with a peace sign, and drove away.

1971

19

PAUL AND JULIA

Spring 1971

P aul Sumner spotted his brother and Valerie crossing the parking lot to Dave's car. Reaching the car
as Dave was backing out, Paul said through the
open window on Dave's side, "Hey man, give me a ride."

Dave eased down on the brake. "Where?"

"Where ya goin'?"

"Wigwam."

"Cool." Paul crawled into the back seat behind
Dave. Shutting the door, eyes settling on Valerie, he
said with a discreet flirt, "Hey, Val."

"Hey, Paul," Valerie returned.

"What's up, Val?"

"Not much, Paul." Valerie's smile was flirtatious.

"We gotta swing by Middle School and pick up
Val's sister," Dave told Paul.

"Finally, I'm going to get to meet little sister?"

With a hint of reservation, Valerie said, "It was destined to happen sooner or later, I suppose."

Julia, seeing Dave's car come into view, rose from the bench. Getting in behind Valerie, her eyes rested on Paul.

With a nod of greeting, Paul said, "Hey."

"Hey," Julia greeted in return, getting settled.

"Julia"—Dave looked at her through the rear-view mirror—"this is my brother, Paul."

Julia made eye contact with Paul again.

Valerie, turning in her seat to face Paul, said, "Meet Julia."

"Nice to finally meet you," Paul told Julia.

Julia smiled. Paul had dreamy eyes like Dave.

Entering the Wigwam, Dave led his group to a table. Sedges Vannhorn was soon there to take orders. She asked Dave and Valerie, "Captured any scarecrows lately?"

"Not lately," Dave answered with good humor.

"I hope to never see another one," Valerie said. "I was never so frightened as that night!"

Sedges looked at Paul. "What's your take on the whole scarecrow monsters?"

Paul shook his head. "I don't know, man. But, what happened to me was real. They're real. We were dragged off into the woods and staked down!"

Captivated, Julia stared at Paul. She believed the

stories. She believed her sister. The whole monster scarecrow invasion on their town was both scary and exciting. It was exciting to listen to the stories and be a part of something supernatural. Nevertheless, it was also scary to think you could be the next victim.

"Were you scared?" Sedges asked Paul.

"Not like Valerie. More like confused. Fearing the unknown. Fearful of what they were going to do next."

"So, in other words, you were scared," Dave pointed out.

Sedges looked at Julia. "What about you? Have you encountered any scarecrows?"

Julia shook her head.

Valerie said, "Once it starts getting dark, she's home behind locked doors."

Julia gave Valerie a disapproving stare. Valerie was always making her appear like a little girl.

Sedges said, "Smart girl."

"You're close to RiverDawg and BootShaker—I mean, StormDancer—what do they think about it all?" Dave asked Sedges.

"RiverDawg isn't saying much. But he takes it seriously. That concerns me. Makes me think there is actually something to fear. StormDancer is nonchalant. He's of the opinion it's more natural than supernatural."

"What do you think?" Valerie asked Sedges.

"I think we should be more like Sunshine. Play it safe and stay behind locked doors." Sedges raised her head at the full room. "What can I get you all?"

After giving orders, Paul pushed his chair back and stood up. "I'm gonna check out the tunes. Any requests?" Paul looked at Valerie.

"Carpenters, please."

Paul turned his eyes to Julia. She shrugged. Paul said, "I'll be back."

"You didn't ask Dave," Valerie taunted.

"That's because, I don't care."

"Maybe, I won't care if you have a ride home," Dave threatened.

Paul ignored the threat, walking away.

After selecting "We've Only Just Begun" for Valerie and his own selections, Paul returned to find his Coke and fries waiting on him.

Dave also had a Coke and fries. Valerie and Julia had malts. Paul, noticing Valerie stealing fries from Dave, offered Julia, "Have some fries." He pushed the order toward her to share.

"Thank you." Julia smiled and took a fry.

Following the Carpenters song came the Who's "Magic Bus." As the song began to play, Paul commented to Julia, "I love this song!"

Julia, sipping her malt and having a fry here and there—'cause they were good and she was hungry—tried not to eat too many. Paul was sociable, well-mannered, and good-natured. Throughout the song, he interacted by singing and drumming to the beat of the song with his two index fingers.

"Magic Bus" was followed by "American Woman"

by the Guess Who. Paul, going into performance mode, interacted with the song. At one point, by happenstance, he looked at Julia. Harmonizing with the vocalist, he sang to her.

Dave said to Julia, "He's into music. Tries to be a singer."

Paul replied, "Rock-and-roll, man! It's my religion."

"He collects albums," Valerie told Julia. "Buys one a week." Interrupting his "performance," Valerie asked, "What album are you buying this week?"

"I thought about Neil Young's *After the Gold Rush*. Critics say it's one of the best albums of the year. But *Led Zeppelin II* seems more appealing." Paul looked at Julia. "You like Zeppelin?"

"I'm not much into hard rock."

"What do you like?"

She wanted to say contemporary concert and symphony, but doubted he'd understand. "The Monkeys, Beach Boys, the Mamas and the Papas, the Carpenters—groups like that."

Paul nodded in polite agreement. "Like the Beatles?"

Julia shrugged. "Some."

"Who's your favorite Beatle?"

Julia shrugged. "George, maybe. I loved the song 'Something.'"

"I'm a John fan, myself. There's none cooler than John." Paul turned to Dave and sang a couple lines from *Instant Karma*.

"I think those words are meant for you," Dave told Paul.

Paul said to Julia, "Older siblings. They're hard to like, but you gotta love 'em. It's like the law or somethin'. Right?"

Julia laughed. Paul was funny. And he did have a voice for singing. "Do you play an instrument?" she asked.

Dave answered, "Are you kidding? He doesn't have the patience. Paul wants to be able to pick up a guitar and start playing like a rock star."

"I can do a mean air-tar," Paul boasted.

"Julia plays an instrument," Valerie told Paul.

"Cool!" Paul shifted his stare to Julia. "Whacha play?"

"The violin."

"She's actually good," Valerie gave as praise.

"Didn't you win in a state competition last year?" Dave asked Julia.

"Placed second."

"Wow!" Paul was impressed.

Julia shrugged. "Second place in my age division."

"Still."

"She's being modest—one of the few areas she is—but she does have a talent for music. She plays the flute too," Valerie said proudly.

"How many albums do you have?" Julia changed the subject.

"Forty or so. I try to buy one a week. I want to have a rock-and-roll library."

"Why?"

Paul shrugged. "'Cause I *love* rock-and-roll. 'Cause it's something to do. I'm looking forward to someday having a room with bookcases, but instead of books, albums. I'll have the best stereo and sound system money can buy. Speakers around the room and in each corner. In the middle of the room, a nice leather recliner so that after a hard day's work I can come home, kick back, space out, and escape reality."

"Instead of buying albums all the time, you could be saving money for a car. Then you wouldn't have to bum rides all the time," Dave challenged.

"I'm saving money towards a ride!" Paul defended. Looking at Julia, he said, "I'm going to buy a hog, man—a motorcycle."

That perked Julia's interest. She had a thing for bikers. "Really?"

"Bikes are cooler than cars. Have you seen the movie *Easy Rider*?"

Julia shook her head.

"That's an 'R'-rated movie. She's too young," Valerie said.

Julia threw her sister another disapproving stare. She hated being only thirteen.

Paul asked Julia, "You ever rode on a motorbike?"

"No."

"When I get mine, I'll give you a ride."

"Can't wait."

"It's a date then."

20

WIELDING OF THE WAND

Flipping through a new magazine, Rita envied the clothes. The look of the seventies was appealing. Colorful. Sexy. Skirts and dresses were super short. Most of her wardrobe was from the fifties. The outfits she had for school were outdated and worn. A couple didn't fit right from her alterations. She was tired of them and felt shame for having to wear them. Practically her entire wardrobe used to belong to her mother. She had done her best with trying to update them and had done a good job considering, but she lacked the true skill and the equipment to do a proper job.

Staring down at the magazine, she was in desperate need for new clothes.

She had never been shopping for new clothes. Her pa surprised her now and then with stuff from his night hunts. However, he hadn't done it in a long time. He hadn't even gone night hunting in a long time. The cold and nasty weather of winter had kept him home.

It had been an oppressive winter. Unbearable at times. A heavy weight of disappointment and frustration suffocating her. Recently, shaving her legs, she cut herself on purpose with the razor. Bleeding brought relief. Releasing the puss of frustration infecting her soul. She had been wanting to do it again, but so far had resisted. Cutting could be scarring, but it was constantly on her mind. Like something she needed to do. A pleasure she needed to have.

A loud snore came from Pa. She glanced at him. She was so tired of Pa.

So tired of the status quo.

However, it had been an interesting few months. Their relationship had changed. More than ever, Pa saw her as the devil's daughter now blossoming into the witch he always knew she was.

Sometimes, he seemed to fear her.

There were times when she feared him. Feared he might set her afire. She sometimes saw the threat in his eyes and the debate on his mind. Pa was crazy and unpredictable. She had been having nightmares about it. It had been a winter for nightmares.

Rita hated Pa. He kept her from having a life. Kept her from Glenn and Paul. Kept her from having dates.

She looked at Pa, wishing he were dead.

He needed to die.

But how would she do it?

Rita's new hobby was learning witchery. Learning how to *wield the wand*. It came natural to her. A hidden talent she had always had, but was unaware of.

She flipped a couple more pages.

She needed new clothes.

Glenn and Paul weren't giving her the attention they used to. More and more they were eyeing girls who were in style and in miniskirts.

She had lost Denny.

She was not gonna lose Glenn and Paul. She was not going to sit idly by and let other girls steal them away. Glenn and Paul were hers.

Spells are weaved in presence and atmosphere— the thought blew across her mind. She wasn't sure how she knew that, but she understood the concept.

Inspired by a dark spirit inside, she put down the magazine. Wasn't she a dark princess, conceived in lust and sin-born? It was time to own it. Like a light coming on, she was a wand to be wielded.

She yielded.

The conjure began with a bath. She hoped Pa would remain asleep. If Pa interrupted the conjure before she was done, the magic would be lost.

After bathing, she misted her body with perfume Pa had brought home to her one night. She put on a pair of dark-colored pantyhose and an old black slip cut into a miniskirt. She finished the conjure with a pair of high-heel knee-high boots.

Looking into the mirror, it was sexy and provoking. The conjure was complete. Of course, on the negative side, the desire provoked in Pa would come with a cost.

She needed new clothes.

She had to do what she had to do for the sake of Glenn and Paul.

Waiting for Pa to wake up, wondering if she should do something to wake him, she heard a peck on the window. It was Johnny. She went out onto the porch.

Johnny asked, "What are you doin'?"

"Nothing."

His eyes flowed down to her boots. And back up, pausing at her chest.

"Like what you see?"

"Huh?" He looked up to make eye contact.

"What are you doing here?"

He shrugged. "Just wanna see you."

"Pa's gonna wake up anytime. Be ready to disappear."

Johnny stepped off the porch and went to the side to be close to the corner of the house. Rita stepped over to where he was. She was on the porch and he was on the ground looking up. She wasn't wearing panties and her pantyhose was see-through. She wondered what he was able to see. By his line of sight, he was seeing something or trying to. The little pervert. Men were so predictable. And easy to cast spells on.

Homer woke up from one of his loud snores. He wasn't sure how long he had been sleeping.

Reaching for his bottle, he looked about, making himself aware of his environment. He yawned and took a sip of whiskey.

He grabbed a cigarette and lit it.

He heard talking.

Outside.

He got up.

Opening the door and stepping outside, Rita was standing at the edge of the porch. Suspiciously, he demanded, "What's going on? Who you talking to?"

Rita turned his way. "No one, Pa. Just talking to myself."

He looked about the yard. He didn't see anyone. He looked at Rita. "Whacha doin' out here?"

"Nothing. Enjoying the warm night. I'm so glad winter is over and spring is come. So glad it is back to being warm again. It makes me want to get out and do something."

She was smiling. She acted happy. She wasn't normally like that. He looked her up and down.

She asked, "How about you, Pa? Does the warm air make you want to get out and do something? You ain't been hunting in such a long time. I bet you're glad it's getting warm again so you can enjoy the night and go hunting again."

"Why are you dressed like that?"

Rita shrugged. "I just wanted to look pretty tonight, is all. I was looking in my magazine at the way girls were dressing now'days." She moved into a flirtatious stance. "I wanted to be pretty too."

"I'll show you," she said, stepping around him and going back inside. She was wearing perfume.

He followed her in.

She went over to the sofa and bent over to pick up a magazine. Her slip-dress rose above her buttocks. Holding the magazine, she turned to him. "See." She stepped over to show him pictures of women in miniskirts and boots.

"I wish I had some new dresses, so I could look pretty like this." She moved in closer. "Pa, would you like to see me in some new dresses so I could look pretty too?" She pressed herself against his hardened rod.

Homer understood it was to get something she wanted. It was good business. A balanced trade-off. He accepted and turning her around, dropping his pants, he bent her over.

21

THE BURNING OF A SCARECROW

P a had gone night hunting. It was liberating. Rita could breathe. She hadn't been able to breathe in such a long time. And even better, Pa promised her new clothes. She felt happy for the first time in a long time. The music on the radio was music to her soul.

A tapping on the window drew her attention to Johnny outside looking in. She grabbed a cold beer and went outside. The air was cool and refreshing. The moon crescent. Sitting on the edge of the porch, they made conversation sharing the beer. Her cheerful mood, heightened by the beer, prompted her to want to dance.

She stepped from the porch into the yard and began swaying and moving to the distant sound of music coming from inside. Johnny, finishing the beer, sat watching her.

"Dance with me." She grabbed at Johnny's hands.

Johnny pulled away. "I'm not dancing. Dancing is stupid. Dancing is for girls."

Sashaying about in front of him, "Be stupid with me." She reached for his hands again.

"No." He pulled them from her grasp.

She stopped and stood before him as a dark shadowy figure. The bright moon behind her sat like a glowing crown of horns on top of her head. Luminous strands of blond hair slithered and flowed about in a dance of their own. She looked like a silhouette. Like a shadow.

The shadow said, "Dance with me and I'll let you touch me."

After dancing and frolicking about for a while, Rita said, "We need more beer." Johnny watched the motion of her hips as she walked away.

Rita returned with a beer. Her blouse was completely unbuttoned. Shocked and staring, he saw she wasn't wearing a bra, but the blouse adequately covered her breasts. Johnny couldn't see anything.

Seated on the edge of the back porch, taking turns taking drinks, Johnny sometimes caught glimpses of Rita's breasts as she moved about.

"It's getting late," she announced, sounding disappointed.

Johnny, feeling lightheaded, took another sip. Rita pulled the beer from his hand, setting it aside. She said, "Give me your hand." She took his hand and placed it on a breast. Letting go, leaving his hand on her breast, she placed a hand on his thigh with a tender massage. "Thanks for coming over tonight. Thanks for dancing with me. I had fun."

His hand was on her breast, but he didn't know what he was supposed to do.

Staring out across the yard toward the woods, she said, "I hate my pa. I wish he were dead." She inched her massage higher on his thigh.

After a moment of silence, she said, "If Pa were dead, you'd come over any time you wanted and we could be free to have fun and do whatever we wanted." She moved her massage next to the bulge in his pants. "You and Betty could come over and spend the night. We could all sleep together in the same bed. It would be fun."

After another moment of silence, "I so wish he was dead."

She placed her hand on his bulge, and squeezed. She turned to look at him. "We have school tomorrow. I need to go to bed. You need to get home." With another hard squeeze, she leaned forward and kissed his lips. Pulling her hand away and pulling his hand off her breast, she scooted away, picked up the beer, and stood.

"Go home." She opened the back door, entered the house, and closed the door.

Johnny stood. He felt woozy. He went to her bedroom window and watched her change into sleepwear. She flipped off the light, crawled into bed, and covered up.

Rita was all he ever thought about anymore.

He wished the monster was dead too.

Seated in a chair in the room where Veggy was kept, Scarecrow Homer watched his friend have another spell of coughing, gurgling, and gagging. His friend wasn't doing well.

Not well at all.

The only light in the room was a candle sitting on top of a dresser. Homer hadn't wanted to turn on any lights. A candle was less likely to draw attention. Next to the door, sitting on the floor, was a sack containing a couple of dresses, a nightgown, and a pair of heels Homer had taken from June's closet.

Veggy coughed and gurgled again.

Homer hadn't visited his friend in weeks. The winter had been cold and nasty. The cold made his body ache. Made his face hurt.

Winter was depressing times.

Spring was a relief. It brought life back to the world. To Homer too. He was ready to get out and have some good times with his friends again.

Some whiskey drinking and philosophizing times.

Some scarecrow times.

Some nightmare gift-giving times to the we're-so-much-better-than-you citizens of the surrounding community. Showering people with gifts of terror was fun.

Good times.

He, Veggy, and Mr. Scarecrow were the talk of the town.

"Remember Halloween night?" Homer made conversation with Veggy. Homer had made Veggy into a scarecrow and had taken him and Mr. Straw Head into town for Halloween. Homer noticed the scarecrow theme was a popular costume. "Would you look at that, boys," Mr. Scarecrow announced. "They love us."

Finding the right place, Homer carried Scarecrow Veggy and laid him on the ground next to a sidewalk. Homer mounted Mr. Straw Head nearby in a way that whoever came across Veggy was more than likely to look up to see Mr. Straw Head standing nearby and looking their way.

It happened like Homer anticipated. A group of teens walking along saw Veggy on the ground.

"Look," one pointed. "What's that?"

Three boys, two girls, all in costumes ... ventured closer. Someone said, "It looks like a scarecrow."

They stopped next to Veggy. Pirate Boy said, "It looks real."

Sexy Cat Girl said, "I don't like this, let's get out of here!"

The vampire said in an attempt at a joke, "Don't be such a scaredy cat."

One of the boys, dressed as a scarecrow himself, bent forward to poke Veggy. About that time Wizard of Oz Dorothy, seeing Mr. Straw Head, raised an arm and pointed. "Look."

When poked, Veggy opened his eyes and grunted.

As they all screamed, Homer jumped from hiding and charged forth, growling.

Sexy Cat Girl fainted. The others, scattering, couldn't run fast enough.

Homer quickly got Veggy and Mr. Straw Head to the truck, laying them in the back. He would have liked to play with Sexy Cat Girl, but feared the risk. For all he knew, she could have been dead.

Homer chuckled at the memory.

Good times indeed.

Veggy went into another coughing, gurgling, and gagging spell.

Homer took a drink of whiskey.

Veggy looked weak. Too weak to survive. He wasn't even aware of Homer's presence.

Homer had brought Mr. Straw Head with him and mounted him against the bedpost at the foot of the bed looking down on Veggy.

Homer hoped for a fun visit with Veggy. The three of them drinking, talking, and sharing memories.

Him, Veggy, and Mr. Straw Head—what a trio. What a crazy, wild freak show of a trio they were.

People looked at men like them with disdain. They were outcasts. Voted out by popular demand. Seen as monsters and freaks. Unworthy of social interaction with the pretty, healthy, and wealthy "good" people of the community. It was even a wonder Homer and his good friends weren't hunted down and killed.

He took a drink of whiskey.

A wind of hate and anger blew across his soul.

His best friend was dying.

Dying from too much neglect.

The room stank of urine and death mingled together. Homer believed it was pneumonia killing his dear friend. His lips were blue; every breath was a struggle.

A pharmacy of meds littered the nightstand next to the bed.

It had been a bad and lonely winter for his friend. Homer felt angry with himself for not visiting him more often. Not being around to take care of him.

Homer took another drink of whiskey to drown the pain.

The real villain in this scenario was Veggy's wife. The whore!

Homer hated women. All he ever wanted was to be loved, touched, and desired.

Women thought only of themselves. Engrossed in their desires and wants. They only "loved" men for what they could pilfer from them. To a woman, a man was a purse. Overall, Rita was no different.

Veggy's wife didn't love Veggy. He was no longer of use to her. No longer could he give her things. Make a living for her to spend. He was useless to her now.

A burden.

And she was letting Veggy die. She probably wanted him to die. Was probably aiding in his death.

Hate and despair simmered inside Homer.

Veggy was dying a hard suffering death. He didn't deserve to die this way.

His wife did, though.

She deserved to be beaten to death. Homer considered allowing the anger and hate to warm his bones like the whiskey he was drinking.

Homer gulped his whiskey.

God didn't want Homer to be happy.Didn't want him to have friends.

No sir.

Not good ole Homer.

Veggy went into another fit.

Homer stood and stepped over to the bed. His good friend's head was hot with fever. No telling how long he'd had the fever. No doubt, his brain was fried.

Homer looked at the clock. Veggy's wife was getting off work. She'd soon be home.

Homer, picking up the bottles of meds, read what they were. He stuffed three bottles into his pocket.

Homer pulled the pillow from underneath Veggy's head. He was too good of a friend to let Veggy suffer any longer.

Homer placed the pillow over Veggy's face. As he kept it there, the life leaving Veggy fed the violent storm of hate and hurt whirling inside his soul.

Homer heard someone entering the house.

Homer continued to press the pillow on Veggy's face.

From behind, "What the ..." Veggy's wife said

entering the room. "What's going on? Who are you … ?"

Homer let go of the pillow and turned.

June saw a scarecrow killing her husband. She let out a bloodcurdling scream, piercing through Homer's ears and into his brain. A violent wind exploded across his soul as he surrendered to the demonic within!

With lightning speed, he charged forth with hate beyond understanding, punching June in the mouth, breaking teeth and bone. It silenced her as she was knocked back against a wall. Grabbing the shocked and dazed woman, he bashed his fist into the side of her head. Swinging her around, he threw her violently into the dresser with the candle, knocking the dresser over.

June lay on the floor next to the dresser. Homer stared down at her. What a dog! Homer kicked her in the gut. Kicked her in the head. Bending down, he took ahold of her to pull her to her feet. She was lifeless.

Unconscious.

That made the demon mad. It wanted to feed on her fear and pain. From Homer's mouth came a fury of demonic growls.

The demon bit into June's throat. Homer tasted the warm blood spurting in his throat.

Demonic Homer, grabbing a fistful of hair, yanked it from her scalp. He threw her across the bed, knocking Veggy off onto the floor.

Demonic Homer jumped onto the bed and off, landing on top of June. He began violently pounding her face.

It wasn't the physical damage of pounding a human's face into mush that was bringing pleasure to the demon, it was the destroying of life! The life being pounded out of June was addictively sweet and intoxicating. If a demon could have a truly rapturous experience, this was it.

However, for demons, there were no such things as joy and satisfaction. Only an eternal pain of starvation for such feelings. This whole experience, as sweet as it promised to be, was no more satisfying than what a droplet of water would be to a parched man dying of thirst in a desert. In fact, it was more torturous than pleasing. It all served to make the demon's hate much greater and the emptiness more hollow. Punch after punch after hate-filled punch.

Finally Homer stopped.

He stood.

Able to put thoughts together again, he stared down at the unrecognizable bloody mess.

He didn't remember doing it.

Realizing the room was on fire, Homer grabbed the sack next to the door and ran.

22

BLOSSOMING

Crawling out of bed to begin the new day, Rita looked her wardrobe over. It was limited and depressing. She would decide later. Leaving the bedroom, Pa, half-naked, was asleep in his chair. A whiskey bottle lying in his lap.

She faked a cough. No response.

She did it again—louder.

Nothing.

He was passed out. She wished he were dead.

In the kitchen there was a sack on the table. Looking into it, it was clothes. Two dresses—a black one and a red one. There was also a nightgown and a pair of heels. A tiny bottle of perfume. She picked up the perfume. *Midnight Pleasure.* She raised it to her nose. She liked it.

Unfolding the dresses, they were cocktail dresses. They weren't new, but they were up-to-date and stylish. She tried on the red one. It felt loose on her.

The relaxed pleat stopped inches above the knee. Whoever owned the dress was probably shorter and perhaps a little heavier. It would be an easy fix.

She held up the black dress. A little different from the red dress. The dresses were paint-the-town dresses.

She would wear the red one today.

The heels were roomy, but she could wear them.

This was exciting. Her spell had worked!

Also on the table were bottles of pills. She picked one up. It was a painkiller. The name of whom the prescription belonged to had been scratched off. Another bottle was for infection. The third bottle was for sleeping. It was open. One of the pills on the table beside it. Pa must have taken one.

She went back into the living room. "Pa?" she said. There was no response. She went over to him. She reached out and with a gentle shake, "Pa?" No reaction. He was still breathing. She frowned. Shaking him harder, "Pa!" she said louder. No response.

Back in the kitchen, she tapped a sleeping pill into her hand. She would hide these. They might come in handy. She took a few of the painkillers too. She took the three bottles and put them into a cabinet out of sight. If she were lucky, Pa wouldn't remember them.

She went to get ready for school.

Hearing the school bus honk down the road at

the Brandts' house, Rita grabbed her things. She paused beside her pa. "Going to school."

No response.

She shoved on his head.

No response.

She pinched his nose closed. His mouth fell open with a gasping-like snore, but slept on. It amazed her.

Rita was standing at the road when the bus stopped. Climbing aboard, she took her normal seat beside Betty Brandt.

"Wow. New outfit?" Betty asked.

"Yeah. I think someone gave it to my pa."

"You look pretty today," Nancy Dayton said.

"Thank you," Rita told her.

Johnny moved from the back of the bus to a seat across the aisle from Rita and Betty. Nick Dayton followed. Rita looked into Johnny's eyes; she wanted to know his thoughts. Reading people's eyes, knowing the thoughts beyond, came natural. A skill she'd developed over the span of her life because of her pa's scarred face. His face being unreadable, she had come to know his thoughts by expressions in his eyes. In her world, being able to read eyes was a skill of survival.

Johnny looked her over. He looked down at her legs and boots. She'd decided on the boots instead of the new heels. He looked back up, eyes filled with lust. "Is that one of your dead mom's dresses?"

Johnny's eyes revealed jealousy and insecurity.

He disapproved—not because he didn't like what he was seeing, but because he didn't want anyone else liking what he was seeing.

"Johnny!" Betty scolded. "You don't say things like that!"

"Shut up, Retardo," Johnny told Betty.

Rita said to Betty, "It's fine." Turning to Johnny, she said, "What if it is. What's it to you?"

"It makes you look like a whore."

"So, you like it then. Huh?"

Getting off the bus, Rita and Betty entered the school together before parting ways. Rita headed to the place where she, Paul and Glenn met every morning. Traveling the hall, Rita noted the turning of heads and approving stares guys were giving her. The boots, tight on her feet, would soon be hurting, but the attention was worth it.

Reaching Paul, Glenn, and Wally, she strategically passed between them before coming to a stop. She wanted them to smell the new perfume.

"Wow!" Paul spoke first. "Look at you. New dress?"

"Yeah. Like?"

"Hot."

Rita smiled. Objective met. She looked at Glenn. The look in his eyes was lust. Wally liked it too. Rita asked, "What are we discussing this morning?"

"The fire!" Glenn was quick to seize her attention.

"Fire?" Rita's stare turned his way.

"A couple of miles or so from where we live as the crow flies, a house fire killed two people," Glenn answered.

"Oh my," Rita said, not out of real concern, but for social acceptance. There were rules for social acceptance. She wanted to be accepted and have friends. "Who was it?" Not that she would know them, but it showed interest.

"The Huschins. Know 'em?" Glenn asked. "A woman and her paralyzed husband."

Rita shook her head. "Her husband was paralyzed?"

"She was probably trying to rescue him," Wally added.

Rita glanced his way, making eye contact.

"That's not all," Paul yearning for her attention. "The rumor is that scarecrows were involved!"

"Scarecrows?" Rita's eyes touched Paul's.

"Yeah, they found the remains of a partially burned scarecrow in the same room as the bodies!"

"Wow."

"I know, right?"

"It's the talk of the town," Glenn reclaiming her attention.

"It's become a serious matter," Wally chimed in.

"The scarecrows are now killing people!" Paul exclaimed, grabbing back her attention.

"Guess I'll have to keep a closer eye on your house from now on," Glenn upped the contest with a comforting touch on her bare upper arm to recapture her attention.

"You do that," Rita encouraged Glenn with a smile of flirtation.

Paul stepped closer to Rita. "You smell good. New perfume?"

"*Midnight Pleasure.*"

"It pleasures me," Paul countering Glenn's move.

A whistle of approval came from a group of varsity football jocks passing by looking Rita over. Rita looked their way. The flirtatious smile and the twinkle of excitement dancing in Rita's eyes was concerning. Until now, Rita had belonged to Paul and Glenn. Others weren't interested in the backward, socially challenged "hill" girl who was somewhat weird. A girl with old, worn, and outdated clothes. But today, their diamond in the rough had been discovered. Their Rita had blossomed. The new look catapulted her into a new social status. She was no longer someone to ignore.

The game had changed.

Going to class, people were looking her over. Even the male teachers weren't immune. Rita found it exciting. Paul and Glenn traveled beside her, being extra-attentive. Extra-protective. Reaching her first class, she said bye to her escorts and entered.

Eyes, locking on her, followed her to her seat. Taking a seat, her dress rising up, displayed even more thigh. She could have adjusted it, pulled it down some, but didn't. She crossed one leg over the other.

In the past, when people took notice of her, it was a look of indifference or negative. In the past, it seemed safer not to be seen. Today, the looks were lingering lustful ones.

She liked it!

Rita understood that certain outfits held seductive powers, but she had never experienced the magic on such a large scale before. The lustful gawkings were intoxicating, creating a warm titillating stirring inside.

She wanted to give the audience more, but there was a balance to maintain.

Paul Sumner could hardly wait for his second-period class. He and Rita had it together. Anxiously, he hurried to make an exchange at his locker, wanting to meet Rita at hers and walk with her to class. Hurrying to her locker, he found an upperclassman standing at her locker talking with her.

She was enjoying it.

That was bothersome.

Paul stepped up beside her. Rita continued giving the upperclassmen her attention.

That was upsetting.

The senior said, "Hey," to Paul.

Rita told the guy, "Gotta go."

"Talk to you later." The guy hurried off.

Walking Rita to class, Paul asked, "What did he want?"

"We were talking."

"About what?" Paul tried not to sound insecure.

"Nothing in particular."

"Did he ask you out?"

"Out?"

"You know, like on a date?"

"No." She made eye contact. "He asked me if I liked basketball. I told him I didn't know. He said I should attend the game this week."

"What did you say?"

"I said I'd think about it."

"Your dad's not gonna let you go to the game," Paul hopefully stated.

"I know that."

Paul fought to be cool and not appear threatened by the looks, smiles, and stares guys gave Rita during class. He was disturbed by how much she liked the attention. Rita was his and Glenn's girlfriend of sorts. There had never been anything official, just a claim. He and Glenn shared her. Not a politically correct thing. Not something society accepted. It was rebel. It was fun and sexy.

Paul did not want to share Rita with the world.

By end of class, Paul decided Rita needed to be taken out of this environment and away from the competition. Escorting her to her locker, he asked, "You want to skip the rest of the day?"

"Skip?"

"Skip school. Take a day off. Go and have fun."

"I've never done that before."

"There's a first time for everything."

"How does it work? What would we do?"

"We walk out the door and leave."

"Where would we go?"

"Where do you want to go?"

"I don't know."

Paul begged Kalvin, "Seriously, man, let me borrow your bike!"

Kalvin shook his head. "You don't have a license. You're not sixteen yet, man."

"Come on, man! I'll soon be. You know I know how to ride. I've rode your bike many times."

"Only checking it out. Only for a few minutes here and there."

"I know what I'm doing, man. You know that."

"Do you know how much trouble I could get into if you had a wreck and someone got hurt?"

"I'll be careful. No stupid stuff. You have my word."

"Still."

"If something happens, say that I took it without asking."

"You mean like you stole it?"

"Fine."

"I don't know, man. It's risky."

"Cut me a break, man." With a head gesture, Paul directed his attention to Rita standing nearby, waiting.

Kalvin looked Rita's way. He looked her over. He said, "I'm feelin' ya."

"What will it take?"

"I thought you were going to buy it off me?"

"I am. I'm saving money toward it."

"How much you got?"

"'Bout a hundred." Paul had more, but didn't want Kalvin to know.

"Give me a thirty-dollar down payment."

"I don't have thirty dollars on me."

"Bring it to me tomorrow and I'll let you have the bike till midnight tonight."

"Seriously?"

"You want it or not? I'm taking a big risk here."

"Fine."

"I'm going to walk away and not realize the key fell out of my pocket."

Kalvin began walking away. Paul stepped over to Rita.

"Well?" Rita asked.

Watching Kalvin, a key fell from his pocket. Paul told Rita, "We steal it."

"What?"

Paul took Rita's hand. Picking the key up off the floor, Paul gave Rita a wink.

"We're just going to take his bike?"

"We are."

Standing next to the motorcycle, Paul handed Rita the helmet. "Put this on." He got on the bike.

"We are really going to do this?"

"We are!" Paul started it. Once Rita had the helmet on, she climbed on behind him.

Driving away from the school, Paul asked above the noise of the bike, "Where you want to go?"

Rita leaned forward, getting as close as possible to his ear. Trying to speak seductively, "Can we go to Springfield?" Squeezing her arms around his waist, emphasizing desire, "I want to visit a plaza?"

"Sure."

Paul felt a sucking kiss on the back of his neck.

In Springfield, Paul decided on an early lunch. "Where would you like to eat?"

After a thoughtful moment, she answered, "Burger King."

Inside the Burger King, Rita didn't know what to do. She had never been to a place like this before. Paul explained how it worked. After getting their food, Rita picked the place she wanted to sit. Beaming with excitement and delight, her enthusiasm was that of a child. It was endearing. Her delight honored Paul, making him proud to be doing this for her.

Rita swallowed her first bite. Paul asked, "Well, what do you think?"

"It's different. Not really what I had expected. But, I think I like it." She glanced around the room. "It's all so clean, fast, and convenient."

"Welcome to modern America and factory dining."

"Factory dining?"

"This is a manufactured assembly-line meal. Fast

food. Nothing is custom. A process of duplication. Every burger is the same."

"What do you mean?"

"That Whopper you are eating wasn't so much made as it was created. Scientifically. By a team of experts. Every time you order that burger, it will taste just like that. Right now, in New York City, someone is eating a Whopper and it looks and tastes just like the one you are eating."

"Wow. That's amazing!"

"We live in an amazing time."

A few bites later, Paul asked, "What made you want to eat here?"

"Advertisements on the radio. *Hold the pickles, Hold the lettuce, special orders don't upset us. All we ask is that you let us serve it your way.* It sounded like a fun place to eat. Warm and friendly. Ya know, *have it your way*. I wanted to know how that would feel."

Paul marveled at her. She was such a contradiction. Ignorant and naive about so many things, yet so smart and so knowledgeable about other things. He said, "I can't believe you've never ate out before."

"Pa won't consider it."

"So you always cook?"

"Always."

"Wow." Paul watched her eat a fry. "Whatcha think about the fries?"

"I don't know. I think I prefer crispy fried potatoes."

"Fast-food is quick and convenient, but it doesn't compare to a good home-cooked customized meal."

Finishing his burger, Paul said, "You'll have to cook for me sometime."

"I would love to."

"It's a date, then. Someday."

Rita's smile was laced with flirtation.

After a little bit, Rita asked, "Is this like being on a date?"

The question surprised Paul. Her eyes revealed the question was sincere and heartfelt. "Exactly," he answered. Sometimes Rita seemed so innocent and vulnerable. Like she needed to be guarded and protected.

Paul said, "A typical date is when a guy asks a girl out to go and do something. To spend time together. To have some fun. Generally, they'll start out having dinner of some sorts. Then go and do something fun. And usually, before the date ends, there will be a time of intimacy—ya know like making out."

"I would love to be able to date." Her eyes suddenly went dark and stormy. In bitterness, she said, "I hate my pa. I wish he were dead. He won't let me do anything. I'm like a prisoner."

Paul, taken aback by the wicked tone in her voice, pushed it aside. He said, "Ya know, we are like being on a date right now. I mean, I did ask you out when I asked you to skip school with me. And we are having dinner. Therefore, my dear, would you honor me in making this your first real date? Like the commercial says, *You can have it your way!*"

The stormy countenance on her face switched to a sunny childlike expression. "Really? We could do that? We can be on a date?" She paused. "You would want to date me? Am I good enough?"

He couldn't believe she would ask such a question. Her stare was intense and probing. He said, "Yes. Rita, if your dad would let you, I would date you all the time."

"I would love for this to be my first date."

"It's done. Welcome to your first date!"

Leaving Burger King, they went in search of a plaza. It didn't take long. Parking and getting off the bike, Paul, slipping an arm around her waist, "Well sexy lady, where would you like to go?"

Rita looked at her options. There were a dozen stores in front of her. She was excited. One store in particular grabbed her attention. It had the *Eternity Tree* image on its sign. Rita pointed. "I would like to go there, Trendy Eve Boutique."

Inside Paul, following Rita, was astonished with her childlike enthusiasm. She was hardly able to contain herself with all there was to see, touch, and feel. He now believed her when she had told him she had never been shopping.

Trendy Eve Boutique was like no other store Paul had ever been in. It was mostly a clothing store, but the clothes were not traditional. Most were very stylish, hip, modern, and sexy. Some were fantasy-theme oriented and inspired. A lot of the apparel was Celtic and witch-like.

Rita went from one outfit to another, from one rack to another.

The store was dark, but had ample lighting. The woman attending the store was attractive and looked college age. Her hair was long and the color of rust. Irish, maybe. She had dark eye makeup and black lips. A black-lacy tight-fitting blouse with detached bell sleeves and a "V" neckline drew one's attention to her bust. Dangling above her cleavage was a necklace displaying what looked to Paul like an Egyptian symbol.

Most of the jewelry and accessories Paul was seeing were cultic, gothic, fantasy, and New Age related. There were a variety of crystals, amulets, pentagrams, and dragons in various forms of jewelry. About the store were displays of table sculptures, paintings, and other items of decoration. All of it relating to the occult, mysticism, and the supernatural.

Paul, looking toward the saleslady again, found her expression pleasant, but her persona intimidating. The entire store was intimidating. Paul didn't feel comfortable being there.

Rita seemed completely oblivious to what kind of store it was. Thinking perhaps she lacked understanding, he quietly said, "Rita."

She interrupted him: "Do you like this?" She pulled an outfit out for him to see.

The dress was short, sexy, and witchy looking. "Yeah, I guess. Rita, do you know what kind of store this is?"

Rita, pushing the dress back in place, ventured to another. "Whatcha mean?"

Whispering he said, "This is a store for witches and devil worshippers."

She glanced at him. "Yes, I know." Taking a step toward him, she kissed him on the cheek. "Thanks for bringing me." She went back to looking.

Paul stared at her in disbelief. He did not expect that. He glanced at the Irish "witch" saleslady. She grinned. Goose bumps popped up on Paul's flesh.

Rita, flipping through a rack of dresses, "Don't you just LOVE these clothes?"

"They're cool."

"If I could, I'd buy them all! I'd love to own a store like this."

"Do you have money?"

It was the wrong question. The joy and wonder beaming from her instantly stopped. Reality gave her a cold slap across her face. "No." She respectfully pushed a dress back in place. "I never have money. I wouldn't know what that was." She stepped over to another rack.

Examining the rack, she whispered, "I hate Pa. I wish him dead."

Paul wished he hadn't said anything. The experience was no longer fun. The dream dead. Destroyed by the dragon of reality. Paul felt bad. It was his fault.

No way could they leave here without her getting something. That was the joy of shopping. Her first date, her first shopping experience, especially with him, needed to be a positive one. He would have to be "chivalry." He didn't have much cash, but he did have a check in his wallet. A check in case of an emergency. This was as good of a reason as any to use it.

Paul spoke softly in Rita's ear: "You're in luck. You are my date. Dates are entitled to a gift. Pick out something and I'll buy it for you."

Rita turned and peered into his eyes. "Really? You would do that for me? You have money?"

"It would be my pleasure. And yes, I have money."

Like sunshine bursting through a cloudy sky, joy spread across her face. She took a moment to give him a sultry kiss.

Now she was on a mission!

A short time later, Rita pulled an outfit from one of the racks. She held it up. "I like this." She put it up against her body as to get a visual. "Do you like it?"

It was a black dress. It had sex appeal. Paul tried to visualize it. "It looks good."

"Would you like to try it on?" The Irish witch was next to them.

"Really? Could I?"

"I think you should. There's a dressing room over there," she pointed. "Follow me."

Rita looked at Paul for permission. He nodded.

Rita followed. Paul too. After Rita disappeared

into the little cubicle, Paul bided his time looking at the witchy paintings mounted on the nearby wall. The salesperson remained nearby, but kept her distance.

Rita stepped out. Directing her question to Paul, "What you think?"

Sleeveless, thin, and sophisticated, the top of the dress lay just above her breasts and was held up by thin straps going over her shoulders. The dress gave accent to her breasts. It was a dress to be worn without a bra. Rita had understood that. It wasn't see-through, but it was revealing. It was arousing.

The bottom half was chiffon, Gypsy-like, and below the hips it was see-through. It had an asymmetrical hem and was short in spots and longer in others. It had Celtic characteristics and was something a witch would wear, but it wasn't so obvious as to being that type of dress. A witch look would come from added accessories.

"It's spellbinding on you!" the Irish woman stated.

"Really? You think so?"

"Oh Honey, with your body and looks, you'll work magic in this dress. It was made for you."

Rita looked at Paul. He was already caught in its spell. Rita did a spin, feeling beautiful and empowered.

The boutique witch, stepping up to Rita, ran fingers through Rita's hair, fixing it into a sultrier look.

She said, "You need to bleach your hair. It would enhance the magic. And bright red lips."

"You think?"

"I know."

Paul watched the witch walk a circle around Rita, taking in her looks and the look of the dress on her. As she was doing it, the lady asked Rita, "Are you a Wiccan?"

Rita's expression showed she didn't understand.

"A student of the Craft? A witch," she explained.

"I am a witch," Rita announced matter-of-factly.

That shocked Paul and he wondered, where did that come from?

"Have you had training? Do you belong to any traditions or covens?"

"No."

"Who do you follow?"

"What do you mean?"

"Are you into the teachings of Gardner? Alex Sanders? Or maybe Crowley? Sybil Leek? Have you heard of Ann Gallagher?"

To all these, Rita shook her head.

"You must be an eclectic Wiccan," the lady determined.

"An eclectic Wiccan?" Rita asked.

"A solitary practitioner. It means you don't follow any single teachings or traditions. You're creating your spiritual path. Are you new to the Craft?"

"As a practitioner," Rita said. "But I was born a witch."

Paul was already shocked and lost by the whole conversation, but Rita's last proclamation even surprised the boutique witch.

The witch asked, "Do you have a spirit guide?"

"A spirit guide?"

"A spirit from the world beyond that helps you. Empowers you. Gives you guidance as it were."

"I don't think so."

"This dress requires a necklace. Come," the saleslady ordered.

Rita followed her to a display case.

"Pick out a necklace."

Paul, trailing, didn't know what to think. The whole thing flabbergasted him. Did he even know Rita at all? Where did the backward, naive, vulnerable girl who needed protecting go? The girl he wanted to take care of and protect. Paul watched Rita look over the selection of jewelry, asking the witch lady questions about pieces.

How was Rita—shy, backwards, and lacking in self-confidence—at the same time flaunting, aggressive, and intimidating? Rita was baffling. A challenge. Paul had spent the day thinking he was in charge.

But was he?

Had Rita been in charge the whole time? With Rita, you could never truly tell. She had a gift of always getting what she wanted, but it was always your idea.

Rita was a puzzle he couldn't figure out. When

he was away from her, she was on his mind. In her presence, he was lost in the fog of her presence.

Perhaps she was a witch. Perhaps this was what a witch was.

While Rita and the boutique witch discussed jewelry, Paul's eyes fell upon a nearby display of rock albums for sale. He stepped over for a closer look. It was a small collection of very specific groups: Black Sabbath's *We Sold Our Souls for Rock 'n' Roll*, Led Zeppelin, Blue Oyster Cult, The Beatles' *Sgt. Pepper*, the Rolling Stones' *Their Satanic Majesties Request*, the Doors, Lucifer Rising, Mousike, House of Boleskine, and others. One album grabbing Paul's attention, because of the cover, was the album *Holy Prostitute* by a group called Minstrels of Pan. It looked like an oil painting displaying a beautiful lady, naked and lying on an altar. Paul wanted to buy it—if nothing else, just for the cover. He fought off the temptation, picking up the Rolling Stones album. He didn't own the album, but had heard some of it.

Paul watched the saleslady get into the display case and pull out a necklace. Rita turned to face Paul as the lady put it around her neck to fasten it. Rita gave him an excited little-girl smile.

Rita asked Paul, "How does it look?"

The necklace was two silver circle rings with writing on them. One circle was bigger than the other, the smaller circle set inside the larger. It looked good and went well with the outfit. Paul nodded. "What's it say?"

The saleslady answered, "It's an Irish blessing: *'May God grant you always a sunbeam to warm you, a moonbeam to charm you, a sheltering angel so nothing can harm you.'*"

"Don't you love it?" Rita asked him.

"It's nice."

"Can I have the necklace to go with the dress? Is it too much to ask?"

Paul looked at the saleslady. "How much are we talking?"

"For the dress and necklace, less than thirty dollars."

"Oh my!" Rita's smile faded. "That's way too much, isn't it?"

It was the expression taking over her face—an expression of, *it's out of my reach. I'm not good enough for something so nice and pretty.* It was far more than what Paul wanted to pay, but how could he deny her? The Celtic witch was right. Rita was enchanting in the dress. "Like I said earlier, you can have it your way. I can afford it. I have a job."

"Really!" In a joyful skip toward him, "You are so wonderful!" Placing hands on the sides of his face, she pressed lips against his. After a French kiss, "Thank you so much."

Looking at how the dress gave reveal to her breasts, "My pleasure. Really."

Rita, turning back to the saleslady, said, "Isn't he wonderful?"

The lady grinned and said, "The outfit comes

with detached sleeves as well." She held them out. "Try 'em on."

Rita took one, pulling the elastic part of the airy chiffon bell sleeves up past her elbow. She did the same with the other. Stretching out her arms side to side, forming a cross, the end of the sleeves hung down at least a foot.

Before Paul, Rita the witch stood.

"Stunning!" the Celtic lady stated. "Can I help you with anything else?"

"Better stop here," Rita told her in a delightful tone.

The saleslady looked at Paul. "Shall I ring it up?"

Reluctantly, Paul nodded, stepping forward to the counter with the Rolling Stones' *Their Satanic Majesties Request* album he decided to buy.

Rita asked, "Can I keep it on?"

Paul lusting her over, "Definitely."

The saleslady took the check and put it away. She walked around the counter with a pair of scissors and removed the tags. "I'll put your other dress in a bag."

"Thank you. That is so nice of you," Rita told her.

The lady left for the dressing room. Returning and

before handing Rita the bag, "Here's a special gift for you." The boutique witch stuck a book in the bag.

Leaving the Trendy Eve Boutique, Paul and Rita

headed back to NuSprings. Once in NuSprings and too early to take Rita home, Paul decided on the city park. He entered the park on the back side.

The back side of the park, the south side of the lake, was forest, woods, and trails. A park road running through the forest led to isolated and private picnic sites along the bluff above the lake. The picnic sites were rustic and consisted of a picnic table, an iron grill, and a view of the lake, and most of the sites had a trail leading down to the water.

Standing near a picnic table and looking out across the lake and the park beyond, Rita asked, "So these are the places where guys take girls for parking and making out?"

"It is." Paul stared at Rita as she stared out across the lake taking in the view. The thin, see-through, asymmetrical gypsy hem danced upon the breezes, making it even more eye-catching and revealing. With the boots and the detached sleeves, she looked very much like a witch. It was a hot look. Paul wasn't sure how he felt about it, but right now, he was too turned on to care. "Shall we walk down to the lake?"

Rita making eye contact, "You're the boss."

Paul led Rita down to the lake's edge. One of the reasons this was Paul's favorite picnic site was the wooden bench near the water's edge. A very secluded spot and great for making out.

"Milady." Paul swung his arm out, offering Rita a seat on the bench.

Rita, taking a seat, smiled. Paul sat down beside

her. She looked out across the lake and on the other side, seeing the concrete teepees, she said, "I would like to visit those teepees some time."

"It can be arranged." Putting an arm around her, Paul leaned forward with a kiss, placing a hand on her leg.

She asked, "Is this the part of the date where we make out?"

"It is."

Having changed back into her red dress, Rita had Paul drop her off down the road from her house. Sliding off the bike, standing next to him, she said, "Thank you for the date. This has absolutely been the greatest day of my life!" She leaned forward with a kiss. "I wish it didn't have to end."

"Me too." Paul took on a serious look. "You know Glenn is going to be furious about us skipping school and spending the day together."

"You think so?"

"Very much."

"I'll have to make it up to him."

"He's in love with you, you know that don't you?"

Smiling her sexy smile, she said, "I gotta go. And you need to disappear." Rita turned and began walking toward home.

After a few steps and not hearing Paul leaving, she turned his way and shooed him. He waved bye, started the bike, and headed the opposite way.

Having never done anything like this before,

Rita wasn't sure how to deal with it. She had beat the school bus home and decided it might be best to hide until the bus passed and then head into the house as if she had been on it.

Sitting behind a tree amidst tall weeds and shrubbery, time seemed to stand still. She reached into the bag and pulled out the book she had gotten from Trendy Eve Boutique.

The book was titled *Blakk Magick.* In smaller text, it said, *Feeding the Shadows.* "Deysi Blakk" was the first chapter. It was a short history of Deysi Blakk, explaining that the contents of the book was a compilation of material taken from the journals of Deysi Blakk. Deysi Blakk, born in 1896, was thought to be an obscure lover and follower of Aleister Crowley. Accusations accused her of breeding. Accused her of having babies for infant sacrifices for the "feeding" of the "shadows." In time, she was institutionalized for insanity and eventually committed suicide in a ritualistic ceremony offering her soul for the "feeding" of the shadows. She believed in doing so, she would be reincarnated with an elevated status.

The school bus interrupted Rita's reading.

Cautiously entering the house, she saw her pa was not in his chair. Looking around and not finding him, she determined he was off somewhere. She sighed with relief.

23

THAT GIRL RITA

In her cheerleader's uniform, Julia Brooks looked Indian. With every visit, the Wigwam offered NuSprings' cheerleaders credit off any order as long as they were in uniform. This allowed the girls a free drink, a burger, or fries or some other selected menu item. NuSprings' cheerleaders brought ambiance to the theme of the establishment. NuSprings was home of the Renegades and the cheerleader's uniform, typical in its overall style and design, was unique in that it was fashioned to look Indian. The material was faux suede, the color of tan, implying a tanned skin. The dress was accented in red and yellow. The sexy short fringe skirt showed more leg than normal pleated skirts. A blouse was sleeveless with a modest "V" neck. Headband and armbands added to the look, giving the uniform additional sex appeal. The girls were a source of eye candy good for business.

Following Dave and Valerie inside, Julia kept an eye out for Paul. She was disappointed when he wasn't in the car when Dave picked her up from school. Paul had gallant elements like his big brother. Dave was proper, well mannered, and strived to do the right thing. Paul was more relaxed. He liked having fun more than doing the right thing. He was daring. The air of excitement hovering around Paul was appealing. For Julia, Dave was a toy; Paul had possibilities of more.

Julia, seated with Dave, Valerie, Quillpen, Tianna RedBird, and Denny York, had fries and a malt, which were free because she was in uniform. Catching a glimpse of Glenn York outside the Wigwam, she told Val she was going to go and mingle.

Finding Glenn but no Paul, she ended up in a group of fellow cheerleaders to socialize and gossip.

Hearing a motorcycle, Julia turned and discovered Paul Sumner. He circled the Wigwam before parking and shutting off the bike. Getting off the bike, he was met by a couple of guys engaging him in conversation. Leaving her friends, Julia sought for an opportunity to cross paths with him.

She saw an unhappy-looking Glenn York marching toward him. Drawing closer to Paul, Glenn shouted something angry. The guys talking to Paul stopped and turned their attention to Glenn advancing their way. Paul, raising arms and hands up, gesturing to Glenn to back off and calm down, began talking. Julia was unable to hear and moved closer.

Glenn shouted more stuff. Others were taking notice. The guys talking to Paul stepped back out of the way. People began moving in for better "seats." Julia did too.

Pushing Paul's hands aside, Glenn gave Paul a hard shove backwards. Paul, stumbling backwards, managed to keep his balance.

Julia moved closer.

The announcement of a fight rang out.

Paul, trying to reason with Glenn, was shoved again. Paul, better prepared this time, took a step backwards but didn't stumble. Shouting at Glenn, Paul stepped forward and shoved Glenn. Glenn bounced back swinging. In seconds they were tangled together and rolling on the ground, both throwing and blocking punches the best they could.

Julia was on the front line with a crowd growing around her.

Dave and Denny, pushing through the crowd, stood briefly for a moment watching their brothers going at each other. Moving forward, Dave took hold of Paul and Denny took hold of Glenn and pulled them apart.

Denny asked Glenn, "What's going on?"

"Nothing."

Dave asked Paul, "Whatcha fighting about?"

"A misunderstanding."

"Yeah. Right." Glenn not buying it.

"If you would just have let me explain, we could have avoided all this," Paul defended.

"You're such a freaking jerk, man."

"You got it all wrong," Paul tried to reason.

"You screw her?"

"It wasn't like that, man."

Glenn shook his head. "You're a liar."

"Forget you, man," Paul said. "You're too jealous to listen to reason."

Dave butting in, "Who are you talking about?"

"No one," Paul answered.

"Is this about that girl Rita?" Denny asked.

Paul and Glenn stared at each other. When neither made a comment, Denny said, "Really? You two gonna throw a lifetime friendship away over some chick trying to screw her way into a better life? The tramp's not worth it, man."

Glenn, jerking free of his brother's hold, turned and punched Denny in the face. Caught off guard, Denny tripped backwards and fell.

"She's not a tramp!" Glenn told him. Looking at the crowd and then Paul. "Screw the both of you!" The crowd parted, allowing Glenn passage as he walked away.

Quillpen Jack extending an arm down to Denny, "Dude, your little brother punched you in the face."

"You think anyone else noticed?" Denny got up.

"Only everyone."

The show being over, the crowd began to disperse. Paul, attending to a busted lip, noticed Julia. She remained where she was.

Dave asked Paul, "You alright, man?"

"Fine."

"This was over a girl named Rita?"

"It was over a misunderstanding."

Julia saw Paul glance her way. She smiled.

"Done with the bike, man?" a guy asked Paul, walking up.

"Thanks, man. Key's in it."

Dave said to the guy, "You loaned him your motorcycle?"

"No. He kind of stole it," the guy answered, walking away.

Dave turned to Paul. "You stole his *bike*?"

Paul sighing, "Creatively borrowed."

Dave, turning to Valerie, shook his head.

Valerie said, "Kalvin didn't seem mad. So it's probably not like he made it sound."

Kalvin, standing next to his bike, called out, "Hey man, is this your album?"

Paul started toward Kalvin.

"I think I just need to walk away right now," Dave said to Valerie.

Dave and Valerie walked away. Julia stayed and waited for Paul.

Walking back toward her, album in hand, "Hey Julia," he greeted. "What's up?"

She shrugged. "You tell me."

"It is what it is."

"Interesting day?"

"Very. I need to sit."

Julia followed Paul to a bench.

Paul sat down. Staring, "Like the outfit."

"It's a one of a kind," Julia joked. "I'm part Indian."

"Yeah?"

"Royal blood, I'm told." She smiled.

"Are you now?" Paul patted the seat for her to sit.

"So I'm told." Julia sat down. "Who's that girl named Rita?"

"A friend."

"Just a friend?"

"It's complicated."

"In love with her?"

"Love's a strong word."

"Uh-huh."

"She's different."

"Is this girl named Rita pretty?"

"She can be."

Julia wanted to know more, but felt it wouldn't be cool. She asked, "What album did you buy this time?"

"Rolling Stones." Paul handed it to her. "You like the Stones?"

"Not so much." The album was cartoonish and psychedelic looking. The band members, sitting side by side on the ground, were dressed in old-style royal-court-type clothes. Mick Jagger was dressed as a wizard. In the background was a castle. Julia read the album's title, "*Their Satanic Majesties Request*? Sounds evil."

"Probably is."

Valerie walked up. "Time to go. We're leaving."

Julia, frowning, rose to her feet. Noting Paul's lustful roaming eyes, "Coming?" she invited.

"I think I will."

This is stupid, thought Glenn York standing in the pasture staring at Rita's house. He wanted to march over and knock on the front door. Instead, he messaged her by tying a yellow ribbon to a specific post in the field. Yellow meant campout. Taking a seat on the ground next to the post, anger resonated within imagining Paul and Rita spending the day together. Like a developing storm, fury had grown with each passing hour. Dark stormy clouds filled with volatile energy. The fight at the Wigwam allowed release of some of the anger.

But not enough.

The storm still brewed.

After reading a few pages of *Blakk Magick*, Rita closed the book. It was not an easy read. Deysi Blakk did not think with normalcy. Her thought pattern was unsystematic and mysterious. Paragraphs didn't always make sense. What Rita did take from her reading was a quotation from Aleister Crowley: "Magick is the science and art of causing change to occur." Deysi added, *"There are secret and unseen forces in nature that when understood and agreed with can bring alterations in perceived reality."*

Rita needed time to think on the statements. What were those secret forces of nature?

Getting off the sofa, she hid the book. If Pa happened to take notice of it, he might be of the notion to burn it.

Rita wondered where Pa was. Stepping outside onto the front porch, she saw someone waving from the York field. Glenn? Seeing a yellow ribbon, she waved and went out into the yard to answer. She stuck a shovel in the ground at the spot, meaning she didn't know, but would try. She went back into the house for fear of Glenn coming to talk with her from across the road.

Glenn was happy Rita saw the message, but it would be a torturous wait to see if she would be able to meet with him. Once she found out, she would message back. Getting a fire going, he crawled into the tent to clean it out. He rarely took it down anymore. It was more convenient just to leave it up.

Satisfied with the tent's condition, he crawled back out. Looking toward Rita's house, her message shovel stated she could come.

Taking a seat next to the fire, he made ready the lantern. Adding another log, he poked at the fire with a stick. Rita spoke of her pa being mean and crazy. She never gave details, only vague statements.

Rita's pa had been badly burned in a fire. His face and parts of his body were terribly scarred. He didn't work and was given to whiskey. He was angry, cynical, and hated people. Rita had described him as being an angry storm cloud with volatile inclinations.

Never, under any circumstances, were he and Paul ever to come to her house. It was a law she had sternly decreed. When they asked why, she'd answered, "Because things could go bad. Really bad!" He and Paul promised never to do it.

Rita was not a gold-digging tramp seeking a better life. Denny didn't know Rita. She lived in poverty. In a bad environment. But, she was a good person. She had a good heart.

Didn't she deserve better? Was it wrong he wanted to love her and give her things? Make her happy?

Didn't Rita deserve to be happy?

Rita was the sexiest girl, perhaps the sexiest woman, he knew. When she was around, life was fun, sexy, and interesting. She saw life differently than anyone he knew. She didn't follow a traditional mindset. Things with her weren't black or white. She made her own rules. Did what made her happy.

Was that so wrong?

Even if it meant she would have two boy-friends? Two lovers? It was a bittersweet scenario. Glenn understood Rita was starved for attention and love. She once told them her pa had never told her that he loved her. She was sure her mom had, but her mother had been killed when she was young and she couldn't remember her mother ever saying it. Could barely remember her mother at all.

As much as he hated it, he was willing, for Rita,

to share her with Paul. He didn't want to. It sometimes killed him to see the affection she gave Paul. He was jealous of Paul. Jealous of Rita's fondness for him.

Glenn wanted Rita to himself. He wanted all her love. All her affection and devotion. He wanted a traditional relationship of one guy and one girl. He wanted a happily- ever-after.

But that wasn't Rita. She wasn't traditional.

Being in love with Rita was hard. It was the greatest thing ever, but terribly frustrating.

Sitting on the ground by the fire, staring toward Rita's house, he was startled by the sudden appearance of Rusty coming up nudging and licking with tail wagging.

"Hey buddy." Glenn petted the dog. "Where did you come from?" Hearing movement, Glenn turned his head to see his sister Jenny walking up.

"You all right?" Jenny asked.

"Yeah. Why wouldn't I be?"

"Whatcha doing?"

"Thinking."

Jenny looked in the direction Glenn was staring, seeing Rita's house. "Heard you and Paul got into a fight today."

Glenn shrugged. "No big deal."

"Yeah?" Jenny walked around to stand in front of Glenn. Her back to Rita's house. "Heard you punched Denny in the face. He may end up with a black eye."

"He deserved it. What you want? What are you doing here?"

"You missed supper. It'll soon be dark. We were worried. I came to see if you were okay."

"I'm fine. You can go back and tell everyone not to worry."

"How long are you going to sit out here, 'thinking'?"

"I don't know, Jen. All night maybe. I need to be alone! I need to think."

Jenny looked about in different directions. "Aren't you worried about scarecrows?"

"Haven't really thought about them."

"Maybe you should. They kidnapped you once— remember? Not to mention, the other night, two people were brutally killed and burned to death. Not far from here."

Glenn shrugged. "If you're so worried, maybe you need to get back to the house, before it gets darker."

"Glenn, you're my little brother and I love you. That Rita girl is not the girl for you."

"Who asked you?"

"Just saying."

When Glenn didn't respond, she said, "She comes from a different world. She has different values. She will only bring you trouble and cause you heartache. In the long run, she'll destroy your happiness."

"Understand. Now leave."

"What do you see in her anyway?"

"She's interesting. I like her."

"She's weird."

"She's different."

"There's something not right about her."

"How would you know?"

"I just know! She's been our neighbor for a few years now. I'm not in love with her. I see what she really is. Things are not right about her and her dad. She gives me the creeps."

"You don't know anything."

"She's pulling you down. She's coming between you and Paul. You and Paul have been best friends since you were kids. You gonna throw that away over someone like her?"

"Like her?"

"She's not like us. She hasn't been raised like us. She's in a different class."

"What are you implying?"

"She hasn't had a proper upbringing. She's more like the Brandts than us."

"No she's not."

"Does she go to church? Does she even believe in God?"

"I don't know. Who cares?"

"It matters! You were raised in church. It used to be important to you. She's changing you."

"No she's not."

"Don't be a fool. You two could never be equally yoked. Your belief systems are different. Your values are different."

There was a moment of silence. "She's no good for you, Glenn."

"Jenny, you need to leave."

"Why? You gonna punch me in the face too?"

"If I have to."

"See! That's what I'm talking about. You were raised never to hit a girl. Guys don't hit girls in our family."

"Go, Jenny! You're getting on my nerves."

"Can't you see what she's doing to you?"

"She's doing nothing."

"She's corrupting you. You used to be a happy-go-lucky guy. You're not anymore. She's coming between you and Paul. Between you and Denny. Between you and me. Between you and our family. Between you and God!"

"She's not doing anything, you guys are."

"None of us like her."

"That's real Christlike of you."

"You're blind. Look at you. What are you doing out here anyway?"

"Waiting for her. I need to talk to her."

"How do you know she's coming?"

"She's walking this way."

Jenny turned and looked. Rita was almost there. She was in a black dress and boots. Rusty had gone and met her. She turned back to Glenn. "She even looks like a witch. She's no good. Please understand that."

"Good-bye, Jenny."

Walking up, Rita greeted Jenny with a smile. "Hi." Jenny frowned and turned back to Glenn. "Dad's not going to let you stay out here all night. It's too dangerous." Walking away, she said, "Rusty." Rusty pulled away from Rita to follow Jenny.

Rita, watching Jenny walking away, turned to Glenn. "Did I do something wrong?"

"You did nothing wrong."

"She doesn't like me."

"She doesn't know you?"

"She hates me. I saw it in her eyes."

"She doesn't matter."

Glenn saw Rita looking for a place to sit. She wasn't dressed to sit on the ground. She was in a nice dress and looked more like she was going out on a date, instead of sitting by a fire in the middle of a field. "Sorry."

"Sorry?"

"I didn't think about having you a place to sit. And you're not dressed for the ground. You look nice."

"I wanted to look good for you. We could sit in the tent," she proposed.

"Are you cold?" Glenn stood.

"If I get cold, perhaps you can warm me?"

"I may anyway." Pulling the tent flap out of the way, "Welcome, to my humble abode."

Rita bent down and carefully crawled into the tent. Glenn followed behind with the lantern. Inside, she began removing her boots, not concerned with the arousing visual she gave. Glenn didn't know if the visual of letting him see up her dress was on purpose or if it was the lack of proper upbringing. Neatly putting the boots to the side, she positioned herself into a modest and comfortable position and made eye contact.

Glenn said, "I'm glad you got to come. I was afraid you wouldn't. I really needed to see you."

"I got lucky. My pa took a sleeping pill and passed out. He has nightmares. The pills help. Hopefully, he'll be dead to the world for the rest of the night."

Glenn watched her stare move from his eyes to his swollen cheek. "Is that a bruise on your cheek?" She reached out with a gentle touch. "Does it hurt?"

"It's fine."

"What happened?"

"Rita, what happened to you today? Where did you go?"

The sternness and seriousness of Glenn's voice caused Rita to pause. Pulling her hand back, she looked hard into his eyes. "Paul took me to Springfield."

"Why?"

"He asked me if I wanted to skip school with him. He said it would be fun. I love fun. I said yes."

"What did you do?"

"He took me to Springfield. We ate at Burger King and then he took me to a plaza. I've never been to a plaza before."

"Then what?"

"We came back."

"Is that all?"

"We made out at the park for a bit."

"Just made out?"

"Yes."

"Nothing more?"

"If you are asking if we had sex, no we didn't."

Glenn, sitting cross-legged, didn't object to Rita placing her hands on his knees. She said, "Paul said you'd be upset. Did you and Paul have a fight? Is that why your jowl is swollen?"

Glenn didn't answer, but Rita read the truth in his eyes. "Are you mad?"

"Not at you."

"Don't be mad at Paul. You don't have to be." Leaning forward, gently placing her lips to his, she kissed him. In a soft whisper, "Why would you be?"

Even if he had wanted to, he didn't have the resolve to resist her. A moment of tender kissing turned into a time of making out.

Pulling away, being in a strain from the position she was in, she moved into a different position. "Glenn, you're important to me. I need you. I want you. You make me happy. You make me feel special. You're the silver lining in my dark stormy life. You don't need to be jealous of Paul. You give me something I need. Something Paul cannot."

"Rita, do you believe in God?"

That surprised her. It showed in her eyes. "Huh?" A cloud passed across her eyes. "Why?"

"I want to know more about you. Do you believe in God?"

"I'm not sure. I suppose I do. My pa does."

"Have you ever been to church?"

"I don't remember ever going. I might have when I was really young. Maybe when my mother was alive. Why?"

"Have you ever read the Bible?"

"My pa reads it to me sometimes. He seems to know some about it. He used to go to church."

"Used to? What happened?"

"The fire. The fire that killed his mom and pa and burned him. He's bitter with God over it. He says God could have stopped it from happening. But God didn't." With a touch of bitterness, she added, "He thinks God is mean and cruel."

"What church did he go to? Do you know?"

"No. I think we are Mormons, though. He once told me we were. He says the Mormons have the best beliefs. What religion are you?"

"Baptist."

The title didn't mean anything to her.

As Glenn contemplated her answers, Rita said, "We used to have money. Back in Kansas my pa and his parents owned a thousand-acre farm."

"Really?" That was many times the York farm. "What happened?"

"God took it from us," she stated bitterly.

"What do you mean?"

"Pa says it's so. It began with the fire. After that

came one bad crop after another. Then a train killed my mom. Bad luck, bad luck, and more bad luck. Finally, we became bankrupt and lost the farm. That was when we moved here. Pa says God is to blame."

"Wow. So sorry. I never knew."

"My pa won't work or try to have a better life. He just lives to drink." With bitterness, Rita went on, "What's the point? God is just going to take it away from us anyway. God does not want us to be happy. So, do I believe in God? I don't believe God is good like your sister says. Jenny told that once. A long time ago. That God is love and He loves me. I'm sure that's easy to believe when you're a York and life is good. It's not so easy to believe when you're me. I made the mistake of telling my pa what Jenny said. He gave me a whooping so I could know how the love of God felt on the bare skin!"

Glenn didn't know what to say.

Rita, staring deep into his eyes, asked, "Glenn, why did God have to kill my mother? How can that be love? If that's the good love of God, I'd rather serve the devil!" Her statement shocked him. There was a darkness in her eyes. Her shadow flickered about in a dance on the tent wall behind her. It wasn't right. The fire in the lantern wasn't flickering. Goose pimples popped out on his skin.

Glenn didn't have an answer. He was out of his league. His relationship with God was more plastic than gold.

Rita had opened up and allowed him to see the

years of pain and bitterness bottled inside. Allowing him to see how lost, vulnerable, and hurt she was. How much she needed love.

Not knowing what to say, Glenn asked, "Rita, can I put my arms around you and hold you?"

The storm faded from her eyes. "Glenn, you never have to ask if you can hold me. I'm yours to hold."

Moving to sit beside her, Glenn put an arm around her and pulled her close to his body, planting a kiss on the side of her head. He held her tight as she rested her head against his chest. After a time of silence, Glenn asked, "Are you okay?"

"I was thinking how I've never been held like this before. It's nice. Like you actually care."

"Rita, I do care." Kissing the top of her head, he whispered, "I love you. I want to love you for the rest of my life." He emphasized his feelings with a squeeze.

Time passed in silence. Rita hadn't moved. Hadn't spoken. Starting to feel apprehensive, Glenn raised her face with his hand to look into her eyes. Her eyes were watery with tears. "What's wrong?"

"I never heard those words spoken to me before."

"I love you, Rita." Glenn lowered his lips onto hers.

After a time of affectionate kissing and hugging, Rita, through watery eyes, pulled Glenn down upon her; she whispered, "Make love to me."

Once spent, Glenn resting atop her, felt her

eddying in climax. She held him in a tight embrace. She told him, "Thank you for loving me. For saying you love me. You and Paul have made this day the greatest of my entire life!"

Ben York, Glenn's father, stood a short distance from the tent. Not taking any chances concerning scarecrows, he was carrying a shotgun. Rusty, sitting beside him, waited for what was to be next

Ben York hadn't been there long and couldn't see into the tent, but understood what had taken place. Loudly clearing his throat, announcing his presence, he called out, "Glenn, it's getting late. Time to come home. Say good night!"

Inside the tent, serious whispering started as the lantern reflected shadows scrambling.

"Dad, is that you?" Glenn asked while trying to be quiet in getting dressed.

"Yes, Son, it is."

Ben patiently waited. The serious whispering continued as the lantern revealed the two dressing.

Glenn in a stern whisper said, "Rita, get it together! Calm down! My dad's not like your dad!"

Moments later, Glenn crawled out of the tent with Rita right behind him. Glenn stood to face his dad. Rita stood to his side and slightly behind him, holding his arm for protection.

Ben, being as intimidating as he could be, stared at them.

Glenn began, "Dad, we were only ..."

"Glenn!" Ben cut him off. "If you're fixing to lie to me, don't!"

When Glenn said no more, Ben turned his stare to the girl beside him. There was immense fear in her eyes. She was nearly shaking. Her stare was on the gun as if she expected they were about to be shot. Ben said, "So you must be Rita." Holding on to Glenn for dear life, she made eye contact, but didn't respond. Ben asked, "You live in the house over there?"

She nodded.

Glenn answered, "Yes she does."

"Does your dad know where you are?"

Glenn said, "No. He has medical problems and is sleeping."

Staring at the two, Ben realized there was no point in a lecture. The girl was way too frightened to hear it. He wanted her respect, but he didn't want her to be in fear of her life. "Well, Rita, I'm Ben York, Glenn's father. It's about time we met. I would have rather it were under different circumstances."

She kept her eye on the gun. Did she really believe she might be shot? Remaining silent, Ben said, "Well Rita, you best be getting home now."

She looked at Glenn.

"See you tomorrow."

Letting go, Rita took off running as fast as her feet would carry her.

Ben and Glenn watched until she made it to her house. After disappearing inside, Ben turned his stare back on Glenn. "Did she really think I would shoot her?"

"I think so. Apparently her dad is crazy like that."

A small fire was still burning in the pit. "You got water to put the fire out?"

"Yes, sir."

As Glenn put out the fire, Ben said, "I always expected to catch Denny in a situation like this. But not you. You were always the good son. The one I felt I never had to worry about. After listening to all Denny and Jenny think and believe about Rita, I was going to demand you to stay away from her. However, after tonight and having seen the girl, I know I'd be wasting my breath in telling you to stay away from her. Am I right?"

Finishing the fire detail, Glenn answered, "Yes, sir."

"I figured as much."

Glenn, standing tall, looked at his dad. "She's not a bad person, Dad."

"I'm sure you see the good in her."

Ben stared down at his son. "I'm going to be honest with you, Son: I'm at a lost on what to do about this affair. I don't approve of it. As your father, I want to protect you. Keep you from making a mistake. But obviously, you're going to continue to pursue this girl. You were never one to lie and be deceitful. I don't want to give you reason to start now.

"You hungry?" Ben asked.

"A little bit."

"I think your mother saved you a plate."

Glenn followed his dad as they walked home. After a period of silence, Ben asked, "What will you do if the girl comes up pregnant?"

"Marry her."

A few steps further, Ben asked, "Do you think she will be a faithful wife?"

Glenn thought a moment. "I think she will be loyal."

"Interesting answer."

A few steps more, Ben said, "Denny says she's promiscuous. From what I'm hearing, she spent the day with your best friend and the night with you. How do you feel about that?"

"It's complicated."

Standing outside the house, Ben paused before entering. "Being promiscuous, if she comes up pregnant, will you still marry her?"

Ben saw that Glenn hadn't really thought it out.

Ben said, "I'm not going to forbid you seeing her. I am against it. I agree with Jenny. I fear she will bring you pain and misery. I fear Rita is going to be your suicide affair! I truly hope you're man enough to handle it."

24

BLAKK MAGICK

reak.

Sounding like a foot stepping across a weak floorboard, it came from the short hall coming from the bathroom. Rita was on the sofa. Pa was passed out in his chair. Other than Rita's reading lamp, dark and silent the house was.

In the silence and darkness there were always things to hear. Spooky creaking noises without origins. Loud pops. Howling noises from the wind and windows. Creepy night noises outside filtering in, adding to the ghostly effects harassing and playing tricks on the mind.

Old houses welcomed ghosts.

Creak.

The spooky, creepy footstep sounded closer.

Rita and Pa were never a family of two. They were a family of three. Mr. Scarecrow from Kansas had come with them to NuSprings. When Rita was a little girl, the shadow played with her. From the corners of her eyes, she would get glimpses of darkness moving. Watching her. When she would take a second look, it would be gone, but goose pimples would pop up on her skin.

Besides Mr. Scarecrow, the attic spooks were always spooking her. It was their fun.

There were the spooky times when she would put her baby doll in its little crib for the day and then go to school only to come home and find it in some weird place.

Pa could have done it. But, she didn't think so. The attic spooks were playing a game of hide-and-seek with her.

There were spookier times. Like coming home from school, Pa off somewhere in the fields, and the baby doll was missing from the crib. She would hear it crying. The doll had no mechanism in it for crying. But crying it did. Soft, whimpery weeping of a baby vulnerable and needing its mother. When Rita saw the baby doll, the crying stopped.

One time, she found her doll at the foot of the steps leading up to the attic. Rita knew it was the spooks playing with her. But creepy and scary it was nonetheless. She forced herself to get the baby and take it back downstairs.

Another time, weeks later, the doll was halfway up the stairs.

The third time, the doll was nearly at the top of the stairs. Rita barely had the courage to rescue it. But the door was shut.

One day, she came home from school, her baby missing. Soft, distraught baby whimpering filled the house. Standing at the bottom of the steps leading to the attic, the attic door was open. The crying was coming from inside the attic. The spooks were inviting her to come and get her baby.

Rita would not. When things went into the attic, they never came out again.

Rita never saw her baby doll again.

Rita began to have nightmares about her baby. In the nightmare, the baby doll, lost and lonely, would cry. A baby needing its mommy.

She asked Pa one day if he would go up into the attic and see if her baby doll was up there. He told her to do it herself.

She would not.

It was just a doll, Rita told herself. A dumb toy.

Still to this day, now and again, she would have the nightmare of her lost abandoned baby crying for her.

Creak.

Rita glanced toward the hall. *Nothing.* Since Pa was home, Rita hadn't turned on the radio. The radio masked a lot of the noises. But, Pa often griped about it being on.

Rita suddenly felt the tug of Deysi Blakk's *Blakk Magick* reaching out to her. Drawing her. It wanted to be read. It needed to be read. It was hungry. She looked over at Pa. He was quietly and rhythmically snoring.

Rita stuck a hand down into the sofa behind the cushion and pulled Deysi Blakk's book out of hiding. She read again the statement at the bottom of the cover: *Warning: undisciplined knowledge can be dangerous and destructive.*

Rita wasn't sure what it meant.

Ignoring the sudden weird *clank* sound from the kitchen like someone—or something—dropped a utensil into the sink, Rita opened the book. Looking down on the page before her, Deysi wrote: There are shadows among us. Angelics fallen. Angelics given to darkness. Spirit beings and sky rulers—sometimes seen as mysterious lights in the night. Other times seen as shadows sitting in the corners where walls and ceilings meet.

Sometimes in corners where walls and floors meet.

They are darkness without solid form. They have no eyes, but they're always watching. I see them now. They see me. They be hungry. Always hungry. They gather waiting to be fed dishes of innocence.

One flies into me—searching my soul for a morsel of innocence.

I have no innocence left inside me.

I surrender anyway.

It chews on that surrender like a starving man chewing on the leather sole of his shoe in hopes of getting some kind of benefit.

I feel the cold in my soul.

I want to be warm, but it don't care. It finds respite in my suffering.

I can feel the empty hollowness of the shadow tortured with cravings never to be satisfied. An emptiness distorting reason and truth.

It feels like myself.

I'm not its lover, but its whore. It cannot love. It can only lust. The shadow uses me.

I need to bleed.

With a scalpel, I make a small incision on my thigh.

Bright red blood appears. I feel a tiny relief from the heavy weight of hollowness threatening to crush me. I don't understand it. But it is something.

I wonder in the human half of my mind if the shadow is somehow feeding off the life that's in the blood that is leaking from my body.

I sense it does.

I wish I had a baby to cut.

Oh gawd, the craving of a baby's innocence is great within.

It's not my wish. But it excites me.

I can taste the sweetness of it.

There's nothing sweeter than the taste of a bleeding baby.

Rita closed the book, her heart thumping in her chest. She felt wicked reading it. Reading it was a sin. Somehow, she had just fed the book. The room wasn't cold, but her body was covered in goose bumps. There was something cold in the room. She shivered. She felt afraid.

She looked at Pa. He was an empty soul. A corpse of a man once alive with hopes and dreams. He looked gray. He looked dead.

Staring at Pa, a dark apparition barely detectable to the human eye rose out of him. Rita followed it with her eyes. It settled in a corner where a wall and ceiling met.

Her heart felt like it was about to explode. She was afraid to move, fearing if she moved it would focus on her. She didn't want to look at it, but was too afraid to close her eyes.

The shadow descended back into her Pa. Pa coughed and then went into a coughing spell that woke him up. He rose up in his chair to get control of the coughing.

Rita pushed the book down behind the sofa cushion to hide it.

Pa turned demonic eyes on her. "What are you looking at?"

"Nothing, Pa."

"Well, stop it!" came an angry growl from within. It happened so fast: Pa picked up the ashtray from the end table next to his chair and threw it. The ashtray smacked her in the chest. It hurt, but was more shocking than painful. Fearful not to obey, she looked away from him and down at the sofa. Giving herself something to do, trying not to act terrified, she reached and picked up a magazine to read. From the corner of her eye, Pa raised a whiskey bottle to his mouth. Pa's demonic eyes staring at her.

Time passed.

Her fear faded with the passing of time as Pa's eyes went back to being normal again.

It now seemed surreal, and if it weren't for the ashtray, she would have wondered if it had happened at all.

Inhaling a deep breath, coming back alive, Pa rose from his chair. He left the room. Rita heard him go into the bathroom.

Flipping through a magazine reading stuff she had previously skipped, Rita heard someone stepping onto the front porch of their house.

A knock came from the front door.

Pa was in the bathroom.

Fearing it might be Glenn or Paul being stupid, she jumped up, raced to the front door, and opened it.

It was Johnny's pa!

"Evening, Princess," George Brandt greeted with a friendly enough smile. "Is your pa 'round?"

"Yes."

Without invite, George stepped past her into the house. "Would you let him know I'm here."

"He's in the bathroom." Closing the door, a smell of alcohol gave evidence he'd been drinking.

Leaving Mr. Brandt standing in the front room,

Rita went down the short hall to the bathroom. With a knock on the door, "Pa, Mr. Brandt, the neighbor down the road, is here to see you."

"What?" her pa asked with a growl.

"George Brandt is here. He wants to talk to you."

Rita heard curse words. "I'll be out in a minute." Rita went back into the living room. "Pa will be out in a minute."

Mr. Brandt nodded. With hungry eyes, he looked her up and down. Rita realized she might not be properly dressed for company. She was only wearing a shirt, but Mr. Brandt didn't look offended. Brandts weren't proper people either. No harm done. Realizing this was an actual visitor, she reminded herself there was a protocol of hospitality to follow. In one of her magazines, she had studied an article on proper hospitality. Searching her memory, she asked, "Would you like to have a seat?"

"That's kind of you, but I'm fine, I won't be long."

"Could I offer you something to drink? A beer perhaps?"

"Well, aren't you the proper lady. I'm good. Thank you anyway."

The moment turned awkward from silence. It was her job to be a good host and entertain her guest. She tried to remember the next act of protocol.

He broke the silence with, "How old are you, dear? Your name is Rita, right?"

"Yes, sir. Fifteen."

The bathroom door opened.

George waited for Homer and saw an expression of surprise at seeing him standing in his front room. George spoke to defuse any offense Homer might have. "Hope you don't mind me stopping by. We're not just neighbors, I consider us friends. However, I'm not here to socialize—I'm here on business."

"Yeah? What business?" Homer sounded irritated.

"You remember June, the barmaid, and her husband Veg?"

Homer nodded.

"Are you aware they died the other night in a fire?"

"The girl told me about it."

"Did she tell you scarecrows were involved?"

"That's what she heard."

"Well, some of us at the bar believe these scarecrows may be a group of psychopaths on LSD and hiding out in these hills somewhere. June was like family to us. We take care of family. She was special and we're pissed off about her death. So a group of us is getting together to do some hunting tonight. We know these woods and hills pretty good. I'm on my way home now to get my rifle. Passing your house, I thought, *Good ole Homer is a man who might enjoy going scarecrow hunting.* We're not like the law; we'll shoot first and ask questions later. How about it, friend? Up for a scarecrow hunt?"

Homer was silent for a moment, but finally said, "A hunt sounds fun, but as you know, I don't do well around people."

"Ah, I know you have issues with the way you look, after the boys get used to ya, you'd be one of us."

"I appreciate your words, George, neighbor down the road, but I'm a loner. I'll grab my gun and do some hunting 'round here. I know the woods around here well enough."

"Sure you wanna be walking around out there alone? This group can be dangerous."

"Not as dangerous as me."

Seeing an unnatural blackness in his eyes, George said, "I think I believe you. Alright then, I'll be on my way. Just wanted you to know you were welcome."

Homer nodded in appreciation.

George lusted over at Rita. "You take care now." Giving Homer a farewell nod, he turned and exited the house. Walking to his truck, he thought how Rita would make a good replacement for June.

Johnny watched his dad looking his rifle over. "Me and the boys are gonna do some huntin' t'night," his dad told his mom.

"Tonight?"

"Yeah. Scarecrows!"

"Scarecrows?"

"There was talk at the bar tonight that the scarecrows might be some kind of cult group wigged out on LSD. You know like that Charles Manson group that's on trial for murdering that pretty little actress and her friends."

Johnny, Betty, and Jimmy stood nearby listening to every word.

"The town's under a curfew. No one under eighteen out past nine. Also heard—" George laid down the rifle. Picking up the bologna sandwich and taking a bite, "June's face was pounded into hamburger meat before she was burned. It wasn't natural."

"How could someone do such evil?" Johnny's mom asked.

"It's like that Manson family. They took that actress, who was pregnant, and while she was still alive, cut the baby out of her belly, and killed it in front of her dying eyes."

"It's hard to believe a human could do such a thing. What would make someone do such evil?"

"It's the LSD they're on. The more they do, the crazier they get." George took another bite. After swallowing, "The belief is that a group of hippies are living out in these hills somewhere in some type of commune having orgies and doing drugs. At first, they just went about stealing scarecrows for whatever reason. But over time, the drugs taking over their minds, they started dressing up like scarecrows going around scaring people. Now, they're so wigged out, the monsters have started killing people.

"Some believed the psychos went into the house to kidnap Veggy and use him in some type of Satan worshipping ritual and June came home catching them. So they beat her to death and then set the house on fire."

Johnny watched his mom shake her head in total dismay, not knowing what to think. Swallowing the last bite of sandwich, his dad said, "One thing for sure, this ain't California. This is the Ozarks! If there's a group of psychos out there, we'll hunt 'em down and kill 'em like we would any rabid animal." George got up and went into the bedroom.

"Mom," Betty asked, "y-you think the-the scarecrows could c-come here?"

Johnny could see the fear on Betty. Even he wished, as much as he hated his dad, that his dad would stay home tonight and protect the family.

"Don't even think such a thing!" Johnny's mom insisted without being convincing.

Johnny's dad, hearing the conversation, came back carrying the shotgun. "The churches in town are having a community prayer time asking for God's help. Like that's gonna do any good. Praying never helped anything."

George turned to Johnny and stuck the gun out to him. "Here, boy, take this." Johnny took the gun. "It's loaded and ready to shoot. If anyone tries to come in, point the gun at 'em, hold it tight against your shoulder, and pull the trigger. You've shot the gun before. It'll probably knock you on your butt like the last time, but it'll do damage and make the psychos think twice about breaking into someone's home."

Satisfied, George turned from Johnny and looked at his wife. "I asked freak Homer down the road, if he wanted to take part in the hunt. He said, he'd go out and hunt the woods around here. So, I guess he'll be on the lookout. Of course, if he runs across 'em, they'll probably end up bashing his head in as well. Wouldn't hurt his looks any."

Grabbing his things, George said, "Hope the pretty little neighbor girl can take care of herself. Alright, gotta go. Don't wait up." Going out the door, he called back, "Lock up."

Johnny's heart was racing inside. His mother locked the door. Betty and Jimmy turned their stares on him with fear in their eyes. Feeling scared too, he needed to man up. His job was to protect the family. He was the Dark Knight. Manning up, he said, "I hope they come knocking on the door. I would love to shoot 'em!" Pointing the gun at Jimmy, he added, "I could do it too! Wouldn't bother me one bit."

"Don't point the gun at us!" Betty yelled.

"Johnny! Boy, you know better than that!" his mother shouted a scold.

Johnny grinned, but obeyed. Carrying the gun with him, he said, "I'm gonna go and tie one of the dogs to the front porch, and one to the back porch— they'll go to barking if anyone comes around."

After tying one dog to the back porch and the other to the front porch, Johnny bravely stood feeling safe at the moment and searching the darkness looking for scarecrows.

Looking toward Rita's house, he wished he could go and see her. Show her the man he was. Show her he could protect her.

He thought about her crazy pa, and what his dad had said. The monster was probably out wandering around somewhere nearby watching. If Rita were lucky, the scarecrows would kill him like his dad said.

Yes. That's an inspiring thought.

25

FREEDOM

Pa disappeared into the woods with fishing gear. Rita exhaled a sigh of relief. Freedom was sweet. She left the bathroom. When Pa was around, she attended him, pleased him, did what he thought she ought to be doing. It was the way of Mormonism, he told her. She was a female. Females, according to Pa, were created to serve males.

Rita never read the Bible. It was the "Law Book." Glancing toward it on the shelf, it had belonged to Pa's parents. Her grandparents. She never knew them.

She should burn it.

The thought made her grin.

After all, she was a sinner.

A witch by birth.

Bound for hell anyway.

What did it matter?

According to Pa, it was a woman's nature to be attracted to the devil. Eve was the first and every woman after her. It is why good girls liked the bad boys.

A sudden craving sprang up in Rita. Now would be a good time for some Deysi Blakk.

"No!" She spoke to the air. To the craving. It wasn't her craving the book, it was the book craving her.

The book scared her. It was causing her to have dreams of Mr. Scarecrow stalking her. Nightmares of her frightened baby crying "Mommy" in the attic. In the nightmares it wasn't a baby doll, but a real baby.

Rita forced her thoughts back on being a woman. Pa preached women were deceitful and cunning creatures. Slithering about, using their womanly ways to manipulate men into sin. Perhaps it was true. Magazines taught as much. There were always articles in the magazines teaching such things like *Ten Ways to Charm a Man*, *The Magic of Flirting*, *Glamour and Beguile*, *Daddy's Girl*, and so on.

Standing next to the sofa, Rita reached down to get Deysi's book, but stopped. A chill went up her spine. The book had almost tricked her into reading it.

The book was sweet-talking her with the promise of knowledge and understanding. It offered her secrets of magic and manipulation. It promised her freedom.

The book was hungry. It wanted a bite of her

soul. She ignored the book, went to the radio, and turned it on.

The song on the radio made her think about friends. What friends she had. Johnny, the sneaky little pervert, was a good friend. Betty too. Nick and Nancy were friends. Glenn and Paul were more than friends, they were lovers.

Rita felt another tug to read just one page. One page couldn't hurt.

No!

In the past week, she had gone to the bathroom three different times to cut herself. To bleed. The book's magic was strong and now she understood the warning on the cover.

Freedom, the book whispered to her soul.

What would freedom feel like? What would it be like not having Pa around? What would it be like to go where she wanted? When she wanted. Doing what she wanted. What would it feel like to be a York?

Rita York.

On the radio, the Three Dog Night song "Joy to the World" came on. It was this week's number one. Rita loved the song. She turned up the volume and sang along.

Rita had no joy. She was a dog on a chain. When Pa was gone, she, like a dog, was free to wander around, but only as far as the length of chain.

The Brandts' dogs were kept on chains. Rita wandered over to the front door, opened it to look toward the Brandts', to look at their dogs and see how her life looked like. What it looked like being chained to an old broken-down house.

There was a man standing on the road in front of her house. He was staring. She felt goose pimples. Normally she would call to her pa and he'd tell her what to do. Her pa was gone. The stranger's gaze fell on her. She recognized him. He was the Indian hippie known as BootShaker. She had seen him one day on a trip into town. Pa had gone into a tirade about hippies and how they were all communist. How he'd like to kill'em. Kill'em all.

She had been intrigued. Hippies were about freedom. Freedom was a hippy's religion.

Rita stared at the Indian staring back. What was she going to do? Why was he there? What did he want? People told wild stories about BootShaker. Some said he was scarier than his witch-doctor pa.

If she did as Pa would want, she would shut the door and pretend not to be at home. However, she had a hippy spirit in her. She stepped out onto the porch. "Can I help you?"

BootShaker asked, "You live here?"

"Yes."

"Are your parents home?"

"It's just me and Pa." *And the devil.* "He's gone fishing."

The man stared. Rita asked, "What do you want?"

After a moment of silence, he answered, "To share with you the Good News."

"What good news?"

"The Good News about life and freedom!"

Rita's lips curled into a smile. He was speaking her language. She stepped off the porch, taking a few steps toward the road. "You want me to become a hippy?" She could picture herself a hippy. Enjoying a life of freedom.

The Indian smiled. "Not exactly."

Rita's smile faded. Was she not even good enough to be a hippy? Would she ever be anything more than a worthless dog? "What then?" The hardness in her voice said that his merchandise might not be welcome.

"Jesus loves you. His desire for you is life and happiness. Do you attend church?"

"No. Pa doesn't believe in church."

"Do you believe in God?"

Rita shrugged her shoulders. Johnny didn't believe in God. He said people who believe in God were fools. Glenn, however, did believe in God. "I've not decided."

"Would you like to believe in God?"

Rita shrugged. Feeling defiant, she answered, "I'd rather believe in a fairy godmother." If she had a fairy godmother, she would ask to be free of Pa.

"God wants to be a Father to you. He doesn't operate through magic, but the supernatural. He is the Creator. He can give you the desires of your heart."

She took a couple more steps toward the Indian. "Pa says God is mean and vengeful. Because Adam and Eve disobeyed God and broke the law, we all became sinners. And God hates sinners."

"God hates sin. Not sinners. God is love. God loves you. He sent Jesus to die on the cross to pay the debt of your sins so you could be free. Free to have a relationship with God in spite of your sins. To experience life instead of death."

"God made his Son die to pay for my sins? Sounds unfair. Mean and vengeful-like."

"It was unfair, but Jesus chose to die for you. It was His choice. He was willing to do that for you."

"You say God loves me? That He is love?"

"He is the origin and First Cause of love."

"What about those stories where God told the Jews to go from one city to another, and kill all men, women, and children? Kill everybody and everything. That sounds to me mean and vengeful. Where's the love there?"

"You are referring to Deuteronomy chapter 3 perhaps?"

Rita didn't know, but her pa had read her the scriptures. He liked those scriptures. He liked the stories of killings and slaughtering. He liked focusing on the meanness and cruelty of God.

BootShaker continued, "You are referring to the Land of Promise God promised to Abraham and his seed after him. Do you know who was occupying the Promised Land at that time?"

Rita shrugged.

"It was the tainted bloodline of the seven giant nations."

That sparked Rita's interest. Giants were spoken about in the Bible, but she never really thought about them as being real or true. Giants were non-human. Freak creatures of legend. She didn't know much about giants other than their association with some ancient time.

"Do you know where the giants came from?" BootShaker asked.Rita shook her head.

"Before God created the earth, before Adam and Eve, He created the angels. Angels are sometimes referred to as the sons of God. The greatest, wisest, and most beautiful was Lucifer. At some point, Lucifer decided, being full of beauty and wisdom, that he should be a god. To be his own god. To have and to pursue his own will and desires. He went about selling himself and his philosophy of freedom from God to the angels. He created a great angelic following which led to a rebellion. The angels who followed him, became the 'Fallen Angels.'

"After God created Adam and Eve, Lucifer, in the form of a serpent, in the form of a dragon, visited them in the garden of Eden. This is why in some cultures, history records dragons as being wise, beautiful, and able to talk. Adam and Eve bought into the dragon's philosophical merchandise of 'self-deity' and '*It's my life.*'

"Allying with the dragon, now known as Satan,

the fallen angels came and dwelled among man. And they, the sons of God, saw that the daughters of men were appealing and they took them for wives. The offspring were giants.

"Giants were a tainted creature of demon and human. Monsters in many aspects. They were big and mean. Evil in nature. They began to breed and multiply upon the earth, creating evil and a tainted bloodline.

"Wickedness upon the earth rapidly grew very great. Violence was everywhere and people's minds and thoughts dwelt on evil continuously. This was why God destroyed the earth in Noah's day. It was to preserve the human bloodline.

"After the flood, fallen angels once again mated with the daughters of men, creating another race of giants that grew into the seven nations mentioned in the seventh chapter of Deuteronomy. This tainted race of humans and giants occupying the Promised Land considered themselves a superior race. This is why God told the children of Israel to kill every man, woman, and child and not to take wives nor marry into these people. God wanted to destroy this tainted bloodline from off the earth. It was evil and would only produce evil-minded and heartless men using violence as a weapon to dominate, oppress, and rule those deemed less superior.

"Now when you say God was being mean and cruel by having every man, woman, and child killed, it was just the opposite. God was protecting the human race through a surgical operation of removing a cancer. It was to protect the human race.

"To protect you.

"You are precious to Him.

"The Good News is that God loves you. He does not wish anyone to perish and go to hell. Hell was created for Satan and the angels who followed him. Not for humans. However, for those who choose to follow Satan, those who reject God's plan of salvation and would rather do their own thing instead of God's, they will also be cast into hell with their king.

"I invite you to accept Christ as payment and ransom for your sins. God's free gift to you. You no longer have to be a sinner. You can be free! Would you like to experience God and freedom? Will you make a decision today to turn to Christ?"

Rita felt confused and anxious. She was in a fog. Her heart was pounding. The Indian was staring. Staring into her soul. She didn't like him seeing her soul. She didn't like this conversation. She needed to think. Reason things out. "My pa doesn't like me talking to strangers. I should go back inside." She turned and headed for the house.

When she stepped up to the porch, BootShaker called, "Rita."

She turned. "How'd you know my name?"

"God whispered it. God wants to prove His love for you. Earlier, you said you would rather believe in a fairy godmother; if you had one, what would you desire?"

"To be a York. Can God do that?"

"All things are possible with God."

"Yeah? Then I want to be a York. And not years from now through marriage. There's nothing supernatural about that. I can make that happen."

"How soon, Rita, do you want to be a York?"

Rita shrugged and then answered, "God created the world in seven days. I'll give Him one week to make me a York."

"Rita, God will do it in three. In three days from now you will be of the household of York. And not by marriage."

"I doubt that," Rita answered with skepticism. She entered the house and shut the door. Her heart was racing. Her hands were trembling. She stepped over to a window and peeked out. BootShaker was gone. She couldn't see him anywhere. She eased open the front door, peeking out. No Indian. She looked in all directions. No Indian anywhere.

She felt a tug from *Blakk Magick*. Ignoring it, she went to the refrigerator, grabbed a beer, opened it and took a gulp. Taking a seat on the sofa, she took another gulp. Setting the beer down, she reached into the sofa and took hold of the book *Blakk Magick*. Realizing what she was doing, she yelled, "No!" and jerked her hand away.

The book was hungry.

She cussed aloud and said, "Why won't everyone just leave me alone!" She got up and went to the bathroom. She opened the medicine cabinet, took out a razorblade, and sat down on the toilet. She ran the blade across the top side of her wrist. Bright red blood appeared on the cut. She sighed, took a breath, and relaxed. And then realized what she had just done. What was happening to her? Everything was getting out of control. She didn't want to be crazy like Pa. She didn't want to be crazy like Deysi Blakk. She didn't want to feed the shadows. She just wanted to be normal. She just wanted to be a York.

Rita began to cry.

Homer cast his rod toward a partially submerged fallen tree. The cast fell short, hitting the trunk and bouncing off. He cursed, wanting the cast to go over the trunk. He reeled the line in and cast again. It was better. He worked the bait and soon reeled in a hand-size bluegill. He carefully freed the fish from the hook. Fish were his friends. He held the fish up before his face, looking at it eye to eye. "You ain't too smart are ya, ya dumb fish? Been skipping school?" Homer snickered. "Ah well, I likes ya anyway." Homer tossed the fish back into the creek.

It was a good day and Homer was in good spirits. He hadn't felt like this in a while. Perhaps it was because it was spring. To a farmer, spring was always a special time of the year.

Homer tried his luck again, but to no avail. He moved on toward another spot. Standing in a foot of water, Homer cast into the deep area next to a fallen tree. Getting no response, he changed the lure.

Popping bugs were okay for fishing in general, but he wanted something more tempting to bass.

Homer took another step toward the deeper water with another cast. This time it hit in the targeted spot. He began the "dance." He had practiced working his lure until he created what he called the "dance." In his mind, he pictured the lure dancing about in a mocking manner that teased and provoked bass. In his mind's eye, the lure was boastful. Homer could hear the lure half talking and half singing,

Come and get me,
Come and eat me,
If you think you can.
Do you think you can?
I don't think you can.
Dumb, dumb fish,
Dumb, dumb fish.
La, la, la.
La, la, la.

Homer felt something take the bait. The vibration and movement suggested bass. The tug-of-war was on! The bass on the end of the line was putting up a worthy and enjoyable fight. Homer played and had a good time, but eventually reeled it in. A smallmouth. Medium size.

Gently freeing the fish, he looked it in the eye. "Homer's my name. Fishing's my game." He looked intently into the fish's eyes searching for intelligence. "You ain't the smartest tuna in the sea, but you got heart and I like that about you." He released the fish.

He watched it swim away, disappearing into deeper water. He wanted another one. There would be more. Bigger ones. More challenging. Homer moved on, looking for another spot.

Homer, making another cast, sensed the presence of something. He turned his head to glance at the stream behind him. He didn't expect to see anything. In truth, he figured it was nothing more than a spook sneaking up on him to haunt him. After killing Veg and June, he had it coming. He figured he'd be sporty about it.

Instead of seeing nothing, he saw an Indian standing nearby. It was unexpected and startling. Indians were such sneaky, creepy people.

"Good day, sir," the sneaky creepy Indian greeted.

Homer turned his attention back to fishing. If he ignored the sneaky creepy Indian, maybe the sneaky creepy Indian would vanish. Or at least go away.

No such luck. The sneaky creepy Indian was sneaking closer. The stream whispered each step the intruder took against its current. This was invasion! This was Homer's little spot in the world. His sanctuary. His place of peace, comfort, and friends. The sneaky creepy Indian had no right being here!

"How's the fishing?" the Indian tried for conversation.

Obviously, the sneaky creepy Indian wasn't just

going to go away. He would have to speak with him. COULD HE NOT JUST EVER HAVE A DAY OF PEACE, ENJOYMENT, AND HAPPINESS WITHOUT INTERRUPTIONS? MUST PEOPLE ALWAYS SPOIL THINGS FOR HIM! DID GOD HATE HIM THAT MUCH!

If he had his hammer, he could wait until the sneaky creepy Indian stepped close enough where he could spin around and greet the intruder with a hammer to the forehead.

That'd be fun!

But he didn't have one. It is so hard to think of everything all the time.

"Caught anything yet?"

"You a reporter?" Homer answered as he worked his line.

"More of a fisher-of-men."

Homer, thinking he said "fisherman," glanced his way. Not seeing any gear, he asked, "Yeah? You catch'em with yer hands, do ya?"

"Not so much."

"I don't see a pole in yer hands." Homer, focused on fishing, tried to be rude hoping the intruder would get the hint and move on.

"My pole isn't natural. It's spiritual."

Homer thought, *Either sneaky creepy Indian had been hitting the peace pipe a bit too much or he's an escapee from the Looney Toon Reservation.* Mockingly Homer asked, "So how's the fishing in your world?"

"I've had a nibble or two."

"Perhaps, you need to change yer bait."

"Perhaps." The Indian, standing beside Homer, watched the line with him. "You live around here?"

"Do you?"

"I sense a spirit of animosity in you."

"Really? Perhaps I just need a little bit of peace and quiet. Some alone time. Maybe do a little fishing. Enjoy some nature."

"I don't think fishing is your answer."

"Yeah? What's your prescription? What magic pill has the big chief got you on?"

"Freedom."

So, here it was. Trying to enjoy what had started out a good day was now being ruined by a sneaky, creepy hippy Indian. Homer hated hippies. Homer hated Indians. Homer hated sneaky creepy people. Homer hated that he didn't have his hammer—that he couldn't bash the intruder's head.

"Do you want to be free, Homer?"

"How you know my name?" Creepier and creepier.

"God told me."

Out of the corner of his eye, Homer could see the Indian studying him. Homer felt a flood of anger rising within.

"Do you believe in God, Homer?"

"Who are you?"

"A man with a message."

"From God?"

"Yes."

Homer snorted. "So what would the Big Guy be wanting me to know?"

"How much He loves you."

First freedom, now love—hippy words. "Love? God doesn't love me! If anything, He hates me."

"Why would you think such a thing?"

Homer, breaking from his stance, turned toward the Indian holding the rod with one hand and pointing to his face with the other. "Look at me! Is this love?"

"It's the work of sin and death. It is not the work of God."

"I think you should walk away while you can, before I commit a work of sin and death on you!" Homer nearly shouted. Angry winds of a dark storm was brewing within. Intensifying by the second.

StormDancer, not intimidated, calmly answered, "You're angry with God. It's understandable. God does not mind that you are angry. But your anger is misplaced. God loves you and wants to free you from your prison of anger and regret. He wants to give you a divine peace going beyond your understanding."

Shouting God's name in vain, Homer threw his rod. He doubled his fist and stepped into punching range of the creepy hippy Indian. Homer shouted, "I was at peace! I was enjoying a moment of happiness and pleasure before you came along! Before God sent you to ruin my day! God hates me with passion! He keeps me alive only to torture me!" Homer, lowering his voice, insanely and calmly added with deadly intent, "Maybe I should share some of that divine love God has shown me on you! Would you like to feel God's love through the pounding of my fists as I bash in your face?"

"God loves you, Homer. He wants to bless you."

Blinding demonic rage erupted deep within Homer. With deadly intent, lightning speed, and suddenness, Homer, no longer in control, charged forward to grasp the Indian by the throat, to choke the life out of him, to crush his windpipe, and then break his neck! And afterwards, pound the Indian's face into mush!

Homer's next coherent thought came as he found himself lying face down in the stream pushing himself up out of the water. What had just happened? On his knees, holding himself out of the water, he shook his head to shake away the confusion. Lifting his head, he glanced around. The Indian stood nearby. His last thought was to kill the Indian. Then everything went black. Staying in the position he was, he tried to gather his senses.

StormDancer spoke: "I apologize. You charged me. I had to put you down. Your speed and power didn't leave room for gentleness."

Homer was feeling disoriented and confused. He needed a drink of whiskey. He couldn't seem to remember where he kept it. Why couldn't he remember? Suddenly he wanted to die. Death seemed his only answer. His only option. He needed to die and he needed to do it now! He needed a knife! He needed to slice open his throat.

Feeling panicked, where was his knife?

The Indian stepped over and placed his hand on top of Homer's head. StormDancer charged, "As a child of God, as a priest and king of the Most High, I, in the name of Christ Jesus, grant you freedom! I command the evil spirit within to release you and go!"

Homer felt intense fear deep in his soul as the Indian kept praying.

Feeling searing heat, a scream of agony came out of Homer's mouth. He convulsed, falling again face first into the water. His soul felt like it was being torn apart. Foul language of a demonic voice screaming out was cursing God. Homer fought to push himself up again. He vomited. The stench was repulsive, filled with death and decay. The odor caused him to vomit again.

And then, feeling his soul ripping apart, the demon was gone.

In the stream, like an animal on all fours, Homer's arms shook under the weight of his body. His mind was reeling. He felt strange. Incomplete.

Who was he?

What was he?

He felt only half a being.

Homer felt someone helping him up. It was the Indian. The Indian was speaking a language he didn't understand. The Indian helped Homer over to the bank. Leaning against a tree, the forest seemed different. It looked different. It was full of life. Homer hadn't noticed the life before. The forest before had always been a place of darkness and covering. A place to hide. A place of seclusion. A sanctuary for the misunderstood and unwanted. A place for wild and dangerous beasts. Now he wasn't feeling so beastly. He wasn't feeling wild and dangerous. He felt weak. Vulnerable.

He felt Human.

He felt shame.

Ashamed of what he had become. He yearned for a drink of whiskey. He didn't seem to have the energy to pursue it.

The Indian spoke: "Homer, God loves and cares about you. Will you accept Him as your Lord and Savior?"

The hate and anger Homer normally had toward God wasn't there. He didn't feel a desire to be friends with God either. Homer tiredly replied, "God doesn't love me."

"Oh, but He does. He is Love."

"Look around. Look at the world. If God is love, then why is there such evil? Why is there disease? Why are innocent children and people stricken with deformities? Why is there so much death, sorrow, and pain? Why was I burned? Why am I cursed with looking like a monster?"

StormDancer answered, "Because, Homer, mankind chose freedom from God. Man chose the law of self-interest and indulgence. To learn evil. To know the pleasures of sin. Sin offers great fun, but the wages of sin is death. The curse of sin is entropy. Entropy is the physical corruption that gives way to death, diseases, sorrow, and pain. This world you see is what freedom from God looks like.

"Homer, will you surrender to God? Will you allow Love to fill your heart and life?"

"You don't understand," Homer challenged. "I've done bad things. Very bad things."

"God's love is greater than any evil you've committed. God loves the person you are meant to be. The person in you." StormDancer stepped over and placed a hand on his shoulder. "Will you, Homer? Will you accept God's love, his forgiveness and salvation?"

Homer, in a moment of clarity, thought back on his teenage years. The memory of an altar call. The pleading of the Spirit drawing him to repentance. The stubbornness of his will. The desire for pleasure. The beautiful big-breasted young woman willing to grant him certain carnal favors. Favors a young Christian man would have to turn away from.

The struggle between flesh and Spirit ended with him deliberately choosing sex instead of salvation. He reasoned, he would choose sin for a season. What would be the harm? Later, after he was married, he would choose God, and like his parents, join the church and raise a family. But, an unexpected chain of events took him into a different direction. He got lost.

The Indian said, "Homer, God is calling you one last time. Your eternal choice will be decided this day. What is going to be your choice?"

Homer bowed his head between his knees. He was tired of all the hate. Tired of feeling dead. He opened his mouth. "I surrender."

He was almost shocked by it. However, it felt good to say. He said it again: "I surrender." The thick blanket of death and darkness wrapped around him like a straightjacket ... loosened.

"I surrender!" he declared more purposely.

The blanket seemed to crack and crumble as rays of love began to penetrate his soul, bringing light and warmth.

"I surrender. I accept Christ!" The straightjacket of death and darkness fell.

Bawling like a baby, he felt himself being wrapped in the arms of God. The intense hate he had known for so long was replaced by love as emotional healing took place.

Time seemed to vanish for a while. And then with excited eyes, Homer looked around. The Indian was gone. He was disappointed. He wanted to hug the Indian! Love was bubbling inside him. He wanted to share it!

Homer stood. The forest was beautiful and alive. Birds were singing. He couldn't remember the last time he'd heard a bird sing. He had forgotten they did. He listened. There were so many wonderful sounds. He wanted to hug the forest. He reached around the tree beside him and in an embrace said, "I love you, tree."

He stepped from the tree and gazed up into the canopy covering him. "I love you, forest!" He looked beyond the canopy into the sky and shouted, "I love God Almighty!"

Rita entered into his thoughts. Suddenly, he was overwhelmed with love for her and felt his heart was going to burst. He wanted to hold her. Squeeze her tight. He would tell her how much he loved her. He would fall to his knees and beg her forgiveness. He had done evil to her. Great evil! He would tell her how wrong he had been. He would share the love of God with her. He would set her free.

There was so much mending he had to do.

It couldn't wait!

Homer began to run. As fast as his old body would allow him. He ran feeling younger than he was. He would run for as long as he could—all the way home if his body allowed. He couldn't get to Rita quick enough to tell her how much he loved her. How much God loved her!

Homer lay on the forest floor, blood running out of his nose. He never saw it coming. Never expected it. The bat, swung into his distorted scarred head as he ran by, busted open his skull.

Homer lay dead.

Shocked by his actions, Johnny Brandt stared down at the monster. He couldn't believe what he had just done. It hadn't seemed real. Something resembling a smirk formed on his lips as the demon grinned within.

Johnny threw straw and a piece of tattered cloth from a scarecrow on the ground next to the body and fled.

26

THE YORKS

Night had come and Pa hadn't come home yet. It was unusual. When he went fishing, he was never gone this long.

A strange day it had been. The Indian. Deysi Blakk's book haunting her. The anxiety. Finally, she had went to drinking beer until drunk and then passing out. Waking up as the sun was going down, she was depressed and queasy. The radio wasn't bringing comfort. She fixed something to eat, but the queasiness didn't go away. Things weren't right.

How had life gotten so out of control?

Where was Pa?

She wanted her pa to show up so things would seem normal. Standing on the back porch, she stared into the woods. There was nothing to see. What was Pa doing? Would he be gone the rest of the night too? Looking in one direction and another, she thought about the scarecrows. Were they out there? Last week people had went hunting the scarecrows. None were found or seen.

Rita went back inside, through the house, and out the front door. No messages from Glenn. She didn't expect to see one, but still felt disappointment. She didn't want to be alone.

Looking toward the Brandts', nothing unusual there.

Where was Johnny? He always seemed to have a sixth sense when Pa was gone. Pa had been gone all day and Johnny hadn't been around.

Things weren't right.

Perhaps Johnny's mom and pa were keeping a tight rein on him because of the scarecrows.

Rita stepped back inside the house and locked the door. She wished she had someone to talk to. She looked around the room, but purposely not in the corners for fear of seeing movement.

All was silent. No eerie noises. Things weren't right.

Looking at the sofa, she felt a tug from Deysi's book. The tug was weak. Perhaps the more she resisted, the weaker the magic became.

Magic was strengthened through agreement.

She decided to take a bath.

After the bath, she read magazines and listened to the radio until bedtime. Deysi Blakk's book left her alone and no ghost haunted her. It was a relief.

The next morning, Rita was up early. She had been awake off and on throughout the night. She got up hoping Pa had come home and was passed out in his easy chair and was truly surprised to see it vacant. Anxiety washed over her. She searched the house and then went outside. No sign of Pa. She went to the edge of the woods and walked a little ways down the path he normally took, calling out to him.

He never answered.

She had never been in the woods for fear of becoming lost. And now there were scarecrow monsters to worry about.

She returned to the house.

Had scarecrows got Pa?

Anxiety grew inside. She didn't know what to do. She needed help. They didn't have a phone. She would need to go either to the Brandts' or to the Yorks'.

Johnny's dad had been nice to her. Mr. Brandt was friends with Pa. She kind of felt comfortable going to him. But he was mean and vicious sometimes and she didn't like that.

She had met Glenn's dad, but at the time, she was scared. Glenn told her the next day at school his dad wasn't even mad. Concerned more than anything. Glenn said his dad was a nice guy.

In her spirit, Mr. York was the best choice. She stepped off the porch in the direction of the York house. The closer she got to the Yorks' house, the greater her anxiety became. The more vulnerable she felt. Something bad had happened. Life had changed.

Rusty met her with tail wagging. It was a small comfort.

Slowly and hesitantly, Rita stepped upon the front porch. Sick with anxiety and a trembling hand, she made herself knock.

The door opened. It was Jenny. A look of shock crossed her face. She asked harshly, "What do you want?"

Trying to remain calm, Rita answered, "Is your pa home?"

Jenny looked confused. "You want my dad?"

"Please." Her voice quivered. She felt a tear slide down her cheek.

"Just a minute." Jenny turned from the door and walked away.

Moments later Mr. York came to the door, opening it. "Come in."

Rita stepped in. Faces were staring in the background. Tears were sliding down her face.

"What can I do for you?" Mr. York asked.

"My pa," and with that she broke down into a sob. She didn't mean to. It just happened. The release of pent-up anxiety. She tried talking, but was sobbing too much to be understood.

Mrs. York, putting arms around her, pulled her into an embrace, whispering words of comfort. For a time all Rita could do was sob.

With the family gathered around, Rita eventually calmed down enough to tell them her pa was missing.

Mr. York asked, "How long has he been missing?"

"Yesterday morning he left to go fishing. I haven't seen him since."

"Where did he go fishing?"

"I don't know. Somewhere in the woods."

"Around here? Did he walk?"

Rita nodded. "Behind our house is a path into the woods and he went down that path."

Through tears, she watched Mr. York say to his wife, "Keep her here." He turned to Denny. "Get the sheriff over here. In the meantime, I'll see if I can find him."

It didn't take Ben York long to find the body of Homer Pierce. He escorted the sheriff to the body.

Ben York spent the day hanging with the sheriff's men, taking part in an area search looking for clues and those who might be responsible.

Returning home around suppertime, he found his wife and Jenny in the kitchen. Knowing Rita had been told, he asked, "How's Rita?"

"As well as expected, I suppose. She's in some form of shock, I'm sure. She mostly just sat and watched TV. Glenn hasn't left her side. I've heard her laugh a few times from the programs they've watched. She said she hadn't watched TV in two years and has never watched colored television before. Nor one with such a clear picture. She seems fascinated by it. I think it helps to keep her mind occupied and off the tragedy."

"The TV is making it easy for her to escape reality. It may be a good thing for now."

"What's the story? What do they think happened?"

Speaking in a whisper, "Evidence suggests scarecrows. From the foot patterns, it looked like Mr. Pierce was running and someone stepped out from behind a tree and swung a club into his head. The evidence isn't conclusive, but the consensus is that Pierce came across the scarecrows or they came across him, and in running to get away, he was ambushed."

"How many are there?"

"No one knows. From the reports over the past year, there are three for sure. Could be several."

"It's the work of the devil!"

"That's for sure."

"What are we going to do about Rita?" Mrs. York asked.

"What can we do? The girl doesn't need to be alone right now. She's too young to be on her own. It's too dangerous for her to return home. This makes the third person killed in this area. In fact, most of the 'scarecrow' activity has taken place on this side of town. It's believed they're hiding out in this area somewhere."

"That frightens me."

"It's worrisome. However, there will be teams out tonight in this area watching and searching. We'll be alright."

Mrs. York proposed, "I guess we can put Rita in with Jenny."

"What?" Jenny wasn't keen on that idea.

"For now anyway. Like it or not, for better or worse, I got a feeling Rita is going to become a part of this family," Ben York told them.

27

TILL DEATH DO US PART

Jared "Thunder" Seelot called for a meeting that included his parents, Chief KnifeWater and Sophia. Also invited were Sedges and her parents, Lewis and Pearline Vannhorn.

"Son, is this it?" the Chief asked. "Are we still waiting on someone?"

"Everyone is here." Jared said, "I have an announcement to make." Jared looked at Sedges. "You may show them."

Sedges stepped up next to Jared, smiling ear to ear. She raised her left hand to display the ring on her finger.

Jared said, "I've asked this lady to marry me."

"And I said yes!" Sedges beamed.

The reaction was that of surprise. After a moment of silence, Jared's expression darkened. "Wow! We were expecting a bit more enthusiasm."

"You have to give us a moment, Son," the Chief declared. "You just dropped a bomb."

Sophia Seelot asked, "Have you two been dating?"

"Secretly. A few months now."

"Why the secret?" Sophia asked.

Jared looked at his mother. "Our romance was personal. People meddle way too much in my life as it is. Sedges and I fell in love. I wanted the romance to be between her and me. Not her, me, and the tribe. I didn't want a 'romance' filled with politics."

The Chief nodded. "I can understand that." Standing up and stepping toward Sedges, he said, "I can't think of a better girl to complement my son. Nor one I'd rather have for a daughter-in-law." Embracing Sedges, he added, "His decision has made me a proud father. There may be hope for him yet."

Lewis and Pearline also giving approval, everyone celebrated with hugs and congratulations.

Politics dictated an open celebratory engagement party for the tribe and town. The event would take place at the city park.

The city park, Three Springs of Hope Memorial Park, was originally established in 1910 by Mayor Thomas Seelot. It was to memorialize and preserve the actual Indian encampment site in which the city was founded. At this time, the park was named "Springs of Hope Park."

Thirty years later in the 1940s, major improvements made on the park included doubling of the park size, adding additional amusements, and the creation of the city's lake, Three Springs Lake. Chief and Mayor Earl "JayBird" Seelot authorized it with the erection of the Earl Hollis Dam south of the city. It was also during this time he authorized the purchase of the tribal grounds east of the city.

Major improvements on the park happened again in the early sixties under the current mayor and chief. KnifeWater changed the named Springs of Hope Park to Three Springs of Hope Memorial Park in honor of the "three" springs creating the lake and the three men the city was founded upon. Improvements included the doubling of the park size again with additional recreational activities and picnic sites. KnifeWater's major addition to the park was the large stone monument in which the top half was sculpted into three statues—in the spirit of Mount Rushmore—featuring the upper bodies of the three celebrated founders of the city: Chief One-Who-Sees-A-Lot, to his left was Tribal Priest ThunderBear, and on his right Quill Pen Jake. The monument included a historical inscription and was erected upon the preserved site of the original encampment. Along with this was the creation of a ceremonial encampment including five life-size concrete teepees. Although teepees were never a part of the city's history nor of the Cherokee culture, teepees are iconic of Native America. Teepees bring ambience and tourists.

Beth Seeker arrived at the park with Quillpen Jack and Tianna RedBird. With a few hours of daylight left, Quillpen parked his car in an obscure place in the shade and away from the crowd. Getting out of the car, Quillpen affectionately patted it on the hood. Tianna shaking her head, "I hope someday you'll love me as much as you do this car."

"A warrior and his horse are one." Quillpen kissed his hand and placed it on the car. "Till death do us part."

"Oh my gawd," Tianna declared.

Beth told Tianna, "I think he just married the car."

"I think you're right." In pretend anger, Tianna pushed Quillpen out of her way as she headed to the celebration.

The celebration was open invitation and there was already a crowd wandering about. The smell of meat cooking from various locations gave Beth an appetite. Tonight's feast was deer, beaver, duck, dove, and squirrel.

Beth found her mother, Chief KnifeWater and Sophia, Jared, Sedges, and Sedges' parents at the hub of activities where there was food, drink, and conversation. After greetings and congratulations, Beth tried the wild-game salad featuring each of the meats. She eventually ended up with RiverDawg, StormDancer, and Tish, who were using one of the concrete teepees as their campsite. She decided to hang with them. RiverDawg was offering his special *Tsgoya* soup for those interested.

Denny York, driving, entered the park from the south entrance, making his way around the lake to the front side where the celebration was taking place. Jenny York was up front beside him. Rita Pierce, excited, was in the back seat next to Glenn. She raised his hand to her lips for a kiss. It was her tenth day living with the Yorks.

Only fourteen people attended the funeral of her pa. Those fourteen were the Yorks, the Brandts, Paul Sumner, and to her surprise BootShaker Quake and his hippy wife. It was a weird, solemn, and uncomfortable day. Although the Yorks and Brandts were polite to one another, it was obvious the families were not friends.

BootShaker, in giving condolence, told Rita he had talked to her pa the day he was killed. BootShaker told Rita her pa had given his life to Jesus and she could at least take comfort knowing he was now at peace and in heaven. Rita didn't say so, but she didn't believe it. She wondered why the Indian would tell her such a lie. Perhaps, it was proper social etiquette for such an event. She didn't know, but she knew Pa. Pa hated God! He hated Indians. No way would he have done what the Indian said. BootShaker was a trickster. Pa was burning in hell just like her mother. It was where he needed to be. She would take comfort in that!

During the funeral, Rita would have liked to have spent some time with Johnny. She could speak honestly with him and get things off her chest. But she never got to talk with him. His pa kept a close rein on him. The whole time Johnny was there, he acted strange. He wasn't being Johnny, but it wasn't a normal event.

Rita was glad when it was all over and done with. She was glad to shut the door on that part of her life.

Denny parked the car and the four got out. Glenn, taking Rita's hand, began leading her. Denny said, "Don't forget the city curfew. Be back here by nine."

"Yeah, yeah," Glenn answered.

Having only seen the teepees from the highway that went by the park running through town, Rita wanted to see them up close and followed Glenn as he led the way.

"I can't believe you've never been here before," Glenn said.

"Not on this side of the lake," Rita remembering her first visit to the park, which was with Paul less than a month ago.

Paul Sumner, arriving, went searching for Rita, finding her with Glenn seated at a picnic table near the lake's edge. They were eating. Paul was somewhat disappointed Rita was in slacks and modestly dressed. Her outfit looked to be one of Jenny's.

Paul greeted, "There you two are. Jenny said you were around somewhere."

With a tone of annoyance, Glenn greeted, "Hey, man."

Rita frowned at Glenn and said with delight, "Hi. Glad you came. Sit."

Paul sat down next to Rita. She leaned and kissed him on the cheek. "I am so happy you're here!"

"Me too. I've been worried about you. Wondering how you've been doing?"

"I'm fine. Really, you guys. Never been better."

"So, I guess you finally got to see the teepees?"

"I did. They're cool. Glenn took me inside one. He's been showing me around and explaining things." Rita leaned over to Glenn with a kiss to the cheek. She said, "I love this park. It is such a great place. I can't wait to have a daughter of my own and bring her here to play."

"A daughter?" Paul questioned.

"I see myself with a daughter."

"And who do you see as the father?"

With a playful smile, Rita evaded the question, saying, "Glenn was just telling me about the Seelots and how every Seelot was married here at this park. That it has become a tribal tradition for members of the tribe to be married here. And as a part of their marriage, they share a drink from the three springs. A kind of good omen for blessings and prosperity."

"Have you met any of the Seelots yet?" Paul asked.

"No. But, Glenn pointed them out to me and told me who they were."

The park's amphitheater used the natural landscape forming tiered seating by way of retaining walls. Julia Brooks, sitting beside her sister, watched Jared Seelot, Quillpen Jack, and others throw hawks at a target made from the cross-section of a tree trunk and mounted on a tripod with a red dot painted in the center. Denny York and Dave Sumner were cajoled into participating. The tribe members were good. Dave and Denny not so much. When their hawks did hit the target, they rarely stuck.

Julia kept an eye out for Paul, who was supposed to be there. She hadn't seen him yet. Finally, she told Valerie, "I'm bored. I'm gonna go and mingle."

"Do not leave this area!" Valerie commanded her, looking down at her watch. "It's almost six o'clock; at seven, meet me in front of the statue so I know where you are and that you're safe."

"Fine. Gee. It's not like I was planning to go off anywhere. I'm not stupid."

"I mean it, Julia! Seven o'clock. If you're not there, I'll have people searching for you!"

"I'll be there!"

Rita, walking between Glenn and Paul, held hands with both of them. The trio stopped to watch the hawk-throwing contest since Glenn and Paul's brothers were participating.

Rita asked, "So the guy getting ready to throw is Jared Seelot who is known as Thunder, who is getting married?"

"Yes," Glenn answered.

Thunder's hawk stuck the target's bull's-eye. Claps and cheers rang out. He bowed and stepped aside.

Quillpen Jack stepped up.

Rita asked, "His name is Quillpen?" The feather quill stuck in his black straight-brim leather cowboy hat made it easy to remember his name. Quillpen looked more Indian in the way he was dressed, but it was still the typical hippy look of the times: bell-bottoms, tie-dyed tee, and dingo boots.

"Correct," Glenn answered.

Paul added, "He's also known as the Dragon Slayer.""The guy who drives the cherry-black car with *Dragon Slayer* painted on it?" Rita sought confirmation.

"Yes," Paul confirmed.

"And he's the guy," Rita continued, "that got into a knife fight and killed a guy." Rita knew the story. Everyone did.

"Right again," Paul answered.

The Dragon Slayer's hawk landed next to Jared's.

Jenny York, watching her brother throw hawks, saw Glenn, Rita, and Paul walk up. Jenny said to Valerie who was seated next to her, "I just don't understand it."

"Understand what?" Valerie asked.

"Glenn and Paul. Look at them," Jenny pointed.

Valerie looked. They were both holding Rita's hands. "What's up with them anyway? Are they both really dating her?"

"I don't know what's going on. It's weird. She's weird."

"Weird?"

"She stares into your eyes when you're talking to her. It's weird. Glenn says she's looking into your soul to see the truth. Creeps me out."

"How is she? She's living with you guys, right?"

"Unfortunately."

"That bad?"

With an annoying sigh, Jenny answered, "No. Not really. I mean, she's nice enough. She's trying to fit in. She does what she's told. She's eager to help with chores and stuff."

"So what's the problem?"

"I don't know. There's something about her. She's a put-on."

"What do you mean?"

"It's like she's playing a game. Like she's trying to be one of us. Trying to be a York. If you ask her a question, she tries to give a York answer, instead of an honest answer. I can't figure her out. I don't know what the truth is with her. I don't trust her. I feel like she's playing us."

Jenny continued, "Watch her. Watch how she plays Glenn and Paul. How she bounces back and forth between them flirting and charming them. She's got them wrapped around her finger."

Jenny was silent a moment, then added, "I think there may be something between her and Denny too."

"Really. Why's that?"

"I don't know. Denny's smart. Sly. I've noticed him hitting on her."

"Sounds like Denny. What's Rita's response to Denny?"

"Encouraging."

"That's not good."

RiverDawg, sitting in front of a concrete teepee in an "X" chair smoking his "peace" pipe, amused himself with passersby.

StormDancer and Tish were also sitting in "X" chairs. Tish commented to her father-in-law, "It seems to me, most people are leery of you."

RiverDawg pulled the pipe from his lips. "They should be."

RiverDawg spotted Julia Brooks. She was with another girl. Both girls were in short dresses and raised-heel sandals. "Sunshine," RiverDawg called out to her in a whisper.

Julia stopped and turned her head toward him. The other girl, stopping two steps later, turned back. Julia said something to her friend. The girls looked his way. He motioned them over.

They acted reluctant, but came.

"My children, this is Sunshine," RiverDawg introduced Julia to StormDancer and Tish.

StormDancer and Tish greeted her with warm smiles and nods.

RiverDawg said, "Is she not a ray of sunshine amidst a world dark and stormy?"

"You are very beautiful," Tish complimented Julia.

"Thank you," Julia responded graciously.

StormDancer asked, "What is the name your parents gave you?"

"Julia."

RiverDawg looked at the girl with Julia. "What do people call you, child?"

"Cheryl."

"Good to make your acquaintance, Cheryl. You're a pretty young lady as well."

"Thank you."

RiverDawg turned back to Julia. "It's been a long time since last I've seen you. How have you been?"

"Good."

"I'm glad to hear that. Will you sit for a bit? I have a story to share with you."

"Sure. I guess."

"Good." RiverDawg turned to StormDancer. "My son, be so kind and go to the sacred springs and bring back a drink of water from all three springs."

StormDancer humbly got up to do as told.

With StormDancer walking away, RiverDawg said to Tish, "Daughter, would you be so kind as to get these ladies a blanket to sit on."

A blanket was produced and Tish spread it out in front of RiverDawg. The blanket was Native American made. Julia and Cheryl carefully took a seat, doing their best to be ladylike in their short skirts.

After a minute of small talk and joking, RiverDawg, pulling the pipe from his lips, looked at Julia. "My daughter, I see within you the spirit of one of your ancestors. Did you know you have the blood of Cherokee in you?"

Julia answered, "I've heard I do."

"Good. You had a Cherokee mother who was born around the birth of this nation. The mother of One-Who-Sees-A-Lot. She was born on a dark gloomy day, but the instant she left her mother's womb a small break in the clouds allowed a ray of sunlight to touch her body. It was a touch from the Great Spirit giving her a cheerful spirit. ThunderBear, the great priest attending the delivery, said she was blessed."

StormDancer returned with the water.

Julia asked, "ThunderBear? As in the guy in the statue?"

"The very same." RiverDawg took the cup of water from his son and set it down. He continued, "ThunderBear said the ray of sunlight touching the child, was the Spirit Beings above placing in her a gift of promise. The child became known as Ray-Of-Sun, Daughter Of Promise. Ray-Of-Sun's cheerful spirit brought joy and hope to her people."

To emphasize what he was about to say,

RiverDawg leaned forward. "I see Ray-Of-Sun's spirit reborn in you. She was full of life and cheer. But you are full of life and song. There's a song in you. It's a gift of hope."

Julia didn't know what to think. RiverDawg leaned back, sticking the pipe into his mouth again. Suddenly, his old wrinkled face inches from hers, he whispered, "A storm brews. But in you the ray of sunshine brings the promise of rainbow."

Julia blinked and RiverDawg was sitting in his chair as he had been. The grin on his face and the stare in his eyes revealed what no one else saw, or heard.

RiverDawg took the cup of spring water and stood up. He held it up before the four directions, speaking in Cherokee.

When finished, he sat down and offered the cup to Julia, who was still seated on the blanket. RiverDawg said, "Drink, my child. The water is sacred. It will bring to life the gift of hope within you."

Julia's stare traveled to the faces watching her. She raised the cup and drank.

Beth Seeker, passing by one of the concrete teepees, heard someone say, "Elizabeth." She stopped. It was Isaac "Inada" Connesawga. He was standing at the teepee's entrance. A smile broke out on her face.

Isaac pulled her into the teepee. After a lengthy kiss, he said, "Sorry, but I've been dreaming of doing that for months."

"I'll forgive you, if you do it again."

RiverDawg reached into the pouch hanging from his belt and pulled out a necklace made of a thin piece of leather with a small claw of an animal hanging from it. He ceremonially hung it around Julia's neck with a chant. He told her, "The claw is from a bear. It's a strong relic from generations ago. It is now yours. Wearing a bear-claw necklace brings protection and good health. The gift in you must be protected."

"Protected from what?" Julia asked playfully.

"Witchery, Sunshine. Witchery."

At seven o'clock Julia and Cheryl, standing in front of the statue, discussed RiverDawg and the things he'd said. The bear claw was small and dainty. "I should have it put on a chain of white gold."

Cheryl said, "It's unique. Not everyone has a bear claw. It looks good on you."

Valerie and Tianna walked up.

"Happy?" Julia asked her sister.

"Just keep in mind it was at this park that Tianna and I, Dave, and Quillpen were attacked by a scarecrow."

"I haven't forgotten. I'm not going anywhere."

"There's going to be a big hawk-throwing contest shortly. Chief KnifeWater, StormDancer, and RiverDawg are supposed to participate. It's a rare event to have those three competing. Everyone will be down at the amphitheater. I want you down there too. It'll soon be dark and too dangerous to be away from the crowd."

"What if I don't want to watch?"

"It's better than dying. I'll be looking for you."

When Valerie and Tianna went on their way, Julia said to Cheryl, "Like I'm stupid enough to go off and get killed."

Cheryl, flicking the claw lying on her chest, said, "But, *Sunshine*, you have protection."

"Protection against witchery. What's that supposed to mean? I don't know of any witches."

Returning from the island, it seemed everyone was gathered at the amphitheater. "Wonder what's going on?" Glenn asked.

Rita, holding both Glenn and Paul's hands, was trying to keep them both happy. A juggling act focusing on each of them without showing either favoritism or neglect. It was a strange game and Rita was playing it well.

Paul enjoyed it.

Glenn did not.

Glenn was aggravated Paul was there. Glenn wanted Rita to himself and Paul was ruining their night out together. The three of them being together and hanging out used to be fun. Now it had gotten awkward. Rita living with Glenn, Glenn seemed to feel she belonged to him. Paul knew that Glenn was wanting him to back off. It was putting their friendship under great strain. Paul wasn't sure if their friendship was going to survive. They had been best friends for a long time, and Paul hated that it was crumbling. He would perhaps be willing to back off, if it was what Rita wanted. However, Rita didn't want him to back off. She liked the relationship the three of them had. Rita was a special type of lady. She was sexy and liked sex. Paul was not ready to give that up. In all honesty, what Rita was offering him was more appealing than what his friendship with Glenn offered.

Beth and Isaac heard clapping and cheering down at the amphitheater where most everyone had gathered. Spotting Tish, Beth and Isaac made their way to her. Taking a seat next to Tish, Beth asked, "What's going on?"

Tish looked at her and Isaac. "Where've you been? I was worrying. I was just about to get Ira and go looking for you."

"I ran into Isaac. We've been talking."

"Don't be disappearing like that!"

Julia and Cheryl, making an appearance before Valerie at the amphitheater, stood off to the side. Searching the crowd, Julia saw Paul.

The tiered seating of the amphitheater was a semicircle of six rows going downhill to the stage area. The majority of the crowd was seated in the first four rows. Staying above the crowd, Glenn, Rita, and Paul were seated at the left end of the fifth row.

Down below, at the "stage" area, Chief KnifeWater Seelot threw his tomahawk with poise and skill. It stuck in the target dead center in the bull's-eye. Cheers and claps rang out. He went to the target and removed his hawk.

When the Chief was clear, StormDancer, with less poise, threw his hawk. It too hit dead center. He also was applauded.

The next contestant was RiverDawg. RiverDawg stepped up to throw. He said, "This is too easy." He turned his back to the target and threw the hawk. The hawk stuck in the target, but missed the bull's-eye. After the cheering died down, RiverDawg said, "I'm getting old. I missed."

RiverDawg didn't remove his hawk and said to StormDancer, "Think you can beat the old man, now?"

The crowd cheered in anticipation of the challenge.

StormDancer, accepting the challenge, stepped up and threw behind his back; the hawk stuck in the target, but far from the bull's-eye. StormDancer said, "I've gotten rusty too."

Rita focused on Paul as he explained how the Chief, the witch doctor, and his son StormDancer were legendary in tomahawk throwing. She didn't care much about hawk throwing or the games of

Indians, but being with Paul and Glenn and not having to worry about Pa or being caught was such an awesome feeling. Finally her life was grand and she was happy. She leaned over and kissed Paul on the cheek.

Stopping his dialogue, Paul asked, "What was that for?"

"Just because." With sparkling eyes and a big smile, she added, "I've never been so happy."

Glenn interrupted, "Don't look now, Paul, but your girlfriend is walking this way."

Rita turned to see two girls. Pretty. Especially the blond. When they got within speaking distance, the blond greeted Glenn, "Hi," and looking past Rita to Paul, "Hi, Paul," she greeted with enthusiasm.

Paul returned, "Hey, Julia. What's up?"

Julia shrugged. "Thunder Seelot and Sedges Vannhorn are engaged."

"I heard the rumor."

The girls were on the same tier, but standing. Paul was sitting and looking up. Short skirts were powerful anyway, but more so when one was able to look up them.

Glenn said to the girls, "This is Rita."

The girls looked at Rita with a polite "Hi."

"Hi," Rita returned.

"Have a seat and join us," Glenn invited.

Julia said, "We would, but I wanted to ask Paul for a favor." She looked at Paul.

"Sure," Paul asked.

"I need my purse and it's in Dave's car. Dave's tied up with the contest and Valerie won't let us go to get it without an escort. She's afraid I'll be kidnapped, killed, and eaten by a scarecrow. Or something. I was wondering, since it's your brother's car, if you would escort us?"

"Sure. No problem." Paul stood up. "Be back in a bit," he said to Rita.

Rita, watching Paul walk away with the girls, didn't like it. Turning to Glenn, Rita asked, "What did you mean, 'his *girlfriend*'?"

Cheryl didn't follow Julia and Paul to the car, but stayed back at the encampment area to have something to eat.

Reaching Dave's car, Paul said, "Well so far so good. No scarecrows yet."

Julia pulled open the car door to the back seat. Paul enjoyed the visual of Julia getting in and scooting to the other side. Looking back to him, "Coming?"

Paul got in beside her.

Julia said, "Close the door." Paul obeyed. "Lock it. Ya know, scarecrows and all." Paul locked the door. "So," making eye contact, Julia asked, "You want to make out?"

"Are you serious?"

"I am."

"You're a seventh-grader. A twelve-year-old. I'm sixteen. I'm in high school. It's against the rules."

"I'm thirteen. I have a late birthday. I should be in the eighth grade."

"Still."

Julia shrugged. "You just turned sixteen and so you're still like fifteen. I'll soon be fourteen, and girls mature faster than boys, so in reality you're only fifteen and I'm fourteen. That's only a year. No rules against that."

Paul stared at her a moment. "You're good with numbers, aren't you?"

"Math's my thing."

"I dig it. What about the law? Aren't you like illegal to me?"

"I thought you were a biker. What do you care? Are you scared to make out with me?"

"You're not like your sister, are you?"

"I'm a biker-boy kind of girl. Besides, there's no rules about a thirteen-year-old making out with a sixteen-year-old. Is there?"

"Never heard of one," Paul said.

"Problem solved."

"You're quite the negotiator."

Julia, grinning, moved to straddle Paul's lap, facing him. "Pucker up. I'm going to make out with you." Leaning forward to kiss Paul, she stopped. "No. Instead, I'm going to pretend you're my sister's boyfriend. That's against the rules for sure."

"I don't know if I'm comfortable with that."

"I didn't ask you. Shut up and pucker up—Dave."

On the stage below, Chief KnifeWater was in competition with his son. "Beat that," Chief KnifeWater told Jared.

Jared stepping up to throw, "You gonna move your hawk?"

"I'm not worried about you hitting it, college boy."

"Your loss." Jared threw. Barely hitting the bull's-eye, his hawk stuck two inches from the Chief's. It was a good throw: people applauded.

Rita wasn't interested in the competition. Her thoughts were on Paul. She felt threatened by Julia after Glenn told her about Paul's fondness for Julia and the chemistry between them. Rita wasn't sure she wanted to share Paul. Julia's beauty was powerful magic. Paul was special. She didn't want to lose Paul.

Rita's thoughts were interrupted by cheering and clapping on the stage below. Sedges had stepped forward with a hawk.

"What are you planning on doing?" Jared asked her.

"The Chief says you throw like a girl. He says I could probably outthrow you." Encouragement for Sedges rang from the crowd.

"Oh, he did, did he?" Jared looked over at his grinning father.

Rita was aware of the competition between Jared and Sedges, and that Sedges had somehow bested Jared on a technicality, but mainly she was wondering why Paul hadn't returned. She wanted to go and look for him, make sure he was okay, and see if he was still with Julia. If he was choosing to be with Julia instead of her.

The hawk games finally ended and the crowd began to disperse. Valerie, remembering Julia, scanned the crowd. Not seeing Julia, she said to Dave, "Where's Julia? Do you see her anywhere?"

When neither could see her anywhere, Valerie grumbled, "I knew before this evening was over with, she would go wandering off. I know that girl!"

Everyone moving about and leaving their seats, Glenn said to Rita, "The show's over."

"Looks like Paul missed it. Wonder where he is?"

"You know Paul. He's probably hanging with Julia."

"I think I could use a snack and maybe something to drink. Do you care?"

"No problem." Glenn stood; taking Rita's hand as she stood, he began leading her toward the food.

Escorted back to the celebration, Julia asked Paul, "The girl you and Glenn are with, is that the Rita you and him got into a fight over?"

"Yeah."

"So, is she your girlfriend or Glenn's?"

"Both."

"Both?"

"Rita thinks differently than most people. She's a progressive thinker."

"Progressive thinker?"

"Why have one boyfriend, when two is better?"

"Huh." Julia considered.

Cheryl walked up. "Did you find what you were looking for?"

"I did!" Julia answered, smiling.

"There you are!"

Paul, Julia, and Cheryl turned to see Valerie and Dave marching their way.

Valerie drawing closer, "Where have you been?"

"Nowhere," Julia defended.

"You were supposed to stay close by and not be wandering about," Valerie accused.

"I got bored. Besides, Paul was with me." In a defiant mockery tone, she added, "To protect me!"

"Like he was able to protect himself."

"Chill, Val," Dave said. "She's fine."

Valerie flashed Dave an angry look. Dave said to Julia, "Stay put. It's almost eight thirty. We'll be leaving in a few." Dave looked at Paul. "And you'll be coming with us."

"I'm down."

To Valerie, Dave said, "I want to congratulate Thunder and Sedges one last time before we leave."

Valerie looked at Julia. "Don't wander off. Anywhere!"

"I'm not. Gee!"

Seeing Glenn and Rita standing nearby, Paul said to Julia, "I need to talk with them before we leave."

Walking away, Paul turned back to Julia. "Don't move."

"You too? Really?" Julia answered back.

Glenn's arm was around Rita. Paul understood the message. Paul said to Rita, "Sorry it took so long."

Rita, staring hard into his eyes, asked, "Did you make out with her?"

Caught off guard by the seriousness of Rita's accusation, Paul stumbled with, "I, uh ..."

"You did. I see it in your eyes. That's why you were gone for so long."

"How can you see it in my eyes?"

Rita gave him a witch's grin. "Glenn told me she was your girlfriend."

Paul looked at Glenn.

He shrugged. "She is."

Paul said to Glenn, "I see how it is." Looking at Rita, Paul said, "She is not my girlfriend."

"You made out with her, though, didn't you?"

"Maybe."

"That's fine. I don't care." Rita turned to Glenn. "It's almost time to leave. Let's go to the car. I want to have sex before we go home." Pulling Glenn with her, she walked away.

Paul watched Rita and Glenn walk away. Rita was angry. That was new. Jealous? He turned. Julia hadn't moved. She had been watching. Probably listening. Paul started toward her.

Everyone had gone. Quillpen Jack, Tianna, Jared,

and Sedges stood in the parking lot in conversation. Jared said, "Again, we want to thank you for taking part in this celebration."

"You all honored us," Sedges concurred.

"It was a good night and an honor to have been a part of it," Tianna said, glancing around.

Seeing a dream-catcher necklace on Quillpen's neck, Jared asked, "What's up with the necklace?"

"RiverDawg gave it to me," Quillpen answered. "He said it was a gift for the Dragon Slayer."

"Your car?"

"That's how I took it."

"Where is your car?" Jared asked.

"It's parked over there." Quillpen pointed to another small parking place down the park road. "It's hard to see because of the trees and the darkness."

"He didn't want to park over here with everyone else. He thinks it's too good to be parked among the 'common' cars," Tianna complained in good nature.

"What can I say, man, the Dragon Slayer is special. I lost my virginity in that car," Quillpen Jack ribbed.

Jared laughed. "How many times now have you lost your virginity in that car?"

"Once with me," Tianna countered, "and once with the car. Not sure which was first."

Jared, noticing Tianna's eyes darting about again, asked, "Are you nervous?"

"I don't like being out after dark."

"The scarecrow thing?" Sedges asked.

"I don't want to be attacked again. I still have nightmares."

"Whatever or whoever is behind this scarecrow thing will eventually get caught," Jared assured.

"Yeah, but who else may have to die first?" Tianna voiced concern.

"It's past nine. We're breaking curfew," Sedges reminded.

"Guess we need to get home." Jared gave Sedges a flirtatious pat on the rear.

"I'm ready," Tianna told Quillpen.

"The lady has spoken. Great evening. Had fun. Live long, prosper, and bare us a chief."

"Thanks, man," Jared replied.

Quillpen took Tianna's hand, leading her away.

"Be safe," Sedges told them. To Jared, she said, "Let's watch and make sure they leave safely."

"Planned on it."

Quillpen Jack and Tianna waved to Jared and Sedges as they drove past them leaving the park. The dream catcher hanging from the car's rearview mirror.

"It was a good evening," Quillpen acknowledged.

"It was," Tianna agreed. "I'm happy for them. They make a good couple."

"It was their destiny."

"How many kids you think they'll have?"

"Hard to say. The Seelots were never ones to have many kids."

"Wonder why?"

"Don't know. Too busy. Too many responsibilities. Too many things always in the way, I guess."

"How many kids do you want to have?" Tianna asked.

"Haven't given it much thought. It would be good to have a couple of sons, though; I'm the last of my name right now."

Quillpen eased to a stop at the curb in front of Tianna's home. Quillpen asked, "Want me to walk to the door?"

"I think I'll be alright." Tianna grinned. "Wouldn't want to make your car jealous."

"To love me is to love the car."

"Yeah, I'm getting that."

"The car is a part of who I am. We share a spirit." Quillpen scooted closer to Tianna, putting an arm around her.

"Like I said before, I hope someday you'll love me as much as this car."

"Who says I don't?" Quillpen leaned her way for a kiss.

After a good long kiss, Tianna said, "Can the car do that?"

"There are things the car cannot do."

"Keep that in mind. The car may be able to take you many places, but there are some places only I can take you."

"Shall we take another drive?"

"Just making a point." Tianna gave one last final

kiss. Stepping out of the car and before closing the door, she said, "Love you. Don't leave till I'm in the house."

"Wasn't going to. Love you too. Almost as much as the car," he provoked teasingly.

Projecting an annoyed look, she said, "Night," closed the door, and hurried to the house.

Once she was safely in, Quillpen drove away.

On his way home, stopping at a stoplight, he took a moment to surf the radio for a good song. It was very unexpected! He had absolutely no warning. No idea where it even came from. Reaching up, Quillpen Jack grabbed at the cord wrapped around his neck strangling him. The cord felt like it was cutting its way into his neck. Unable to pull on the cord to find relief, he tried to grab hold of whoever it was strangling him.

It was no use.

Quillpen Jack struggled and fought in vain until his last dying breath!

Once dead, his body was pulled and pushed over to the passenger side. Garth Rygersmith crawled over the seat, got behind the wheel. He put the car in gear and drove on.

Tuning off the static noise coming from the radio, Garth looked at the dead Indian slumped over in the seat next to him. The Indian was half in the seat and half on the floor. It wasn't a very dignified position. Garth, the gentleman he was, reached over to pull and tug on the corpse to get it into a more noble position. His efforts didn't help much. He gave up. It didn't much matter anyway.

With a sigh of relief, Garth asked, "How ya doing, Jack? Not so well, it seems. Sorry to have rained on your parade, but business is business."

After a moment of silence, Garth said, "Funny how unpredictable life can be. Under the circumstance, I'm sure you're in agreement.

"You have a nice car. I understand your love for it. I've heard about this car. Like the color, what I've been able to see of it. I noticed the inscription *The Dragon Slayer* and the dream catcher on the rear fenders. It makes a statement. Kind of a bold one. You killed a dragon, got away with it, and you're boasting about it. I rather dig that. I do. I'd do the same. Plan to actually.

"But the problem, Jack, Tommy Morris was my friend. Not just a friend—Tommy was family! He was the little brother I never had. I couldn't just let you kill him and get away with it. He only wanted what everyone wants. A little piece of the American dream.

"But life can be cruel.

"Don't you think, Jack? Of course you do. Look at you. Just when you thought life was going great, look at what happened.

"Something I've come to know and understand: life is a villain, Jack. It's true. A cruel mistress of sorts—promising you the world and then when you think you're on top, riding her for all she's got, she reaches forth and cuts off your nuts.

"Life sucks, Jack, and when she does, she bites!

"Are you feeling a little castrated, Jack? The Quillpen line just came into extinction. How you feel about that?"

After a moment of thought, "It's a dog-eat-dog world. Make no mistake about it. I've been all over the world. Seen some really disturbing stuff. Here in America, people don't see the evil ruling the world. If the American people did, it would destroy their belief in God.

"It truly would.

"Can you keep a secret, Jack?" Garth looked over at the dead Indian. "I'm thinking you can. You know what I do for a living? I work for the United States government. That's right. My job is to kill people who pose a threat to the ruling machine. To democracy. Can you imagine that? Been trained and everything. There's a secret war going on in our government. I'm on assignment right now. Not with you. I just popped into town for a moment to take you out. To avenge Tommy. A little personal matter I wanted to attend to.

"I'm on my way up north to take out a university professor who is using his job and position for a political agenda. He's on the wrong side, ya see. That's politics for you."

Garth, heading out of town, was driving toward a specific place. A place he knew about. A place where he could dispose of the body. A place where the body might never be found.

Heading toward his destiny, still in a dialogue, Garth said, "You know, I've had a real hate for you over the years and especially since you killed Tommy, but spending some time with you sharing feelings, I don't really hate you like I thought I did.

"But, you are dead now. That could be the difference. You know what they say: 'The only good injun is a dead injun.' Now I understand that may be a little offensive to you. It may sound a little racist on my part, but being racist is believing in evolution.

"I'm an evolutionist, Jack! All the way! You cannot truly believe in evolution and not have the spirit of racism in you. It's what the whole concept is built upon. One animal evolving above another. One animal superior to another. Lower forms serving the higher forms.

"We're all animals, Jack. It's science. The ugly side of the nature of things. When you think about it, racism via evolution is taught in school, served up in little sugary bowls to camouflage the bitter taste. If evolution is being taught, racism is being implied. That's the facts, Jack!

"Evolution, man, it's a beautiful thing!"

Garth pulled off the road onto a dirt path going into the woods. After a little ways, he stopped the car, turning the engine off. "Can't take you with me, Jack. This is where we part ways. Where you and your car part ways. I'm kidnapping the car by the way. I like it. Gonna keep it as a souvenir. That bold statement thing, ya know."

Garth got out of the car and went around to the passenger side. He opened the car door. "Good talk, Jack. I've enjoyed it. One last thing—THOU SHALT NOT POKE THE DRAGON!"

Lightning Source UK Ltd.
Milton Keynes UK
UKHW020659180121
377244UK00012B/1382